PRAISE FOR SHARON POTTS

"This is thriller writing the way it is supposed to be."

—Michael Connelly, *New York Times* bestselling author, on *In Their Blood*

"Rich with high-concept, captivating characters, and a relentless plot that simply won't go away."

—Jeffery Deaver, *New York Times* bestselling author, on *The Devil's Madonna*

"Resourceful and emotionally strong characters boost this satisfying domestic thriller from Potts."

—*Publishers Weekly*, on *Someone Must Die*

"A complex plot that builds believable suspense on every page."

—*Sacramento Bee* on *In Their Blood*

"With lean, spare writing that maintains suspense throughout, the author deftly weaves the various characters' stories into a plot that explodes in revelations."

—*San Francisco Book Review* on *Someone's Watching*

OTHER TITLES BY SHARON POTTS

SUSPENSE
Someone Must Die
The Devil's Madonna
Someone's Watching
In Their Blood

CONTEMPORARY FICTION
South Beach Cinderella
Goodbye Neverland

THE OTHER TRAITOR

Sharon Potts

Churlish Press

First Edition

ISBN 978-0692690598

In memory of Hannah Mariasha Adler (1916-2010), whose stories occasionally frightened, always enthralled, and ultimately inspired me.

And for Ben, Sarah, Julie, David, Josh, and Michael—her legacy.

PROLOGUE

June 12, 1953

His eyes were wrong. Sepia gray and filled with hate. She knew his eyes were a luminous blue, much like the cat's-eye marble she had played with as a child.

And the grainy face. It didn't belong here, staring at her from the screen of her television in the dimness of her living room. It was all wrong. The receding hairline, bulldog jaw, angry mouth. One eyelid drooped like a falling curtain over his right eye. This was the man Americans had been taught to hate. It was not the man Mariasha had known.

The camera pulled back to reveal the entire vile placard carried by one of the demonstrators marching outside Sing-Sing Prison awaiting the execution. Above the unrecognizable face, the printed words shouted DEATH TO GOLDSTEIN!

Mariasha winced. How could things have gone so wrong?

The newscaster's televised voice rang out, each word a painful jolt.

Head of spy ring. Passed atomic-bomb secrets to the Soviets. Sentenced to death by electric chair.

Traitor!

Mariasha tried to breathe, vaguely aware of the sunken sofa cushion beneath her, the warm stagnant air, her husband's hand clasping hers. His soft and strong, a few age spots and wrinkles appearing among the golden hairs. Hers, numb.

The voice coming from the television stopped abruptly. Aaron's hand tightened over hers. This was it.

A shuffle of paper. The newscaster looked up. "I just received word that at 8:17 this evening, Isaac Goldstein died in the electric chair." He ran his tongue over his lips. "Once again. Atomic spy Isaac Goldstein has gone to meet his maker."

She squeezed her eyes shut, so tight she became dizzy. She had made her choice.

Her young daughter ran into the living room and threw her arms around Mariasha. "What's going to happen to Sally?" Essie asked.

Mariasha stroked her daughter's golden curls, so like her father's hair. Essie had been friends with Isaac Goldstein's daughter since they'd been babies.

She met her husband's eyes.

Aaron nodded. He knew. He understood.

"I'm sure Sally's mother will take good care of her," Aaron said. He gently lifted the little girl. "Come, Esseleh. I'll tuck you into bed."

There was no air left in the room. Mariasha grabbed her handbag and fled the apartment into a crumbling fortress of brick and concrete. This was the old Manhattan neighborhood where Isaac Goldstein had lived much of his life. His people. Most had never wavered in their support of him. But they were only a small minority. In the street, neighbors huddled, moaning, crying. Old men and women, many others younger, Mariasha's age. Some carried lit candles as they marched in their solemn vigil. It was after sundown. *Shabbos.* The executioners had even violated the holy Sabbath.

She hurried down Ridge Street, past the dilapidated Lower East Side tenements, away from the people. A bulldozer blocked a street where they'd started knocking down older buildings to make room for a government housing project. Mariasha could smell the stale East River and remembered the park. The bench where they'd sat together, the world frozen as though they were sealed inside a snow globe. But she couldn't go there. The memory was too close. It would be like staring into a solar eclipse.

She walked instead to Delancey Street and got on the train to Brooklyn.

The train car jerked and yawed, lights flashing off and on as it screamed through the tunnel, until it finally surfaced to cross the Williamsburg Bridge.

Beneath her, the black river was still. The muted Brooklyn skyline rose ahead of her, low buildings silhouetted against a faded sky. No stars tonight. All brightness had been sucked out of the world by too many bolts of killing electricity.

The train crossed Brooklyn. Crossed Mariasha's life. A too-short childhood picnicking with her parents in Prospect Park, a few happy moments at Coney Island, her years as a politically active student at Brooklyn College.

She got off the train at the Alabama Avenue station, then picked her way down cracked, deserted sidewalks past red brick buildings, the shoemaker and butcher shops, maple and elm trees thick with broad green leaves.

Her old street was quiet. Tenement windows open to catch a nonexistent breeze. A few cars parked along the curb. Smudged chalk on the sidewalk from a game of hopscotch. A broken stickball bat stuck out of a garbage can.

She sat down on the stoop of her childhood apartment building, remembering how the neighborhood women would gather outside with their baby carriages and fan themselves against the summer heat, listening to the off-key carnival sounds of an organ grinder. How Mama would drop a small paper bag down to her from their second-floor kitchen window. In it, a sandwich of pumpernickel bread smeared with delicious *schmaltz* and sprinkled with salt.

Mariasha leaned back against the cool stone steps and looked up at the rusting fire escapes. Diapers hung from the clotheslines like limp flags of surrender.

Her heart ached so much she could hardly breathe. She had made her choice.

But had it been the right one?

CHAPTER 1

Over sixty years later

Here in the kitchen. *La cuisine*. That's where Annette Revoir could still feel her grandmother more than anywhere else in the old Paris apartment. Grandma Betty had always been in the kitchen, surrounded by hanging copper pans, making *chocolat chaud*, baking croissants, or cleaning a chicken in the chipped porcelain sink.

As a child, Annette would watch from her perch on the rickety ladder-back chair, boosted up by a couple of thick telephone books. Grandma Betty would boil hot milk in a saucepan, fold in finely chopped pieces of bittersweet chocolate, then add brown sugar. After they finished drinking their cocoa, Grandma Betty would wash her hands and dry them on her plain white apron. Then she would stand behind Annette and carefully separate her thick blonde hair into sections. Annette would grow sleepy in the warm kitchen that smelled like melted chocolate. Sometimes Grandma Betty would call her Sally, forgetting that her daughter was a grown-up woman and Annette her daughter's child. She would plait Annette's hair into braids so tight they felt like forever hugs.

Annette's eyes stung. The kitchen was cold and smelled like disinfectant. No one had cooked here in a long time. And no one was ever again going to braid her hair into forever hugs.

She wiped away her tears. Dear, sweet Grandma Betty was gone and it was time to say goodbye. Annette snatched another sheet of yesterday's *Le Figaro* to wrap the last copper saucepan. A familiar face in smudged newsprint near the bottom of the page stopped her. She started to wad up the newspaper. That face did not belong here in her grandmother's house, especially not now, so soon after her death. But like someone hypnotized by a public hanging, Annette couldn't help herself. She flattened out the page and glanced at the article beside the old photo. Two short paragraphs about a newly published memoir by a former KGB agent who had been involved with U.S. atomic-bomb spy rings back in the 1940s.

She heard the front door opening. Mama returning from the *boulangerie* with lunch. Annette ripped out the article and shoved it into the pocket of her jeans as her mother stepped into the kitchen, placing a canvas bag of groceries on the table.

Mama fluffed out her short white hair. "*Il pleut,*" she said. She shook off her old camelhair coat, scattering a few droplets of rain over the cartons lined up on the wood floor.

"*Pas de pot,*" Annette said. "At least it isn't snowing yet."

"*Fini*?" Mama asked.

"*Oui.*" She put the wrapped pan into a carton. "I finished packing up the kitchen," she said, switching from French to English. She and her mother usually spoke in a mélange of their two languages. "Dishes. Pots and pans. Everything's in boxes for the men from the Emmaus charity to take."

"*Bien.*" Her mother laid her coat over one of the ladder-back chairs. "I bought some brie and grapes for us. And a little wine."

Annette pulled the long baguette from the satchel. The bread was wet with rain on its exposed half. She broke off an end. "Do you want to go through the cartons?"

"No," her mother said. She opened the bottle of burgundy with the corkscrew Annette had left out with a couple of plates and glasses for their lunch. She seemed smaller than the year before when Annette had returned to Paris for a visit, just after she'd finished her master's degree in journalism. Grandma Betty's slow deterioration and finally her death almost two weeks ago, a few days before Christmas, had taken its toll. Her mother's once-plump face was gaunt and her blue eyes sunken, reminding Annette of photos she'd seen of concentration-camp victims.

Mama poured wine into two glasses, handed one to Annette, and took a long sip from her glass. She gestured with her chin at the pile Annette had assembled on one of the kitchen chairs. A folded embroidered tablecloth with matching napkins, brass candleholders, and a book with yellowed pages, missing its cover, called *The Jewish Home Beautiful*. It had been published in 1941 and had recipes and tidbits about Jewish living, like table settings for the different Jewish holidays. There was an inscription on the first page. *To my dearest sister Betty. Love, Irene.* "What's all this?" her mother asked.

"I thought you might want it," Annette said. "Grandma Betty kept it, so it must have meant something to her. Reminders of our family."

"I don't need any reminders."

"But Mama..."

Her mother backed out of the kitchen carrying her glass and the bottle of wine. "I want nothing from the past."

Annette wanted to shout, *Grandma Betty's gone. We only have each other now.* But she said nothing. Mama was incapable of showing affection. The past had killed that in her.

Annette finished her bread, cheese and wine, rinsed off the plate and wine glass, then packed them away. She ran her hand over the top of the butcher-block kitchen table. Grandma Betty was gone. She had lived in this same apartment all of Annette's life, and for many years before. She and Mama had moved to the Marais district in the 1950s, when they had first come to Paris from New York. Annette couldn't say if this had been their original apartment, or if they'd moved in after Grandma married her second husband, the very French Simon Revoir, whom Annette had called Grand-Père.

She stood in the entrance to the living room, taking in everything for the last time. The walls, high ceilings, and crown moldings were all painted white, the sofa and chairs were covered in an ivory fabric, and sheer, floor-length drapes hung in front of the tall windows. Everything was clean and colorless, and it occurred to her that perhaps the purpose of all the white had been to erase something.

Her mother sat on the sofa surrounded by cartons, the wine bottle on the parquet floor in front of her. She sipped from her glass as she stared at the rain splattering against the window panes.

Annette bent over and kissed her head. Her mother squirmed, hating to be touched, but Annette held tight and kissed her again. The short white hair had thinned and Annette could see her pink scalp. Mama was getting old, almost sixty-nine. She'd had Annette, an only child, late in life, and Annette often felt as though she'd been raised by two grandmothers.

She released her mother and went to finish packing up the master bedroom. Her grandmother's high bed with its white iron headboard was in the center of the room beneath a beautiful old crystal chandelier that hung from an ornate ceiling medallion. The real estate woman had suggested that they strip the apartment of all personal items, but leave the furniture and fixtures in case someone wanted to buy them, as well.

Even after most everything had been packed away, the apartment still felt as it had when her grandmother was alive. There had never been much of a personal nature. No paintings, knickknacks, or books. Only three photos had sat on the now-empty nightstand. One of Grand-Père, a spindly little man with a black goatee whom she hardly remembered, the second of Annette's mother in her nurse's uniform, and the third of Annette when she had graduated from the University of Michigan four years before. Maybe her grandmother hadn't wanted to settle in, perhaps for fear of having to someday leave it all behind.

She brought the stepladder and a damp dust rag over to the floor-to-ceiling closets. The day before, she had cleared out all of her grandmother's clothes and taken them to a Catholic charity. But there were several high shelves that she had been unable to reach. She climbed up the steps with the rag and peered into the first shelf. Nothing but dustballs and a couple of dead bugs. She wiped it clean, stepped down and moved the ladder to the next section. Also empty. She cleaned it, then went to the final closet. There was a box pushed all the way back, so it hadn't been visible when she was standing on the floor.

Annette felt a trill of excitement. Had this belonged to Grand-Père or her grandmother? She reached in and pulled out a small leather suitcase with no luggage tag. She wiped off the dust, carried it down the stepladder, and laid it on the bed.

If it had belonged to Grandma Betty, perhaps the suitcase contained some link to a past that had been carefully hidden from Annette. She had a vague recollection from her childhood of her grandmother reading pale-blue tissue-thin letters, tears running down her cheeks, but didn't know what had upset her, or what had become of those letters.

She ran her fingers over the worn brown suitcase. She flipped up the two locks and pried the top open, releasing the smell of camphor.

Women's clothes. She carefully laid out each item on the bed. A ruffled black apron—very different from the plain white one her grandmother had always worn. A sexy satin aqua nightgown with beige lace around the neck. Had this been Grandma Betty's? She shook out a long, yellowed wedding veil, fingering the small holes in the sheer fabric, eaten away by time. Beneath the veil, in the bottom of the suitcase, was a large rectangular book with a black leather cover.

Her heart bounced. A photo album.

She opened it, fascinated. Black-and-white photos of smiling people she didn't recognize were pasted onto black construction paper, each labeled with names and dates.

On the first page was an eight-by-ten portrait of Grandma Betty wearing a long satin bridal gown that fell in waves on the floor. She held a bouquet of white orchids. Her grandmother's face was pursed in a shy smile that minimized her overbite, and her medium brown hair was arranged in a rolled page-boy. Although she wasn't a pretty woman, she looked radiant. On her head was the veil that now lay on the bed.

Mama needed to see these, even if she didn't want to.

Annette carried the album into the living room and sat down beside her on the sofa. Her mother was still looking out the window. The rain had turned to snow and flakes were sticking to the panes.

"Mama, I found photos of Grandma Betty when she was young. You have to look at these."

"No," her mother said, but her eyes turned to the book on Annette's lap.

Annette opened to the portrait of her grandmother as a bride, let her mother study it for a minute, then turned to the next page.

She was confused. This one was of Grandma Betty and the groom. But the man that stood a head taller than her grandmother was a handsome, sparkling young man. He was dressed in a formal U.S. Army uniform with a number of ribbons and medals over his breast pocket. In the shadow of his billed cap, she could tell he had light eyes, probably blue like hers and her mother's, a hint of pale hair, and a broad open smile. Annette had never imagined her real grandfather once looked like this.

Her mother made a small noise, like a bird about to be crushed.

"I'm sorry, Mama. We don't have to look at these."

Her mother patted her throat. "Show me."

Annette turned to the next page. There he was again. Much younger, a grinning teenager wearing an old-fashioned bathing suit with a striped top. *1932. Upstate New York*, the label read.

The face was open and pure. How could that be? These photos contradicted everything Annette believed.

She slowly turned the pages as her mother studied each photo with her. Her grandparents wrapped in a plaid blanket on a toboggan, wearing ice skates at the side of a frozen lake, laughing with another couple whose faces were blurry. December 1943, Laurels Hotel, Catskill Mountains, New York.

She turned the page. Another picture of her grandparents with the same couple seated around a table in a restaurant. Her grandfather was in his military uniform, the others in evening dress. In this photo, Annette could see the faces of the other couple clearly. An older man with thinning hair and a much younger-looking woman. The woman had dark hair and eyes, high cheekbones, and a movie-star smile. A cluster of large stones that looked like rhinestones sparkled in her ears. She was stunning. Next to her, Grandma Betty with her small eyes and pronounced upper jaw looked like a mouse, despite the white orchid she wore on a velvet ribbon around her neck. Annette read the caption. *With Mariasha and Aaron Lowe. December 1944. Dinner and dancing at the Starlight Roof Supper Club.*

She wasn't sure why she was so taken aback that her grandparents had had friends. Yet here was a photo of four people out for an evening. None of these people looked like monsters. Certainly not her grandfather.

Her mother took the album from Annette and turned the pages. She stopped on the last page. Annette looked over her mother's shoulder at the photo of two little girls, both blonde, holding hands in front of a brick apartment building. They could have been sisters.

"This is me," her mother said. "And I think I remember the other girl."

Annette read the caption. *1950. Our Sally with classmate Essie Lowe. In front of our apartment on 120 Columbia Street.*

Essie Lowe. Probably the daughter of her grandparents' friends, Mariasha and Aaron Lowe. And if the girls were classmates, they'd probably all lived in the same Manhattan neighborhood.

"Essie was my friend," her mother said, in a voice that sounded childlike and plaintive.

Annette's heart ached for her. Her mother had once been a happy child until one day her ordinary life was publicly shattered. Then, probably to escape a vicious world, Grandma Betty bundled herself and little Sally off to Paris, away from friends, family, their old neighborhood, and a familiar language.

But why had it happened? Because her grandfather had been a monster or because it was convenient for people to believe he was?

Annette reached into the pocket of her jeans, pulled out the article she had torn from the newspaper, and looked at the smudged photo of Isaac Goldstein. His hooded eye glared at her. A monster?

She quickly read the two short paragraphs about the KGB agent's memoir. According to the agent, Isaac Goldstein had no involvement in passing secret atomic-bomb information on to the Soviets. *Goldstein was never a major player in communist spy circles,* the agent had written. *He didn't have access to crucial material. That all came from another source.*

What if there was something to the Soviet agent's story? Annette was a journalist, someone who didn't accept things at face value, and yet that's exactly what she had been doing all these years.

She took the album from her mother and looked again at the photo of the smiling bridegroom, a decorated army hero. Her real grandfather. Isaac Goldstein. He looked nothing like the smudged picture of the angry man from *Le Figaro*, a traitor with a squinty eye. The hateful photo had been on 'Death to Goldstein' posters in 1953 and was the one that popped up hundreds of times if you searched on Google Images. But did that make it true?

Who had this man really been? A hero or a traitor?

Annette put her arm around her mother, holding tight even as Mama shrank from her touch. Perhaps the truth about Isaac Goldstein could help Mama reclaim her life.

And then his granddaughter could finally reclaim hers.

CHAPTER 2

Who the hell was this person? Everything about him was wrong.

Julian Sandman stared at his distorted reflection in the black lacquered door to his apartment. He'd been standing there for so long that the caked snow that had accumulated on his dress shoes during his walk home from his Midtown office had melted and soaked through to his feet.

Happy thirtieth b-day, man, whoever you really are.

A thumping bass beat leaked through the apartment door, which meant Sephora was probably inside getting dressed for her spinning class. Well, he'd made the first move and there was no going back. Might as well get this over with.

He jabbed his key into the lock, opened the door, and was hit by a blast of cold air from the open balcony door. Sephora preferred fresh air, even when it was freezing outside. He pulled off his soaked shoes and socks in the front foyer. His feet had turned white and crinkly and looked grotesque against the polished black marble floor.

But then, this entire apartment was grotesque. He and Sephora had been here a year, but it still felt more like a trendy hotel suite than a place where people actually lived. He took in the stiff black leather sofa, ebony brick wall, media console and giant flat-screen TV. A fake white Christmas tree with crystal ornaments stood in the corner of the room topped by a Jewish star, Sephora's big concession to Julian. Beyond the open balcony door, the snow was coming down so thick it obscured the view of the Hudson River. Not that you could see the river even on a clear day, thanks to the new highrise that was under construction across the street. You didn't get much for five thousand dollars a month in Manhattan's West Village these days.

What the hell was he doing here?

He loosened his tie and dropped his wet cashmere coat, wool hat, and briefcase on the leather chair by the rarely used glass desk. The plain wood chess set Julian's father had gotten him when he was five sat on a corner of the desk, though Julian never played chess anymore. There were lots of things he didn't do anymore.

He followed the rhythmic beat of hip-hop music into the bedroom, recognizing Lil Wayne rapping.

Sephora sat on the bed, yanking on a pair of tight black high-heeled boots, her silky reddish-blonde hair falling across her face.

"It's slippery out there," he said. "Not high-heel weather."

She tossed the hair out of her eye and stood up. "I'll take a taxi."

Julian watched her examine herself in the full-length mirror. Blue jeans over a black leotard. A body most guys drooled over, as he once did.

When they'd first met a couple of years before, Sephora had been one of the HR recruiters at the company's corporate office and had taken him out to lunch. For two hours over martinis and tuna tartare, she had tried to impress him with what an amazing opportunity was in store for him with one of the largest pharmaceutical companies in the world. The company invested more in R&D than any of its competitors, she'd told him, and that meant Julian would work in a state-of-the-art lab on projects that could transform the health and well-being of the world.

While Sephora hadn't been the main reason he had accepted the employment offer, that lunch certainly hadn't hurt. A few weeks after Julian joined the company, he and Sephora started dating. A year later, she moved in with him, and then dropped her corporate career.

"You're home early," she said, studying him in the mirror. She rubbed gloss on her lips with her pinkie. "Getting a head start on the big celebration?"

"Not exactly. Can we talk?"

"My class is in twenty minutes," she said.

Lil Wayne's voice pounded in the small room.

"Aww, come here, big boy. Let me give you a birthday hug." Sephora pulled him toward her, swung her back against his chest in a spooning position, then crisscrossed his long arms around her breasts so that both their reflections were framed in the mirror. Her face was fresh and pink-cheeked, her green eyes sparkly. He, on the other hand, looked like he'd been dragged in from a shipwreck. Short black hair plastered to his skull like a swimming cap. His face a collage of pasty white skin, five o'clock shadow, and dark smudges around his sunken blue eyes.

"Lovely," he said in a flat voice. "An award-winning couple."

"You'll feel better after you take a hot shower."

"Can you skip your exercise class? I really need to talk to you."

She dropped his hands and rubbed an invisible imperfection on her cheek that she must have noticed in the mirror. "We can talk when I get back. Should be around eight. We're having dinner with Brent and Camilla at eight-thirty at a new restaurant in the Meatpacking District. I know you don't want a big fuss over your birthday, but after that we're meeting up with the rest of our friends at the Gansevoort bar."

Her friends, she meant. "I'd rather we just stay home and order in a pizza or something."

She cocked her head and frowned, as though he was speaking in a foreign language. "A pizza? For your birthday?"

"Or sushi. Whatever you want. I've got a lot on my mind."

She checked her watch. "I have to go." She started across the room toward the dresser.

"I quit."

She stopped and looked at him.

"I quit my job."

"What are you talking about?"

"I've been miserable there with all the bureaucracy and bullshit." He went over to the sliding glass door and watched the snow piling up on their balcony. The hibachi they'd bought and never used was almost completely buried. "This was never what I wanted to do with my life."

"So you have something else lined up?"

He turned back toward her and shook his head.

She scowled and played with a strand of apricot hair. "I know some people at Pfizer and Merck. I'm sure they'd love to hire a brilliant guy like you. MD from Cornell, PhD in biophysics from MIT. Top of his class at both. Two years in new-product development." She seemed to be warming to her subject, but she'd always had a knack as a recruiter.

"I'm leaving the corporate world."

She glanced at her watch again. "I can live without the suspense. Where are you going? Some startup? Back to the academic world?"

"I'm not sure. I haven't gotten that far. Maybe I'll take up painting again."

She squeezed her eyes closed like she'd gotten a sudden headache pain, then opened them. "Painting? What, houses?"

He'd been stupid to hope she'd understand.

"Jesus, Julian. You're working for one of the top pharmaceutical companies in the world developing products that will change the health and well-being of the world."

"I'm making a goddamn face cream. I think the world can do without one more of those."

She opened a dresser drawer, pulled out a black silk scarf, then slammed the drawer. "I just don't know where you get off quitting your job without even discussing it with me."

"I'm sorry. I would have talked it over with you first, but it just happened. I was sitting in my office filling out yet another useless report and I thought, 'What the hell am I doing here?' So I went in to give two weeks' notice. They told me thanks very much, but company policy was for me to leave today. So I left."

Sephora wrapped the scarf around her neck. He followed her to the living room where she grabbed her fur coat from the front closet.

"And what are you going to do about money?" she asked. "Or is your dream to be a starving artist?"

"I have a little saved."

"But you have financial responsibilities, Julian. This apartment. Stuff. You know."

"We'll move someplace cheaper. Maybe Brooklyn. We can make this work."

"Whoa, Brooklyn?" She held up her hand. "Since when did you become in charge of my life's decisions? I happen to like this apartment."

He felt a spurt of rage. "Then how about you going back to work to pay for it while I 'find myself' like you did this past year?"

Her nostrils flared as she held his stare. "So that's how it is." She pushed past him and opened the front door.

His reflex was to tell her he was sorry, but nothing came out.

She glanced down at his shoes and socks in front of the door. "Happy birthday, asshole," she said, and then was gone.

He clenched his fists, quaking in the frigid air that blew in through the open balcony door. What had he been thinking? Sephora was interested in his earning potential, not in his happiness. He paced in his bare feet in his ridiculous apartment with its high ceilings, purported Hudson-River view, and ugly black furniture that Sephora had persuaded him to buy. How the hell had he gotten to this place in his life? In a hated career, an alien apartment, with a girlfriend he didn't much like? Living an inauthentic life to please everyone except himself.

And then his fists relaxed. Sephora wasn't the problem, and he knew it.

He picked up the black queen on the wooden chess board and turned it over in his fingers. One minute he'd been a happy kid playing chess with his dad, reading comic books, and sketching his favorite superheroes. Then Dad died and nothing felt right after that.

The chiseled face of the black queen stared up at him. For most of his life he had ignored the truth, but deep inside he knew exactly how he'd gotten to this place. Excelling in all the things he thought would please his mother. Trying to get her to finally notice him, maybe even love him.

Well, he was thirty years old. Time to grow up. But in order to go forward, he would first have to go back.

He set the black queen on its square and caught his reflection in the glass desktop. A little blurry, but he could almost recognize the person that hadn't been there for a long, long time.

Himself.

CHAPTER 3

Annette was jetlagged, woozy from fatigue. It was midnight back in Paris, seven pm here in Manhattan, and she knew she should try to get back on a normal schedule. Probably eat something and stay awake at least until ten.

She had called her mother when she'd landed at JFK. With Grandma Betty gone, Annette worried that Mama, who had no close friends, would be terribly lonely. Before she'd left, Annette had asked her to come to New York with her, but Mama had looked at her as though she'd gone insane. "New York?" She made it sound like a curse. "I'll never go back."

Annette sank against the blue-chenille sofa that doubled as the bed in her studio apartment, and checked her phone. Bill had texted her two hours ago. *Call when you get in. Dinner?* But she'd been too busy researching Mariasha and Aaron Lowe on the internet, looking for possible connections to Isaac Goldstein. Now, her eyes were practically crossing from staring at her computer screen and her stomach grumbled. She hit speed dial on her phone, hoping Bill hadn't given up on having dinner with her. He was her go-to person when she had a problem, either personal or professional.

"Yo," Bill said. "If it isn't Annie-get-your-gun."

Bill insisted that Annette resembled Annie Oakley. Probably the frantic blonde hair she occasionally wore in braids like the famous sharpshooter. Or maybe he was joking about Annette's attitude about life.

"You still want dinner?" she asked.

"Absolutely. The Black Sheep?"

"Sure. See you there in fifteen minutes or so."

She quickly straightened up the room, more out of compulsion than because she thought Bill might come back here later. She shoved her empty suitcase into the back of the closet and stowed away her grandmother's clothes and tablecloth in a drawer of the armoire. Her grandmother's photo album, brass candle holders, and coverless book of Jewish recipes and traditions now sat on top of the wood steamer trunk. She'd picked up the battered trunk at a flea market and used it as a table and to store the books she couldn't fit on the two bookcases on either side of the bricked-in fireplace. She would have loved a working fireplace, but could appreciate that the building's owner was concerned about a fire hazard.

Her apartment had originally been the front parlor of an 1890s brownstone in a neighborhood just north of Morningside Heights that was now on the verge of a comeback. Annette had moved in three years before, because the rent was cheap and it was pretty close to Columbia University. After she graduated last year with her master's in journalism and started work as a freelance writer, she hadn't wanted to move, loving the light from the large bay window, the original oak floors, and the proximity to laid-back restaurants, old bookstores, and vintage shops. Perhaps it also reminded her of Paris.

She slipped on a red ski jacket and a pair of well-worn Ugg boots over her jeans, and locked the apartment door behind her. Snow was falling lightly so she pulled the hood over her head and walked through slush to the restaurant three blocks away. Discarded Christmas trees with tangled tinsel lay on their sides near the gutter, shedding brown pine needles. The air smelled of smoke and fir and garbage.

She stepped inside the crowded entryway of The Black Sheep and stomped the snow from her boots. The restaurant was a former bar turned vegan restaurant with a full liquor license and still looked like a saloon with a tall bar and stools in front of a mirrored wall of booze. Along the opposite brick wall were oak booths with at least fifty years of initials and hearts scratched into the wood. Definitely not a white-tablecloth kind of place, which made it popular with students from Columbia and City College, residents and interns from St. Luke's, and locals from Harlem and Morningside Heights.

All the barstools were taken and the booths occupied. Then Annette saw a large dark-skinned hand waving to her from a booth in the back. Bill gave her a smile and pushed his tortoise-shell frames up on his nose. He was wearing his usual nerdy-professor outfit—navy crew-neck sweater over a white button-down, and probably loafers, which she couldn't see under the table. His prematurely gray afro was cut close to his scalp, like a low-pile carpet.

"Hey," she said. She slid into the booth opposite Bill and shrugged out of her ski jacket. There was a pot of tea, a mug, and four used teabags leaking brownish liquid on a small plate. "How'd you score a booth?"

"I've been here for two hours holding this table."

"*Mon dieu*! Seriously?"

"I figured you'd have to eat sooner or later."

She waved at the teabags. "That's all you're drinking?"

He pursed his lips, as though considering what to tell her. "I thought it best to take a break. I had a little episode early this week."

"*C'est affreux*," she said, concerned for her friend. Bill's dark moods had taken him to bad places in the past. "I'm sorry I wasn't here for you. Are you okay?"

"I'm great," he said. "Stop being a mother hen." He signaled to the waiter. "But you should have a drink. I understand their special tonight is a rum punch smoothie made with fennel and plums."

Bill seemed okay, so she relaxed. "Sounds like the chef had too much leftover plum pie from Christmas."

The waiter came over. Annette ordered a glass of sauvignon blanc, Bill asked for another pot of water and a couple more teabags, and they got a platter of tofu and black bean nachos and two brown rice avocado rolls.

Bill put the four used teabags into his mug and poured what was left of the water over them. He had the same purposeful expression she remembered from the first class she'd taken with him in Twentieth-Century Political Journalism. At the time, Professor Bill Turner had looked like another student, but the last year had aged him and he now seemed more than his forty years.

"Tell me about Paris," Bill said.

"You're in an awfully big hurry to make this about me. Can we first talk about what happened to you this week?" She wanted to know what had set him off on a drinking binge. "Was it Kylie?"

He took a sip of his tea and made a face. "Cold." He put the mug down. A few tea leaves floated to the top. One of the teabags had broken open. "It's not really her fault," he said. "I blindsided her. Here she thought she was in a forever marriage and she learns that her husband has a sick alternative preference for men."

"Stop acting like you have a disease," Annette said. "There's nothing wrong or immoral about being gay."

The waiter set the wine, hot water and teabags on the table, then left.

"But if I had understood it sooner," Bill said, "I could have avoided the pain I've caused everyone."

"And you wouldn't have your beautiful son."

Bill took his glasses off, rubbed his eyes, took in a deep breath, then slowly exhaled. "She doesn't want me to see him," he said. "She's talking about moving away. She's concerned I'm a bad influence."

"That's bullshit," Annette said.

Bill waved his hand for her to keep her voice down.

"You're a wonderful influence, Bill. A brilliant man and an amazing human being. Billy is lucky to have you for a father."

He put his glasses back on and gave her a closed-mouthed smile. "Okay, Annie-get-your-gun. Pipe down. You don't have to right all the wrongs of the world in one day. Let's give Kylie a little time to adjust to the idea. The wound is still fresh."

"It's not a wound and it's been almost six months."

He smiled broadly this time, his strong, even teeth strikingly white against his dark skin. "I love you, Annette Revoir. I'm sorry I only gave you an A-minus."

Annette let go of her anger and laughed. It was an ongoing joke between them. The A-minus on a paper she'd written about Alger Hiss that Annette felt should have been an A.

He pulled the old teabags out of his mug, put a fresh one in and poured water over it. This time it steamed. "Ah, better," he said. "Now tell me about Paris and your mother."

Annette took a long sip from her glass of wine as the waiter put their food down on the table. Bill was the only person Annette had entrusted with her secret that Isaac Goldstein was her grandfather. Bill knew about her shock when she'd learned of her grandfather's existence when she was sixteen. Her shame when she searched the internet and learned Isaac Goldstein was a hated man who had betrayed his country. And her anger at her mother for never trusting her with the truth. He had told Annette to read beyond the headlines, to be a journalist and dig deeper. But Annette hadn't wanted to learn more. Every time she read her grandfather's name and thought about her roots, she felt dirty.

She stared at one of the hearts carved into the wood tabletop. *TJ Loves LM. '83.*

“I found a photo album that my grandmother had hidden away,” she said. “There were these incredible photos I’d never seen before. My grandparents’ wedding picture, pictures taken on their honeymoon, my mother as a little girl. The photos ended in 1950.”

“The year your grandfather was arrested.” Bill was widely read, especially in twentieth-century politics, but Annette was always surprised when he would recite what seemed to her to be arcane details. “Your mother was how old? Seven or eight when your grandmother took her to live in Paris?”

“Eight.”

“That’s tough. She not only lost her father that year, but she must have sensed he was someone she should be ashamed of.” Bill stared into his mug, as though he was trying to read the floating bits of tea leaves.

“It’s not the same thing as you and Billy,” she said. “Isaac Goldstein was viewed as one of the most hated men in America. A communist who passed on atomic-bomb secrets to the Soviets. An enemy to all that was good.”

“Hate and fear come in many different flavors, my Annie.” He gave her a sad smile. “Tell me more about the album.”

Bill was right. As much as she wanted to, she couldn’t fix everything and everyone overnight.

“In the wedding photo, Isaac Goldstein was dressed in his military best with medals and ribbons,” she said. “The photo…” she searched for the right words. “It made me question everything I’d once accepted as irrefutable. Isaac Goldstein was a decorated war hero—how could he have been a traitor to his country?”

“An interesting dichotomy,” Bill said.

“He was also so normal-looking. I’d say ordinary, but that’s not quite right, because even through the photos I could tell he must have been very charismatic. And handsome. Nothing like the photo of him that’s plastered all over the internet. Death to Goldstein! That man looked like something straight out of Orwell's *1984.*"

Bill raised an eyebrow. "You don't believe that's a coincidence, do you?"

Annette leaned against the hard booth, taken aback. She'd read *1984* in high school, the year before she'd learned about her grandfather. There was a character in the novel, Emmanuel Goldstein, who was used as the focal point of hatred. His ugly, distorted face was broadcast on all telescreens each day so the masses could yell and scream and direct their fury and resentment toward him in what was known as 'Two Minutes Hate.'

"*Merde*," Annette said. "Do you think the government created the 'Death to Goldstein' posters with that awful picture so people would identify him with Orwell's monster?"

"I've always thought so," Bill said. "*1984* was popular during the peak of the anti-communist frenzy. Everyone was reading it at the time your grandfather was executed. If Emmanuel Goldstein was 'the number one enemy of the state,' as he was called in the book, then wouldn't people conflate his image with this other Goldstein?"

"So you don't believe my grandfather was a spy?"

"I'm not saying that." He swished his teabag back and forth in the mug. "He was a known member of the Communist Party. But I've told you before there's a lot more to Isaac Goldstein's execution than is taught in schools. Many theories and speculation. One supposition is the government was trying to create fear in the form of a communist threat in order to garner support for the Korean War."

A group of burly young men had pushed in from outside and were crowding the bar to watch the football game on the hanging TV. They shouted and cheered.

Bill leaned closer to her across the table so as to be heard. "Even at the time, a contingent was against his execution. And now recently released KGB documents suggest Goldstein wasn't as deeply involved as believed. A few political experts theorize he was executed as an example, because they couldn't catch the real spy."

"So you believe there was someone else?" Annette asked.

"Don't know." Bill pushed his glasses up. "Problem is no one's ever identified anyone who might have done what Goldstein was accused of."

"A memoir just came out by a former KGB agent," Annette said. "He claims someone else was involved but doesn't name names. Still, there may be something useful in the book. I'll get hold of it tomorrow."

"Good. I was wondering when you'd get off your ass and approach this like a journalist."

"That's not fair," she said. "This hits too close to home. Especially when I saw how it scarred my mother and grandmother."

"I know it's not fair, but just because it's personal doesn't mean you should shy away from investigating. The key to being a good journalist is to be able to view any situation objectively."

"You can take the professor out of the classroom, but…"

He waved her joke away with his hand. "I'm glad you're finally able to talk about this without getting angry and defensive."

"I wasn't defens…" She stopped herself. "Okay, maybe a little. Anyway, there was something in the album I'm following up on. Photos of my grandparents with a couple named Mariasha and Aaron Lowe."

Bill scrunched up his face and shook his head to indicate that he didn't recognize the names.

"They had a daughter named Essie Lowe who'd been my mother's friend," she said. "I started researching the Lowes looking for other connections between them and my grandfather. "

Bill nodded, as though to encourage her, just like he used to do in class.

"Aaron Lowe died thirty years ago, at the age of eighty," she said. "I found an obit online. He was survived by his wife, Mariasha, daughter Esther, also known as Essie, and two grandchildren. He'd been an economics professor at NYU."

"Hmmm."

"You think that's significant?"

Bill took off his glasses and examined them. "If he was teaching at NYU in the 1930s, there's a good chance he was a communist or at least a socialist. Most of the professors were left-wing back then. There wasn't the stigma of being a communist that developed years later. I can research him for you. Did you find anything on Mariasha?"

"Quite a bit, actually. She was a sculptress. Worked primarily in metal. Has several pieces on display at a few small museums."

"Is she alive?"

"At least as of an hour ago," Annette said.

"She must be pretty old."

"Ninety-five. A bio mentioned that she's still in the same apartment in the Lower East Side that she lived in with her husband. I looked it up. It's on Ridge Street, one of the few buildings that haven't been bulldozed."

"I take it you're planning to pay her a visit."

"I am."

"Interesting," Bill said. "You'll be returning to the same neighborhood where your grandparents and mother once lived."

“That’s right.” The place her mother refused to revisit.

Annette ran her fingertips over the carved initials, hearts, and dates in the wood tabletop. ‘63. ‘79. ‘48. Had any of these people been back? And if so, were they happy they had returned, or sorry they disturbed their memories of the past?

CHAPTER 4

The thought of going back to his childhood house in Forest Hills, Queens always caused a knot in his stomach. Even now, almost twenty years after his father's death, Julian still felt the same hollow ache knowing Dad wouldn't be there. Would never be there again. But as much as he didn't want to return, he needed to see his mother and clear away the past.

A blast of cold air sliced through the army-surplus jacket that he'd dug out of the back of his closet after Sephora had stomped out of their apartment. The old jacket was special to him, a souvenir from the brief period when he'd lived in Paris. Despite his hat, his ears felt like they might freeze and crack off, but at least it had stopped snowing. He turned up his collar and ducked his head down into his jacket like a turtle as he entered his old neighborhood. Streetlights brightened the snow that was neatly piled against the curbs and around the bases of thick oak trees.

He turned the corner. He slowed his pace as his heart sped up. His childhood house was down the street. A rambling white Colonial with peeling paint, it stuck out from among the large, elegant brick and stucco Tudors as much as Julian had stuck out among the other kids. He'd been the fatherless geek, the kid who preferred homework to teamwork.

Smoke circled up from the red brick chimney into a pewter sky. He blinked. No. There was no smoke. That had been a memory, or maybe an illusion. His mother never made a fire in the fireplace.

He turned down his collar, pulled his head up out of his jacket, and opened the front door with the rarely used key he kept on his key ring. "Essie," he called, stepping into the small foyer. There had been a time when he called her Mom, but that had been when Dad was alive and Julian had felt like he was part of a family.

The house had its customary sterile smell and the entranceway was still covered with the paisley-patterned wallpaper from his childhood. There was a piece missing at the bottom that he'd torn off when he was a kid. He didn't think his mom even noticed.

He hung his jacket and hat on one of the wooden pegs that were almost too low for coats. His dad had screwed those pegs into the wall and probably set them at a height that Julian and his sister Rhonda could reach when they were kids.

He heard the slam of a cupboard door in the kitchen and tentative footsteps crossing the planked dining-room floor.

His mother stood in the arched foyer doorway, her arms crossed over her chest. She was tall, almost his height, and as erect as a model balancing a book on her head. She wore a white button-down blouse and black slacks, her wavy hair cut along her jawline like she'd always styled it, except there were now streaks of white mixed with the dark blonde.

"Your call was certainly a surprise." Her blue eyes were slightly unfocused, and Julian picked up a vague scent that could have been antiseptics. She must have just gotten back from the hospital. Dr. Essie Sandman. Not Esther. Odd that she used her childhood nickname professionally, but maybe it appealed to her kid patients, who called her Dr. Essie.

"A nice surprise, I hope," he said.

"So do I."

Essie was such a downer, always expecting the worst. But that could have been because she was an oncologist and many of her young patients died. Or maybe her negative disposition had led her to her chosen profession.

"I figured you'd be out celebrating your big day with friends," she said.

She had remembered his birthday. He hadn't expected that.

"I'll get you a beer. We can sit in the living room." She headed toward the kitchen before he could remark on how odd it was that she had beer in the house.

He stepped into the "dead room" as he thought of it, since it was anything but a living room. It hadn't changed in his lifetime and was rarely used since Dad died. His eyes roamed over the leather Chesterfield sofa and two navy-and-green plaid club chairs. Built-in bookshelves faced the windows, which were flanked with heavy drapes that matched the chairs. In the corner of the room was the game table where Julian and his dad once played chess every evening, until they didn't. That ended when Julian was ten.

The heart attack had come while Dad was making dinner. Julian had heard a crash in the kitchen and ran in to find his father unconscious on the floor. Julian tried to shake his father awake, then called 911. Terrified, he left an urgent message for his mother, who'd been at the hospital working. If she'd been home, would that have changed anything? Probably, but unfortunately you couldn't change the past.

Julian crossed to the white brick fireplace that hadn't had a fire going since his father's death. At least he could change that. He jiggled the flue open. A basket of logs sat on the hearthstone. They were probably twenty years old, but wood was wood. Julian laid the fire like he remembered his father doing, broke off a piece of kindling and lit it with a match from the matchbox. The fire caught.

He fanned it and watched the flames flick against the logs, just as they had when he was a kid. He stood up, pleased with himself, and took a step back from the fireplace.

The familiar watercolor painting confronted him from above the mantel. It was a large piece, about two feet by three, and framed behind non-reflective glass. Julian had always been fascinated by the dark red stain that seemed to explode like a blood-tinged geyser. On the bottom of the composition lay mysterious, three-dimensional black shapes that looked like rotten potatoes, and everywhere were neon green dots that practically glowed. The painting was unsigned, but Julian could tell, even as a child, that the artist was very skilled. He had once asked his mother why she kept such a disturbing painting in the living room, but she had ignored his question.

"Here you go." Essie seemed a bit wobbly as she came into the room and handed him one of the pewter steins she was carrying. She glanced at the fire in the hearth, then perched on the arm of the leather sofa and took a swig of her beer. Had she been drinking before he got here? But his mother never drank, did she? Julian knew very little about what his mother did or didn't do.

He sat on the club chair closest to her, feeling awkward. He saw her every few months or so, usually at a restaurant in Manhattan. She'd call him when she was coming into the City to see a play or visit a museum.

Essie took another swallow, then rested the beer stein on her thigh. "Well, you must have something on your mind to make the long trek out here. What's wrong?"

Where to begin? "I quit my job."

She tilted her head, as he imagined she did when she examined an x-ray to determine how serious her patient's condition was. "What triggered that?"

"I hated what I was doing. I guess I finally reached the saturation point."

"Milestone birthdays can do that. Are you thinking of practicing medicine? Would you like me to make some calls?"

"No," he said, a little too harshly. He softened his voice. "But thank you. That's not why I'm here."

"Then why are you here?"

He stared across the room at the table where he and his father once played chess. "I've decided it's time to change my life. To try to make myself happy for once."

"I thought you were happy."

He shook his head. She obviously didn't know him very well, either.

"Well, I hope you find what you're looking for," she said.

"That's it?"

"What do you expect me to say?"

Julian got up and went over to bookshelves. The upper shelves were filled with dozens of medical books, the bottom two with his dad's favorites— Clancy, King, Turow, Michener, Ken Follett's *Pillars of the Earth.*

What had he been expecting from her? That she'd finally react? Finally notice him? "I wonder if you have any idea how badly I wanted your approval when I was growing up."

"You had my approval."

"It sure never felt that way," he said. "After Dad died, I remember when you'd come home from the hospital, I'd show you my drawings. Dad always told me how much potential I had as an artist, but you hardly looked at them."

She took a sip of beer. "It was a difficult time for me, too."

"I know that, and all I wanted to do was make you happy. Rhonda was off at college, so it was just the two of us. And when I saw that my art meant nothing to you, I started working harder in school."

She gave him a funny look that he didn't know how to interpret.

"I thought if I went to medical school, that would make you proud, but you didn't even come to my graduation. So I went for a PhD at one of the top biophysics programs in the country, but you didn't make it to that ceremony either. Only Nana came. Only Nana cared about me."

"Pfff," she said, pushing the air away with her hand. "Your grandmother only cares about herself."

"That's not true. It's Nana who's been around for me since Dad died." A collection of his father's pipes were lying on a shelf. He picked one up, feeling the weight of the polished bowl in his hand. "I spent my whole life trying to get your attention, but you were too busy to notice."

"That's just your perception, Julian."

"Really? So help me fix my perception. Tell me that whatever path I choose, you'll still be proud of me. Even if I decide to take up painting again."

She looked away. "Is that what you're planning to do?"

"Yes," he said, even though up until this moment he had been unsure of his next move. Still wasn't sure of it.

"You're thirty years old. You don't need my approval."

"I know that, but I would like it. And I'd finally like to understand why you never seemed to care about me when I was a kid."

"I did the best I could." She stared into her beer stein. "I'm not a warm, hugging person. That was your father's role. I was the breadwinner and I enabled him to be the nurturer. It was an arrangement we both wanted."

But was it the arrangement Julian had wanted? Sure, he understood it. His dad had been a fifth-grade teacher and was always home early. He made dinner, reviewed

Julian's homework, took care of Julian when he was hurt. Julian held the pipe to his nose, imagining he could still smell cherry tobacco smoke.

"That's why we worked as a family," his mother said. "We each had our own areas of responsibility." She took another gulp and set the stein on the end table. "Then your father died. And I didn't know how to do the things he'd been so good at. So I just kept doing the part I knew. It wasn't like I had much instruction on being a good mother from my own."

"I know you and Nana have issues, but…"

"It wasn't just your grandmother and me. She had problems with her brother, too." Essie got up from the arm of the sofa and went over to the fireplace, where she gazed up at the watercolor above the mantel. "He painted this," she said. "My Uncle Saul."

"Are you kidding?" he said. "This has been here my entire life. You never mentioned someone in the family made it."

"Didn't I?" she said. "Uncle Saul gave it to me as a present. On my thirteenth birthday. My mother was very angry about that."

Saul had been his grandmother's younger brother. Nana occasionally talked about him, but she never said he'd been an artist or that they'd had issues.

"Why are you telling me this now?" he asked.

"To give you some understanding of what your grandmother's really like. You see, she took the painting away from me and hid it. I found it years later."

"Why would she hide it?"

"She hides a lot of things."

It was hard to believe how different Essie's perceptions of his grandmother were from his own. "What you're saying about Nana makes no sense to me."

"Your grandmother shows you a different side of herself. She loves you." She leaned against the mantel, as though she needed support to keep from falling. "But she hates me. Always has."

"Hates you?" he said. "No, she doesn't."

She gave him a sad smile, looking like a hurt child.

He got that knot in his stomach again, but this time it felt like he'd read something he shouldn't have in his mother's hidden diary. Some dirty little secret he'd have been better off not knowing.

CHAPTER 5

Annette had a problem. It was one thing to start an investigation, quite another to execute it effectively. Barging in on Mariasha Lowe and asking if she believed her old friend Isaac Goldstein was innocent, probably wasn't the best way to get information. Mariasha would likely get defensive and kick Annette out on her butt. If she could even kick. Annette had spent the morning researching the once-famous sculptress, but had found no references to her in the last few years. Even if she was physically and mentally okay—a big 'if' for a ninety-five-year-old, Mariasha might not be willing to meet. So before she tried to set something up, Annette needed a good reason to persuade the old woman to grant her an interview.

After exhausting all links to Mariasha Lowe on the internet, Annette decided to head down to the Barnes & Noble in Union Square. She hoped they would have art books that contained examples of Mariasha's sculptures, or better still, personal info about the sculptress or a hook for an article that Annette could claim she was writing. Once she had a plausible approach nailed down, she could then figure out how to get Mariasha to agree to see her.

The bookstore was crowded, not surprising for a Saturday morning. Annette pushed past the shoppers rummaging through discount tables laden with books to the Art and Architecture section in the rear of the store. She found several coffee table books featuring one or two pieces of Mariasha Lowe's work, but none contained much insight into the artist. Then, she came across a small book called *Evoking the Great Depression*. It featured art projects primarily by New Deal artists, but included Mariasha Lowe because of her themes. The book was broken into chapters on Social Realism, The American Worker, and America at Play and Rest. Mariasha's work was discussed in the last section complete with photos of several of her pieces. Very promising.

She went to the 'Non-Fiction New Releases' section to look for the book by the Soviet agent that had referenced Isaac Goldstein. She took the clipping from *Le Figaro* out of her wallet—*A Soviet Spy in America* by Boris Yaklisov. She found it, paid for both books, then went to the upstairs café where she bought a cappuccino. Someone was getting up from a window table with a view of Union Square Park and Annette quickly nabbed the table.

Outside, beyond the skeletal trees, she could see the tops of white tents set up for the Saturday greenmarket and hundreds of people milling about the fresh produce stalls. The snow from last night had been shoveled into mounds near the street, though there were still patches of white at the bases of the trees and near the colonnaded arcade. In the distance, she could make out the equestrian statue of George Washington. This wasn't far from where her grandparents had lived, and she wondered if her grandfather had come by the park seventy or eighty years ago. Would he have admired the statue of America's first president or had Isaac Goldstein been too enamored of communist ideals?

She flipped through the index of the Soviet agent's book, looking for the name Isaac Goldstein. There were far fewer references to her grandfather than Annette had been hoping for. But then she read that Yaklisov hadn't been Goldstein's primary point of contact. The Soviet agent had only met Goldstein on two occasions, but those had been enough to form Yaklisov's impression of him.

She found the passage that had been quoted in the *Le Figaro* review.

> Goldstein was never a major player in communist spy circles. He was charming and enthusiastic, but frankly, he did not seem altogether serious about the communist mission. He was more interested in acting the part of a spy than actually doing any serious work. It was obvious to me and other handlers that Goldstein didn't have access to atomic-bomb secrets that he allegedly stole and passed on to the communists. That all came from another source.

Allegedly stole. Annette reread the words. So he'd probably been set up. But by whom? The government? Trusted friends?

She skimmed the next few paragraphs, but the author hadn't said anything further about who this other "source" could be.

She closed the book. Would Mariasha Lowe have known Isaac Goldstein's circle of friends well enough to be able to hypothesize on a possible traitor?

Annette pulled the photo album out of her satchel and flipped to the page of her grandparents with the Lowes in December 1943 at the Laurels Hotel. The two smiling couples were posed in front of a toboggan. Had they met for the first time at this resort in the Catskill Mountains, or had they already been friends before this photo was taken?

She turned to the page of the four of them at the Starlight Roof restaurant. December 1944, one year later. But the photo of the two little girls—her mother Sally and Essie Lowe—was taken in 1950. *In front of our apartment on 120 Columbia Street,* the caption read.

The Lowes and the Goldsteins would have been friends from at least 1943 through 1950, so there was a very good chance that Mariasha was acquainted with others who associated with Isaac Goldstein. Would she know the person who had committed atomic espionage and let Isaac Goldstein take the fall in his place?

She put aside the photo album, picked up *Evoking the Great Depression*, and turned to the section on Mariasha Lowe. There was a general description of her work, her major pieces, where they were on display, and then a biographical sketch, which was consistent with much of what Annette had already learned in her previous internet research.

She tapped her notes into her laptop as she sipped her cappuccino, hoping to find an inspiration for an article.

Born in Brooklyn, 1918 as Mariasha Hirsch, the older of two children. Brother Saul, born 1922. Father died in 1925, mother in 1939.

Annette did the math. Mariasha would have been seven when her father died, twenty-one when her mother died. That would have been tough. Her brother would have been seventeen. Had Mariasha been close to her brother? But even if she was, it was unlikely that he had a connection to Isaac Goldstein.

She continued reading and taking notes.

Attended Brooklyn College 1935-39. Married Aaron Lowe, economics professor at NYU, in December 1943.

Same as her grandparents. So the two couples were most likely both on their honeymoons in the photo at the Laurels Hotel.

She read on.

Mariasha's daughter Esther was born in 1945, but Annette already knew that. Essie had been her mother's friend and classmate.

Then nothing for the next eight years. What was Mariasha doing? Raising Essie? Sculpting?

Mariasha's first show was in 1954, which just happened to be the year after Isaac Goldstein's execution.

Then the article moved into a discussion of Mariasha's work.

> Mariasha Lowe's sculptures are evocative of Depression-era America. However her pieces of men, women, and children at work and play differ from the thick, brooding artwork one typically associates with the WPA Depression-era artists. Lowe's work has a lightness and an energy, as though her creations are about to step off their marble bases and finish what they've begun.

Annette studied a picture of one of Mariasha's sculptures called *Girl Playing Hopscotch* and quickly understood the comment about lightness and energy. The sculpture was composed of only metal pipes and spheres, but in it Annette could see a child poised on one leg, about to jump through the air to the next square.

As a journalist, Annette could appreciate how difficult it was to convey so much so sparingly. Bill always said, "Make everything count in your writing," and that was exactly what Mariasha had accomplished with her art.

She browsed through a few more pages, her admiration growing for this woman who had once known her grandfather.

But who was Mariasha Lowe and what had motivated her to create such powerful sculptures? Was this the hook she should use to approach Mariasha for a story? How people from her past influenced her? Or maybe Annette could use the angle of how growing up during the Depression inspired her work, then use that as a lead into communism. From there, she could ask Mariasha if she knew the Goldsteins, since they were from the same neighborhood, then move on to friends and common interests. That could work. She felt a tingle of excitement as often happened when an idea for an article began to jell. Now she was ready to meet the woman.

She had found Mariasha Lowe's street address and phone number in her earlier research. Should she call and tell her about the article she was planning to write, then ask if she could come by? But what if Mariasha refused to see her?

She finished the cappuccino. Maybe it would be better to just show up. Bill always joked about how hard it was to say no to Annette in person. And if Mariasha still refused, well, how hard could it be to wrestle down a ninety-five-year old?

CHAPTER 6

Julian's head felt like it was being squashed under the arm of an angry linebacker as he buried it beneath his pillow. Too much to drink. *What doesn't kill us makes us stronger.* At least that's what Nietzsche said, but Julian wasn't so sure.

After leaving his mother's house last night, he had decided to celebrate his birthday by heading over to a seedy bar in the East Village. Sephora kept texting him, *Where the hell r u?* but he didn't answer. Finally she wrote, *U r a giant asshole*, at which point he turned his phone off.

The bar was frequented mostly by NYU students and a few derelicts and he ended up downing shots with a bunch of communications majors until he was feeling no pain. He vaguely remembered giving his wool hat to a blonde with a Lauren-Bacall sneer, then somehow getting home, saying hi to his doorman and collapsing on his bed.

A hell of a way to celebrate his thirtieth birthday.

But now he was thirty and a day. He opened his eyes, blinking against the late morning light that came in through the balcony sliding doors, cursing himself for not closing the blinds the night before. At least the door was shut, so it wasn't freezing inside. He checked the other side of the bed. No Sephora. Was she sleeping out in the living room? That wasn't exactly her style.

He brought his legs over to the side of the bed trying not to set off an explosive chain reaction in his head. Slowly, he stood up, then went to the kitchen to grab some Advil, bracing himself for a mega-confrontation with his girlfriend. But Sephora wasn't stretched out on the sofa, sipping coffee and thumbing through one of her fashion magazines. Thank you, God. Of course, this was simply a postponement of the inevitable. Sephora wasn't one to pass up an opportunity to fight.

He took three Advils, ate a couple of bananas, then went to shower. The steam and pounding water cleared his head. Last night, his mother had said she wasn't feeling well shortly after her emotional remarks about Nana, and had asked him to leave. He had been peeved by her abrupt dismissal, but now he processed what she had told him. He had a great-uncle who had painted. That made two family members who had been artists—Nana and Saul—so maybe his plan to pursue painting wasn't all that far-fetched. If that's what he really wanted, because on some level he wondered if he had latched onto painting in order to spite his mother. And then, what was really going on between his mother and Nana? He hadn't realized how hurt she'd been by Nana and how much it resembled his own pain. Were he and his mother more alike than he wanted to admit? No way. He and Essie were about as different as two people could be.

He turned off the water and dried himself with a towel as he returned to his bedroom. He opened the closet door. What the hell? There was a pile of clothes on the floor. His clothes. Sephora's shoes, bags, dresses, pants and shirts were all gone, but she'd scrawled a note on the closet wall. GO TO HELL. He stepped closer. She had used red nail polish.

He sat down on the bed. Sephora had left him. Shouldn't he be sad or angry or disappointed? Some reaction to show that his relationship with this woman over the last two years had meant something to him? But whatever love or attraction he once felt for her had faded a long time ago. And then he started to laugh. Nail polish. Sephora had said goodbye to him with red nail polish.

Probably last season's shade. He fell back against the bed and laughed until his stomach hurt. His head started pounding again. He caught his breath, wiped away the tears of laughter, and sat back up.

She was gone. But that was okay. He no longer had to put on an act for anyone. He was free to start over.

He reached into the heap of clothes in his closet and pulled out a pair of worn jeans and a stretched-out crew neck sweater that Sephora hated. He dressed quickly, grabbed his army-surplus jacket, and took the stairs down the nine flights to the lobby.

Sephora was gone.

What doesn't kill us makes us stronger.

CHAPTER 7

Stronger. He was already feeling stronger. Just a little, but it was a start. Goodbye job. Goodbye Sephora. But Essie was a tougher nut to crack. He had taken one step forward with her, but it felt like he had fallen back two. Maybe his grandmother could get him on track.

Most of the slush had been cleared off the sidewalks from yesterday's storm and Julian walked through the West Village passing hip new restaurants and yuppie bars, double-parked BMWs, doormen flagging down taxis in front of renovated luxury apartment buildings like his. It was like he was seeing his neighborhood for the first time. Damn. Why had it taken him so long to realize he didn't belong here?

He walked farther and farther from this phony place, stepping over a 'Happy New Year' tiara, a crushed gold horn, and silver streamers, crossing Houston Street into the Lower East Side and the rich, spicy smells of his childhood. Rusted fire escapes clung to old tenement buildings like vines. Some of the restaurants had been here for a hundred years—Yonah Shimmel's Knishes, Russ & Daughters Appetizers, Katz's Deli. His grandmother's world.

He turned south and went down the familiar streets. Her apartment building was just as it had always been. Brick and solid, with bay windows overlooking the front courtyard where Julian used to throw a rubber ball against the wall when he was a kid.

The outer door was oak, abraded and darkened with age. Julian ran his finger over the buzzers on the adjacent wall. The name beside Apt. 4B was barely legible. The paper it was written on had probably been there for the last sixty or seventy years. Aaron Lowe, it still said, even though he'd been dead thirty years, since shortly before Julian was born.

He pressed the buzzer and waited, knowing it sometimes took her awhile to get to the intercom.

"Yes?" her sweet scratchy voice said. "Who's there?"

"It's me, Nana." And for the first time in a long while, he was where he belonged.

A comforting staleness, reminding him of the *Musée de la Vie Romantique* in Paris, hit Julian when his grandmother opened the door to her apartment. She had to hold her head back to look up at him. Her dark eyes were clouded by cataracts and her short chaotic hair looked like silver tinsel.

"Hi, Nana." He took in her quirky outfit, typical for her—leopard-print pants, a red sweater that was way too big, and earrings with clusters of magenta stones. She was so tiny that he had to stoop all the way over to kiss her soft crepe-skinned cheek. She smelled citrusy, like she always did. How could his mother speak about this woman as though she was the devil?

"I think you're growing and I'm shrinking," Nana said. "At this rate, in another ten years you'll be a giant and I'll be no bigger than a mouse."

Julian laughed. His grandmother was in her nineties, but she liked to joke about the future as though she was going to be around forever. And he wished she could be. The thought of a world without Mariasha Lowe left him with a hollow feeling inside.

"How does that song go?" she said. "If I knew you were coming I'd have baked you a birthday cake."

"Sorry. I should have called. But you never have to do anything special for me."

"I can still make you something to eat. It's almost lunchtime."

"I'm good. I had a couple of bananas." He took of his army jacket and hooked it on the coat rack.

"How about some nice French toast or macaroni and cheese?"

His childhood favorites. "Thank you, Nana, but I'm not really hungry. Can we talk?"

"Of course."

Julian left his shoes in the foyer, not wanting to get scolded for messing up his grandmother's rugs. It was kind of funny that here, with his grandmother, he felt like a child again—safe and loved.

He followed her into the living room. She moved cautiously, her eyes on her feet as she tottered across the wood floor and pale pink area rug. The soft leather of her flats bulged from her bunions. She hoisted herself up into one of the two turquoise leather chairs closest to the windowed alcove where three of her sculptures stood.

The apartment hadn't changed since Julian's earliest memories. It was like stepping into a circa 1945 time capsule, where every object seemed important because of the absence of clutter. Nana still had a wind-up Victor Victrola in one corner and, against the long wall, a large wood console with its original black-and-white television. The TV hadn't worked even when he was a kid and he wondered why she kept it. Julian had gotten her a flat-screen TV for her bedroom that he knew she watched because she was always up-to-date on the latest episodes of *Downton Abbey.*

The walls were the same mint green they had always been, and in front of the console was a crimson art deco sofa with bulbous arms and the two turquoise chairs. He remembered Sephora's reaction the first time she came here. She'd pinched Julian's arm and whispered, not realizing Nana's hearing was excellent. "This stuff is so retro. I'd love it in our place."

His grandmother had called out in her sweetest voice. "I'm not dead yet, darling."

"How's your girlfriend?" Nana asked now, as though reading Julian's mind. "Cremora? Remora? I never remember her name."

"Sephora."

"That's right. Sephora. What kind of people name their child after a make-up store?"

"We broke up."

"I'm sorry to hear that," she said. "Sorry if it makes you sad. Not sorry about the girl."

"I know you didn't like her much."

"She was pretty," Nana said. "There are plenty of pretty girls out there."

"She was a symptom of the wrong choices I've been making."

His grandmother nodded, as though she knew what he was referring to.

"Somehow I got myself into the wrong life," he said. "Wrong girlfriend. Wrong apartment. Wrong career."

He went over to the sculptures that Nana had created with her own hands. Most of her work had been sold or given to museums, but she had kept these three for herself. Each one was a four-foot-high representation of a person made of steel rods and bronze golf-ball joints, a bit like the Tinkertoy set he'd played with as a kid. The brass plaques on their bases read: *Woman Wearing New Hat. Man Reading. Boy Playing Stickball.*

They'd been there his entire life, but Julian had never paid much attention to them. Of course, Julian was realizing there was quite a bit he hadn't noticed growing up.

"Anyway," he said. "I'm trying to fix all that. I quit my job and now that Sephora's gone, I can start looking for a new apartment."

"And will that make everything better?" she asked.

He turned back to her. "Not everything." He sat down in the chair next to hers. "I went to see Essie last night."

"Good," she said. "You should spend more time with your mother."

"That's never been easy for me."

"Your mother loves you."

"So you've been telling me my whole life, but I'm trying to understand why she never seemed to want to be around me."

His grandmother closed her eyes. Her wrinkled cheeks and mouth sagged and she looked terribly sad.

Julian rested his elbows on his knees. "Nana, I need your help."

She opened her eyes. "You know I'd do anything for you."

"Then please explain to me why she's so cold and angry. Did she not want me? Rhonda's ten years older. Was I a mistake she can't get over?"

"Oh, Julian. It's nothing like that. I'm telling you, your mother loves you."

"Then what's going on?"

"Sometimes that happens between parents and children. An inability to communicate."

A dull light came in through the windows making the three sculptures seem forlorn. "Was that what happened between you and Essie?" he asked.

His grandmother rubbed her pointer finger with her thumb.

"Nana, I'm not completely blind. My mother never visits you. Why is that? And I remember the two of you fighting all the time when I was a child."

"What can I say, Julian? My daughter and I never got along."

"But why not?"

She sighed. "I wasn't a good mother. I wish I could have been, but the world I grew up in molded me. I made promises to my parents. I had responsibilities to my brother. Maybe I just didn't have enough left over to be a good mother, too."

"I don't buy that," he said.

She turned her gold wedding band around. Her fingers were knobby from arthritis. These were the hands that had once created intricate sculptures; now they resembled her work.

"My mother told me about your brother Saul."

His grandmother started, as though she'd heard a sudden noise. "What did she tell you about him?"

"That he was an artist."

"He liked to paint, but he was never an artist."

He looked at the walls, unadorned except for a purple neon clock and fan-shaped sconces. "Do you have any of his paintings?"

"No."

"Did you know Essie has one?"

Her face grew pale.

"Saul gave her the painting that's hanging in our living room."

"She has that?" Her voice was practically a whisper.

"Yes," he said. "And she told me you hid it from her. Why did you do that?"

"It was a terrible painting."

"It was her birthday present."

She shook her head, angry about something.

"Essie told me that you and she fought about it," he said. "Is that why you're still upset with each other? Because of the painting?"

"I wanted to protect her. That's all I ever hoped to do."

"She said you and Saul didn't get along."

Her face hardened, her lips forming a straight line. "Your mother knows nothing about my relationship with Saul. He was my baby brother. I sacrificed everything for him."

"Then tell me, Nana." He sat forward on the chair. "Tell me about your parents and your brother. Tell me so I can understand my mother. So I can understand myself."

She squeezed her eyes shut and shook her head.

"Why not? Is there something you don't want me to know?"

Her eyelids opened. She licked her lips. "It's all in the past. Nothing in the past can help you."

"But I think it can."

She seemed to shrink into the big turquoise chair. Her eyes clouded over as she stared at the three sculptures.

"Please, Nana."

Finally, she let out a heavy sigh. "Okay, Julian. I'll tell you our story. I only hope it will help, not hurt you."

He almost reminded his grandmother about Nietzsche's words—*What doesn't kill us makes us stronger*—but he had a feeling she wouldn't appreciate them.

CHAPTER 8

She didn't want to tell him any of it, but her grandson had a point. How could he ever be himself if he didn't know where he had come from? So she would tell him some of the story, but never would she reveal everything. Not to Julian, not to anyone.

Mariasha looked across the room at the sculptures she had created. Mama adjusting the treasured hat she had made for herself. Papa immersed in a favorite book. And Saulie, poor Saulie, playing a momentous game of stickball. The frozen figures had emerged from her desperate effort to preserve the people she loved in a moment of happiness, so she wouldn't have to dwell on how she had failed them.

Julian was on the edge of the other chair, his stocking foot tapping on the floor, impatient and frustrated, just like her brother had once been.

She studied the optimistic swoop of the rods that formed the shoulders of *Boy Playing Stickball.* "First, I would like to clear something up, Julian," she said.

He looked at her expectantly, his blue eyes reminding her of his mother's, just like the cat's-eye marble Mariasha had had as a child.

"I loved my brother," she said. "Maybe too much."

"What do you mean?"

"You want to hear our story, so I'm going to tell it to you from the beginning. Then, maybe you'll understand."

The clanking sound of the radiator started up and the room filled with stale heat.

"My parents came from Russia in the early 1900s," she began. "They ran away to escape the pogroms against the Jews, hoping to find safety in America. A place to raise their children." She ran her tongue over her lips. "My father, I think, was in love with America. The land of liberty, he used to say. But he also felt, like many of the other immigrants, that he had to do his part to help shape America. He was very active as a social democrat. And that was how my little brother and I were taught to see our country. As a place where equality should prevail. Where everyone deserved a fair shake—black, white, immigrant. Everyone."

She told him about how poor her family had been, how her father had gotten sick when she was a little girl. That after she'd heard the doctor talking about germs and using separate plates, she was always reluctant to eat food her mother hadn't prepared. She recounted how her father had been a thinking man, an educated man, who wanted her to study, to learn, to teach her brother. He would read books to her and made her promise to read them to Saul.

"My father died when I was seven," she said. "My mother was left alone with little money to raise two young children. She took in laundry and sold eggs to neighbors from our tiny apartment."

Julian's face was in a frown, as though he was picturing this.

"Saul was not even three when Papa died," Mariasha said. "Mama was busy trying to support us and my brother became my responsibility."

She looked at the sculpture of *Boy Playing Stickball*. They were a couple of ragamuffins, she and her brother, living their childhoods with practically no supervision.

"I read him the books my father had read to me. Stories by Sholem Aleichem. Books and pamphlets I didn't fully understand at the time. About equality for all."

She leaned her head against the chair and closed her eyes. "They have a name for children who grew up like my brother and me," she said. "Red-diaper babies. Children whose fathers or mothers were sympathizers with certain communist ideals."

Julian looked startled. "So were you a communist?"

Mariasha released a long heavy breath. "Let me tell you the whole story, then you be the judge of what I was."

June 1932

Mari watched the stickball game from the stoop of their apartment building. Last inning. Man on second. Saulie's team behind by one.

It was hot and there was no breeze. Even the diapers on the clotheslines between the tenements hung motionless. Mari's heavy black braid made her back sweaty. She threw it in front of her shoulder and fanned herself with the book she'd borrowed from the public library. *Campfire Girls at Work.* Next month, she was going to camp for a week and she wanted to learn everything she could about camping. This was the fourth *Campfire Girls* book she'd read. She couldn't wait to hike in the woods and learn how to build a fire, where she'd roast marshmallows and tell spooky stories.

Saulie was up at bat, clutching the broom handle low, his dirty white shirt pulling out of his overalls. He was four years younger than Mari—ten and small for his age—but he was one of the best hitters on the street. He could win the game for them now.

The pitcher, a twelve-year-old named Louie from around the corner, threw the rubber ball. Saul swung. The stick connected with a thwap and the ball went flying over the second baseman's head toward the butcher shop.

Mari jumped up. “Go Saulie!” she shouted.

Saulie raced the bases marked in chalk, red curls bouncing, his short sturdy legs churning up and down like engine pistons.

The ball bounced behind a parked car and two boys ran to get it. The second baseman got there first. He fumbled the ball, trying to throw it to Irving, who was standing in front of home base waving his arms. “Throw, you *shmendrick!*” Irving screamed.

Saulie was nearing home base, a chalk mark on the rough asphalt. The second baseman wound up his arm and threw.

Don’t slide, Saulie, don’t slide. Stop trying to be a hero. Her brother had already torn up his other pair of overalls, and his legs were covered with scabs.

Saulie slid into home.

“Safe,” the umpire said.

Saulie got up, a wide grin on his face. Blood darkened the fabric on his freshly torn pants. The other kids surrounded him, patting his back.

She shook her head, even though she was proud of him. “Saulie, come inside,” she called. “I need to get that cut cleaned up.” She closed her book and went to get him. She knew how stubborn he could get.

“Good game,” a man said to Saulie. He was standing near a small truck with *Portraits* written on its side, and he had a camera box and a folded tripod under his arm. “Let me take a picture of you swinging. Maybe your ma would like it.” He handed Saulie the broomstick, which had been lying on the curb.

“But his pants are torn,” Mari said.

“You’ll hardly notice in the picture.” The man opened the wood camera box like an accordion and set it up on the tripod in the street. “Ready?”

Saulie went into a swing pose, hamming it up with a fake serious expression.

"Say *toochis*!" the man said, smacking his butt.

"*Toochis*." Saul's face broke into a grin, revealing his too-big front teeth that made him resemble a beaver.

The man took the picture, then glanced at Mari. "What about you? You're awfully pretty with those big dark eyes, especially when you smile."

Mari covered her mouth with her hand. Mama had told her she shouldn't smile so wide, so as not to tempt the evil spirits, but Mari couldn't help it sometimes. "No thank you."

The man shrugged. "What apartment are you in? I'll bring the photo up to your mother after I've developed it."

"2B," Saul said.

Mama was making stuffed cabbage and it stank all the way into the outside hall. The apartment was different from when Papa had been alive. Mama had sold the velvet drapes, rugs from the living room and dining room, and a few of the pretty cut glass bowls that she'd kept in the china cabinet and on the coffee table.

Mari had done her best to fill the empty spaces. She had turned broken broomsticks, rusty pipes, cracked dishes, rubber balls, and whatever else she could find, into tiny people. She chose not to dress them in scraps of fabric, preferring to leave their elegant attire to her imagination. They stood in the corners of the rooms, arms extended to give her a hug whenever she passed them.

Saulie pulled off his overalls in the bathroom and sat on the edge of the clawfoot bathtub as she examined them. He'd torn a section she'd already darned before and it was damp with blood.

"Hold still while I clean the cut."

"I'm going to play for the Yankees someday," he said. "Ouch."

"I've told you not to slide anymore." She dabbed an old clean diaper they used as a rag against his knee, soaking up blood. Luckily it wasn't too deep a cut.

"I want to be like Lou Gehrig."

"Last week you said Babe Ruth," Mari said. "I'm putting on the iodine."

"I changed my mind. I know Babe batted 373 last year and Gehrig only batted 341, but this year Gehrig's on track to beat him. And anyway, I've got Gehrig's consistency. OUCH!"

"I'll bet neither of them screams like a baby. Go put your other pants on."

Mari took the torn overalls to the kitchen to scrub them with lye soap.

The photographer was there with Mama and was showing her the photo of Saulie. He had put it in a nice paper frame. "Two dollars," the man said.

"Ha," Mama said. "I should live so long that I'd have two dollars to spend on a picture." She spoke in Yiddish, the language they all used at home.

Mari looked at the photo. The photographer had captured Saulie's impish grin, the wild curls, the tough-boy pose. It was a wonderful picture.

"And why would I want a picture of my son in torn pants?" Mama said. "He looks like a little *trombenik*."

"A dollar then," the man said. "I can't do better than that."

"I'm sorry," Mama said. "For a dollar, I could practically feed my family for a week."

The man shook his head and left with the photo.

Mama fiercely scooped chopped meat mixed with rice into a cooked cabbage leaf. "Such a nerve," she said. "A dollar for a picture of a dirty boy in torn pants."

"Saulie hit a homerun," Mari said. "He won the game."

"Better he should sell newspapers and make a little money."

Mari filled the washbasin with water and put the overalls in to soak. Even with the windows open, it was steamy in the house. Canisters of rice, flour and sugar, and a tin of tea lined the cupboard shelves. Mama always seemed to worry when the canisters got low.

"A dollar," Mama said, stuffing another cabbage roll. "Does he think I'm made of money?" Her hands stopped moving, bits of pink chopped meat stuck to them. She stared out the window at the hanging clothes. "I don't have a single picture of him. Not even a baby picture. Papa got sick. Who could think of pictures at such a time?"

She turned to Mari, her eyes wide as though she'd seen a ghost. She wiped her hand on her apron and took a few coins out of the money jar on the oak icebox. "Come quickly, Mari. We have to catch the man."

Mama ran ahead down the stairs. Mari had a hard time keeping up. She'd never seen her mother move so fast.

Mama went out into the street and looked both ways. There was no sign of the photographer. "Which way did he go?"

Mari pointed in the direction the truck must have headed. They both ran down the street, past the drugstore and the grocer and shoemaker. At the corner, Mama looked around, a wild expression on her face. "Come," she said. And she ran down the next street, dodging pushcarts laden with fruits and vegetables, pickles and halvah. The photographer's truck wasn't anywhere to be seen.

Mari was panting. She put her hand on Mama's arm. "He'll be back another time. We'll have him take Saulie's picture next time."

But Mama just stood in the middle of the intersection, her white apron dirtied with pink chopped meat. She looked forlorn. As though she had lost more than a photograph.

"Is this Saul?" Julian asked, pulling Mariasha out of the past. He was gesturing toward the sculpture of *Boy Playing Stickball*. "Is that why you made this? Because you didn't have any photos of him as a child?"

She nodded, hoping that would satisfy him for now. Her memories had drained her.

Julian seemed to sense her exhaustion. He kissed her goodbye and promised to come back the next day and bring lunch. *Blinchiki* and caviar, he said, making a little joke. "Isn't that what communists eat?" She laughed with him, trying to ignore the uneasiness in her gut. She had opened the door to the past, just a little this time. But could she keep the torrent of memories from throwing it all the way open?

She had to watch her words, even if it was the last thing she ever did.

CHAPTER 9

Mariasha Lowe's Lower East Side apartment was about two miles from Barnes & Noble, but it had warmed up outside, so Annette decided to walk.

She went down side streets passing restaurants, groceries, hardware stores, and apartment buildings that had been converted to NYU dorms. It was an eclectic blend of old brick buildings with an occasional eruption of modern glass and steel. Sections of the streets were slippery with ice despite the salt that had been sprinkled by shopkeepers. It reminded Annette of where she lived uptown, but it was also very much like Grandma Betty's neighborhood in the Marais district. A wonderful fusion of the new growing out of the old.

This was also the neighborhood where her own grandparents had lived and her mother had been a little girl. Columbia Street. That's what was written beneath the photo of the two little girls. *Our Sally with classmate Essie Lowe. In front of our apartment on 120 Columbia Street.*

Annette entered the address in her phone, then followed the walking directions, zigzagging toward her mother's old block. But as she approached, she felt a stab in the pit of her stomach. All the tenement buildings were gone. She was in the midst of a public housing complex of tall, almost identical brown buildings, with air conditioning units jutting from their dirty windows. There was nothing here for her to connect to. The shops and smells of her mother's childhood had been bulldozed away.

She stared at the featureless highrises, no longer sure about this mission she had planned. How could an old woman like Mariasha Lowe accurately recall the past when so much time had gone by? Even if she remembered Isaac Goldstein, Mariasha's memories were likely to be tinged with the last sixty years of public condemnation.

Clearing her grandfather's name was just another one of Annette's stupid ideas. She'd had many of them over the years, each one designed to fix some unhappiness in her life. Like when she was eight and had written her father a long letter about how much she missed him and then signed her mother's name. The letter came back because of insufficient postage. Mama had read it and torn it up with a warning to Annette never to do such a thing again.

Or there was the time when Annette was twelve and had begged Mama to adopt Tsega, the Ethiopian girl who'd been her pen pal. Even after Mama said no, Annette contacted an international adoption agency, posing as her mother. When a woman from the agency came by to interview the Revoir family, Mama had been furious. "Our family is fine the way it is," she'd said. But later that night, Annette heard her mother crying in her room.

Now, once again, Annette was hoping to fix things. But would she only end up hurting her mother yet again?

She found herself standing in front of an older five-story building. She checked the street sign on the corner and the building number. Her subconscious had led her to where Mariasha Lowe lived.

She took a step back. It was a pretty building with bay windows overlooking a courtyard. Against the beige and brown bricks, the fire escapes were freshly painted and there was a giant oak tree in front of the building that probably provided wonderful shade when it had leaves.

Annette was filled with a physical sense of the past. Her grandparents had probably come here to visit their friends, the Lowes. Did Mama have sleepovers with Essie? Perhaps little Sally had played hopscotch with Essie in the shade of the oak tree while their parents watched.

At last, a tangible link to her mother's childhood and her grandparents' world. Maybe Mariasha Lowe's memories hadn't been twisted by the ugliness around her. Maybe she could help.

Annette walked through the courtyard and examined the intercom board beside the door. It took her a moment to recognize a barely legible name on a yellowed paper. *Aaron Lowe*. Mariasha's husband. Beside the name was the buzzer for Apartment 4B.

She felt a rush of anxiety, like bees swarming in her belly, and took a breath to settle herself. Why was she reacting like this? She'd interviewed people before. But she knew why. This time it was personal.

The outer door to the building opened and a tall guy in a faded green jacket came out. He was probably around thirty with a couple of days' beard growth and a preoccupied scowl. They caught each other's eye and Annette felt the kind of static electric shock you sometimes get when you touch another person on a cold, dry day. The guy seemed thrown off balance as well. He pulled his head back like a shying horse and blinked a couple of times. His bloodshot blue eyes were piercing.

Then he half-smiled at her. There was a tiny cleft in his chin. "Can I help you?"

"I'm not sure. I'm looking for a woman...Mariasha Lowe."

His smile turned into a frown. "May I ask what it's about?"

She didn't like being interrogated by some stranger. "That's really between me and her."

"Actually, it's between you and me. I'm her grandson."

"Oh." She hadn't been expecting that, but it made sense. Aaron Lowe's obit mentioned grandchildren.

"My grandmother has all the life insurance and long-term care policies she needs."

She realized his misunderstanding. "That's not why I'm here."

"And she's happy with her Part B Medicare coverage."

"I'm not a solicitor," she said. "I'm a journalist. I'm doing a piece on her sculptures." She felt uncomfortable swapping one lie for another, but maybe she would write a piece on Mariasha's work, too.

His eyes rolled over her satchel, her Barnes & Noble bag. "You probably should have called first."

She was about to argue, but it would be better to have this grandson on her side. "You're right," she said. "But I was in the neighborhood and thought I'd stop by."

"Well, I'm sorry. You can't see her now."

Arrogant jerk, she thought. "Wouldn't that be her decision?"

"I just came from her apartment. She's not up to seeing anyone today."

"*Ce trou du cul*," she mumbled.

He raised his eyebrows as though he knew she'd just called him an asshole. "What's that?" he said.

"Nothing." She tried to control her disappointment and be professional. "Well, I guess I'll call her and set something up for another time."

He ran his fingers through his short black hair. "Or I can arrange it. She doesn't like to talk to strangers, but if I tell her we've met, she's more likely to see you."

Well, at least he was trying. "That would be great, thanks."

"Do you have a card?" he asked.

"Um, sure." She dug through her satchel, pulled out a purse-worn business card and handed it to him. It had her name, cell number, email, website, and said Freelance Journalist. No address. She wasn't interested in attracting stalkers.

He examined it like a bar doorman checking for fake IDs. Apparently, he still didn't believe her.

"You can check out my website, too," she said. "It has links to my published articles and references."

He nodded, still looking at the card. "Annette Revoir." He pronounced it as though he'd studied French. "Is that a real name or did you choose it because you like saying goodbye?"

"*Revoir* means to see again, not goodbye. And yes, it's a real name."

"You're French?"

"Born in Paris, but I live here now."

He put the card in his pocket. "I'll give you a call after I talk to her."

"Thanks." She started walking away.

"Julian Sandman," he said.

She turned. "What?"

"My name. So you know who I am when I call."

"*Bien.*" She continued walking.

He loped after her. "I can probably give you some background on her."

"That's okay, but thanks." She started walking more quickly.

He kept up with her. She didn't like his persistence. Maybe he wasn't really Mariasha Lowe's grandson. He hadn't actually given her any information outside of what a stranger would have figured out during their conversation.

"I can tell you about what it's like having a famous sculptress for a grandmother," he said. "The art projects we did together when I was a kid. Nana was big on pipe cleaners and buttons."

He'd called her Nana. That was sweet. And she didn't think he'd made up the detail about pipe cleaners and buttons. He probably was her grandson, but Annette was still picking up a vibe that made her uncomfortable. Of course, that was probably because he was an attractive guy who was showing an interest in her. Historically a huge deal breaker for her.

"Would you like to go for a cup of coffee?" he asked.

"I don't think so, but thanks." She reached the corner of Houston Street. The car traffic was heavy and the street was teeming with people. The guy was no longer walking beside her. She stopped and turned.

He stood a few feet behind her with his thumbs hooked on his jacket pockets. "Are you really a journalist, Annette Revoir?"

"Of course."

"You sure as hell don't act like one."

She felt her cheeks grow warm, but he was right. This grandson was a potential source of information and she was racing away from him like he had ebola.

She took a step toward him. "I've already had coffee."

He took a step toward her. "Then how about a drink?"

"Too early."

They stared at each other for a moment.

"Do you like knishes?" he asked.

"Knishes?"

"Don't they have them in Paris? Like hot pockets. Turnovers filled with mashed potatoes. There's a place nearby that's been around since the early 1900s."

"Really? I'd like that."

He looked surprised, clearly not expecting her to agree. "Okay then," he said.

Okay then, she thought.

She followed him up Houston Street, passing old tenement buildings and restaurants that had been there forever. Katz's Delicatessen, a giant sign read. Since 1888. Russ & Daughters, Appetizers, Established 1914. Except for the electronics stores and occasional boutique, the wide boulevard might have looked a lot like this sixty, seventy years ago. Her grandparents and mother would have walked here, maybe eaten at the deli or bought herring from the appetizing store. It was only a few blocks from their apartment building. And Mariasha Lowe must have come this way, too. Maybe she'd walked on this street at the same time as her grandfather, perhaps even going to get knishes.

"Yonah Shimmel's just a little farther," Mariasha's grandson said, and gave her that half smile.

And once again, Annette marveled at how the new grew out of the old.

CHAPTER 10

Julian sat across from the girl in the red ski jacket at a small table near the front of Yonah Shimmel's waiting for their knishes. He wasn't sure what to make of her. No question she was attractive with those huge blue eyes, waves of long blonde hair, and the slight French accent that came from those pouty lips. She reminded him of the sexy urchin paintings they sold in Montmartre near the apartment he'd rented when he lived in Paris. But there was something off about her story. Was she really writing an article about his grandmother's sculptures? But if not, what the heck had she been doing outside Nana's building?

He doodled on a napkin with his mechanical pencil, watching her without being obvious. She was ignoring her Dr. Brown's root beer and plate of coleslaw and pickles, as she examined the yellowed newspaper clippings and old photos that hung on the wall. The ones of New York in the early 1900s seemed to particularly interest her. She had unzipped her ski jacket and left it on so he couldn't tell what was underneath, but he had a feeling it was real nice.

Annette sat back in her seat and frowned at him as though she was reading his mind. She had a small beauty mark just above her lip, kind of like Marilyn Monroe. Julian was a sucker for the actresses of classic films.

"So did you grow up around here?" she asked.

"Queens. Forest Hills." He pointed in the direction of the cardboard cartons that were stacked almost to the ceiling in the east corner of the restaurant.

"But you know the neighborhood very well." She picked up the pickle and nibbled on its end.

He forced himself to stop gaping at her and looked down at his sketch. "I used to visit Nana when I was a kid. Now I live over in the West Village." He decided not to get into how he would be moving out sometime soon, probably to Brooklyn.

"You must get to see your grandmother a lot."

"Not as much as I should," he said. "What about you? Do you have family here?"

Annette gave him a hard look, as though she thought he was going somewhere with the question. The restaurant door opened, letting in a few customers and a burst of cold air. She pulled her ski jacket closed and gave her head a little shake. "My mother's in Paris. My dad's up in Connecticut. "

"Were they both French?"

"I thought you were going to give me background on your grandmother."

"I was just curious, but if you…"

"My dad's American. He worked in IBM's Paris office, but moved back to the U.S. when I was six. My mom's a nurse." She took a sip of soda, then put it back down on the fake-marble tabletop.

Neither of them spoke. Julian shaded in the face—all frowns and pouts. It had been a mistake coming here. He didn't need another complication while he tried to figure out what to do next with his life. Why hadn't he just let her go her own way?

"What's with the doodling?" she asked.

He covered the napkin with his hand. "Just something I do."

"It looked pretty awesome from what I could see."

No reason to hide it. He pushed the napkin toward her. He'd sketched out an action figure that resembled Batwoman.

"This is amazing," she said. "Are you an artist like your grandmother?"

He was taken aback. In all the time he'd known Sephora, she had never remarked on his drawings or doodles. "I've done it for fun most of my life," he said, "but I'm thinking of going professional."

"Doing what? Graphic novels?"

"Possibly," he said. He hadn't taken it that far.

"I imagine your grandmother's been very encouraging."

"Actually, she hasn't been." He thrummed his fingers against the table. Did that have something to do with Saul? "My grandmother never pushed me in any particular direction, but she's always been supportive of anything I've decided to do."

"And what have you been doing?"

He smiled. "Is this going to be in the article you're writing on my grandmother's sculptures?"

She blushed and pushed her hair behind one ear. A perfect ear like the inside of a small conch shell.

What the hell was wrong with him? Only a few hours after Sephora walked out, he was already into someone new? Maybe he was an insensitive prick like she once said he was. But with Sephora, he was always on edge, and with this girl, he felt different. Almost like he'd always known her.

"Two potato knishes," the guy behind the counter called out.

"I'll get them," Julian said, pushing out his chair. When he returned a moment later, Annette had her laptop open. He set the knishes on the table and sat down.

"Sorry about getting carried away," she said. "I promise to keep my questions focused on your grandmother. May I take notes?"

"If you want." He took a bite of knish. "But to answer your question, I got an MD when I was planning to practice medicine, then changed my mind and went for a PhD in biophysics. After two years hating my job, I decided to quit yesterday."

"Whoa," she said. "I thought we were going to stick to your grandmother."

"That was your idea, not mine." He gestured at her knish. "Eat it before it gets cold."

She cut off a piece and tasted it. "This is good."

"You don't stay in business for over a hundred years making crap."

"I suppose not." She smiled. She had a great smile that lit up her face like a kid getting a present. "You don't look old enough to have completed an MD and PhD."

"I'm thirty," he said. "Yesterday was my birthday."

"Happy birthday," she said softly.

"Thank you." His throat closed up. No one had wished him a happy birthday quite as sweetly.

"That's still awfully young to have done so much."

"I finished college at nineteen," he said.

"Ah, I get it. You're a genius."

"Good in school, maybe. Not so brilliant in life."

She looked down at her laptop. "Maybe we should talk about your grandmother."

He picked up on the brush off. "Fine."

She took another sip of soda. "So tell me about her." She kept her eyes on her computer. "Her sculptures were influenced by the Great Depression, does she ever talk about what it was like growing up then?"

Julian felt a strange letdown, but this was the reason she'd come here with him.

"She talks a lot about her childhood," he said. "She was very poor. Her parents died when she was young."

Annette nodded. "I read that. And she still went to college. She must be an amazing person to have done that with all the adversity in her life."

"Nana is amazing," Julian said.

She reached for the Barnes & Noble bag on the table and pulled out a book. *Evoking the Great Depression.* She opened and turned it so they could both see the page. It showed a photograph of a sculpture. *Girl Playing Hopscotch.* 'This is a lovely piece," Annette said. "I sense the girl is happy despite the difficult time she grew up in."

"Nana's like that," Julian said. "Always optimistic."

"Not so much in this piece." Annette turned to the next page. "It's called *Boy Singing*. I don't know why, but it makes me sad. See how he holds his hands?"

Julian had never seen this sculpture before, or even a picture of it, but she was right. The boy's arms were extended in an embrace, but his hands were angled down, rather than up. As though he had given up hope of something.

The back of Julian's hand touched the Barnes & Noble bag. There was a second book. "Does this have more of her work?" he asked, as he reached for it.

"No." She tried to push the book back in the bag, but it was already out. *A Soviet Spy in America* by Boris Yaklisov.

Julian picked it up. "Does this have something to do with my grandmother?"

"It's for something else I'm working on. A piece on American communists. Nothing directly related to your grandmother." She rubbed the beauty mark over her lip. "Of course, she would have been a young woman when the communists were prominent in the thirties and forties. Does she ever talk about that?"

Julian leaned back in his chair. Nana had been telling him about being a "red-diaper baby" and the influence of communism in her life, but why would a journalist writing about Nana's sculptures care about that? "What do you really want from my grandmother?"

Her face turned red. "I told you, I'm writing an article about her sculptures. Did you really intend to give me background on your grandmother or did you ask me here under false pretenses?"

"I'm sorry, but your questions seem a bit off-point."

"I'm trying to get background and context. But maybe you don't even believe I'm a journalist. Maybe you need to study my website and confirm my credentials before you'll grant me an interview with your grandmother." She stuffed both books back in the Barnes & Noble bag. "So please, go ahead and do that. Check my references. And when you're satisfied, I hope you'll call me." She was definitely pissed at him. Even her beauty mark was quivering. "Because I would very much like to meet your grandmother. From what I've read about her, she's a remarkable person." She slammed her laptop closed and stood up with her books and satchel. "And I don't have my own grandparents anymore. My grandmother just died and you're damn lucky to have yours."

She left the restaurant.

A cold wave of outside air rushed over him. And all Julian could think of was that he didn't give a shit if Annette Revoir had some hidden agenda.

He really wanted to see her again.

CHAPTER 11

No matter how you tried to hide from it, the past was always with you. Mariasha could see it in her grandson's eyes, hear it in his voice. His lingering frustration at having a mother who didn't know how to love him. But it wasn't Essie's fault. She had only the example of her own cold mother.

But what was done was done. Mariasha couldn't change the past. She could only let it taunt her with memories of how it all started. In innocence. An exciting adventure to camp. A bite from an apple. But that was how it had been between Adam and Eve—how could it have been otherwise for Yitzy and her?

She closed her eyes. She could smell the pine needles, the freshly mowed grass, the turned earth in the vegetable garden. She could see his smile, hear his wonderful laugh. For a short while, she was a girl again. For a short while, she was still innocent.

August 1932

They took the subway into Manhattan. Mama, Saul, and Mari. Mari had reminded Mama that she was fourteen, old enough to go by herself, but Mama wouldn't hear of it.

Her mother had a small shopping bag over her arm. She was wearing an old felt hat and one of her high-necked dresses from when Papa had been alive. She had combed Saul's hair, but Saul kept rubbing his head and by now, his orange curls looked like carrot salad.

Mari clutched her bundle against her. Clothes for the week wrapped in a scarf. Shorts. Clean underwear. Blouses Mari had made herself cut down from old dresses. A bathing suit borrowed from Mrs. Silverman's daughter, who was married and pregnant and had no need for it.

At the corner, Mari looked in all directions. Tall buildings, way taller than the ones in Brooklyn, blocked the sun, but held in the heat. She felt as if she was standing at the bottom of a furnace.

An old yellow school bus was pulled up in the street where the children who were going to camp had been told to meet. A few boys and girls were hugging their mothers goodbye and getting on the bus. They came from *Arbeter Ring schules* around the city and Mari didn't recognize anyone. That was good.

I can be anyone I want to be at Camp Kindervelt. Daring and exciting and interesting, just like the Campfire Girls.

"I have to go," Mari said.

Her mother looked at the bus like it was a ship leaving for the other side of the world. When Mari had told Mama how much she wanted to go to camp, she'd been surprised when Mama had reached into the pouch she kept pinned to her brassiere. It held the 'emergency money' she'd gotten from selling their furniture. Once there had been five twenty-dollar bills, but now there was only one bill left. Was Mama sorry she'd given her the money?

"Make sure you eat," Mama said. "You're already too skinny."

"I will, Mama." Mari turned to her brother. "Goodbye, *trombenik*." She hugged him hard, until he squirmed out of her arms. His face was flushed. "Try not to slide. At least not until I come back and can stitch up your knickers."

He grinned, showing his chipmunk teeth.

"Okay, well, goodbye then." Mari felt the tightness in her throat. Why did she want to cry when this was the most wonderful thing that had ever happened to her? She reached the bus and glanced back. Mama's hand was on Saul's shoulder. They looked small and far away.

She bolted from the bus, ran to her mother, and hugged her, inhaling deeply her mother's familiar scent of lilacs and talcum powder. "Thank you, Mama. Thank you for letting me go."

Then she hurried onto the bus without looking back.

The bus drove along the East River. Mari sat on the right side, in the middle of the bus, on a seat by herself. Most of the other girls and boys seemed to know each other and sat in pairs. At least they were dressed like her in old, clean clothes. She clutched the bundle in her lap.

She was going someplace new and wonderful. Away from hot sidewalks and drab brick buildings and laundry hanging from clotheslines behind the fire escapes. *I can be anyone I want to be. Just as special as a Campfire Girl.*

Across the East River, she could see the smokestacks of the factories in Queens. She'd been to this other borough with Mama and Saul, and it had seemed very far from Brooklyn—practically the other side of the world. They went every year to visit Papa's grave at the Mount Hebron Cemetery. There was a small cameo picture of Papa on his headstone looking very serious. Different from how she remembered him. It had been seven years since he died, and she was having a hard time holding onto the memory of him smiling. But she knew he would have been happy about her taking this adventure to Camp Kindervelt.

A group of girls in the back of the bus had begun singing the Ruth Etting song about eating an apple every day and taking good care of yourself.

Mari hummed along. Yes, Papa would have been very pleased about this adventure.

One of the counselors called out that they were passing Yankee Stadium and several of the boys and girls rushed to Mari's side of the bus to look out.

There it was in the distance, towering over the nearby brownstone apartment houses. The curved facade reminded her of pictures she'd seen of the Coliseum in Rome. Next to it loomed what looked like a giant baseball bat.

She remembered how excited everyone had been when the new stadium first opened, just before Papa died. Mari chewed on the end of her long braid. Saulie wanted to see a game at Yankee Stadium. Why shouldn't they go? Now she knew where it was. She'd been out in the world. An adventuress.

The bus left the smokestacks and dense brick buildings of the city behind. It felt as though they were driving through a magical forest, everything green. Little houses appeared on the tree-covered hills. The girls had stopped singing. A few of them were sleeping, their heads resting on their neighbors' shoulders.

The bus got off the main road. Its windows were open wide and the air smelled different. Fresh and earthy like Brooklyn's Prospect Park. Branches scratched the side of the bus as it bounced over potholes, making its way down a winding unpaved road.

The bus came to a stop. "We're here," one of the counselors called.

Mari got off the bus, dizzy and disoriented after the three-hour ride. It was warm in the sun, but there was a cool breeze. She stretched her arms and neck. Tall trees everywhere—oaks, maples, and pines, and many she didn't know the names of. Several unpainted wooden buildings encircled an open, grassy area. In the distance, Mari could see a large lake reflecting thick woods and the blue sky.

She held her bundle tightly as the counselor called out names and organized the girls in small groups. Mari was in the Emma Lazarus Bunk. It looked like a broken down shed where really poor people lived. Even Mari wasn't that poor. Had she made a terrible mistake coming here? A week in the country. But this was nothing like the *Campfire Girls* books.

Everyone changed into shorts and went to a big wooden community house to eat. It smelled awful. Worse than the cafeteria at school. Mari always brought her own lunch to school, afraid of getting sick if she ate what someone else had prepared. *Use separate plates, cups, and silverware, so the germs don't spread.* That's what the doctor said when Papa was sick.

She sat at a picnic-style table with two other girls. She said hi, but the girls ignored her. Everyone seemed to know each other. Mari picked at the grayish green beans on her plate. She felt sick inside.

Grownups were making speeches, welcoming everyone to camp. In a corner of the room was a bust of Lenin, bearded and stern, like the poster in the classroom at the *Arbeter Ring*. It was the only thing familiar to her.

She sensed a change in the energy around her. The boys and girls were touching each other's arms, whispering and gesturing.

A tall, narrow boy with a jumble of blond hair marched to the front of the room, head high, shoulders back. Golden legs extended beneath his khaki shorts.

Several of other boys cat-whistled and began to chant. "Yitzy. Yitzy."

The girls joined in, banging their hands against the wood tabletops. "Yitzy, Yitzy."

The boy turned to face the group. He was probably fourteen or so. She could see that he didn't shave yet. With his upturned nose and blond hair, he didn't look anything like the other boys she knew. Was he Jewish? If not, what was he doing here?

He frowned at the boys and girls, his hooded eyelids making him look half asleep.

"Yitzy, Yitzy," everyone chanted.

Suddenly the boy smiled widely, waking up his face with shiny white teeth. He nodded, raised his pointer finger and began to sing in the sweetest voice Mari had ever heard.

Arise ye workers from your slumbers,
Arise ye prisoners of want
For reason in revolt now thunders,
And at last ends the age of cant.

The *Internationale*. The song of the Socialist movement.

Her father once sang it.

The other boys and girls joined in, locking arms and rocking from side to side. Mari got goosebumps. She wasn't alone.

The blond boy climbed up on a chair, and swung his arms as though he was conducting an orchestra. He was a god.

Look at me. Please look at me.

His eyes connected with hers for an instant, blue and sharp. Mari felt as though she was freefalling through the air.

The song ended. The boy jumped down from the chair and took a bow. Everyone applauded wildly and he went to get food.

She watched him out of the corner of her eye and toyed with the brown meat on her plate. He was talking to a few boys and girls as he made his way down the big room. She willed him to keep walking her way.

And then, there he was, at her table. Her heart bounced. She tried to look like she didn't care when he sat down across from her. He was holding a red apple with his teeth. He took a bite, swallowed, then smiled at her.

The two other girls at the table giggled.

He ignored them, his blue eyes focused on Mari. "Hi. I'm Yitzy."

"Mari," she said, heart fluttering. "It's short for Mariasha."

The two girls whispered to each other, got up and left with their trays.

"Mariasha," he said. His skin was clear. No pimples like most of the other boys had. "I like that better than your nickname."

"Yitzy," Mari said in a voice more confident than she felt. "That's a Jewish name, but you look like a *shegetz* with your blond hair and blue eyes." Mari couldn't believe her sassiness, but something about being around him allowed her to be this other, confident person.

Yitzy drew his head back and frowned. Then he burst out laughing. "A *shegetz*," he said. "Imagine me a goy. And you, Mariasha, with your black eyes and raven hair look like a *shiksa*. Very likely a Spanish flamenco dancer."

She grinned back at him, aware as she did that she wasn't covering her mouth with her hand. So he was a poet, too.

"Mariasha's an unusual name," he said. "You know it means 'bitters' in Hebrew. Like *maror*, the bitters we eat on *Pesach* to remind us of the bitterness of slavery in Egypt. So we'll never forget what it's like to be a slave."

"How do you know so much?"

He shrugged and took a bite out of his apple. "Hebrew school." He looked down at the uneaten food on Mari's tray. "So is this your first time away from home?"

Mari nodded.

"It's not so bad. We do all kinds of things. Folk dancing, swimming, canoeing. And of course there are the classes in social justice. It's all very communal." He swallowed another bite of apple. His eyes were the same shade of blue as her favorite cat's-eye marble. "What's wrong?" he asked.

"I don't swim." Then she added quickly. "I plan to learn."

"Almost no one can swim when they get here. I can teach you, if you'd like."

"Sure," she said. "Have you been coming to Camp Kindervelt a long time?"

"Just since last year. I used my own money, since my parents don't believe in extravagances." He smiled again, as though pleased with himself for using a big word. "But next year, I'll be fifteen and I can come for the whole summer as an assistant counselor." He reached out with his fork and speared a green bean from Mari's plate. He chewed it, then made a face, as though in terrible pain. "*Got in himmel*! Who could eat this *drek*?"

Mari laughed.

Yitzy held out his half-eaten apple. "Here, take this."

"Oh no, thank you. I'm fine."

He pressed the apple into Mari's hand. "Eat."

It had his saliva. His germs. Mari was momentarily revolted by the thought of biting into it. Then she dug her teeth into the apple.

Mariasha put her hand over her chest, felt her heart pumping. Yitzy. Such a charmer. Some called him an opportunist, but she knew what had been most important to him was being liked. Playing a role in which he could be admired.

She thought about how special Yitzy made her feel, like she could be anyone she wanted to be. And yes, even do the unthinkable.

The days at Camp Kindervelt went too quickly. At first, Mari catalogued every hour, reviewing each experience, hoping to make it last forever. Breakfast, when Yitzy would share his toast and make her eat a few forkfuls of his eggs. Then study group, where they would sit on blankets under the old oak trees and learn about Karl Marx and the system of socialized democracy. Then came waterfront. Mari would change into her wool bathing suit, damp from the day before and so stretched out that she tied the straps together behind her shoulder blades with a piece of twine to keep them from falling down. Yitzy wore a bathing suit with a blue and white striped top that showed off his long golden arms. He taught her how to swim in the freezing cold lake, how to canoe, how to kiss with the scent of pine needles all around them.

And then it was all over.

On the bus ride home, she sat by herself and stared out the window. The trees went past her in a blur. She thought about Yitzy. How he had taken her into the woods while the other campers sat around the campfire singing Socialist work anthems. How they kissed over and over, his lips soft and full.

She touched her own lips now with her fingers. They felt bruised and sore. She sucked them in, and closed her eyes, remembering the way he tasted.

They had agreed to meet in two weeks. At the smokestack shaped like a giant baseball bat just outside Yankee Stadium. September 4th. Mari would bring Saul so Mama wouldn't get suspicious.

That's what she had to hold onto. Yitzy and Mariasha in two weeks.

But how could she live without him until then?

The bus became hotter as they got closer to the city. The smell of smoke and burning coal replaced the pine needles and fresh air. Then, there was Yankee Stadium and the giant baseball bat where she'd be meeting Yitzy in two weeks. Thirteen more days.

The bus turned off the highway. The buildings were taller, closer together, the air thicker. Her heart ached more than she believed possible. When Papa died, she'd been too young to fully understand her loss. And it hadn't been sudden. Papa had been dying a long time, so she had already started to heal by the time the scab came off. But this—saying goodbye to Yitzy after only just getting to know him—felt like her heart had been ripped out.

The bus stopped by the building where she'd said goodbye to Mama and Saul the week before. The campers bundled off, hugging each other goodbye, then went toward their mothers and fathers.

No sign of Mama or Saul. Mari couldn't wait to tell her brother all about camp. Next year he would come with her. Yitzy might even be his counselor.

She sat on a fire hydrant, her bundle of clothes on her lap. It was so hot that she couldn't take a deep breath without feeling as though she was scorching her lungs. Everyone left. The bus pulled away.

Could Mama have gotten the date wrong? The time? She waited another half hour, then went to the subway station and took the train to Brooklyn. She walked the three blocks from Alabama Avenue, passing brick buildings she'd seen her entire life, but that now looked alien to her. She missed the thick green woods, the crisp blue sky, and cool sweet air. She missed Yitzy.

There was a black car double-parked in front of her apartment building.

She said hello to Mrs. Silverman, who was rocking her daughter's new baby in the carriage. Mrs. Silverman shook her head and looked away.

Something wasn't right.

Mari ran upstairs to their second floor apartment. A wave of heat hit her when she opened the door. The apartment smelled strange. Like medicine and sickness.

"Mama? Saulie?"

She dropped her bundle of clothes on the easy chair and searched the rooms. No one in the kitchen. Nothing cooking on the stove. She peeked into the bedroom she shared with Mama. The brass bed was made up with the bedspread Mama had crocheted before Papa got sick.

Then she heard Mama and a man talking quietly, just outside the little bedroom. The doctor who had taken care of Papa.

"There are new cures we can try," the doctor said.

Mari stopped breathing. *Cures? No. Please. Not again.*

She pushed between the doctor and her mother and looked into the spare bedroom. The room was dark. Saul was propped up on two pillows, his eyes closed, his curls dull like tarnished bronze. Even in the dim light, Mari could see the uneven flush of red on his cheeks.

Her abdomen convulsed, as though she'd been punched. Papa had stayed in this very room. She remembered sitting beside him, as he taught her to read letters and words. Then how he had closed the book and hugged her against him. *You are the strong one, my Mariasha. Promise me you'll always take care of your Mama and little brother.*

I promise, Papa.

Saulie opened his eyes and gave her a little smile. His breathing was ragged. "You know I love you, Mari."

"I love you more," she said, but he had already closed his eyes, as though he hadn't heard her.

She stepped back into the hall, heart pounding. "What's wrong with Saulie?"

"Shhhh," Mama said.

"I'll be back tomorrow, Mrs. Hirsch," the doctor said, then left the apartment.

"Tell me," Mari said, hearing the panic in her voice. "What's the matter with Saulie?"

Mama perched on the edge of the pink sofa that no one was ever allowed to sit on. Streaks of gray wound through her reddish hair. She looked much older than when Mari had left a week before.

"His throat hurt," Mama said, turning a button on her housedress around and around. "But Saulie always gets sore throats. Now the doctor says it's something worse. Much worse."

Worse? But then Saulie wouldn't be able to go with her to Yankee Stadium. She wouldn't be seeing Yitzy, after all. She clenched her fists, wanting to scream. This was all Saul's fault. How could he do this to her?

"His heart may be ruined," Mama was saying. "He could even die."

"What are you talking about?" Mari felt her legs go weak. "Saulie can't die."

"He's my baby," Mama whispered, "and I don't even have a picture of him."

The edge of an icicle slid down her spine. Here she was thinking about herself when her brother might die. She had promised Papa she would take care of Saul, but she had forsaken him.

What if God punished her for her selfish, sinful thoughts? What if Saulie died because of her?

She had to make a choice. She closed her eyes and said a silent prayer.

Please, God. If you save Saulie, I promise never to see Yitzy again.

CHAPTER 12

Sunday morning was glorious, which made Annette uneasy. It was the combination of an intense blue sky and crisp air that created the illusion that everything was clean and beautiful. As she walked through Central Park, even the snow blanketing the gentle hills seemed to sparkle in the sunlight.

Prime real-estate-selling weather, her father had jokingly referred to it the Christmas she was seventeen. She'd been visiting him at his old rambling house in Danbury, Connecticut that backed up to a wooded lot. That's when she noticed the discreet 'House for Sale' sign and her father told her he was marrying a wonderful woman with two great kids and moving into the woman's house. That was the last time Annette visited him, and after that she'd grown to mistrust beautiful weather. Which she knew was silly. Today will be a glorious day, she told herself. Even though yesterday had been a near bust.

She was still annoyed about how she'd handled Julian Sandman. It was no wonder he had questioned her true purpose. She had done a lousy job with her attempt at subterfuge, trying to get him to talk about communism when she was supposedly interested in his grandmother's sculptures. She had probably blown the chance of ever meeting Mariasha Lowe, but hopefully Bill would have some ideas on what she should do next.

She waited for a group of bicyclists to cross the winding path in front of her and took in a breath of cool fresh air. It was almost eleven and she had her regular

Sunday date with Bill at the Reservoir, a one-point-six-mile running track that surrounded what had once been the source of water for Manhattanites, but now was a favorite gathering place for mallards, geese and joggers.

Bill was a far more serious runner than Annette and competed in marathons, so he liked to run the two miles from his apartment near Columbia University to another jogging trail in the park and end up at the Reservoir for his last leg. Annette lived a little farther away and preferred to walk rather than run to Central Park from home. She was usually satisfied with one lap around the Reservoir before she and Bill headed over to the Boathouse for coffee and cinnamon buns.

She reached the broad marble stairs at 90th Street and Fifth and climbed them to the Runners' Gate. Bill was already running in place in front of the magnificent elm that had been there since the late 1800s. He wore a black jogging suit, emerald-green gloves and a red, green and white reindeer-patterned headband around his ears. Bill was still self-conscious about his recent "coming out" and she was pleased he was at least getting a bit more brazen with his accessories.

"Good morning," he said. "You're right on time."

"I hate you," Annette said. "You're not even panting or sweating. And you've already gone what? Five miles?"

"Seven. I started early."

"Nice jogging attire," she said, "unlike me." She glanced down at her red jacket, old Nikes, and purple leggings with a small hole in the knee. Her hair was in braids to keep it out of the way while she ran.

"It's important to keep up the right appearances." He adjusted his tortoise-framed glasses, held in place by a croakie. "Do you need to stretch or are you ready to go?"

"I'm good." She fell in beside him and they took off around the path. It was free of snow and ice thanks to the hundreds of jogging feet that kept it clear. On their left, the water looked like a giant lake and reflected the clear blue sky. Bill maintained a gentle, even pace so that they could actually hold a conversation. "You look happy this morning," she said.

"I am. Kylie's bringing Billy to the ice-skating rink at one. She said I can have him for the entire afternoon without supervision."

Annette was frustrated by Bill's acceptance of his ex-wife's meager concessions regarding their son, but she didn't want to ruin his good mood.

"And how are you doing?" he asked. "Did you meet the woman who's going to tell you all about your grandfather?"

"Not yet, but I finished the book by the Soviet spy last night." She'd tell him about Mariasha Lowe's grandson later.

"And?" he asked.

They passed a copse of leafless trees. Just beyond, a couple of horses with bundled up riders were loping down the bridle path.

"I learned a lot about being a spy in the 1930s and 40s," she said. "It was pretty unsophisticated. They actually did dorky things like greet each other with secret passwords. You know like, 'Bobo sent me.' They even cut up Jell-O boxes and matched up the pieces to confirm who they were. I thought that was just in Grade-B spy movies."

"Spying's become a lot more sophisticated in the last sixty or seventy years, thanks to technology and the internet. Anything in the book that ties to your grandfather?"

"Indirectly," she said. "The author, Boris Yaklisov, worked for the Soviet Embassy in New York, but he was also a case officer for the communists. He went to college rallies and recruited students who were sympathetic to the communist movement."

"That wouldn't have been too difficult," Bill said. "Back in the thirties, college students in New York were even more left-wing than today. City College and NYU were both fertile recruiting grounds for the communists." A group of joggers going the wrong way forced her and Bill to squeeze to the right as they passed. "In fact, some of the most prominent people accused of being atomic spies came out of CCNY," Bill continued. "Morton Sobell, Alfred Sarant, Julius Rosenberg."

"Interesting," she said. "Yaklisov recalled meeting Isaac Goldstein at a meeting around 1938. But Yaklisov wasn't impressed with him. He called Goldstein a dilettante and didn't think he had much value for the Party. He didn't see him again until after the war. And then, only briefly."

They passed the midway point around the reservoir and she looked across the water at the eastern and southern skylines of Manhattan, staircases of flat and pointed rooftops clearly visible behind the skeletal trees.

"I suppose Goldstein became more valuable to the communists after the war," Bill said.

"What do you mean?"

"As you saw in your grandmother's old photo, he was quite the war hero. He rescued a soldier from drowning and was seriously injured in 1943. He received the Soldier's Medal, Purple Heart, and a medical discharge."

Bill was right. Recruiting an American war hero would have been quite a coup for the Soviets.

"Then he went to work for the Army Signal Corps as an engineer," Bill said. "His job was to inspect electrical equipment manufactured by defense contractors for the government. A couple of witnesses at his trial claimed Goldstein stole confidential information from the Signal Corps and passed it on to the Russians." Bill took off his headband and gloves and stuffed them into a pocket. "Have you read anything about the trial?"

"I started reading the transcript, but it's almost three thousand pages. I tried to find a concise summary, but there's a ton of material out there. I can't figure out what's been verified and what's been shown to be false."

"It can be overwhelming," he said. "But here's one thing you may find helpful." He slowed down to a fast walk. "The key witness against Goldstein was a woman named Florence Heller. She claimed Goldstein was the head of the spy ring she was part of and that Goldstein received documents from a contact in Los Alamos, New Mexico, where the major work on the atomic bomb was done. She said Goldstein passed these documents on to the Russians. Most trial analysts now believe she lied to protect her boyfriend."

"I read that. Could the boyfriend have been the spy?"

"Not likely. During the years after the trial, it was pretty much confirmed that no one in this alleged spy ring had access to any significant details relating to the construction of the bomb."

They reached the end of the jogging path. "One other thing I wanted to ask you about," she said. "Yaklisov claimed in his book that someone with the code name of Slugger was delivering vital atomic-bomb documents to the Soviets."

"Slugger? How spylike."

"I know," she said. "Yaklisov insisted that Goldstein wasn't Slugger, but wouldn't say who was."

"That's interesting." Bill took off his glasses and rubbed the lenses with a cloth from his pocket. "I'd never heard Slugger mentioned in connection with the Goldstein case."

He put his glasses back on and they started down the winding road toward the Boathouse. "So where do you go from here?"

"Obviously, it would be great if I could track down this Slugger person, but I'm not egotistical enough to believe I'll be able to decode something that stumped the FBI and CIA." She took a sip of water from the bottle she had in her pocket. "For now, I'll settle for trying to understand what kind of person my grandfather really was."

"I checked into Aaron Lowe for you."

"Oh good. Did you find anything?"

"He published a number of papers while he was at NYU. Mostly theorizing on how economic central planning would work in America."

"So Aaron Lowe was a communist?"

"Probably."

"That might explain why his grandson was a little rattled when I asked him if Mariasha Lowe had communist leanings."

"Whoa." Bill stopped walking and stepped to the side of the road to study her. "Back up. Grandson?"

"I met her grandson yesterday." Her cheeks grew warm.

Bill scrunched up his eyebrows. "He'd be the son of the woman you said was friends with your mother. Essie Lowe?"

"Good memory."

"I imagine he's a lot older than you."

Bill knew Annette's mother had had her late in life. "Actually, he's around thirty."

"Ooooo."

"Don't start, Bill."

"From the way you're blushing, I'm guessing he's not married and he's hot."

"It's a nonissue," she said. "I was hoping to use him to get to Mariasha, but I probably blew that."

"I doubt that."

"I'm not very good at lying," she said. "He seemed to pick up that I wasn't interested in Mariasha for her sculptures."

"That's what you told him?"

"Well, I didn't think she'd talk to me if I came out and said I was trying to clear Goldstein's name and did she happen to have any ideas who the real spy was?"

"Maybe not."

"Oh come on, Bill. You're the one who taught me to be cagey as a journalist."

"Not cagey. Subtle."

"Fine. I don't think subtlety is the best approach here."

"And what's the deal with the grandson?"

"I think he was more interested in me than in giving me background on his grandmother." She continued walking.

"And that's a bad thing?" Bill got in step with her.

"I'm not interested in him."

"Of course you're not. You haven't had a love interest since when? Oh that's right. Since never. You write off every guy thinking he's going to drop you like your father dropped your mom."

"Enough," she said. "How about we stay away from my love life and I promise I won't give you life advice?"

He held up his hands in surrender. "Fine."

They reached the Boathouse. There was a line of people buying coffee at the Express Café window. They went to stand at the end.

"Anyway," Annette said. "His name is Julian Sandman. There's a remote possibility he'll contact you for a reference on me."

"A reference?" Bill grinned. "I'll tell him you're very lovable, but you can be a real pain in the ass."

"A professional reference," she said.

"Really?"

"Since he didn't seem to believe my story, I told him to check my references."

"Next time don't interview people in your Annie-Oakley braids." He reached over and gave one of hers a tug.

"I had my hair down."

"Then you probably looked pretty hot yourself."

"*Ras le bol*!" she said. "Enough."

"Okay, okay."

They got to the take-out window and ordered two cinnamon buns and two coffees, then they sat at one of the outdoor tables that overlooked the lake. There were a few white swans gathered at the edge of the bank, basking in the sunshine. A short distance from them, a large duckling, or maybe it was a black swan, paddled alone in the tall brownish weeds.

"The thing is," she said. "I hate lying about what I'm really after."

Bill took a big bite of cinnamon bun, then licked his lips. "So tell him."

She shook her head. "I think it's better if I play it this way."

Her cell phone rang and she dug it out of her inner pocket. She didn't recognize the caller. "Hello?" she said.

"Hi. It's Julian Sandman."

"Oh, hi, Julian." Her heart bounced. She glanced at Bill, who winked.

"If you're free around one," Julian said, "I'm planning on heading over to my grandmother's. You can join us, if you'd like."

"Yes, I would. Thank you." The swans had waddled down into the water and were floating away. The black swan had joined them, hanging back just a little. The sky was even bluer. The air crisper.

"Do you eat pastrami?" Julian asked.

"Pastrami?"

"Yeah. I guess they don't have that in Paris. It's a kind of meat that…"

"I know what pastrami is. I didn't understand your question."

"I'm bringing lunch."

"Oh. Pastrami's fine."

"Good. I'll meet you outside her building at one." He clicked off.

Annette pressed 'End.' She looked up. Bill was grinning at her with the biggest smile.

"Okay, fine," she said. "He's cute. But don't start annoying me about him."

He just kept smiling.

And Annette couldn't help it. She smiled, too.

It really was a glorious day.

CHAPTER 13

The A train had been stuck in the tunnel for twenty minutes just before the Washington Square station. Something about debris on the track, the conductor had announced. Annette thrummed her fingers against her cell phone. She was going to be late and there was nothing she could do about it. Even though she now had Julian's number, thanks to his earlier call to her, there was no service in the bowels of New York's subway system. Technology only got you so far.

She tried to focus on her interview with Mariasha Lowe, not the delay or the people pushing in around her in the crowded subway car. She ran a series of questions through her head about how the Depression had inspired Mariasha's sculptures, then about the backdrop of communism, and finally about Mariasha's friendship with Isaac Goldstein. What had seemed like a simple segue when Annette had come up with the plan at Barnes & Noble, now felt more like a giant leap. How could she introduce Isaac Goldstein into the conversation without revealing who she really was and her goal of clearing her grandfather? And what if Mariasha wanted to distance herself from her friendship with a despised traitor? Annette couldn't afford to blow this important link to the past. She needed to stay sharp when she spoke to Mariasha to be sure she guided the conversation to the information she needed. Of course, if she didn't get out of this damn subway soon, there would be no interview.

By the time the A train pulled into the station and Annette transferred to the F, she was sweating profusely beneath her ski jacket from the heat in the packed train. It was bad enough she hadn't had time to go home, shower, and change after her jog. Now she'd also probably smell like a construction worker.

She emerged at Delancey Street at 1:13 and redialed Julian's number, but the call went straight to voicemail. He'd either turned off his phone or the battery was dead. She sprinted to Mariasha Lowe's apartment, concerned that Julian would give up on her and go inside without her. Her sneakers pounded on the sidewalk as she turned into Ridge Street. She pulled up short at the courtyard of Mariasha's building.

Julian, his army jacket hanging open, was leaning against one of the brick walls holding a brown paper bag in each hand. She caught the sides of his mouth lift up as though he was about to smile, but that turned quickly into a grimace.

"I'm so sorry," she said, breathless. "The train was stuck."

"I thought you decided not to come."

"Why wouldn't I come? I want to interview your grandmother."

Julian turned to the buzzer panel and pushed a button.

"What do you think I'm doing here?" she asked.

He gave her a quick glance, then looked away.

Was he onto her agenda? But how could he possibly be?

"Is that you, Julian?" asked a scratchy voice through the intercom.

"My grandmother doesn't always follow the best security procedures," Julian mumbled, then he spoke into the intercom. "Yes, it's me Nana. And I brought a friend."

There seemed to be a moment's hesitation, then there was a buzz and Julian pushed open the door. Annette followed him into a dark, overheated lobby.

"Didn't you tell her I was coming?" she asked.

"I didn't want to disappoint her if you decided not to show."

Annette wondered if he was actually talking about himself being disappointed.

The elevator was small and quickly filled with the spicy aroma of pastrami as they rode up to the fourth floor. At least it was better than smelling like her sweat.

The elevator door opened, and she followed Julian down a narrow hallway covered with swirls of thick paint. A head with short silvery hair popped out from a doorway, then a small, stooped woman emerged. She wore a tie-dyed sweatshirt that was much too big for her, baggy red stretch pants and black ballet flats. An assortment of gold and silver necklaces covered her chest and sparkly hoop earrings hung from her long earlobes.

"Hi Nana." Julian swooped and gave his grandmother a kiss on the top of her head. "Meet Annette Revoir." He glanced back at Annette. "This is my grandma Mariasha Lowe."

Annette felt a jolt of excitement and brushed aside the misgivings of her conscience. She would do whatever was necessary to learn the truth about her grandfather.

"It's a pleasure to meet you, Mrs. Lowe." Annette was surprised how much she resembled the photos from when she'd been a young woman. Large recessed dark eyes, high cheekbones, patrician nose. Mariasha Lowe was beautiful, even at ninety-five.

The old woman extended her hand. The joints of her fingers were swollen with arthritis, but her hand was cool and dry. "You may call me Mariasha," she said, then winked. "If I may call you Annette."

Annette laughed. "Of course."

"Annette was born in Paris, Nana, in case you can't understand her through her thick accent."

"It's a charming accent," Mariasha said. "And I understand her perfectly, Mr. Wiseguy."

Annette couldn't tell if Julian was insulting her or flirting. Not that it mattered. She was here to interview the grandmother, not get involved with the grandson.

"I brought pastrami, Nana," Julian said. "No *blinchiki* and caviar this time."

Mariasha chuckled and took the bags of food from Julian into another room.

"Inside joke?" Annette asked, as they hung up their jackets on a mahogany coat rack.

"I told her I might bring that for lunch, but pastrami was easier." He wore jeans and a long-sleeved, light-blue T-shirt that made his eyes appear even bluer. He was built like someone who rowed crew, stretched-out with broad shoulders. She realized he was taking her in, as well, and felt a twinge of self-consciousness. She didn't look much like a professional journalist in her braids, tight turtleneck, and purple leggings with a hole in the knee.

"I was out jogging when you called," she said. "I didn't have a chance to go home and change."

"Works for me." He kicked off his shoes, and must have noticed Annette's expression. "Old habit," he said. "I always used to track dirt into the apartment as a kid. You can leave yours on." He started out of the foyer. "I'll show you around."

The living room was bright with art deco chairs and a sofa in crimson and turquoise jewel tones, the walls painted mint green. But of course, Mariasha was an artist. She would have had a flair for decorating.

An old-fashioned wind-up record player stood on a table in the corner of the living room. At the far end was an alcove with three double windows. In front of each was an almost-life-size sculpture. The outside light spotlighted one of them with a halo effect that caused her to gasp. It appeared to be a young boy swinging a bat.

"*Ah, c'est incroyable*!" she said softly.

"That piece is my grandmother's younger brother Saul," Julian said. "He played stickball as a kid."

"And worshipped Babe Ruth," Mariasha said. She took halting steps into the living room, carrying a tray with napkins and a jar of mustard. Before Annette could go to help her, Julian was there. He took the tray from his grandmother and set it on the boomerang-shaped coffee table.

"Poor Saul," Mariasha said. "He dreamed of playing for the Yankees. I'll bet he would have made the team."

"So what happened, Nana?" Julian asked. "You didn't finish the story you were telling me yesterday. Did he quit sports?"

"He got rheumatic fever when he was ten." Mariasha toddled over to the sculpture of *Boy Playing Stickball*. "He almost died."

Julian pursed his lips. "Is that when he took up painting?"

"He did a little sketching, but mostly he studied." She smiled at Annette. "My brother was brilliant. A lot like Julian."

Julian shook his head, looking embarrassed. "I'll get the food," he said, and headed toward the kitchen.

"I've seen your work in photos." Annette stepped closer to the sculptures. "But in person, they take my breath away."

"They help me remember where I came from."

The perfect lead-in. Annette's heart sped up. "Julian hasn't had a chance to tell you, but I'm a journalist. I'd like to do an article on your work and what inspired you. Would that be okay?" It wasn't exactly a lie. She hoped to write such a piece.

"Why not?" Mariasha said. "It's been a long time since anyone showed an interest in my sculptures."

Julian returned from the kitchen and put a platter of pastrami sandwiches on the table with three cans of Dr.

Brown's soda with straws in them. "Annette's done some really good articles on being a bi-national," he said. "Also on the comparative merits of living in upper Manhattan versus the Paris Marais district."

So he had read her stuff.

"She also wrote an exposé on political corruption in local government, and a rant against small-minded prejudice. Nothing on art, though." He glanced at Annette and raised one eyebrow.

"It's nice that my grandson prequalifies anyone who wants to talk to me," Mariasha said, settling herself in one of the big turquoise chairs. "I'm not so fussy. Shall we eat those delicious-smelling sandwiches?"

Annette sank into the down sofa cushion, self-conscious about the hole in the knee of her leggings. She covered it with her hand.

Julian squirted mustard on a half sandwich, then handed the plate to his grandmother. He sat down next to Annette, even though he could have spread out at the other end of the sofa. "Help yourself," he said. "Unless you'd like me to serve you."

"I can manage. Thanks." Annette reached for half a sandwich. There was a photo in a simple silver frame on the coffee table. A man and woman and two children, a plain-looking, frizzy-haired teenage girl and an adorable little boy of about nine or ten with blue eyes and black hair. "This is you," she said to Julian.

"Why are you surprised? This is my grandmother's apartment."

"But you're so cute here."

Mariasha chortled and Julian scowled.

Annette studied his parents. The attractive blonde woman was Essie Lowe. She bore a resemblance to the little girl in the photo with Annette's mother, but she seemed stiff and unsmiling. The man beside her, on the other hand, had his mouth wide open and seemed to be horsing around. He had bushy black hair and eyebrows like Groucho Marx.

"I think that's the last picture anyone ever took of my father," Julian said.

Annette heard the hitch in his voice.

"He taught Julian how to play chess," Mariasha said. "Julian won all the championships."

"It's okay Nana. Annette's not here to learn about me."

That's right, she reminded herself. Not here for Julian. She picked up on his cue, feeling a flurry in her stomach, and tossed out her first question. "I've read a bit about how your work was inspired by the Depression. What was it like growing up then?"

Mariasha nibbled on her sandwich, as though she was thinking. "Things were simpler in many ways. At least when I was a child. You needed money to eat. To pay the rent. So you did what you had to do. My mother sold eggs to neighbors. She took in ironing. We didn't starve. We always had a chicken on Friday night."

"Your sculptures seem very optimistic," Annette said. "I love the one of *Girl Playing Hopscotch.*"

Mariasha smiled. "We were optimistic, even without much money." Her eyes looked dreamy, but it could have been her cataracts. "We young people had so much energy. We believed we could change the world."

"Change it in what way?" Annette asked.

Mariasha took another small bite and chewed it slowly. "Oh, we were going to right all the injustices. Better wages. Equal opportunity for all. A fair and just system."

Communist principles, Annette thought.

"It was how I was raised," Mariasha said. "When I was a girl, I went to a Workmen's Circle school in the afternoons to study Yiddish. *Der Arbeter Ring Schule*, it was called. What a wonderful organization *Der Arbeter*

Ring was! They even had a summer camp in the Catskill Mountains for children from poor families. I went one summer for a week." She had that faraway look again. "One of the sweetest weeks of my life."

"Did your brother Saul go, too?" Julian asked.

She shook her head. "Not to camp. Only to the *schule*. Our father had wanted us to read and write in Yiddish, as well as English, but it was just as important to Papa that we study the ideas of social democracy at *Der Arbeter Ring*."

"Is that where you learned about communism?" Julian asked.

Annette was surprised that Julian brought up communism after appearing defensive about it the day before.

"We learned about Marx and Lenin," Mariasha said. "They were heroes to many in the 1920s, especially the Jews who'd run away from Russia. But worthy ideals change over time, distorted by those who try to exploit them for their own agenda."

What an interesting perspective, Annette thought. Would Mariasha have been sympathetic to Isaac Goldstein or have seen him as someone with an exploitative agenda?

"In those days there were many wrongs to right," Mariasha said. "Like the injustice of the Sacco and Vanzetti trial. They were foreigners, like most of our parents, and they were executed because of their political beliefs, not for any crime they committed. Because they were said to be anarchists. That made us young people very angry because we were developing our own opinions about how our country should be run."

Annette leaned closer to her. Was this how her grandfather had felt, too?

"We talked about these injustices with great passion," Mariasha said. "But we were still children. And as deeply as we may have felt, I don't think any of us believed such things could ever happen to us."

"So you were practically steeped in communism growing up," Annette said.

"It was the world we lived in," Mariasha said. "The air we breathed. We didn't consider it any more alien than people today find the environmental movement." She smiled at Annette. "I'm sorry, dear. You're being very polite and looking very interested, but this isn't what you came here to ask me about."

"No, please continue," Annette said. "I'm getting a real sense of how these experiences must have influenced your work."

"Not so much experiences. It's people who shape us. People who inspire us or give us courage to do the unthinkable." Mariasha turned her head toward the windows. Annette couldn't tell if she was looking at her sculptures or remembering someone.

"Who inspired you?" Annette asked.

"What's that? Who inspired me?" Mariasha shook her head, as though to clear away whatever she'd been thinking about. "My parents, of course." She took a sip of soda. "I was very blessed, you know. My mother insisted I go to college even though it would have been better for her if I'd gotten a job. Tuition was practically nothing at Brooklyn College. Maybe a couple of dollars a year." She put the soda and sandwich plate down on the table. She seemed lost in thought, again.

"What was college like back then?" Annette asked.

"What's that?" Mariasha said. "College? Oh, we students were all very passionate. We went to Paul Robeson concerts and sang his songs of justice. We attended meetings. We knew the government would make terrible mistakes if we left things in their hands. So we marched. We always seemed to be marching in protest of some wrongdoing." She jangled her silver and gold necklaces with one swollen finger. "It was a heady time. We genuinely believed we could do things that would make a difference."

"But you did," Annette said. "Your generation changed the world for the better."

Mariasha looked at Annette with an intensity that hadn't been there before. "Did we?"

Annette debated asking her what she meant, but Mariasha had continued her story.

"My best friend Flossie and I started at Brooklyn College together in 1935, when we were seventeen. We became fast friends. Believe it or not, I was the adventurous one, always dragging poor Flossie off on a fresh mission."

Mariasha's gaze drifted to the window. "Change. That was our goal. We didn't realize how much we would change ourselves in the process."

CHAPTER 14

November 1935

The train rattled through the tunnel. Mari had to shout to be heard. "There's supposed to be a big turnout at the rally."

"I'd rather be at the movies." Flossie rolled her eyes and pouted, making her look like Betty Boop and Greta Garbo rolled into one, if that was possible. But Mari's best friend was many things. Vivacious and mysterious. Tiny but voluptuous. Self-doubting, but occasionally daring. Like today, Flossie had the nerve to wear a dress just barely covering her knees.

"It will be good for you," Mari said. "An eye-opening experience."

"Or the malt shop," Flossie said. "We could have gone to the malt shop. You know I'm not politically inclined." Flossie crossed her legs, showing off her silk stockings and new high heels. Not rayon stockings and old pumps like Mari wore. A few men on the other side of the subway car seemed to be watching Flossie over their newspapers.

But that was always the case with Flossie. Men couldn't take their eyes off her, while they barely registered Mari's existence. Not that Mari could blame them. She was skinny with stick-straight black hair, which she hated, and had taken to wearing in a bun in the hope of looking older than seventeen. Why would anyone be interested in Olive Oyl when they could look at Mata Hari?

"And to make matters worse," Flossie said, "you're dragging me to the other end of the world for god-knows-what purpose."

"It's uptown Manhattan. Only an hour from Brooklyn. And I told you, the anti-war demonstration will make a wonderful article for the *Spotlight*."

"I suppose." Flossie rolled her finger around one of the chestnut pin curls that framed her round face, then let out a long, unhappy sigh.

"I don't understand you, Flossie. This is an opportunity for us to put up a united front with our brothers at City College. A chance to do something important."

"Oh Mari. Don't scowl and ruin your pretty face." Flossie reached over and gave her a hug. "You know I'm kidding you. Where you go, I go." She gave her a big smile, revealing overlapping front teeth, which on Flossie looked adorable.

At the 145th Street station, Mari and Flossie got off the train with several other young people, probably students like themselves going to the demonstration. The autumn air was crisp and the girls left their winter coats unbuttoned. Several unemployed men were on the street corner hawking apples from carts to the people getting out of the subway. Others held signs offering to work at odd jobs. No one was singing *Happy Days Are Here Again,* like they did when Roosevelt was first elected. Maybe they were tired of waiting for the New Deal. And just maybe there was something Mari and the others of her generation could do about it.

The trees along the wide avenue were almost bare. Leaves crunched beneath Mari's feet and she felt her excitement build. In the near distance, she could see spires rising into the blue sky. As they approached the big gate to City College, the crowds thickened. Mari gasped at the beauty of the Neo-Gothic buildings with their turrets, arched windows, and jutting gargoyles. She was only just learning about such things in her Art Appreciation class, and here it was, more than pictures in a book.

Hundreds of students pushed through the gate, chanting slogans, many carrying signs and banners. *Scholarships Not Battleships*, one banner read. *Take the Oxford Pledge*, said another.

"Oh my goodness," Flossie said, stopping to look around her. "I've never seen so many young men. It's too bad City College doesn't let women attend."

"Come on, you silly girl. We're here to pursue loftier ideals than finding a husband."

"Maybe you are," Flossie mumbled.

Mari grabbed her arm and pulled her through the crowd until they reached a large grassy commons where people were gathered as far as Mari could see. For an instant, she was back in Coney Island, clutching her father's hand, afraid of being swallowed up by the horde. And then, she remembered her father lifting her up high on his shoulders, above the crowd where she felt safe and exhilarated.

"Come on," Mari said. "Let's get closer to the speakers."

They pressed through the throng of mostly young men, who didn't seem to mind a couple of girls getting in front of them. "Excuse us," Flossie said with her most charming smile. "Pardon us."

Mari could see a stage with red, white and blue bunting that had been set up in the center of the quad. Several chairs flanked a podium, but none of the speakers had arrived yet.

About twenty feet from the stage, she decided that the crowd in front of them was too dense to penetrate. "This should be close enough," she said.

"Thank god," Flossie said. "Now all we have to worry about is how to get out of here without getting trampled to death. I hope the article is worth this." She took out a steno pad and pencil from her handbag and checked her lipstick in her compact mirror.

Mari sensed a commotion around her, people gesturing at the stage. Someone had vaulted up from the audience onto the platform. She tried to see between the shifting and bobbing heads.

A tall, broad-shouldered young man with too-long blond hair and a poorly fitting suit ran to the podium. He grabbed the microphone and looked out toward the crowd.

Mari's heart lurched. It couldn't be him.

The young man grinned, looking utterly delighted at being in front of so many people.

Was it possible? After three years, she couldn't be sure. The smile was the same, but the face was different from the teenage boy she remembered. Sculpted and shadowed now, with a hint of a beard.

"My goodness," Flossie said, her head next to Mari's. "He's cute as a bug's ear."

The young man surveyed the crowd, smiling and waving, probably at friends or classmates. His eyes locked on hers. Held her gaze as she held her breath.

His mouth fell open, recognition in his eyes.

Dear god, it was he.

Two policemen were climbing up on the stage. The young man tore his eyes away from her.

Mari grabbed Flossie's arm for support. It wasn't possible.

"What's wrong?" Flossie asked. "You look like you're going to faint."

"Comrades," the young man shouted into the microphone. His voice was mechanical sounding, not at all familiar. "We are gathered here today for peace, but let us not forget our brothers who have been unfairly condemned by an imperialistic society, which—"

The two policemen briskly approached him.

"Oh my goodness," Flossie said. "I think they're going to arrest him. Do you think he's a communist?"

The young man gave the policemen a quick salute, then jumped off the stage. He was swallowed up by the pack of students.

No. Don't disappear again.

The two officers went to the edge of the stage and scowled into the crowd.

Please come back. Mari searched the faces in front of her.

A minute later, the policemen shook their heads and took up posts on either side of the platform to make sure no other troublemakers tried to pull a stunt.

"Mind if I stow away here?" said a soft, low voice near Mari's ear.

She jumped at the unexpected closeness of the young man crouched down beside her.

"Goodness gracious," Flossie said.

"Sorry," he said. "I didn't mean to startle you." He straightened up to his full height, a few inches taller than Mari, even in her heels, then looked down into her eyes.

Her heart pounded as they stared at each other. Three years. Why didn't he say something? Unless he hated her for standing him up at the Yankee

Stadium. Then why had he sought her out after jumping off the stage?

"Better duck down," Flossie said. "The police will see you."

He took a tweed cap out of his jacket pocket and put it on, pulling the brim down to shade his eyes. "How's this?" he asked. "Now I'm incognito. Like a spy."

Flossie was patting her bosom. "Goodness. This is wonderful. A real scoop." She held up her steno pad. "I'm a reporter. We're from Brooklyn College."

Mari felt a stab of annoyance at her friend's sudden enthusiasm for being here.

"Hmmm. Brooklyn College girls," he said, with a wink at Flossie. "I hear you're quite the radicals down there."

Mari stood taller. "Only if you define radicals as people who have the courage to protest wrongdoings."

He touched his cap and grinned at her. "Touché."

"Would you mind if I interview you for our college paper?" Flossie asked.

"My pleasure, Miss Nellie Bly."

Flossie gave a cute little pout and tapped her lip with the back of her pencil. "I think of myself as more of an amateur investigator like Nora Charles. My name's Flossie, by the by." She smiled. "And this is Mari."

"Flossie and Mari," he said. "Isn't Mari short for Mariasha?"

Why was he acting like he didn't know her?

"Like *maror*," he said, "the bitters we eat on *Pesach* to remind us of the bitterness of slavery in Egypt. So we'll never forget what it's like to be a slave."

It was what he'd said the first time they'd met.

"And may I ask your name?" Flossie said.

"Call me Yitzy." He gave a little bow. "Ace student at City College, engineering major, human rights advocate, ardent Yankee fan." He glanced at Mari. "In fact, I was once slugged over the head by a giant baseball bat at Yankee Stadium. But that was a long time ago."

Mari felt her face grow warm. So he was still angry with her. That's what his odd aloofness was all about. "I'm sorry," she said. "My brother..."

A harsh, fake-sounding voice boomed over the microphone welcoming everyone to the 'Mobilization for Peace' demonstration. Hushing rippled through the crowd.

Now was not the time to explain why she hadn't gone to meet him that day.

The man at the podium introduced City College President Robinson, who was greeted by boos and jeering until, frustrated or angry, he took his seat. The other speakers were more sympathetic to the cause for peace and solidarity, but Mari was only vaguely aware of the proceedings up on the stage, more interested in watching Yitzy out of the corner of her eye. She could feel the waves of intensity that came off him, but they seemed to be directed at the podium, not at her. Yitzy's lips worked as though he was repeating to himself those sentiments that he wanted to memorize.

When Student President Robert Brown got up to speak, the crowd cheered, Yitzy most loudly. Brown talked about the importance of American neutrality and urged the crowd to take the Oxford Pledge, an oath that was being taken by students around the country. He held up a piece of paper and read, "We will refuse to support the government of the United States in any war it may undertake."

The crowd went wild, their cheers deafening. Yitzy's face was red as he pumped the air. "No war! No war!"

The cheering went on and on. The crowd pressed against Mari from all sides, pulsing like a giant monster, moving forward, toward the stage. "No war! No war!" Mari joined the chant, feeling flush with power and energy. Yitzy was at her side, his arm brushing against hers. "No war! No war!"

The shouting grew louder, carrying her away. She couldn't breathe.

Yitzy's hand squeezed hers. "Are you all right?"

"Are you all right, Nana?"

Mariasha looked up at the blue eyes, confused. Julian. Her grandson. She was home, not at a long-ago peace rally. But her hand was throbbing, or maybe she was merely imagining Yitzy's touch.

Julian's pretty friend had gotten up. "I'll get you some water," the girl said. Annette. Her name was Annette, Mariasha remembered now.

"I'll be okay." She could hear the breathlessness in her own voice. "I got caught up in my memories."

The girl went to the kitchen and returned with a glass of water.

Mariasha took a sip. "Thank you."

"So you had met Yitzy before?" Julian asked.

"At camp," she said. "When we were fourteen."

"The *Arbeter Ring* camp?" he asked.

She nodded.

"What happened at Yankee Stadium?" Julian asked.

"We were supposed to meet at the giant bat, but my brother got sick." Mariasha closed her eyes. She wasn't quite ready to leave her memories of Yitzy at the rally.

"I think we'd better go," Julian said.

"*Oui*," Annette said.

Mariasha opened her heavy eyelids. "You'll come back tomorrow, won't you?"

"Of course, Nana."

She leaned back in her chair as they cleared the dishes away and then said their goodbyes. She could feel the charge they left in the air. Two young people just discovering each other. Perhaps the beginning of something. She hoped whatever it was turned out better for them than for her and Yitzy.

Yitzy, Yitzy.

Her story left her feeling exposed, scattering old dried leaves that had covered what she tried to bury. But the memories also made her long for what had been.

The days of tasting the forbidden fruit.

Yitzy held Mari's and Flossie's hands the entire walk away from City College, up Amsterdam Avenue. Flossie laughed and spoke in a high-pitched, excited voice, but Mari remained quiet. She wished her friend would disappear, but of course, that wasn't possible. Maybe if Yitzy had at least acknowledged that he and Mari had once known each other, she would have felt less unsettled, but for some reason, Yitzy wanted to keep their past a secret from Flossie.

"Here we are," Yitzy said. He guided Mari and Flossie into a coffee shop that smelled like coffee and cigarettes. A couple of people were sitting at the counter, but the tables and booths were empty. Yitzy led the way across the cracked black-and-white-checkered floor to a booth in the back. Mari and Flossie sat on one side and Yitzy across from them.

After they ordered three cups of coffee and one piece of apple pie to share in the interest of saving money, Flossie took out her steno pad. She twirled one of her pin curls with the point of her pencil and asked him a few questions about his background. Where he lived. Not far from City College. Why he chose engineering. Because he was good in science and math and probably couldn't get a job as a singer.

"My goodness," Flossie said. "You sing?"

"Not for a few years," he said. "I lost my best audience." He exchanged a look with Mari, perhaps to see if she remembered their week at Camp Kindervelt.

"So, Yitzy," Flossie said, "our readers are curious to know. Are you a communist?"

Mari was aghast. "Don't ask him that, Flossie. You know he can get in trouble if you write that he is."

Yitzy played with the brim of his cap, which he'd taken off when they sat down. "May I ask what prompted the question?"

"When you were on the stage, you said something about our brothers, condemned by an imperialistic society. That's Red talk."

He smiled at Mari. "Or maybe I'm just someone who has the courage to protest wrongdoings, like Mariasha."

"Fair enough," Flossie said, clapping her hands together. "But can you at least tell us what you think of communism?"

The waitress put three coffees and a slice of apple pie down on the table, then went to take another table's order. Yitzy stuck his fork into the pie and sawed off a big piece for himself, which he promptly shoved into his mouth.

"Here's what I think," he said, his mouth full. "In this country, we have a problem with freedom of speech. If someone dares speak out against the government or its policies, that person is branded a communist. The American government has tried to turn progressive views into heresy. They want people to associate communism with evil and to fear it."

Flossie was scribbling on her pad.

"So you don't fear communism?" Mari asked.

"Fear it? I embrace it. Why should we fear trying to free the slaves? Isn't that what Moses did in Egypt? Isn't that why your parents chose your name, Mariasha?"

His eyes held hers. Her heart was beating so loudly, she could hardly hear anything else.

"There's so much unfairness in the current system." His voice trembled with conviction. "Terrible working conditions—that's if you can even find a job. Unfair trials because people are immigrants or don't have the right color skin. Sacco and Vanzetti. The Scottsboro Boys. The Herndon case. When will it end?"

It had gotten noisy in the coffee shop, now filled with other students who had been at the rally. Mari noticed that Flossie had stopped writing and was staring at him, mouth open like a hungry puppy.

Yitzy continued talking, his words turning to music, one flowing into the next like a rousing anthem. But this new Yitzy was consumed with the passion of his mission. Sure, he remembered her, but he had also forgotten her. And it was better that way. She had made a deal with God and she wouldn't break it now. What the two of them had started a few years before was over.

Yitzy had stopped talking and was studying her. His fork was extended. On the tip of the tines was a piece of apple. Mari's heart began to pound. She felt like that fourteen-year-old girl on her first day of camp falling in love with a blond, blue-eyed boy with a red apple in his mouth.

"I was wondering, Mariasha," Yitzy said with a smile. "If you would like to take a bite of my apple."

CHAPTER 15

Julian studied Annette out of the corner of his eye as they rode the elevator down from his grandmother's apartment. She was tugging on one of her braids, chewing on her lower lip. She had appeared fascinated by Nana's stories even though they didn't have much to do with her sculptures. He wished Nana would have talked more about Saul, but he had a feeling she would tell him her brother's story in her own way.

The elevator came to a stop with a bounce and they stepped into the overheated lobby. Annette glanced around as though she was trying to memorize every detail. The large gold-framed mirror above an old scratched mahogany table. The Egyptian-pattern border surrounding the cracked tile floor.

She caught him watching her. "Thank you for letting me meet your grandmother," she said. "She's a remarkable woman."

"She is that."

"What a wonderful coincidence that the young man at the college rally was a boy she had met at camp," Annette said.

"The best week of her life."

"That's right. She did say that. I would have loved to hear the story of how she and Yitzy first met."

"Maybe she'll tell us tomorrow."

"So I can see your grandmother again? Does that mean I passed my test?"

"The multiple-choice section," he said. "You still have to complete the essays."

She smiled. A good sign. He didn't want to frighten her off like he'd done the day before.

"Do you want to grab a beer?" he asked.

She ran her fingers over the zipper of her ski jacket. "I don't do well on tests when I'm drinking," she said. "How about we just walk around for a while?"

"Sure." He held open the door for her and they stepped outside. He blinked against the sharpness of the sun in the cloudless blue sky.

Annette stretched her shoulders back, as though waking up. "*Il fait beau! Magnifique*!"

Yes, you are. "There's a park along the East River," he said.

"Did your grandmother take you there when you were little?"

"No. My dad did a few times. Then when I was older, I'd go by myself."

They started walking in the direction of the park. The air had warmed up from earlier and smelled like hotdogs, Cracker Jacks, and orange soda. Or was he imagining that because of the association with his dad?

"It's hard growing up without a father," Annette said.

Julian felt a tightening in his gut.

"I was very young when my father left," she said. "Only six. I kept asking when is Daddy coming home, but my mother would clam up. I couldn't tell if she was angry or hurt. I decided he must have done something wrong and I stopped asking about him."

Something Julian certainly understood.

"My mother and grandmother pretty much raised me," Annette said. "My Grandma Betty loved plaiting my hair." She gave one of her braids a tug. "Maybe that's why I still do it."

"You miss her."

"*Oui*."

"And your father? Did you see him again after he left?"

"Occasionally, during vacations. But he seemed more like a friendly stranger than my dad."

"Do you see him now?"

"Not for a few years." She rubbed the beauty mark over her lip. "Not since he remarried." They walked beneath a scaffold, in shadows for the moment. The mounds of snow near the street curbs were melting and the sidewalk was wet. "It's not that I'm angry with him, or anything. It's just, he has a new family now. A wife and a couple of kids. Besides, he hasn't tried very hard to see me."

Julian felt the urge to put his arm around her, but held back. "I was ten when my dad died."

Annette slipped her hand through his arm, as though it was the most natural thing in the world. They reached the curb and the sunlight.

"My mom never remarried," he said. "I guess that's a good thing."

"You guess?"

"I don't know where she'd have found time for a husband. She works a lot. It was pretty lonely at home."

"I'm sorry."

"I don't mean to sound like I'm complaining. Nana's always been around for me. I went to high school near here. Stuyvesant. So after school, I'd go to Nana's apartment. We usually had dinner together."

They stopped at a red light on the corner of Columbia Street. The massive government-project apartment buildings across the street blocked the sun and cast a shadow over them.

"My grandparents and mother used to live there," Annette said.

Julian felt a sudden chill in the air. "In the projects?"

She shook her head and let go of his arm. "No. Way before. In an old building."

"They knocked down many of the tenements back in the fifties," Julian said. "Is that when they went to France?"

She nodded.

"Not a bad move," he said. "Interesting coincidence though. I wonder if they knew my grandparents."

Annette shrugged. Her cheeks were flushed like she was too warm, or maybe embarrassed.

"Yeah, I know," he said. "That's one of those dumb things people say. New York has like eight million people, but we always ask if someone knows someone else."

The light changed and a dog walker holding the leashes of half a dozen small dogs hurried past them. Julian sensed that Annette's mood had shifted. She was glancing around, as though she wanted to bolt. Had he said something wrong?

"We don't have to go all the way to the park if you have to be somewhere else," he said.

She met his eyes and seemed to be weighing something. "I don't have any place else to be."

"Good," he said. They continued walking. He wanted to get her out of this funky state. "Do you like being a journalist?"

She gave him that child's bright smile again. "I love it. I pick and choose what I want to write about and get to learn all about subjects that interest me."

"Like New York Depression-era art," he said, before realizing she'd probably think he was teasing her again. "Wait. I think I get it. Your roots are here. You're looking for connections to your family, aren't you?"

She stared ahead at the Williamsburg Bridge that stretched across the East River toward Brooklyn. "That's right."

They crossed the wide avenue to the park. Neither of them spoke. Snow-covered fields spread out to the north and south, and benches lined a jogging path. They chose a bench beside a towering oak tree that had probably been here even before the park, and watched the joggers and bicyclists pass by on the waterfront path. Beyond, cars crossed the bridge. The low-rise apartment buildings and warehouses of Brooklyn and Queens formed a purple skyline.

"You're lucky," she said softly.

"How do you mean?"

"You have your grandmother, your mother, a sister. You know where you came from. You feel loved."

"Don't you?"

"I think my mother loves me," she said. "But she has a tough time showing it. She never even hugs me."

Just like his mother.

"I'm sorry," he said.

She gave her head a shake. "Please, don't be. I'm used it. But then when I was walking around this neighborhood earlier, I felt something. A sense of family. Of belonging. And then your grandmother's stories really touched me. I could totally imagine my own grandparents having similar experiences."

"Don't you have stories from their past?"

She rubbed her beauty mark. "My mother and grandmother never talked about the past."

"Well then, I'm glad you got to meet Nana."

She turned toward him. "But why do you look so sad? You have real roots. You don't have to imagine someone else's stories are your own. And you have a wonderful grandmother."

He looked out toward the Circle Line boat, which was slowly heading up the river. Several people were on the outer deck pressed against the railing. A child leaned over and waved. An adult pulled the child back to safety.

"I do have Nana," he said. "But I never really had my mother."

"No?"

He met her eyes. "When you said your mother has a tough time showing her feelings, well, my mother does, too."

She twirled a braid around her finger. "So you and I are the same."

"Yes," he said. "I believe we are."

CHAPTER 16

Mariasha could still remember how that bite of apple tasted. Sweet, but tart, as though the apple pie hadn't been completely baked through. But once she had swallowed the piece of apple that Yitzy placed on her tongue, she knew the promise she'd made to God was meaningless. There was no way she would ever give up Yitzy again. Not for Saulie, not for anyone.

Yitzy would remain a part of her from that day on. They shared the same ideals, the same pleasures, the same dreams. Equality for all. Nathan's frankfurters. Coney Island when it was too cold for ordinary people.

And that was probably what attracted her most to Yitzy. When she was near him, she never felt ordinary. She was daring, dazzling, a risk-taker, even. Like the Campfire Girls in the books she'd read as a child. All she cared about was shining in his eyes. She hadn't appreciated until much later that he had felt the same about her. And she should have seen it right from the start.

She got up from her chair and went over to the ancient Victrola. It was one of the few things she still had from her girlhood and she had kept it because no other record player would ever be right for playing their song.

She tried to move the leather box of records from the shelf beneath, but it was far too heavy. When did that happen? She used to pick up the record container with very little effort. She managed to open the lid and pulled out several large, heavy records, which she set on the floor. Then, she felt around until her fingers touched a record that was smaller and lighter than the others. She lifted it out, and carefully removed it from its plain brown paper wrapper. *Whatever You Choose* was the name of the song. It had been popular back when she was a college student, but the words took on an entirely different meaning for her once it became her and Yitzy's song.

Her fingers trembled as she set it on the turntable, wound up the Victrola, then placed the needle in its groove.

His voice came to her, a cappella. It was as though he was here beside her once again, grinning as though the world would be theirs forever.

December 1935

Mari waited across the street from the Coney Island train station on the corner of Stillman Avenue so she could see the passengers as they disembarked from both stairwells. She scanned the men's faces, but Yitzy's wasn't among them. The train roared away, tracks and platform reverberating. It was three-fifteen, and he hadn't been on either of the two previous trains that had pulled into the station from Manhattan.

A salty iciness blew in on the ocean air. Mari pulled the red wool Basque beret she'd knitted for herself over her ears. She stamped her feet, impractically clad in heels and stockings, and dug her gloved hands deeper into the pockets of her thin wool coat. The smell of frankfurters and knishes from the Nathan's stand on the opposite corner made her stomach grumble.

Was Yitzy all right? Had something happened to detain him? She was certain she had the time, date and place right. When they had last met at the Manhattan 42nd Street Library, they had worked out all the details. Friday at three sharp at the Stillman

Avenue station in Coney Island. Yitzy had joked he'd be wearing a red flower in his lapel and carrying a copy of Thomas Paine's *Common Sense* to be certain she didn't mistake another man for him.

Mari had laughed and written the time and date in her notebook calendar, even though there was no way she would forget. The hour they'd spent together at the library had been too short, too unsatisfying, with people at the other tables hushing them every time Yitzy spoke with fervor or Mari giggled at one of his witticisms. They'd settled on Coney Island where they'd be able to stroll the boardwalk without interruption. Neither had anticipated the shift to frigid weather.

She walked down the deserted street hoping the movement would help her warm up. Just beyond, she could see the Wonder Wheel ride, a roller coaster, the grinning clownish face that was synonymous with Steeplechase Park. What was missing were the crowds of parents and children pushing against each other to get to the ocean edge. What was missing was Papa lifting her high above the crowds.

She felt the vibration in the air before the sound of another train began to shriek toward the station. Mari returned to her post on the corner. A moment later, a few people came hurrying down the stairs. Then, there he was, moving jauntily toward the street, a red flower in the lapel of his broad-shouldered brown overcoat and a book tucked under his arm.

The train roared out of the station.

He saw her, waved his tweed cap, and then crossed the street without breaking his stride. Big smile. He looked like he wanted to hug her. Maybe kiss her. She wondered if he remembered their kisses three years before. But instead, he awkwardly took her hand and shook it vigorously. "Hello, hello. I'm so glad you're here. I'm late, I know. But I couldn't find a flower. My god, it's good to see you, Mariasha."

Mari laughed. "Okay. You're forgiven for being late. Now, catch your breath."

"But the flower," Yitzy said. "I have to explain. I couldn't find a red one anywhere and I was afraid you'd walk right past me if I didn't follow our plan. But then I had an idea. I'd picked up a flyer this morning protesting American participation in the Olympic games in Germany. It was just the right shade of red, so I decided to fold it and stick a pipe cleaner through it, like my mother taught me to do when I was little. I'm afraid it isn't very good." He pulled it out of his lapel and twirled it between his fingers.

"It's perfect," Mari said.

"Then you shall have it, my fine lady." Yitzy made a show of bowing, then handed the paper flower to her. She admired the sharp creases, noting the angry words between the folds. *Fascists. International propaganda. Nazis.*

"And of course, I couldn't forget this," Yitzy said. "Part of your education Mariasha. Thomas Paine's *Common Sense.*" He held out the thin booklet.

"Thank you, kind sir." Mari took it and shivered.

"But you're freezing and here I am blabbering." He sniffed the air like a hunting dog. "Are you hungry? We can grab a couple of frankfurters at Nathan's and get out of the cold."

"I'd like that."

Yitzy wrapped his arm around her and they walked huddled together. Mari would happily remain in the freezing cold forever, if it could be like this.

Only a few people were waiting at the counter. Although Nathan's was mostly open-air, steamy heat from the kitchen permeated the covered area where they stood. Yitzy ordered two frankfurters smothered in mustard and sauerkraut at a nickel each.

Mari wasn't sure if he expected her to pay for hers. "Dutch treat?" she asked.

"Absolutely not." Yitzy handed her one of the hotdogs. "My treat and my pleasure."

They sat close to each other at a picnic-style table, their legs touching. Yitzy shoved about half of his hot dog into his mouth and picked up the *Common Sense* pamphlet. "Read this," he said, his words garbled as he chewed. "Written for ordinary people—the common man, as they used to say. It inspired them to fight for freedom and independence from British rule."

Mari nibbled on her frankfurter. "So you're a patriot, too."

"A patriot above all. As Thomas Paine states so eloquently, one can disagree with the ruling power and still be very much a patriot." He wiped his mouth with his fingers, noticed mustard on his pinkie and licked it off.

Mari was charmed by his apparent disregard for etiquette.

"So, ready for our stroll?" he asked, when she'd finished her hot dog. "I'll do my best to protect you from the elements."

She was delighted that Yitzy once again put his arm around her shoulders and held her close. She hardly noticed the freezing wind whipping around them.

The boardwalk was practically deserted, just a handful of people out for a bracing walk. They went past shuttered concession stands, souvenir shops, freak-show posters, and the closed entrances to the Bath Houses. There were no people on the giant Wonder Wheel, whose colorful baskets trembled in the wind like the last few leaves of autumn, or on the Cyclone roller coaster, which looked like it had been built from a child's Erector Set.

A weak sun tried to push through the blanket of gray clouds. Waves crashed against the expanse of sandy beach, the sound wonderfully deafening, changing the shoreline with each ebb and flow.

Mari could make out pieces of wood stuck in the sand, a broken beach chair, a page of a newspaper blowing along the mounds of sand. No people.

"I came here once with my father," she said. Yitzy leaned closer to hear her over the thundering waves. "I was very young, but I remember all the people. They were everywhere. On the boardwalk, on the sand, in the ocean. I'd never seen so many people. It was terrifying. I was afraid my father would let go of my hand and I'd lose him forever."

"But he didn't let go."

"Not of my hand."

He stopped and turned her toward him, taking her hands in his. Her heart went into its rapid-beat performance that his nearness always seemed to trigger.

A mist of snowflakes surrounded them, settling on Yitzy's tweed cap, on his brown overcoat, on the tip of his red nose. Mari felt the sting of ice on her cheeks and blinked the flakes out of her eyes.

"My god, you're going to turn into a snow woman," he said. "Come on. Let's get out of the cold."

They clung to each other as they ran down the boardwalk. Yitzy ushered her into a store she hadn't noticed was open.

It was dark and smelled like oil, rubber and something burning, and was almost as cold as outside, except at least it wasn't snowing. She looked around the cluttered wood-planked room. Dusty radios, phonographs, stacks of records. A sign, 'Make your very own recording.'

A white-haired old man, wearing an apron over a heavy sweater, was bent over a worktable covered with pieces of electronics. A wisp of smoke floated up from something in the man's hand. He was soldering some wires together.

"Good afternoon, sir," Yitzy said. "Sorry to disturb you. I would like to make a recording for my young lady."

The man set down the tool he was holding and wiped his fingers on his stained apron. He came out from behind the worktable and led Yitzy into a windowed booth in the back of the room.

She watched through the glass as Yitzy sat down at a small table, a microphone in front of him. There were large white squares that looked like ceiling tiles covering the walls and ceiling of the booth. The old man left the booth, then went to a table near Mari, where he fumbled with switches on a large machine that looked a bit like a phonograph, except more mechanical.

She rubbed her hands together in front of the machine's glowing tubes, hoping to warm up.

"You'll be able to hear him," the old man said to her. "I put in a speaker up there." He pointed to a funnel shape coming out of the ceiling by the booth. "In the summer, people like to come and listen to the singers. Good for business. Not much going on in the winter, though, so I take in repair work."

He signaled to Yitzy and Yitzy gave him a nod.

Over the speaker, Mari heard Yitzy give a little cough to clear his throat. And then he smiled at her, so warm and full that the coldness melted around her.

He began to sing.

Embrace me, disgrace me
Just don't erase me.
You are the apple of my soul
If you love me, don't let me go.

Believe me, deceive me
Darling, just don't leave me.
You are the apple of my soul
If you love me, don't let me go.

One promise I will make to you
Wherever I am, whatever you choose
I will love you till my last breath's drawn
I will love you long after my time is gone.

Mariasha was startled out of her reverie by the sound of the needle going around and around in the run-out groove. She lifted the arm from the record.

Yitzy was still smiling at her with his clear blue eyes.

When she was with him, she had felt charmed, special, no longer ordinary. As though, with Yitzy by her side, she could do anything, be anyone. Untouchable. Invulnerable. But that had been her downfall.

And his, as well.

CHAPTER 17

The afternoon seemed charmed, almost magical, as Annette sat on the park bench with Julian talking about their childhoods, their families, how much he loved painting, and she journalism. But the hours went by too quickly. The crisp blue faded from the sky, replaced by pink and orange hues from the setting sun. Then, the last ray of pinkish light disappeared and the temperature dropped suddenly. The chill bit through Annette's leggings and even her ski jacket.

"I'd better get home," she said.

The streetlights had come on along the jogging path, reflecting the disappointment in Julian's face. "You sure?" he asked. "It's almost five. We can have that beer now."

She laughed. She wanted to say yes, and yet she was afraid of where this was going. Their friendship had started with a lie and at this point she didn't know how to tell Julian the truth. For now, she needed to keep some distance. "Another time."

"Tomorrow then," he said. "We'll have lunch with Nana. One o'clock?"

"Does that mean I passed the essay part of my exam?"

"With flying colors."

"One o'clock tomorrow," she said. "I'll bring the food this time."

"Croque-monsieur? Coq au vin?"

"A surprise."

"As long as it isn't escargot," he said. "Those slimy little guys creep me out."

"No snails. I promise."

He walked her to the subway station on Delancey Street and waited at the upper railing while she went down. She looked up when she reached the midpoint of the stairs and waved to him.

He gave her a salute, then turned and disappeared into the darkness.

When Annette got home, she wrapped herself in the afghan Grandma Betty had made her years ago and curled up on the sofa. She felt homesick for family, for her mother. She could call her, but it was just after eleven in Paris and Mama would probably be asleep. Besides, what could Annette say to her? That she was lonely? That she wished Mama would finally talk to her? That she missed her?

Sitting on the park bench with Julian had awakened feelings and realizations, not the least of which was the awareness that she liked Julian more than any guy she had ever known. The prospect of seeing him again tomorrow was thrilling and terrifying. What if she let him in and then he dropped her? But wasn't she doing what her mother had always done? Blocking out any possible happiness for fear of losing it?

She opened Grandma Betty's photo album. There was a great deal of happiness captured in these pages. The photos ended when there was no longer anything to be joyful about. No one wanted to remember the family stories that came once Isaac Goldstein was arrested. Not Grandma Betty, not Mama.

She studied the photos of Mariasha Lowe with her husband and Annette's grandparents. Annette had been able to glean something of her grandparents' world from

Mariasha's stories, but she desperately wanted a closer connection to her family.

She turned to the group wedding photo taken of the bride and groom and their immediate families. Everyone in the picture was dead—Betty, Isaac, their parents, Betty's only sister Irene and her husband. Irene had given her sister *The Jewish Home Beautiful* book that Annette had taken from Grandma Betty's house. The book now sat in front of her on the trunk. She looked again at the inscription. *To my dearest sister Betty. Love, Irene.*

She knew the sisters had been close. Irene, her daughter Linda, and Linda's daughter Jen, had visited them several times in Paris. Jen, who was a year younger than Annette, was a nasty, spiteful child who liked finding ways to hurt Annette. So it was with mixed feelings that Annette would say goodbye to these people who were the closest ones she had to a family besides her mother and grandmother. But the parting between Betty and Irene was always heart-wrenching. She could remember the two sisters clinging to each other until Linda and Mama finally pulled them apart.

A few years ago, when Irene was too frail to live alone, she moved in with Linda and remained in her daughter's house until she passed away.

Might Irene have told Linda stories about Isaac? After all, Isaac had been Linda's uncle. But although Annette had stayed in touch with Linda, they never brought up Isaac Goldstein. The subject had been a source of humiliation for Annette and embarrassment for Linda, and neither liked to recall the day when Annette first learned who her real grandfather had been.

It had been over winter break and Annette was spending the holiday with her father. She'd been mopey, and with reason. At sixteen, she hadn't wanted to come to the States that winter. There was a boy she liked in Paris and she hated being apart from him. Her dad brought her to Linda's house for the day, perhaps hoping the visit would distract her. He had no inkling how far his wish would be fulfilled.

Annette had been working on a half-completed puzzle on the bridge table when Linda's daughter Jen skulked into the family room. She was fifteen, messy black hair down to her waist, wearing worn jeans that were so tight that a roll of baby fat was visible beneath her pink sweater and hung over her waistband.

"I already did that one," Jen said, hovering over the table. She smelled unwashed. "I don't know why my mom keeps taking it out."

Annette kept her eyes on the puzzle, not interested in having a conversation with Jen. She tried to fit a piece into an open spot.

Jen pulled it out of Annette's hand. "It goes here." She slammed the piece into its correct place near the top of the puzzle.

"Thanks," Annette said, though she would have liked to tell her to go away.

"I'm working on a project for school," Jen said. "A family tree. Mom says I can't show it to you."

Annette looked up from the puzzle slowly. Jen's pale eyes were on Annette, her lower jaw pushed out like a bulldog's.

"Why not?" Annette asked.

Jen shrugged. "I don't know. Granny Irene's been helping me. She and your grandmother are sisters, so I even have your side of the family.

Annette couldn't help herself. She was curious. Her mother and grandmother never spoke about family. And Annette, being an only child, often felt very alone.

Jen examined a handful of her long, greasy hair for split ends. "If I show you, do you promise not to tell my mother?"

Annette couldn't imagine why Linda would object, but decided to play along. "I promise."

Jen released her hair and grinned. The sight caught Annette off-guard. She couldn't remember ever seeing Jen smile and her second cousin was almost pretty. If she lost weight, she'd be very attractive.

"Come on," Jen said in a stage whisper, though there was no one aside from Annette to hear her, then hurried up the stairs with exaggerated tip-toe steps.

Annette followed, wondering what Jen was up to. Her friendliness was out of character, but maybe she was lonely or bored.

Jen's room was at the end of the hall. They passed an open door and Annette saw great-aunt Irene sitting on her bed rifling through a pile of envelopes. On a perch beside the bed was Irene's parrot, Prettybird.

Annette continued on to Jen's room. She hadn't been here in years. The Danish-wood bed, desk and dresser were the same, but the room was completely transformed from a neat little girl's room. The bed was unmade, clothes were piled on the floor, and there were food wrappers and Coke cans scattered everywhere.

She was surprised Linda didn't make Jen clean up, but Linda's style had always leaned toward permissive, unlike Annette's own upbringing, which bordered on oppressive.

Even the posters on the walls were far more risqué than anything Annette's mom would have been permitted. There was one of Madonna and Britney Spears kissing. Another of a bikini-clad Paris Hilton in a provocative pose.

Jen picked up a piece of white poster board covered with words and diagonal lines. "I was really confused when I made this," Jen said, scrunching up her forehead. "Especially your grandmother's part of the tree."

Annette stepped around a pile of sneakers and a black lace bra and went over to the desk.

Jen held the poster board against the wall. “You see here it shows the sisters—Betty and Irene Lustig. Your grandmother Betty’s older, born in 1920. My Granny Irene was born in 1925. But here’s the part that confused me at first,” Jen said. “Betty married Simon Revoir in 1955.”

Jen’s hand blocked part of the family tree, but Annette felt unsettled. She knew where this was going. The timing of Grandma Betty’s marriage didn’t make sense.

“Your mother was born in 1945, wasn’t she?” Jen said. “Ten years before Betty married Simon Revoir.”

“What’s the big deal?” Annette hoped her face hadn’t turned red. She hated that Jen knew more about her background than she did. “Maybe my grandmother was married before. Maybe her first husband died.”

Jen smiled broadly, like she was having the best time of her life. She took her hand away from the poster board. “You’re right about that. He sure did die.” She made a loud buzzing sound and pointed to a name attached to Betty’s with another line. It said ‘Isaac Goldstein (b.1918—d.1953)’

The name didn’t mean anything to Annette. The line extending down from the union of Betty Lustig to Isaac Goldstein showed Annette’s mother, Sally Goldstein Revoir (b. 1945--)

So Grandma Betty had been married to someone named Isaac Goldstein and this man, not Grand-Père, had been Annette’s mother’s real father, making him Annette’s grandfather. But why had her mother and Grandma Betty kept this from Annette?

Another line joined her mother Sally to Michael Carter in 1986 and from their union came a downward line showing Annette Revoir Carter (b. 1987--)

Seeing her name on this family tree was a little eerie, but 'Annette Revoir Carter' felt like some other person. Annette had never used her father's last name. She didn't understand why Linda wouldn't have wanted her to see this. Maybe Linda thought she'd be upset that Grandma Betty had been married before.

"Isaac Goldstein." Jen jabbed her finger against the scribbled words on the family tree. "Do you recognize the name?"

"Not really," Annette said.

"You never heard of Isaac Goldstein the spy? The biggest traitor in history? The man who gave the Russians the secret to the atomic bomb?"

Annette felt a flush of heat. They talked about traitors in history class. Judas, Brutus, Marie Antoinette, Benedict Arnold… Isaac Goldstein.

But Isaac Goldstein couldn't be related to her. Jen was making it up to upset her.

"Look here." Jen turned her computer screen so Annette could see it. The face of a monstrous man with one drooping eyelid. "Isaac Goldstein, the notorious American spy, died in the electric chair in 1953," Jen read, then looked back at Annette. "Didn't your grandmother move to Paris in 1953? That's what Granny Irene told me."

"That isn't my grandfather," Annette said, kicking aside a sneaker as she stormed toward the bedroom door.

"Don't believe me?" Jen said to her back. "Ask my mom. She'll tell you. Or why don't you ask your own mother?"

Annette left the room, slamming the door behind her. "*Menteuse*," she muttered. "Liar. Jen's a liar." But her face was hot with a deep-burning shame as Annette sensed Jen had told her the truth. Isaac Goldstein was her grandfather. She was descended from a monster.

Annette turned to the photo of her grandfather—a decorated army hero. Not a monster. It had taken her many years to realize that.

She closed the photo album. Whenever she remembered that day, she was filled with shame. But this time, she felt something different. There was a detail in the memory that she had never paid attention to before. Irene sitting on her bed sorting through letters. Was it possibly those letters had been from Grandma Betty and contained insights into the persecution of Isaac Goldstein?

Annette took out her cellphone to call Linda.

It was time to find her own family's stories.

CHAPTER 18

Annette got off the train at the Dobbs Ferry station with a few other people. When Linda had called this morning to say she'd found letters Betty had sent her sister Irene, Annette had rushed to dress and catch the next train out of Grand Central.

It was colder in Westchester than in Manhattan. A sharp breeze blew in from the Hudson River. She pulled up her hood as she crossed the train platform to the exit stairs. Mounds of snow were piled up by the street where a few cars waited for train passengers, exhaust fumes rising from their tail pipes.

She saw Linda waving from beside an old yellow Volkswagen Beetle. Her mother's first cousin was a grinning beanpole with orange wool mittens and ripples of long curly brown hair flying around her.

"Hey," Annette said, when she reached the car. "Thanks for coming to get me."

"Are you kidding? This is my pleasure." Linda's gray eyes beamed. "It's around fifteen degrees and they're expecting more snow or sleety rain. Hop in the car." She still had a Boston accent from her childhood and pronounced the word 'caaa.'

Annette got in, glad to get out of the chill, and rubbed her hands together. "How's everyone?"

"Good." Linda pulled into the street and started up a hill that had been recently snowplowed. "It snowed last night, so Kenny was up early shoveling out the driveway so he could get to a Corvair club meeting. You know Kenny. He's more determined than a mailman. Neither snow nor rain nor heat nor gloom of night will keep my dear husband away from his old cars."

"And what's Jen doing?" Annette asked, to be polite.

"Still in L.A. Auditioning for a couple of commercials." Linda stopped at a red light and tugged on a dropped stitch in her mitten with her teeth.

"Did she make it home for the holidays?"

"Not this year. Just me and Kenny."

The light turned green. Linda continued past the main street, then turned down a hilly, winding street with white lawns, trees laden with snow, Christmas lights still up.

"How's your mom doing?" Linda asked.

Annette looked out the side window at a snowman wearing a baseball cap, a broomstick over its frozen shoulder like a baseball bat. Its icy face had partially fallen off and it had only one button eye. "You know," Annette said. "She's sad. Always sad."

Linda reached over and patted Annette's hand.

A couple more turns, then Linda pulled into the driveway of their two-story brick house. There was a side entrance that Linda used for her practice as a psychotherapist, though recently, she'd cut back to a part-time schedule.

Annette got out of the car and followed Linda to the front of the house. She could hear a woman's voice shouting. "Mail's here. Mail's here." They stepped inside the foyer. From another room, the woman's voice continued calling, "Mail's here."

"There goes Prettybird, again." Linda shrugged her head in the direction of the kitchen as she took Annette's coat. "You know, my mom's been gone almost two years and I think Prettybird's getting worse. She's very old—close to seventy—and I wonder if it's senility. The bird's been talking more. Saying things in my mother's voice I didn't even know it knew."

"Maybe you could teach it to say, 'Quiet, please."

Linda gave her a playful thonk on the head, then led the way down a narrow hallway, her long curly hair flying out around her from static electricity. Annette smelled fresh-brewed coffee and the sweet, buttery scent of recent baking.

The large eat-in kitchen was the same as when Annette had first visited as a little girl. Lots of oak cabinets, a brick wall with hanging copper pans, and a wraparound benchseat in the corner that overlooked the snow-covered backyard. Prettybird was on her perch in the center of the room.

Annette slid onto the benchseat.

"Here are the letters." Linda picked up a faded blue stationery box from the counter and set it down on the table in front of Annette.

Annette felt a mix of excitement and dread.

"It took me hours to find them after you called." Linda took the cover off the box, exposing tissue-paper-thin envelopes. "Wouldn't you know it, they were in the last carton up in the attic?"

Annette touched the top envelope. "May I?"

"Of course. As far as I'm concerned, they're yours." Linda squeezed her hand. "Losing a relative is always difficult, so I understand why you want to have your grandmother's things."

Annette looked away, embarrassed. Although she did value these letters because her grandmother had written them, she hadn't told Linda the real reason she wanted to see them.

Linda set two mugs of coffee and a platter of muffins on the table. "I read them all this morning. I hope you don't mind."

"I'm glad you did."

"It was a painful time for your grandmother, but as you'll soon read, she and your mother were able to move on with their lives."

Annette studied the envelope. *Par avion.* Sent airmail to Mrs. Irene Lustig in Boston. She recognized the handwriting. It was the same as in Grandma Betty's photo album. The return address was a hotel in Paris. The letter was postmarked September 1953, three months after her grandfather had been executed.

Annette removed the thin paper from the envelope, aware that her hands were trembling.

My dear Irene:

I hope you are well. Sally and I are settling in. My high school French is coming in very handy! You know how I always wanted to visit Paris, but I never dreamed it would be under these circumstances.

Sally and I are staying in a small hotel and the woman who runs it is very nice. She thinks I'm a widow named Elizabeth Gold and has no idea who I really am. She's helped me enroll Sally in school. Sally is quiet and cries in her sleep, but I'm sure once she makes new friends, she'll be fine. Eight-year-olds adjust quickly, or so I'm told.

Annette felt an ache deep inside. She didn't believe her mother had ever adjusted to the trauma of losing her father and relocating to a foreign country. "My poor mother."

"I know," Linda said.

The letters appeared to be in chronological order. Annette read through several. There were details about everyday life. Post-war Paris lacked many of the things Betty had once considered commonplace—toilet paper, silk stockings. She got a job at a hotel. She wrote very little about Sally other than an occasional remark. *Sally still crying. Sally eating a little better this week. I wish Sally would make friends.*

Annette tried to imagine what it was like for the eight-year-old girl to be so far removed from everything familiar. No wonder her mom was always sad and distant.

If only there were something in these letters to help Annette ease her mother's old wounds. Something to point to Isaac Goldstein's innocence. But so far, Annette found no reference to Grandma Betty's first husband.

A year after arriving in Paris, Betty wrote to her sister.

Please don't judge me, Irene. I met a man. He manages the hotel where I work. His name is Simon Revoir and we're going to get married. He's a quiet man, but very nice to Sally. She seems to like him. Of course, Sally doesn't talk much so it's difficult to know. Perhaps you'd find him a little boring and not terribly attractive, but I don't care about that. He's devoted to me.

And no, I don't love him. Love is poison. I never want to love a man again.

Annette took in a sharp breath. So Grandma Betty had loved Isaac. Of course she had. Her blissful face in the photos revealed as much. But what had killed her love? Was it because she believed Isaac was a traitor to his country or was there something else?

She read on. *My heart was broken once. It isn't strong enough to survive another deception.*

Annette pointed to the lines in the letter. "This seems like an odd thing to say. That her heart was broken by deception. It sounds like Isaac wounded her personally, not because he was executed as a spy."

"Whatever she meant, it was an awful time for poor Betty."

"Poor Betty," the bird repeated, like a Greek chorus.

Poor Betty indeed, Annette thought. "Did your mother ever talk about him?"

"About Isaac?" Linda sipped coffee from her mug. "No, I don't think so."

"She must have been very angry about how his execution affected her sister and niece. Did she believe he was guilty?"

"Well of course he was guilty. The government doesn't go and execute an innocent man."

Annette looked down at the letter. *Don't they?*

"He was a terrible person, Annette. Even your grandmother finally admitted that he was a cruel, heartless man."

Cruel, heartless man.

Linda sat down on the benchseat next to her and picked on a muffin. "I never apologized to you for what Jen did."

"No need. I was glad someone finally told me I was related to Isaac Goldstein."

"But that was no way to find out. I just want you to know how sorry I was that Jen hurt you."

"Well, thank you, but I'm okay now."

"Are you?" Linda gave her one of those intense soul-searching looks that Annette imagined she used on her patients.

Annette stared back. "I am."

"Well good." Linda patted her hand, then got up to pour more coffee for herself.

Annette returned to the letters, fascinated to find tidbits about her mother, but also aware that the later letters took her farther and farther from Isaac Goldstein and his possible motivations. There were no letters after the mid-1980s, when the sisters probably began communicating through phone calls.

She jogged the letters into alignment and put them back in the box. She wanted to read about her mother's childhood at her leisure. "May I take these with me?"

"Of course," Linda said. "Like I said, they're yours."

"Did you find anything else?"

"What do you mean?"

"Other letters. These are all from Paris. What about the letters Grandma Betty wrote when she lived in New York and Aunt Irene was in Boston?"

"I didn't find any other letters." Linda went over to the sink and began running water over the muffin pan.

Annette was a little taken aback by the abrupt dismissal. Linda was usually more patient. She looked out the window at the backyard. It was still overcast and dreary. A bluejay settled on the edge of the birdfeeder that hung from a low-hanging tree branch. Annette noticed scattered bird feed and the confusion of dozens of crisscrossed marks in the frozen snow.

She felt certain Betty had sent Irene letters while Isaac was in prison. The sisters were close and from the later letters, it was apparent that Betty used Irene as a confidante. It seemed odd that Irene would have only kept letters from her sister's time in Paris.

The muffin pan clanked against the sink as Linda washed it. What would Irene have done with those earlier letters? Could she have destroyed them? It seemed unlikely. Was there something in the letters that she didn't want anyone to read? Something incriminating? Or was Annette letting her imagination run away with her?

She thought again of that day when she had passed Irene's bedroom on the way to Jen's room. Irene had been sitting on her bed going through letters. But they could have been letters from anyone, not necessarily from Grandma Betty in the early 1950s.

"Did you check her bedroom?" she called to Linda over the running water.

"What's that?" Linda turned off the water and grabbed a dishtowel to dry her hands.

"Did you go through the stuff in your mom's bedroom? Maybe the letters Grandma Betty sent while Isaac was in prison are in there."

Linda gave her head a little shake, as she hung the dishtowel on a hook. "Don't you think you're taking this too far?"

Annette was rankled by her tone. The psychotherapist soothing a hysterical patient. But Annette wasn't hysterical and she wasn't taking this too far.

Then it occurred to her that she'd been insensitive to Linda's feelings about going through Irene's things. "I'm sorry," Annette said. "I appreciate that you slogged through all those cartons in the attic, but I'm sure there are more letters. Please let me have a look in her room. I promise not to upset any of her things."

Linda sat down on the benchseat beside Annette. "I've already been through my mom's room. There are no letters from your grandmother."

"But..."

"Annette. I know you're disappointed not finding what you were hoping to, but I'm afraid those letters just doesn't exist. If they ever did."

She opened her mouth, ready to argue, then closed it. Linda didn't have the letters. Maybe Irene had destroyed them, after all.

"I understand what you're doing," Linda said. "You feel a burden in being descended from Isaac Goldstein. You want to believe he wasn't as terrible as history portrays him. But you need to face the facts. Your grandfather was a horrible person who did horrible things."

Annette flinched.

"But that has nothing to do with who you are."

Annette picked up the box of letters and clutched them against her chest. "You're wrong, Linda. Who my grandfather really was has everything to do with who I am."

CHAPTER 19

The charging theme from *The Dark Knight* awakened Julian. He hit the 'off' button on his cell phone alarm interrupting the pounding of the drums. Sephora's half of the bed was undisturbed, but he felt no remorse that she was gone. He was no longer that person who had lived a false life with a woman he didn't even like. He was just an ordinary guy who wanted to understand where he came from.

He leaned back against his pillow, noticing it was damp with sweat. He vaguely remembered having disturbing dreams. Exploding bursts of red. Had someone been bleeding or was he thinking about the geyser in Saul's painting?

He rubbed his neck and shoulders as he got out of bed. Several of his drawings were scattered over the floor where he'd left them last night. He gathered them up along with the wrappings from a sub sandwich and the four bottles of beer he'd drunk as he had examined his early attempts at art.

He dumped the beer bottles and garbage in the wastebasket and put the drawings back in his old portfolio.

When he'd gotten home after saying goodbye to Annette last night, he had been filled with nostalgia. The conversations with her about his father, his childhood, and how much he had loved painting had brought on an urge to look at his old art work, so he had searched every closet for the carton he had stashed away when Sephora wrinkled her nose at the contents. He had found it at the back of the hallway closet beneath a couple of tennis rackets and some canvas tote bags that Sephora had accumulated at conventions.

In the carton were old, worn favorite clothes of his, an outmoded phone and computer, assorted art supplies, and a pile of comic books. There was also his portfolio.

He had spread the drawings and paintings out on his bed and on the floor, arranged in the order he had made them, starting from when he was around five. The neon green figures bore a striking resemblance to Ninja Turtles. The later drawings were from his Star Wars period, and the last ones he made, when he was around ten, were of Batman and Superman. By then, Julian could see that he had developed a strong technique, but of greater interest to him was that the style—the shading, the three-dimensionality, even the blending of colors—was very similar to Saul's in the painting that hung in Julian's childhood living room.

Saul and Julian had a lot in common. Their fathers had died when they were young, their mothers worked all the time, and they had older sisters. They were both smart and they both painted. But as similar as their art styles were, there was something notably angry and black in Saul's work that wasn't present in Julian's. Whatever had sent Saul over to the dark side seemed to have affected Julian's mother and indirectly, Julian. He needed to find out what that was.

He gobbled down a couple of frozen waffles and a banana, showered, dressed and headed out to see Nana before Annette arrived for lunch. His grandmother had been reluctant to speak about Saul the other day and Julian figured she'd be more likely to tell him whatever she was holding back if Annette wasn't there.

He walked crosstown through a steady drizzle and got to his grandmother's apartment just after eleven. She seemed delighted by his early arrival.

"Would you like something to eat?" she asked, as he stepped into the foyer. She was wearing an old faded man's shirt, which hung on her small frame, making her look like a child in her father's clothes.

"I'm good, thanks." He kissed her head, then hung up his wet jacket and took off his hiking shoes.

He noticed the living room was in a slight state of disarray. The record box beneath the old Victrola was open and there were records scattered over the carpet.

He crouched down to examine them. Big, heavy 78-rpm records. Bing Crosby. Irving Berlin. Ruth Etting.

"What a mess I made," his grandmother said. "It's a sign I'm in my dotage, I suppose." She held out her hand for the record he was holding, then squinted as she examined the label. "*Button up Your Overcoat.* This was one of my favorites." She teetered over to the Victrola. There was a record lying on the turntable. It was much smaller than the shellac ones on the floor. Nana picked it up, handling it as though it was rare and precious.

"What's that?" he asked.

"Oh, nothing." She put the small record in a plain brown paper wrapper, set it aside on the credenza, then placed the record by Ruth Etting on the turntable.

A bouncy voice sang over the scratches about eating an apple a day and taking care of yourself.

Nana sang along, and went to sit down in her big, comfortable chair.

Julian was having a tough time reconciling his mother's portrayal of Nana over fifty years ago with his spunky old woman. In fact, nothing his mother had said the other night made sense. "I want to hear more about your brother, Nana. You told me how much he loved stickball, but then he got sick. What happened to him? Why did he become so embittered?"

"Can't we talk about something else?"

"I suppose we could." He met her eyes.

She blinked and looked away. "But you won't leave me alone until I tell you what you want to hear."

"Something like that."

She absently tugged on one of the buttons on her shirt. "I used to believe if I hadn't gone away to camp that week, Saul would never have gotten rheumatic fever. He might have become a professional baseball player. Everything would have turned out differently."

"You didn't seriously blame yourself that he got sick."

"He was my little brother. My responsibility."

"But you were a child yourself."

"I was, but even children experience guilt."

Julian felt a twinge. Did he feel guilt over his father's death?

The record was over and the needle made a jarring noise as it went around in the run-out groove. Julian parked the arm, then went to sit on the sofa near his grandmother.

"My poor brother," Nana said. "Once he realized he'd never be Babe Ruth, he spent all of his time reading."

"I thought you said he did some sketching."

She frowned and pursed her lips as though she was trying to remember. "That's right. I bought him special pencils. Sometimes, he would make sketches, but mostly he read and studied. He finished all the high school requirements by the time he was thirteen, but Brooklyn College wouldn't let him start until he was fifteen."

"I imagine he felt a bit like a freak," Julian said, knowing from experience. He had started college at sixteen. "Being so much younger than everyone."

"You think?" Nana seemed to be considering this for the first time. "I remember him being happy in those days. I always tried to include him when I went out with my friends, even though he was younger. He was as smart as the next one. Smarter." She folded her hands and looked off in the distance. "I hadn't really thought about his immaturity. But you're right. Maybe he wasn't ready for the adult world."

"So he started college in 1937, right?" Julian said. "What were you doing then? Were you still at Brooklyn College? You told me about the anti-war rally where you met Yitzy. Did you stay friends with him?"

"Yitzy," she said softly. "Yes. We were still friends. He'd come by the apartment all the time. Mama adored him." She glanced over at the sculpture of the woman with the hat.

"And Saul?" he asked, trying to keep her on track.

"Oh, Saul loved him like a brother. Looked up to him like Yitzy could do no wrong. And of course, Yitzy was delighted to have such an ardent protégé. He brought Saul *The Communist Manifesto* and *Das Kapital* and encouraged him to read the *Daily Worker*. The two of them loved to argue, just like a couple of rabbinical students."

"You were talking about the adult world. How Saul might not have been ready for it. What did you mean?"

"We would sometimes go to meetings."

"Communist meetings?" It seemed likely based on the reading material Yitzy brought Saul.

"Some of them." She moistened her lips. "I remember the first time Saul came with us to a Popular Front meeting uptown, not far from City College. That would have been, let's see. 1938. Saul was sixteen. I can still picture him. Still a child, really, stunted by his illness. Smooth-cheeked and small-boned. No bigger than a twelve-year-old."

His grandmother's face became transformed at the memory. She looked sad, wistful, something else. Almost like she was in terrible pain.

"I can only imagine how elated Saul must have felt being in the midst of all the camaraderie," she said. "We were young and naïve. We trusted everyone. How could we know they were already watching us? Sizing us up?"

Julian started. "Sizing you up for what?"

CHAPTER 20

1938

Mari clung to Yitzy's arm as they walked carefully down the dark narrow staircase that led to the basement gathering place. Saul had raced ahead of them, eager to immerse himself in his first meeting of the Popular Front. The din grew louder and she was overcome by a smell that was sweet and sour, like apple cider gone bad.

"This place used to be a speakeasy," Yitzy said. "They closed it in thirty-three, right after prohibition was repealed. Apparently they couldn't compete with all the other neighborhood blind pigs that had gone legit."

Mari's eyes adjusted to the dimness. The large room was low-ceilinged with wood-paneled walls and a mosaic-tiled floor. Along one wall was the now-dull counter of the former bar covered with pamphlets, not cocktails. The mottled mirrored wall behind the bar reflected several dozen people talking in small groups. Only about fifty chairs were arranged in rows facing a speaker's stand, not nearly enough for the attendees milling about.

"Big crowd tonight," Mari said.

"Yeah," Yitzy said. "The speaker is supposed to be a big shot with the Party. There were flyers all around City College promising a good show."

Mari looked around to see if she recognized anyone. Mostly young men, a lot like Yitzy, in three-piece suits and fedoras. Her eyes lighted on a splash of red in the midst of the sea of navy, brown and black. She felt her heart rise, then abruptly drop at the sight of Flossie across the room. Her old friend was striking a Greta-Garbo pose in her flimsy red silk dress and a red slouch fedora hat, as she delicately puffed on the end of a cigarette holder.

Mari hadn't seen much of her since Flossie had abandoned her for a group of uptown girls. And recently she'd heard Flossie had dropped out of Brooklyn College and gotten a good secretarial job in the garment district.

Flossie was staring back at her. It took Mari a moment to realize that Yitzy, not herself, was the object of her friend's attention.

Mari took a step closer to Yitzy. Flossie's eyes flitted to hers and held them. Then she smiled, crooked teeth shining between bright red lips, as she made her way through the crowd, followed by a plume of smoke from the cigarette she held above her head.

"My goodness, Mari," Flossie said in her tinkling voice. "It's been ages." She gave Mari a light hug, then quickly pulled away, leaving behind a scent of Chanel. Flossie looked as though she'd stepped off the cover of a fashion magazine and Mari forced herself not to look down at her own plain navy cotton dress.

"So nice to see you," Mari said, hoping her voice didn't sound hurt or angry, because the truth was, it was nice to see her. Mari missed the girlish intimacy they'd once shared.

"And aren't you a sight for sore eyes?" Flossie smiled adorably at Yitzy, twirling one of her dark pin curls with the tip of her finger. "I hope Mari is taking good care of you."

"Mariasha takes great care of me." Yitzy put his arm around Mari and gave her a squeeze.

"Isn't that sweet?" Flossie said, her lips still set in a smile.

"So what brings you here?" Mari asked. "You've never been interested in politics."

"Oh you know me." She giggled. "I'm always interested in expanding my horizons, so I asked my cousin Bertie to bring me along tonight." She pointed with her cigarette holder at an overweight young man who was standing with several men near the bar counter, dabbing his forehead with a handkerchief. Smoke from their cigarettes hung in a haze around them.

"My cousin says he knows you, Yitzy," Flossie said. "That you're in a few classes together."

"Sure," Yitzy said. "I know Bertie. He's a swell fellow."

Mari was surprised to see Saul in the midst of the small group. He was staring, seemingly transfixed, at a tall, brooding young man with a Clark-Gable moustache, who was speaking passionately and making dramatic hand gestures.

"Who's that with Saul?" Mari asked.

Flossie scrunched up her forehead. "Goodness, isn't he a dreamboat? Do you know him, Yitzy?"

"Oh, that's just Joey. A bit of a scrub when it comes to his classes, but he thinks he knows more about communist doctrine than Karl Marx."

"I don't care if he's not a genius," Flossie said. "He's got himself a nice way about him. Introduce me, won't you, Yitzy? My cousin's useless. And that's why I'm here, after all." She winked at Mari. A conspiratorial wink, just like when they'd been friends.

The three of them waded through the crowd to get to the bar. Flossie whispered something to Yitzy that made him laugh. A year ago, the exchange might have charmed Mari, but for some reason, tonight it irked her.

Saul saw them approaching, grinned and waved them over. His face was flushed and locks of his curly red hair stuck to his forehead. For an instant Mari felt panic. Was her brother getting sick again? But quickly she realized it was more likely caused by the excitement of being here at the forefront of an important movement, surrounded by like-minded people.

"Comrade Joey, this is my sister Mari and her boyfriend Yitzy." Saul looked particularly childlike standing beside the tall young man.

"I know Yitzy," Joey said.

"Aren't you going to introduce me?" Flossie said, raising a penciled-in eyebrow.

"Joey, Flossie," Yitzy said. "Flossie, Joey."

"Pleased to make your acquaintance." Flossie blew out a stream of cigarette smoke.

"You're Bertie's cousin," Joey said.

"That's right." Flossie glanced at the bar counter, taking in the piles of leaflets, and let out a deep sigh. "I wish they still served giggle juice here. Anyone know where a girl could get a drink?"

Joey rubbed his moustache. "If you'd like, I could take you for one after the meeting."

Flossie smiled. "That would be swell, comrade."

"So Yitzy." Saul tugged on his arm to get his attention away from Flossie. "Joey was just telling me about the Steinmetz Society he started at CCNY for engineering students. It's an affiliate of the Young Communist League. I'm going to start one at Brooklyn College."

Mari noticed a man standing beside Joey turn and look at Saul curiously. He was older than most of the people in the room, probably early thirties, with thinning blond hair and a strong jaw. “So you’re a college student?” the man asked. He had a slight accent. Yiddish, or perhaps Russian.

“I am.” Saul straightened up, though he still looked no more than twelve. “My name is Saul Hirsch and I’m a sophomore at Brooklyn College studying applied math and physics with a minor in engineering.”

“I’m impressed.” The man extended his hand. “I’m Anton Dubrovski.”

“Wow. Tonight’s speaker,” Yitzy said, reaching across Saul to introduce himself and shake the man’s hand. “What a pleasure it is to meet you, sir.”

Another stiff-looking man came up to Dubrovski, and whispered something in his ear.

“Boris tells me it’s time for me to give my talk,” Dubrovski said. “Please excuse me.”

Yitzy shook his hand again. “I just want to say, comrade Dubrovski, how pleased I am that the Communist Party has embraced the Popular Front and its commitment to the tradition of Washington and Lincoln.” He pumped his fist in the air. “Communism is twentieth century Americanism!”

The man called Boris gave a tight smile. “He’s stealing your thunder, Anton. We’d better slip away before this young man recites your entire speech.”

Dubrovski winked at Saul; then the two men headed toward the podium.

People started taking their seats. Voices and the scraping of wooden chairs against tile echoed through the old speakeasy.

Yitzy patted Saul on the shoulder. "Isn't that something? Your first meeting and you've made an impression on Anton Dubrovski."

"Who is he?" Saul asked.

"I've met him and Boris at a couple of rallies," Joey said. "They're recruiters for the Party. Important people to know."

"Sounds like you already know them, comrade Joey." Flossie finished refreshing her lipstick and snapped her compact closed. "How about we scram before he makes his boring speech?"

"Well." Joey glanced at his friends, who were heading off to find seats.

"Oh, nuts," Flossie said. "Don't you have any moxie?"

"Sure I do." Joey touched his fedora and nodded at Yitzy, Saul and Mari. "Well, so long. I'm sure we'll meet again."

Mari watched as the swish of red disappeared up the dark staircase, then she took a seat between Yitzy and Saul. Maybe it was childish for her to feel this way, but she was relieved that Flossie was gone.

A smoky haze settled over the room. Mari reached for Yitzy's and Saul's hands and squeezed them hard, sensing as she did so that there were eyes watching her.

She glanced up quickly, just in time to see the man standing at the podium look away.

"So what happened to them, Nana?"

"What?" Mariasha blinked her eyes, unable to get the vision of the man at the podium out of her head. And that terrible smell. Sweet and sour like cider gone bad.

Her grandson was looking at her, waiting for an answer. "What happened to Saul, Yitzy, Flossie, the communist recruiters, all of them?" he asked again. "You said at the beginning of your story that people were watching you. Sizing you up."

Mariasha ran her fingers through her short silver hair.

"Did they recruit Saul?" Julian asked. "Did he work for the communists? Is that why he became so embittered?"

"I told you it's not so simple."

Julian drew back.

She softened her voice. "Mama died and everything changed."

"Changed how?"

She closed her eyes, trying to block out the memory.

"Should I leave, Nana? Would you rather I come back tomorrow?"

She opened her eyes. "Yes, yes, tomorrow would be better." Her brain felt muddled. That terrible smell, she couldn't get it out of her lungs.

"I'll bring Annette, if that's okay."

Annette. His pretty friend. She was supposed to come today with a special lunch.

"I'm sorry, Julian. Tell her I'm sorry, but I'm too tired to see her today."

"I'm sure she'll understand." Julian kissed her forehead, then left the apartment.

Mariasha took a deep breath, but the awful smell was still with her. She tried to think about something else.

Lilacs and talcum powder. Mama's scent.

If Mama hadn't died when she did, would things have turned out differently?

CHAPTER 21

June 1939

"Mariasha Hirsch," the booming voice called out.

Beneath the billowing black graduation gown, sweat ran down Mari's back as she crossed the stage to receive her college diploma.

She turned to the audience's applause and searched the smiling faces of proud relatives. For one crazy instant, she was certain she spotted Mama dabbing her eye with a lace handkerchief, her new straw hat perched jauntily in her upsweep. Then Mari blinked, stabbed by the cold blade of reality. Of course it wasn't Mama. No one who meant anything to Mari was in the audience.

Despite the heat, Mari walked home from the graduation ceremony. She was filled with a desolation she had never known before. This should have been an occasion to celebrate. A chance for Mama to dress in her best, wearing the hat she had so lovingly made for the occasion. They would have gone to an ice cream parlor—Mama, Mari and Saul—and talked about Papa. How proud he would have been. Yitzy would have joined them afterwards. Maybe he would still come. He had his own graduation from City College today, his own family to celebrate with, but surely he knew how important it was to Mari for him to be with her today.

She climbed the stoop of her apartment building. Several neighbors were sitting outside on folding chairs, fanning themselves, drinking lemonade, rocking baby carriages. Freshly washed clothes hung from the clotheslines between the buildings, motionless in the absent breeze. She heard the thwack of a stick connecting with a rubber ball. Several little boys shouted and jumped up and down as other boys raced around in the street.

Was there a God? If there was, why had he forsaken her?

Mari went up to her apartment and let herself in. The windows were open, just as she'd left them, but the air was stale and heavy. She first checked on Saul in the small bedroom. He pretended he was asleep, as he'd been doing whenever she entered his room. She took out the tray of uneaten food and left a fresh glass of water.

Melancholia, the doctor had reported after she'd called him when Saul had refused to leave his room after three days. *It's how some people deal with bereavement. He should come out of it soon.*

But it had been two weeks, and although Saul would occasionally nibble at the bread and jam or egg-salad sandwiches she made for him, he would neither meet her eyes nor speak to her. It was as though he blamed her. And maybe she was to blame.

Mari stepped into the bedroom, where she still slept in the high brass bed, even though some nights she found the emptiness in the room unbearable. The room still smelled like Mama, lilacs and talcum powder, though less and less each day. And Mari feared the day Mama's scent completely evaporated would be the day Mari could no longer face the world.

She picked up the wide-brimmed straw hat from the dresser, touching the green velvet ribbon Mama had tied so smartly in a bow.

"I'll wear this at your graduation," Mama had said, placing it on her head at just the right angle. Her eyes were too bright, too sunken in her pale face.

"You'll be the prettiest mother there," Mari said.

Her mother looked at Mari in the mirror. "I wish I could have given you more."

"Don't talk that way. You've given me everything, Mama."

Her mother turned and faced her. "I don't know how much longer I'll be in this world, Mariasha."

"Mama, please."

Her mother held up her hand. "Let me speak, child." She took off the hat and ran her finger over the velvet. "I'm dying, Mariasha. You know that. The cancer has eaten through my insides. But I need to talk to you about when I'm gone."

"You're not going anywhere," Mari said.

"You're the strong one," Mama said. "You've always been the strong one, even when you were a little girl. You held the family together when Papa was gone."

Mari went to the window and stared out at the diapers hanging from the neighbor's clothesline. She recalled her father's words. *Promise me you'll always take care of your mama and little brother, Mariasha.*

It was too much responsibility for a little girl.

"Saul doesn't have your strength," Mama said.

"Saul is fine."

"Promise me," Mama said. "Promise me you'll always take care of your brother."

"Oh, Mama." Mari threw her arms around her mother's thin shoulders and hugged her tightly. She could feel her bones, smell the lilacs and talcum powder.

"Promise me, Mariasha."

"I promise, Mama."

Mari put the hat back down on the dresser. Mama never got to wear it outside this room. Was it destiny, or could Mari have somehow saved her?

Maybe if Mari had gotten a job instead of going to college. Maybe if Mari had done the cooking and the washing and the ironing, Mama would have had the strength to fight the cancer. Or maybe if Mari had been paying more attention to her mother's failing appetite, the pallor of her skin, and the way she sometimes grimaced in pain, she could have gotten Mama to a doctor sooner.

Maybe if she had tried harder and done more, Mari could have kept her promise to her father and Mama would still be alive.

Yitzy came by later that evening in an exuberant mood, talking about so many things that Mari could hardly process what he was saying.

They sat on the stoop, while Mari turned her mother's straw hat around and around in her hands.

"The world is falling apart," Yitzy said.

Yes, it is, Mari thought. The heat surrounded her like the mist from a boiling teakettle.

"It's our responsibility to stop the Fascists." Yitzy had taken off his jacket and rolled up his sleeves. His forearms were covered with golden hairs. "We've lost Spain to Franco and now Hitler and Mussolini have banded together with their 'Pact of Steel' and who knows what that will lead to?"

Fascists. Her father once spoke out against the Fascists and that didn't help anything. Papa was dead. Mama was dead.

"Hitler is already occupying Czechoslovakia, and Poland is very likely next," Yitzy was saying. "Thank god that Churchill has agreed to support Russia. But even with France, their alliance won't be strong enough to withstand our enemies."

"Saul still won't get out of bed," Mari said. The edge of the green velvet was starting to unravel. "I can barely get him to eat anything."

"He's grieving," Yitzy said. "Like the doctor said. But soon he'll be back on his feet. We need every able-bodied soul to take up the fight. That's why we're going to California."

Mari studied the edge of velvet. She would cut it and stitch it with tiny stitches. Would that work? Mama would know. She looked up suddenly. "What? Who's going to California?"

"We are," Yitzy said. "You and me. You've read the new book by John Steinbeck. *The Grapes of Wrath.* All the Okies have headed out west, looking for a better life, ripe for the Party. We can talk to them about uniting with their communist brothers to fight Fascism. For a better world."

A stray dog walked down the street and sniffed at a garbage can. A broken stickball bat was lying in the middle of the street.

"You want us to go to California?"

"Yes. We can leave in a few days. Now that we've both graduated, there's nothing to hold us back." He took her hand. "Come with me, Mariasha. Let's save the world together."

"Come with you?" The heat was making her dizzy. Or maybe it was hunger. She didn't recall if she'd eaten today.

"Yes, of course. We're wonderful together. And Saul can join us when he finishes college."

"What are you talking about? Saul won't even get out of bed."

"Saul will be fine. He just needs a fresh purpose."

Mari shook her head, wondering if she was stuck in some nightmare. But there sat Yitzy, as real as ever, blue eyes wide with excitement, one eyelid drooping as though about to wink, a sheen of sweat on his forehead.

"You want me to just pick up and leave my brother?" she said. "Do you have any idea what I've been going through the last couple of weeks? My mother is dead, Yitzy. Saul won't eat, won't speak to me."

"Hey, take it easy."

"I won't take it easy." The rage bubbled up inside. "My world is falling apart and you want us to run off and save someone else's world?"

"I'm sorry, Mariasha." He rubbed the back of his neck. "You know I loved your mother, but she's gone. You have to move on."

"Leave my brother? Leave my home? Don't you understand, I'm still grieving and I'm scared."

"You're not listening," he said. "Everything's coming to a head. If we don't pull together now, the world will fall to the Fascists. Sometimes you have to make a choice—the individual or the collective."

"Stop spitting doctrine at me. You have a choice to make, too, Yitzy. I need you here with me. Will you stay?"

A car went down the street, making an ugly crack as it ran over the stickball bat.

"Oh Mariasha." Yitzy closed his eyes. He seemed to be in pain. "I can't stay." He opened his eyes. "You know I can't. Not when the world needs me."

Mari stood up, clutching her mother's hat against her chest. "And I won't leave my brother. Not for the collective. And not even for you."

CHAPTER 22

Annette had just finished paying for her basket of groceries at the Grand Central Market when her phone rang. Caller ID displayed Julian's name.

She stepped aside, as people rushed past her to root through counters piled with fresh produce, dried fruit, bread, cheese.

"Hi," she said, realizing she wasn't doing a very good job of hiding her delight. "I just picked up our lunch. Baguettes, camembert, and fromage de Meaux, which you'd probably call brie. I hope your grandmother will forgive me if I bring wine. It's a pretty good cabernet from the Limoux region."

He didn't answer right away. The smell of cheese and smoked fish drifted toward her.

"Julian?"

"I'm sorry. I just left Nana's apartment." His voice sounded down.

"Oh no. Is she okay?"

"Yeah, yeah, she's fine. It's just, I went over a little early and she started talking about the past and now she's exhausted. She was very apologetic, but she can't see you today."

Annette felt a tightening in her chest. He was giving her a line. Pushing her away. Well, maybe it was better this way. If not now, it would happen later. Men never stuck around.

"I feel like a jerk," he said. "I should have waited for you. Now I've messed up your meeting with her."

"It's fine." The tightness turned into a lump of chilly ice. This day was a disaster. First, nothing in Grandma Betty's letters and now it looked like she'd also lost Mariasha Lowe as a resource. She had known from the beginning how things with Julian would end up.

"Can we still have lunch?" he asked. "I know it's my grandmother you're interested in, but I'd hate that food and wine to go to waste."

So his grandmother really was tired?

"If you'd rather not," he said, "that's okay. I understand."

Tell him no. Save yourself the inevitable heartache. "I'd love to have lunch with you," she said.

He released a deep breath. "Good. Very good."

"I'm at Grand Central. I was visiting my cousin in Westchester this morning," she explained. "Where do you want to meet?"

"It's miserable outside." She could hear him make little puffs into the phone, like a motor trying to catch. "Do you want to come to my place?"

His place? Did she?

"I know the West Village is a hassle to get to from Grand Central. Take a taxi. I'll pay for it. After all, you already bought the food." His sentences ran into each other. "I can tell you more of my grandmother's stories so it's not a waste for you."

"Give me your address."

"You'll come?"

"*Oui*. Why not? There's too much for me to eat alone."

The taxi let her out in front of a modern building and she ran through the rain to the black marble steps. A doorman held open the door for her. Low, pulsing music that she associated with the club scene filled the high-ceilinged lobby.

She was disappointed. This wasn't the kind of place where she had expected Julian to live. It was too hip. Nothing like him. Or was it? Despite their candid conversation in the park the afternoon before, there was obviously a lot about Julian she didn't know.

"Mr. Sandman just called," the doorman said, after she told him who she was visiting. "He'll be here in a couple of minutes. You can wait there." He gestured to a backless gray sofa.

She sat down with her bundles. She had the food and wine in a shopping bag and Grandma Betty's letters in her satchel. She had reread them on the train back to Grand Central after she'd left Linda's house, but had found no fresh insights into Betty and Isaac's marriage or her grandmother's feelings about her husband's guilt or innocence.

The outer door opened and Julian came into the lobby dripping with rain. As he walked toward her, he shook himself like a dog, a big smile on his face.

"I was afraid you might beat me here," he said.

"You told me to take a taxi but you walked?"

"I always walk." He reached for the grocery bag. "Come on up."

The elevator whisked them to the tenth floor, then Julian let them into an apartment that looked like it was out of an episode of *Cribs* on the coolest bachelor pads.

He slid off his wet hiking boots and jacket and held out his hand. "Do you want to give me your coat or are you still deciding if you want to stay?"

She shrugged out of her ski jacket.

"No torn leggings today," he said, as he checked out her yellow sweater and corduroy jeans.

"I wasn't summoned directly from my jog today. I actually had a chance to shower and get dressed."

He hung her jacket in the front closet, but left his dripping wet coat hooked on the doorknob.

She took in the black sofa, high-back leather chairs around a glass dining-room table, a black wall with an entertainment center. In the corner of the room stood a white Christmas tree with a Jewish star at the top. Gray rain was beating against the balcony door behind an austere glass desk. There was a chess set on the desk that looked old and out of place.

"Not what you were expecting?" Julian asked, as he carried the groceries into the kitchen.

Through the pass-through above the granite counter, she could see him opening the bottle of wine. "Nothing about you fits with this place."

He brought two glasses of wine back into the living room and handed her one. "So you pictured me living in a ratty old tenement walk-up?"

She took a sip of wine. "Something like that."

"Honestly, I'd be a lot more comfortable in a place like that. In fact, I'm planning to move to Brooklyn."

"So what are you doing here?"

He shrugged. "I made a mistake. I was living with a girl. This was all her idea."

"Living? Past tense?"

"She's gone," Julian said. "That relationship is completely over."

"What happened? Did she get fed up when she couldn't change you to match the apartment?"

"Pretty good guess," he said.

"Why would you become involved with someone who didn't want you for yourself?"

"I seem to have a problem with trying to please others and not thinking about what's good for me." He went over to the desk and picked up a chess piece, which he turned over in his hand.

"Do you still play?"

"Not since my dad died." He straightened up abruptly and put the chess piece back down. "So, you hungry? I am. Let's have that *fromage et pain* you bought."

They sat on the sofa nibbling on the cheese and baguettes as they sipped wine and talked about themselves. Julian told her about the time he'd run away from home when he was eleven. He'd camped out by the carousel in Central Park but was found by a couple of concerned gay guys who promptly turned him in to the cops. Annette shared with him the loneliness she'd felt when she stayed with her father in America the first time. How she had called a taxi to take her to the airport to go home, but her father had intervened before she could sneak out.

"Sounds like you and I were pretty desperate to escape from our lives," he said.

"Or maybe we were just looking for a place where we'd fit in."

He poured the rest of the wine into her glass. "I'll get another bottle," he said, with a little grin. "It's not from the Limoux region, but it isn't too bad."

He returned with the second bottle, topped off her glass, refilled his, and sat back down beside her on the sofa.

They'd been talking for over two hours and it was almost four, but she was happy that he didn't want her to leave. "So what did your grandmother tell you about that was so draining for her?"

"She talked a little about her kid brother Saul." He smeared camembert on a piece of bread and chewed it slowly. "She told me they went to meetings together."

"What kind of meetings?"

"Well, it sounded to me like they were communist meetings." He wiped his mouth with the back of his hand.

"They went with that guy she'd met at the City College rally."

"Yitzy," she said.

"That's right."

Annette was moving into dangerous territory. "Did she become a communist?"

He rubbed his cheek. It was shadowed by a light beard. "Things were different back then. Communism didn't carry the stigma it acquired later. Especially if you were a college student in New York."

He hadn't answered her question. Or maybe he had, by not answering. She decided not to press it.

"Anyway." He poured more wine into their glasses. "Tell me about your morning. You said you were visiting your cousin."

Her satchel was on the floor beside the sofa. It couldn't hurt to tell him about the letters, could it? But only the part about what it was like for her mother and Grandma Betty to be in an alien place. Julian would understand that.

"I went to pick up letters my grandmother had written when she first moved to Paris."

"Your cousin had the letters?"

"*Oui.* My Grandma Betty and Cousin Linda's mother Irene were sisters. Irene lived in Boston and that's how they kept in touch."

"You told me your mom was a little girl when she moved to France."

"That's right. Only eight. In the letters I see what a difficult time she had adjusting. They're very sad to read."

"What made your grandmother move so far from her family? Was it just the two of them?"

"Yes. Just Grandma Betty and my mother." She looked out the balcony window. The rain was pummeling the glass. How much could she say without him realizing she had misled him and his grandmother?

"What about your grandfather?" he asked. "Did he stay in the U.S.?"

This was it. Would she tell him the truth? All of it? "My grandfather was dead."

"Ouch."

Her heart was pounding. Her mother had once told her, once you tell someone something, you can never take the words back. "My grandfather was Isaac Goldstein."

Julian cocked his head. "Isaac Goldstein?"

"He was executed in 1953 for being a spy."

"Oh my god—that Isaac Goldstein? He passed atomic-bomb secrets to the Soviets, right?"

"Allegedly." She was breathless from her confession. What had she done?

Julian's eyes focused on the black wall. "So that's why you had that book. *A Soviet Spy in America*." He frowned. "Interesting coincidence. My grandmother was hanging around at communist rallies and your grandfather was this notorious communist spy."

"Not such a coincidence," she said. "As you were saying, lots of young people were communists back then."

"Especially the Jews who lived on the Lower East Side and in Brooklyn," he said. "Nana told me how they were raised to believe in social democracy. She even called herself a 'red-diaper baby.'"

"I've heard that term." Annette's heart rate was returning to normal. Julian had hardly reacted to her revelation. But then Isaac Goldstein's execution had been so long ago that Julian probably viewed it as an interesting anecdote rather than as part of who she was.

"So your grandfather was executed, then your Grandma Betty and your mom moved to Paris. That makes sense now. They would have wanted to get away and start over."

He tapped on the side of his wine glass. “Hey wait. They lived a few blocks from my grandparents. You showed me where their building had been.”

Her heart began pounding once again. She never should have opened this door.

“Is that why you came to see my grandmother? To find out if she knew your grandfather?”

“Yes.”

“But why?”

“I was hoping she knew some of the people he knew. To learn the truth about him. I don’t believe he was a traitor.”

His brow formed a scowl and he stared out at the dark rain. “But you said you were doing an article about her sculptures.” He faced her. “Why did you lie about it?”

“I’m sorry. I shouldn’t have. I was afraid if I told her the truth, she wouldn’t talk to me.”

“But you could have told me the truth.”

“When we first met, I didn’t know what you were like so I told you the story I’d prepared. And then, it became awkward to tell you the real reason. I didn’t want you to think I was a liar.”

“You mean like now.”

Her abdomen clenched at the jab. “I’m sorry. I’m not like that. It just happened.”

“Just happened? You lied to me.”

She was startled by the sound of a key turning in the front door.

A gorgeous redhead in a black fur coat walked in. “Hey, big boy,” she called out. “I’m home.”

“Jesus, Sephora,” Julian said.

The woman stepped into the living room and met Annette’s gaze. “Who the hell are you?” the redhead asked.

Annette’s cheeks got hot. Not embarrassment this time. More like rage. She gathered up her things and turned back to Julian. “So tell me,” she said. “Who’s actually the liar here?”

CHAPTER 23

Julian was on his feet, but Sephora blocked his path so he couldn't reach Annette before she'd grabbed her jacket and stormed out of the apartment.

"What are you doing here, Sephora?"

"What do you mean? I live here." She dropped her keys into her handbag and started to take her fur off. "God, it's hot. How can you stand it?"

"Don't get comfortable. You're not welcome here."

"Isn't that a bit harsh?" She threw her coat over the sofa and then went to slide open the balcony door. Cold air rushed into the room with gusting rain. "I mean sure, we had a little fight, but all couples fight. It's just a test of the strength of the relationship."

"We don't have a relationship anymore."

"Of course we do." She picked up one of the bottles of wine, checking to see if it was empty. It was. "Because lucky for you, I happen to be the forgiving type. And I'm not going to make a thing about you bringing some girl back here."

"This is my apartment and it's over between us."

She waggled the empty wine bottle and looked down at the half-full one. "What is it, like seventy-two hours, and you're working on getting laid again? Not that she wasn't cute. A little unsophisticated maybe, but I can see you rebounding with someone simple like that."

He picked up the heavy fur coat and pressed it into her arms. "Goodbye, Sephora." He released the coat, but she let it drop to the floor.

"Julian, baby. Let's sit down for a minute." She took him by the arm, but he resisted. "I had no idea you were so hurt. I mean, I'm the one who should be upset here. First you come home Friday to tell me you've quit your job and we're moving to Brooklyn. No discussion, just the done deal. Of course I got angry. We're a team. We're supposed to talk things through together." She touched his arm again. "Then you skip your birthday party and don't respond to my texts and I have to make excuses for you with all my friends." She squeezed his arm. "I was angry, Julian. I was deeply hurt."

The fury he had been feeling evaporated. He sagged against the sofa, not sure what he had been reacting to. Annette's deviousness? Sephora barging in on them? Or maybe it was simply too much wine. All he knew was that now he felt deflated. And very much alone.

Sephora sidled up in front of him and began massaging his shoulders. "I know you've been under a lot of stress, baby, but we can work it out."

Her skin was practically iridescent, her eyes a glittering green. She leaned in to kiss him. Gently, he held her back. "Sephora, I'm sorry. It's me, not you. I can't be in a relationship right now. Not with you or anyone else."

"Sure you can." She stroked his chest, then reached for his hand. "Let me show you how good I can be for you."

He tugged his hand out of hers. "Please go."

She cocked her head, making a cute, pouty face as she studied him. Then her expression hardened and she pulled back. "Fine," she said. "I just wanted to give you a chance not to be such a dick, but I can see you're beyond help." She leaned over and scooped up her coat, then headed out the door. "Enjoy your misery, asshole," she called over her shoulder. "You deserve it."

Julian slammed the balcony door closed and toweled up the rain that had sprayed inside. Sephora had become a nuisance. An infection that occurred if you didn't clean a wound properly. But she wasn't what had gotten under his skin.

He cleared away the wine bottles, uneaten bread and cheese, and dumped it all in a garbage bag. It wasn't that he was a neat freak. He just didn't want to be reminded of Annette's presence. He rinsed out the wine glasses, put them away, then took the garbage out. He could hear the sound of glass breaking as the wine bottles smashed against the garbage chute. Yeah— he should have put them in the recycle bin, but it was too late now.

There were lots of things he should have done that it was probably too late for.

Annette had lied to him. Sure, he had suspected from the beginning that she hadn't really been interested in writing about his grandmother's sculptures, but she had used him. And worse, she had used his grandmother. She was no better than Sephora. Annette had her agenda and she didn't care whom she hurt in getting what she wanted.

But Julian was done with trying to please women and losing himself in the process. He went into the bedroom and took his old sketchbook and pencils from the carton. He stretched out on the bed and began to draw. A few strong lines, a jaw, a nose, a frowning brow, pouty lips, a beauty mark above the mouth.

He stared at the face, then ripped the page from the sketchbook and tore it up.

CHAPTER 24

Annette could hardly breathe as the rush-hour crowd pressed against her and carried her through the subway tunnel beneath Bryant Park. The wine was finally dissipating from her head along with the blurry numbness that had helped her get through the last hour. There had been major delays on two train lines and she'd been shuffling through the subway system trying to get home since leaving Julian and his red-haired harpy.

She felt as though she'd descended through Dante's *Inferno,* and was now hovering over the Eighth Circle of Hell—Fraud.

She should have known the moment she stepped into his ridiculous apartment that a relationship with Julian was hopeless. The man in the army-surplus jacket didn't belong in a place like that. So either the apartment was a lapse for him or Julian was a fraud. Clearly, it was the latter. Julian Sandman was an even bigger liar than she was.

She reached the platform for the northbound A Line just as a train was pulling into the station. The crowd swarmed around her, pushing her as they got off or on the train. She clutched her satchel as the train door closed behind her. The corner of the letter box stabbed her in the chest, a painful reminder of where she stood in her investigation.

There had been nothing useful about Isaac Goldstein in her grandmother's letters, and now, on top of that, Annette would never have the opportunity to interview

Mariasha Lowe again. But that was her own fault. She should have known better than to drop her guard.

What kind of journalist was she? She had lost sight of her objective and been taken in by the sincere-looking guy who called his grandmother 'Nana.'

The train jerked and yawed and she fell against a man in business attire. He smiled at her. She quickly looked away.

How could she have been so stupid? Hadn't she learned anything from her mother's experience with her dad, not to mention every one of her own disaster relationships? Men were not to be trusted.

But she wasn't going to obsess over her mistakes. She would find a fresh angle for learning the truth about her grandfather or go to Hell trying.

It was dark when she got out of the subway station. She pulled up her hood and hurried home in the sleety rain. She ran up the stoop to her brownstone, stomped the slush off her boots. Once inside, she changed into sweat clothes and sat down on the sofa with the box of letters. She reread them, understanding at an even deeper level the feeling of isolation, loss and sadness her mother and Grandma Betty must have experienced. The letters made her more determined than ever to prove her grandfather had been a victim. Perhaps then her mother would have some consolation for her unhappy childhood. She put the letters back in their faded box and set it on the steamer trunk.

Without Mariasha Lowe or any letters that Grandma Betty may have written while her husband was in prison, she needed to pursue a different route.

The radiator clanked and a fresh wave of heat filled the room.

Bill's voice from her first journalism class came back to her. *Don't rely on one source, no matter how great you think it is. Put out lots of feelers. Remember, the more shit you throw against the wall, the more will stick.*

She had been foolish to put so much faith in Mariasha Lowe's connection to her grandfather. Just because Mariasha and her husband had appeared in Grandma Betty's photo album didn't mean that Mariasha was privy to Isaac Goldstein's possibly subversive activities. Annette had reacted to the old photos and then to the woman more based on feeling than on logic. And while Bill had also taught her to value her intuition, she knew that nothing replaced solid research.

She pulled out her computer and began to do what she should have been doing all along. She found articles and books on Isaac Goldstein and made lists of everyone who had been supportive of her grandfather and/or believed he'd been set up. There were dozens of journalists, politicians, film makers, historians, biographers and, in recent years, former KGB agents. She assembled a bibliography of all of them. Then, where she could, she read articles and excerpts from their books online, hoping to find a fresh perspective or lead.

Unfortunately, everything she read seemed to be a regurgitation of the same material. Many of Isaac Goldstein's advocates believed he had been a scapegoat for the government. Others put the blame for his execution on his lawyer, David Weissman, who they claimed wasn't qualified to represent Goldstein and had botched the defense.

One by one, she went through her list, making sure she had identified everything they'd written on Goldstein, and then ascertaining if they were still alive so she could interview them.

She was dismayed to discover that the majority of Goldstein's early supporters were dead, as were all of the principals at his trial. Florence Heller, who had been the key witness against him, had been killed in a car accident a few months after the trial. David Weissman, the attorney, who would have been a terrific source of information on Goldstein, had died of a heart attack in 1954 and written nothing on Goldstein or his defense of him prior to his death. She found an article by his son, Arnold Weissman, from 1968. In it, the son defended his father's handling of the case. It was a well-argued, informed piece and she learned in the brief bio that accompanied the article that Arnold Weissman was a lawyer as well, at least back when he wrote the article.

She leaned back on the counter stool in her kitchen. Might the son have information about Isaac Goldstein that his father had passed on to him?

Google revealed that Arnold Weissman was a name partner in an uptown Manhattan boutique law firm. She called the number on the firm's website and asked to speak with him. When the woman said he wasn't in, Annette asked for his email address, rather than leave a voice message.

She began to type:

Dear Mr. Weissman: I'm a journalist researching Isaac Goldstein, hoping to prove Goldstein's innocence. I understand your father was his attorney.

She paused. Would an impersonal plea from a journalist motivate the son of Goldstein's lawyer to talk to her? She deleted the sentence and started again.

I'm Isaac Goldstein's granddaughter and I want to learn the truth about my grandfather. Can you help me?

Annette Revoir

Less than a minute later, she received a reply.

Dear Ms. Revoir:

I don't know whether I can help or not, but I'm happy to talk to you. I'm recently retired and no longer have an office, but you're welcome to come by my apartment tomorrow around 2.

He signed the email Arnold Weissman and gave an address on Central Park West.

I'll be there, she replied, feeling a rush of adrenaline.

She was taking her investigation to the next level. Hopefully, it wouldn't lead her into Dante's Ninth and last Circle of Hell. The one called Treachery.

CHAPTER 25

It was dark in the room. How long had she been sitting here? Mariasha touched her face. Damp with tears from reliving that awful day when she and Yitzy said goodbye. Remembering her utter despair. Believing she would never see him again. Never be happy again.

But God, or whoever was controlling destiny, wasn't quite finished with taunting her. He had a few more tricks up his sleeve.

She hoisted her stiff body to the edge of the chair and stood up shakily. So tired. She needed to lie down. Just for a few minutes. She wobbled like a drunk as she made her way to her bedroom and sat on the edge of the bed she had shared with Aaron. Forty years. They had been married forty years before he died. She had been twenty-five when they married and Aaron thirty-nine. A fourteen-year age difference, but they never felt it. She picked up their honeymoon photo from the nightstand. It was too dark in the room to see it clearly, but she knew the pose by heart. The two of them sitting in a toboggan wrapped in a plaid blanket at the Laurels Hotel. How happy and secure they had been at that moment, unaware that in just a few minutes their lives would begin their descent into disorder.

She stretched out on the bed and kissed the picture of Aaron's smiling face.

"I loved you, my darling," she whispered. "I hope you know that."

December 1943

Mari let Aaron help her out of the toboggan. She was exhilarated from the ride down the gentle hill and had happily posed with her new husband for the hotel photographer. Around her, fir trees and the leafless branches of maples and oaks held pillows of white from the first snowfall of the season, and the lake was covered with a glaze of ice that glittered in the sunlight. There was a hush in the air, with an occasional eruption from the raucous scream of a bluejay.

She and Aaron had arrived late last night from Manhattan to find the Laurels Hotel, a favorite honeymoon getaway, practically devoid of guests. Not surprising given so many young men had gone off to Europe and the Pacific in the last year. Her own Aaron was thirty-nine, just above the upper draft age, though to look at him with his freckled skin and laughing eyes, you would think he was much younger.

"Ready for some hot chocolate, darling?" Aaron asked, snuggling her against him.

How protected she felt in his arms. She was his wife now, completely safe for the first time in her life.

"Excuse me," a breathless young woman called out as she ran to their toboggan. "Are you still using this?" She pronounced her words in a flat, unfamiliar way, as though she was from someplace other than New York.

"It's all yours," Aaron said.

"Oh, thank you." The woman smiled, transforming her plain face. Then she waved to a man, who dragged his leg as he approached. "Over here, Isaac," she called. "This one is free."

Mari froze in place. Even across the span of snowy field, even with the limp, she recognized him.

"Are you on your honeymoon, too?" the young woman asked.

When Mari didn't answer, Aaron filled the void. "We are. This is my wife Mariasha and I'm Aaron Lowe."

"I'm Betty Goldstein." She giggled. "I'm still not used to my new name, even though I've had it for three whole days. And here comes my husband," she said, just as the limping man joined them. "Isaac Goldstein."

Mari's eyes met Yitzy's. He started at the sight of her. His face was leaner and his lazy right eyelid had a more pronounced droop than the last time she'd seen him four years before.

Aaron and the woman continued chatting, but Mari couldn't follow what they were saying over the pounding in her ears. She couldn't believe fate had thrown them together once again. And how was it possible, after convincing herself Yitzy meant nothing to her, that she should feel dizzy and light-headed at the sight of him?

Yitzy regained his composure before Mari did. "It's certainly nice to meet you both," he said.

She processed his words. *Nice to meet you both.* Just as when their paths had crossed at the anti-war rally, Yitzy was again choosing not to make their previous relationship known. Well, that would make things easier. She had erased Yitzy from her life, and she would be careful to keep out this man named Isaac Goldstein.

"How lovely to find another couple our age," Betty said. "We've been here three days and there's no one to talk to. Just a group of old folks, but they keep to themselves and their card games."

Mari appraised Isaac Goldstein's wife wondering why he had chosen her. Her eyes were too small, she had a pronounced overbite like Eleanor Roosevelt, and her pageboy-styled brown hair lacked sheen. And yet when Betty looked at him, her face was filled with an adoration that made her attractive despite her imperfections.

The photographer, who'd been hanging back near a fir tree, approached. "Can I interest you in a group photo?"

"Sure thing," Betty said. "My sister Irene told me this was a boring place to go for our honeymoon. I want her to see how wrong she is."

They posed for the photo, spouses' arms appropriately entwined with spouses, as a brisk wind kicked up loose snow around them like sawdust.

"Got it," said the photographer. "I'll have your photos displayed in the lobby later today."

"We were just going in for hot chocolate," Aaron said to the Goldsteins. "Would you like to join us after your toboggan ride?"

"Oh, we'll come along now," Betty said. "It feels like the temperature just dropped. No reason to freeze to death when we can enjoy some nice conversation and warm ourselves by the fire."

Mari walked with Betty a few feet behind Aaron and Yitzy on the narrow snow-crusted road. The two men seemed to have engaged easily in conversation. She was unable to hear what they were talking about as Betty chatted about her wedding, their apartment in a Lower East Side tenement that looked like it could come crumbling down around them, and how sad she was to be away from her family in Boston.

"You're from Boston?" As much as Mari wanted to distance herself from Yitzy and his wife, curiosity got the better of her. "How did you and Isaac meet?"

"Oh, it's very romantic," Betty said, holding her mittened hands against her heart. "Isaac was convalescing at a military hospital in Boston where I volunteered. He'd been injured during the landings in Sicily, but he was a real hero. Got a Purple Heart and the Soldier's Medal for rescuing a drowning soldier. When I first saw him, he was trying to walk with his new crutches and he looked so frustrated that I couldn't help myself and I started to laugh. He looked at me, angry at first. Then he laughed, too, and my heart just melted."

The snow had seeped into Mari's oxfords, freezing her toes. A war hero. Soldier's Medal. Purple Heart. Injured in combat. So much had happened since her Yitzy had gone off to California to recruit Okies for the communist cause. He wasn't the same man. Certainly not the man she'd once loved. He was Isaac Goldstein now.

"What about your Aaron?" Betty asked in a quiet voice, glancing ahead at the men. "Did he also get a medical discharge?"

Mari's face got warm, as it did when people questioned why her seemingly able-bodied husband wasn't off fighting. "He wasn't drafted," she said. "Too old. He tried to enlist anyway, but they rejected him because he has flat feet. He's a professor," she added, not sure why she felt it important that this stranger think well of her husband. "Does what he can to support the war effort."

"Well, lucky for you," Betty said. "I can only imagine how hard it is for women whose husbands are overseas. I don't think I'd be able to bear it if Isaac had to go away." Betty stopped walking and looked at her husband with an intensity that surprised Mari. "I love him more than anything."

The words stung Mari like a slap. Yitzy was Betty's husband. She loved him. He probably loved her, too.

"But tell me about you." Betty slipped her arm through Mari's, and continued trudging down the snowy path toward the rambling Tudor-style main building. "You're so gorgeous. Are you a model or an actress?"

"Gosh, no." Mari shook her head, hoping to toss out any remnants of what might have been with Yitzy. "I'm a high-school French teacher."

"French? *Ooh la la*!" Betty's face got a dreamy look. "I've always wanted to go to Paris. Maybe Isaac will take me after the war."

The four of them sat on cushy chairs in front of the fireplace and sipped hot chocolates. The large, paneled common room was practically empty except for a group of older men playing cards, a foursome of middle-age women engaged in mahjong, and two young boys playing table tennis in the far corner that overlooked the lake.

Mari stole glances at Yitzy, who was talking to Aaron passionately about the U.S.'s responsibility in the war. It seemed ironic to her that Yitzy, once ardently anti-war, had changed his views so diametrically. Of course, different circumstances could easily flip your attitudes. In matters of war…and love.

"It took the U.S. a while to come around," Yitzy said. "I was in California in thirty-nine trying to recruit new blood for the Party when the Soviets signed the non-aggression pact with Germany. As you can imagine, when that happened, no one was interested in jumping aboard the Red Train."

"That's for sure," Aaron said. The two men had apparently learned during their walk that they shared beliefs as communist sympathizers. "Most everyone I knew who'd been a Party supporter was jumping off that train. It felt like a huge deception that the communists would join forces with the Fascists."

"No one would listen to me," Yitzy said. "I told them it was a ploy by the Soviets to buy time while they built up their military strength. They also were far better situated to defend themselves against Germany when they annexed half of Poland. The Soviets never trusted the Germans. They knew it was only a matter of time before the Nazis would invade and they wanted to be in the best possible position."

The sound of a ping-pong ball echoed in the room.

"Maybe," Aaron said, sipping his chocolate.

"Not maybe," Yitzy said. "History has proven me right. But even after the Axis powers invaded Russia with four million troops back in forty-one, still the U.S. stayed out of the war."

"The Soviets were able to withstand Operation Barbarossa without our help," Aaron said.

"Only just," Yitzy said. "And it was at a huge cost to the Soviets. Over three million soldiers dead or taken as POWs." He rubbed his leg that was extended uselessly in front of the glowing stone hearth. "I spent the next six months agitating for the U.S. to get into the war."

"Mahjong," a woman across the room called out.

"Isaac enlisted on December 8, right after Pearl Harbor," Betty said. "He went straight into officer training."

"Very commendable," Aaron said, though Mari could hear the discomfort in his voice.

"The point is," Yitzy said, "the U.S. finally committed to get those Fascist bastards and I was determined to be on the first deployment out of here."

"Isaac was a big hero, you know," Betty said.

"I'm sure." Aaron gave a little smile.

Yitzy frowned and glanced around the room. "Oh look, Betty," he said. "Those boys have finished their game. Didn't you want to play table tennis?"

"Oh I did." Betty clapped her hands together and looked from Mari to Aaron. "Do either of you play? I'm not very good."

Aaron set his mug of chocolate of the coffee table and stood up. "Then we should be evenly matched." He caught Mari's eye. "You'll excuse us for a game or two, darling?"

Mari nodded and watched her new husband cross the room with Yitzy's new wife.

"I hope you're not angry with me," Yitzy said in a soft voice.

"About what?" Her heart sped up, though she willed it not to.

"That I acted like I didn't know you."

She shrugged and looked into the bottom of her mug. The dregs of the chocolate had settled like mud. She had once loved him. He had left her when she needed him most. Now he was married to another.

"I'm hoping the four of us can be friends," Yitzy said. "Aaron told me you'll be living on Ridge Street, a few blocks from us. We'll be neighbors and it will be nice for Betty to know someone."

"And you didn't want her to know our history?"

Mahjong tiles chinked against each other making sharp little sounds. "I was afraid she'd be jealous of you if she knew."

"Jealous?" Mari looked up. "She's the one who married you."

Their eyes held each other's, until Yitzy turned away. "She's not beautiful like you. She doesn't have your strength."

"Yet you married her."

"She's good for me. Her gentleness grounds me." Yitzy leaned forward in his chair, his bad leg stiff, like rigor mortis had set in. "Will you be her friend?"

"I don't like lying to Aaron," she said.

The ping-pong ball went back and forth. Betty let out a squeal of delight. Mari and Yitzy both turned to look at her.

"Please, Mariasha," he said. "For my sake."

Mari took in a breath that burned her lungs. "I can only promise to try."

CHAPTER 26

Washington Square Park was practically deserted. It was just before noon on Tuesday, so where were all the NYU students? This was the university's urban-campus equivalent of a gathering place, and Julian was accustomed to seeing kids swarming through the park even in frigid weather like today. But this morning, the benches along the paths were covered with an inch of icy snow and the only inhabitants were a couple of people with dogs and an old woman pushing a shopping cart filled with rags.

And then it hit him. It was still winter break. His sister might not be here after all, despite her posted office hours, which showed her in today between twelve and two pm.

He walked through the park, hands buried deep in his pockets, the wool hat he'd picked up at a thrift store this morning pulled low over his ears. The temperatures were again in the single digits, making this one of the coldest winters on record. Those global-warming-mongers might do well to recheck their calculations.

He hurried under the modern archway and through the courtyard into Vanderbilt Hall, relieved to get out of the freeze into the heated lobby.

A gray-haired uniformed guard was seated at a desk.

So much for the surprise-his-sister approach. "I'm here to see Professor Rhonda Berkowitz," Julian said.

"ID, please," the guard said.

Julian pulled out his rarely used driver's license with cold, stiff fingers. "I'm not a student here, will this be okay?"

The guard turned it over in his wrinkled hands, then dialed a number on his phone and waited. "Hello, Professor. I have a Julian Sandman to see you."

She must have said something unexpected to the guard because he looked up at Julian and scowled. "Well he looks like the photo on the driver's license. Not a bit like you, though. What's that?" he said into the phone. "Wait. Let me write that down." He turned to Julian and chuckled. "How much is 8763 times 3529 times 1753?"

"Are you kidding me?" This was a game Rhonda used to play with him when they were kids. Accelerating mathematical challenges to see just how far he could go with mental math. "I have no idea."

Julian thought he heard low laughter coming through the phone, then his sister's speaking voice.

"Okay," the guard said. "She wants to know how much they add up to."

So Rhonda decided to give him an easy one. Julian thought for a second. 8763, 3529, 1753. "14045," he said.

His sister must have heard him, because Julian could hear her voice coming through the phone.

"I guess you passed the test," the old man said with a wink. "Professor Berkowitz said you can go on up." He gave Julian a pass and her room number. "End of the hall, on the left."

Julian took the elevator up to the third floor and walked down the empty hallway. All of the office doors were closed except for his sister's. He stepped inside. It was a large room with a view of the park, not surprising considering Rhonda's reputation as a brilliant constitutional lawyer, but with all the piles of books and files, it looked more like a storage room than an office.

There was a conference table with six chairs, also loaded with files. His sister was nowhere to be seen.

Then, on the other side of a tower of law books, he saw something move. A head popped up, covered with frizzy graying black hair, then a pair of piercing pale blue eyes, small pursed lips, and finally a dumpy body wearing a ratty brown sweater over a black wool jumper. His sister had never been a fashion-plate, but it seemed she'd deteriorated even further in the year since he'd last seen her.

She stood up with an effort, brushed off her jumper and trundled over to her desk carrying a book.

"Stop looking shell-shocked, Julian, and sit down." Her voice hadn't changed. Soft, languid and quivering, like a very old person, not a forty-year old. It was remarkable to him that Rhonda Berkowitz had once been a formidable presence in a courtroom, though she'd stopped trying cases four years ago to dedicate herself to research and teaching full-time.

The two mahogany guest chairs were both covered with files. Julian picked up a stack and looked for a place to put them.

"Anywhere," his sister said.

He set them on the floor, then sat down, leaving his jacket on.

She watched him with alert crane-eyes, her hands folded on the desk, a thumb and pointer finger worrying each other. It was a nervous habit she'd had, even as a kid. There was one photo on her desk, of Rhonda and her husband Gary, another well-known attorney who was always spearheading high-profile liberal causes.

Finally, Rhonda released a deep sigh. "I assume our mother and grandmother are fine, or you would have called rather than taken a chance that I wouldn't be in my office over winter break."

Her condescending, indifferent tone irked him. "Yeah. They're okay. Though it would probably be nice if you visited Nana once in a while since your office is only about a mile from her apartment."

"Jewish guilt doesn't become you, Julian." She sighed again, as though the burden of this conversation was wearing her down. "I have issues with our grandmother," she said in her unhurried shaky voice.

"Duh."

"Don't be cute, Julian. You're thirty years old, not a child."

"And Nana's ninety-five. Are you going to wait until she's dead to confront her about your issues?"

"Is that why you're here? To play family peacemaker?"

"This is pointless." He stood up to leave.

"Ahh, Jules." Another tormented breath. "My poor little Jules."

"I'm no one's poor anything."

"I'm sorry. I spend so much time arguing and debating with my students that I think I've forgotten how to be civil."

He rested his hands on the arms of the chair. The wood was deeply scratched. "I saw Essie the other night," he said. "She's still angry with Nana, too."

"Can't blame her. Our grandmother wasn't the warmest of mothers."

"Oh, like our mother was?"

Her lips twitched in a little half-smile. "Touché. You would have made a good lawyer, Jules."

"You already have that covered, Ronnie."

"Fair enough," she said, still smiling. "Now please tell me why you're here."

"I know you stay in touch with Essie, so I'm guessing she told you I quit my job."

"Even if she hadn't I could have deduced it looking at you. It's a Tuesday and you're not wearing one of your snazzy suits."

"I also broke up with my girlfriend."

"No great loss there," she said. "But I understand you're walking away from two advanced degrees to take up finger painting."

"Really, Ronnie? Are you still fourteen?"

"Sorry."

"Between your abuse and Essie mostly ignoring me, it was a real pain in the ass growing up."

"I can believe that."

He took a deep breath. Being with his sister always set him on edge, but he needed to find out what he'd come here for. "Did you know that Nana's brother made the painting in our living room?"

She pulled on a loose thread in her sweater. "I remember Mom mentioning that."

"Not to me," he said. "Friday was the first time I learned that someone else in the family had been an artist."

She didn't say anything for a minute. "Mom's always been very proud of you, Julian. I have, too."

"Right. I've heard that refrain from Nana."

"It's true."

"You could have been a great physician." She sighed. "You could have been a great anything."

"You're changing the subject," he said. "What's the deal with Saul? Was Essie afraid if I knew he'd made the painting, I wouldn't have pursued my higher education?"

"I don't think that was it."

"Something happened with Essie, Nana and Saul. I think it's the reason Essie's the way she is. Why she's so angry at Nana."

Rhonda stood up and began to pace.

"Tell me, Ronnie. You know something."

She went over to the credenza behind her desk and began digging through papers and files. Finally, she pulled out a large, brown folder, held closed by a string. "This is something you might want." She handed him the folder.

It looked like it might disintegrate in his hands, so he opened it carefully. He slid out a stack of papers. Sketches done in pencil. He recognized the style. "Saul made these?"

"That's right." She took the files off the other guest chair, dropped them on the floor, then pulled the chair close to Julian's and sat down.

The paper was yellowed and fragile. The first few drawings were of comic-strip characters—Dick Tracy, Popeye, and Buck Rogers—the heroes of Saul's day. He noted the three-dimensional aspect, which wouldn't have been in the original comics, but was very similar to Julian's own work.

He set each paper down on Rhonda's desk after he studied it. There were several of the Buck Rogers character wearing a strange spacesuit, surrounded by objects that appeared to be glowing. They reminded him of something.

"Do you know the character?" his sister asked.

"Buck Rogers? Just that he travelled to the future. Early sci-fi."

"Very early. He first appeared in the pulp magazine *Amazing Stories* in 1928."

"Saul got rheumatic fever when he was ten, so these sketches are probably from around 1932 or '33."

"Well, he chose an interesting subject," she said. "As the story goes, Buck was exposed to radioactive gas when a coal mine caved in around him. He fell into a state of suspended animation and awakened in the twenty-fifth century. That's where he has all his adventures."

"Very cool," Julian said. "I forget that radiation made it into popular culture in the early 1900s." He looked again at the glowing objects. “So Saul was probably trying to convey radioactive rays here. It’s a lot like in the painting in the living room. I guess there’s a bit of Buck Rogers in that painting.”

He put the Buck Rogers sketches on the desk with the others, and looked at the next one. It was a study of a woman with her hair pulled into a loose bun. She had large eyes and a sad expression on her face and looked like the Madonna.

“This is our great-grandmother, isn’t it?” he asked.

“Yes.”

“I’ve never seen a picture of her.”

“I think this is the only one.”

He turned to the next page. Another study. This one of a girl with a long slender neck and a thick braid draped over her shoulder.

“Nana?” he asked.

“That’s right.”

Julian put the last sketch on Rhonda’s desk with the others. “Saul was very gifted.”

“Like you.”

“Nana’s been telling me stories about him.”

“Really?” Rhonda plucked on her wiry hair. “What kind of stories?”

“That he played stickball as a kid, then became a communist.”

“That’s all?” she said.

“Is there something else?”

Rhonda looked away.

“What do you know about Saul?” he asked.

“Very little.”

“But you have his sketches,” he said. “Did he give them to Essie? Did she give them to you?”

Rhonda shook her head. “I got them from our grandmother.”

"Nana gave these to you? She doesn't even talk to you."

"Years ago," Rhonda said. "She asked me to take them away before she burned them."

"Burned them? Are you serious? But her brother made them. They're a tangible part of her past."

Rhonda put the sketches back into the folder. "I guess she didn't want a reminder of that past."

"Why not?"

"Maybe you should ask her." Rhonda's gaze pierced him.

What was his sister suggesting? That Nana had some terrible secret? Essie had said she was deceptive, but he had refused to believe her. Now, Rhonda's story was matching up with their mother's.

But that didn't make sense. Nana was kind and wise and loving. It wasn't in her nature to deceive. And yet, he sensed she'd been holding something back from him.

Julian took the folder of sketches from Rhonda. Sketches Saul had made. That Nana had wanted to destroy. Just like she'd hoped to do away with the painting Saul had made for Essie's thirteenth birthday. But why? What was Nana hiding?

He shivered in the cold room. And despite the nearness of his sister, he felt more alone than ever.

CHAPTER 27

Annette was relieved to step out of the frigid weather into the dim lobby of Arnie Weissman's apartment building. The son of Isaac Goldstein's attorney lived in an old building, probably built in the 1920s or 30s, but it was well maintained, with two matching Queen Anne sofas beneath a crystal chandelier. She gave her name to the doorman, who called ahead, then directed her to the elevator. She found the apartment number and rang the bell.

A nice-looking older man in a burgundy cardigan and pressed gray slacks opened the door. With his thin graying hair and intelligent brown eyes, he resembled photos she'd seen of his father, David Weissman.

"Please come in, Ms. Revoir." He had a rich, melodious voice.

"Annette," she said.

"Of course. And please call me Arnie." He took her coat and led her to the living room. It had wood floors covered with rugs, comfortable sofas and easy chairs, and walls of books. On top of the baby grand piano in the corner of the room were framed colored photos of smiling adults and children and a couple of black-and-whites, which reminded Annette of the photos in Grandma Betty's album.

"I apologize for the informality," Arnie Weissman said. "I'm accustomed to meeting in my office or boardroom. I only recently retired and I'm still adjusting to my new situation. May I get you something to drink? A soda? Water?"

"I'm fine. Thank you." She sat on the sofa with her satchel as he took the chair cattycorner to her. Through the large windows behind him, she could see the leafless trees of Central Park. "I appreciate you seeing me."

"I was intrigued by your email," he said. "I haven't thought about Isaac Goldstein in years."

"I imagine you're too young to have met him."

He smiled. There was a narrow gap between his front teeth that she found endearing. "Don't be misled by my recent retirement. I held onto my practice many years after most of my peers had retired. I just turned eighty. And I did meet Isaac Goldstein."

She felt a flutter in her chest. "Please, tell me."

"First, if you don't mind, I'm a little curious about you. With my father's very heavy involvement in the case, you can understand I have a bit of a vested interest in learning what became of Isaac Goldstein's family." He ran his hand over his smooth-shaven cheek and stroked his chin. "You see, I knew he had a wife and daughter who left the country after his execution, but they seemed to have disappeared."

Annette nodded. "They tried to disappear. They moved to Paris and my grandmother changed her name."

"So you're French? I thought I detected a slight accent."

"And American. My father's from the U.S."

"And what made you decide to look into your grandfather's death?"

"This." She took out the photo album from her satchel and opened to her grandparents' wedding photo. "I found it when I was packing up my grandmother's apartment. She died a few weeks ago."

"I'm truly sorry to hear that."

"Thank you." Annette felt the sting of tears. She hadn't cried when she'd first learned of her grandmother's death or while she packed up her things. Why was it hitting her now?

Arnie got up and left the room, so she had a moment to compose herself. It was probably the anguish she'd read in Grandma Betty's letters that made her feel even closer to her grandmother than when she'd been alive.

Arnie returned with two glasses of water and a box of tissues, which he put down on the coffee table. He picked up the photo album and studied the wedding picture.

"This is much closer to what Isaac looked like in person than the photos and posters the public got to see," he said.

"That's why I decided to find out who he really was." She dabbed her eyes with the tissue, then crumpled it up. "This man doesn't look like a monster."

Arnie put the album down on the table, then leaned back against his chair. "How much have you read about my father's defense of Isaac?"

"I read the article you wrote in 1968 about your father. That's how I found you."

"So you've done your homework, but let me give you a little more background." He pursed his lips, a faraway look in his eyes. "There are some who believe my father wasn't qualified to handle the case. That it was way beyond his experience. And it's true that my father had a small, family practice and that the Goldstein trial was at a Federal level and required someone knowledgeable in constitutional law. But my father was a brilliant and dedicated man. What he didn't know, he taught himself." Arnie stood up and paced in front of the window. Outside, the sky was a dull gray. "No attorney could have been more committed to defending Isaac Goldstein than my father. Not that they were beating down the door for the privilege."

"What do you mean?"

"Why do you think Goldstein came to my father in the first place? None of the big firms would have anything to do with him. This was back in the early fifties. McCarthyism was in full flare. No one wanted to be seen as a communist sympathizer. And defending Isaac Goldstein would have cast suspicion on the firm that took him on."

"Wasn't your father afraid of being tainted?"

Arnie took in a deep breath, then slowly let it out. "My father was a great man. An independent thinker. Mass hysteria infuriated him, especially the Red Scare. He was determined to give Goldstein the best defense he was capable of. He worked tirelessly during the trial and through two years of appeals." Arnie picked on a button on his cardigan. "My father was determined to defend Goldstein even knowing that he himself was under FBI surveillance as a possible communist. Even when the bar association threatened to have him disbarred."

"For defending my grandfather?"

He nodded. "It was probably what led to his early death. At least that's what my mother always maintained. That the stress of the trial, the appeals, and the harassment by the government caused my father's fatal heart attack."

"I'm sorry," she said softly.

"Well, we all make choices." There was anger or frustration in his voice. "I believe even if my father had known the outcome, he would still have taken on the case and worked it just as hard. Maybe harder, if that was possible."

It hadn't occurred to her that more than her own family had suffered from Isaac Goldstein's persecution. She tried to bring down the tension. "You said you met my grandfather. Can you tell me about that?"

Arnie sat back down. "Sorry for getting emotional. This subject obviously pulls up a lot of painful memories for me."

"I'm grateful to you for sharing them."

He gave her a little smile. "Isaac Goldstein came to my father's office in 1950, shortly before he was picked up by the FBI."

"So he must have known he was going to be arrested."

"He did. He was a communist. He never denied that. Many of his friends and associates were being arrested, so he knew it was just a matter of time for him. But I don't believe he ever imagined how the charges would multiply and take on a life of their own."

"And that's when you first met him, at your father's office?"

"That's right. My father had a small suite in Midtown. Just Dad, a couple of associates and a secretary. I would often help out after school and occasionally my father would invite me to sit in with his client meetings, if they didn't mind. I was sixteen back in 1950, a senior in high school, a baseball star." He smiled at Annette. "That was a long time ago."

"So you were at the meeting with my grandfather?"

He nodded. "And I remember thinking what a handsome, charismatic man Isaac Goldstein was. He commanded the room, even with his limp."

"Limp?"

"War injury. That's why he'd been given a medical discharge and ended up working at the Army Signal Corps toward the end of the war."

She glanced at the photo of her grandfather in the open album on the coffee table. Bill had mentioned the war injury, but not the specifics.

"I recall him joking with my father, who was a serious man," Arnie said. "And my father warning him. 'Don't take this lightly, Mr. Goldstein. If the government arrests you, it's like falling into quicksand.'"

"Your father was prescient," she said.

"No. He was a pragmatist who understood the seriousness of the situation."

"Do you remember anything else about my grandfather?" She craved details from someone who had actually met him.

He thought for a minute. "He asked me about myself. I told him I'd been accepted to Brooklyn College and was going to play on their baseball team. And I remember he became pensive and then he said, 'Sports. Stay with sports. I've always been a Yankee fan myself." He took a sip of water from one of the glasses. "The next time I saw him was at the trial. My father had gotten me in to watch." He shook his head. "Your grandfather hadn't been able to make his hundred-thousand-dollar bail and was being held at the Men's House of Detention on West Street. I remember how different he looked from the first time I'd met him. Tense and anxious, even hostile. Much more like the photos that appeared in the newspapers. But by then, it was apparent to my father and very likely to Goldstein that the trial was a witch hunt."

She sat up straight. "How so?"

"My father had gone into the trial believing he had a very strong chance of an acquittal. The prosecutor's case was shoddy and mostly circumstantial. But then, Dad realized what he was up against."

She felt tiny fingers crawling up the back of her neck.

"Dad was convinced the prosecutor and judge were in cahoots with the government. The judge wouldn't allow important testimony that my father tried to get in and always favored the prosecution. It was apparent to Dad that they railroaded Goldstein's conviction."

"But why would they have done that?"

"You have to remember the times. In 1949, the U.S.S.R. had detonated their first atomic bomb. McCarthy was terrorizing Americans with the Red Scare. The Cold War was in full swing and the government decided to unite the masses in common hate, so they executed Isaac Goldstein as a symbol of evil communism."

Bill had also believed that the 'Death to Goldstein' posters had likely been designed as an allusion to George Orwell's *1984*.

"So what you're saying is there was no real case against my grandfather."

"That's right. Florence Heller, the key witness against him, claimed that Goldstein was the mastermind of a spy ring that included her, her boyfriend Joseph Bartow and Albert Shevsky, who worked at Los Alamos. Goldstein knew Bartow and Shevsky from City College, but he insisted that he had only a superficial involvement with them during the war."

She was familiar with the testimony. "But why would Heller have fingered him?"

"Goldstein told my father that Heller was carrying out a personal vendetta against him because he had once wounded her female pride. You know the expression—Hell hath no fury like that of a woman scorned. Unfortunately, there was no way of substantiating this."

A personal vendetta? There was nothing about this in anything she had read. "But I recall testimony where Florence Heller produced copies of atomic-bomb sketches," she said. "They were very basic and not of particular value to the Russians, but they carried a lot of sway at the trial. Heller claimed she had received the sketches from Shevsky, and then given them to my grandfather to pass on to the Russians."

"My father believed Florence was protecting Joseph Bartow and that she had actually given the sketches and other documents to him."

"So most likely Bartow and Shevsky were the real spies," she said.

Arnie turned his wedding band around on his finger. "That's what my father believed. But years after the trial, it was revealed that Shevsky only had intermediate clearance, which wouldn't have gotten him near important secret material. And yet it's known there were leaked documents coming out of Los Alamos that were crucial to the Russians."

"Do you think my grandfather was involved with a spy ring?"

He rubbed his chin. "It's possible."

His words bit into her. Was she deceiving herself trying to prove her grandfather was a victim when he really had been a perpetrator?

"But Annette," he said. "Even if your grandfather had been aiding the Russians, it was certainly not at a level that would have justified his demonization and execution. And remember, during World War II, Russia and the United States were allies. So it could have been argued that at that time he was helping an ally."

She thought about Yaklisov's book, that someone who went by the code name Slugger was the real spy. "Did Slugger ever come up at the trial or after?"

"Slugger?" Arnie frowned. "Like Babe Ruth's bat? No. I can't say I ever heard that name in connection with Isaac Goldstein."

"Did your father retain any correspondence from the trial? Either letters my grandfather may have written him or letters he may have received in prison?"

Arnie shook his head. "I'm sorry. I don't know of any letters Goldstein sent my father and any personal letters he had in prison would have been sent back to his wife with his other personal effects."

Which Grandma Betty had most likely destroyed.

"Do you believe my grandfather knew who was leaking the documents?"

"I don't, but the government was convinced he did. In fact, my father theorized that the government threatened him with execution because they were certain he would break under pressure and reveal the true spy. My father confronted him about it." Arnie's gaze fell on the family photos on top of the piano. "I remember my father coming home from visiting Goldstein at Sing-Sing during the appeal process. Dad told me he'd begged him to reveal who was actually passing atomic-bomb secrets to the Russians. He reminded Goldstein that if he was convicted, his family would not only lose him but would spend their lives in the shadow of his guilt." Arnie picked up the glass of water and took a sip. "Goldstein said to my father, 'I swear to God I don't know.'"

Annette looked out the window. The sky had turned a darker gray, like pewter. "So my grandfather wasn't involved with anyone who had access to atomic-bomb secrets and didn't know who the real spy was, yet he was condemned as one of the biggest traitors in American history. How could that have happened?"

"Because it was expedient," Arnie said.

She turned to him. "Expedient?"

"Pure and simple, the Isaac Goldstein trial and execution was a government conspiracy to unite the public against a common enemy. When your grandfather didn't give them a name, they still needed to demonize someone."

She pulled in a painful breath as she considered this. "So what you're saying is my grandfather just happened to be low-hanging fruit."

CHAPTER 28

It was snowing when Julian left Rhonda's office. He stuck Saul's portfolio beneath his jacket to protect it, as he walked to his grandmother's building. How would Nana react when she saw the sketches her brother had made? He hoped she was ready to reveal whatever secrets she'd been keeping from him.

There was no answer when he rang the outside buzzer to her apartment. Could she have gone out shopping? But Nana wasn't crazy. She never went out when it was this cold. Maybe she was showering. He used his emergency key to let himself into the building, then took the elevator up to the fourth floor. He rang the bell, not wanting to frighten her by barging in. He waited a moment, then knocked hard. "Nana? It's me."

No answer.

He unlocked the door, worried at this point. A ninety-five-year-old woman shouldn't be living alone. He should have insisted she hire an aide to stay with her. He could have helped pay for it. It would have been a better use of his money than his expensive loft apartment. He stepped into the foyer, dropping Saul's folder on the table. "Nana, are you okay?"

She wasn't in the living room. He checked the kitchen. Empty. He hurried toward the bedroom. "Nana?"

The door was ajar. The room was dim, curtains partially drawn. A slight figure lying on top of the faded quilt. She didn't seem to be moving.

"Nana?" He stepped closer. Her head turned toward him and she opened her eyes.

Thank god.

He sat on the edge of the bed and examined her. She was breathing okay, but her skin looked grayish. He took her hand. Cold. He squeezed it. She squeezed back weakly. “Are you feeling okay?” he asked.

“Perfect.”

Her pulse was forty-eight beats a minute. A little low, but not terrible. He reached into the drawer in the nightstand where he’d stashed a blood pressure cuff and stethoscope in case of an emergency. Her blood pressure was in an acceptable range. He checked her lungs. Clear. He listened to her heart.

“Nana, can you raise your right arm for me?”

“Still a physician at heart,” she said, raising her arm.

“Now the left.”

She did, then moved her legs and arms up and down as though she was swimming. “See? I’m perfectly fine. What are you doing here?”

“Why are you in bed?”

She pushed herself up against the mahogany headboard. He adjusted her pillows. She was wearing the same old blue shirt she’d had on the day before.

“Memories,” she said. “I needed to lie down for a few minutes.”

A black-and-white framed photo of Nana and his grandfather that she usually kept on the nightstand lay on the bed beside her. It hadn’t occurred to Julian that thirty years after his death, Nana still missed her husband.

“This was taken on our honeymoon,” she said, picking up the photo. “He was a wonderful man.”

“I’m sorry I never got to meet him.”

“Me too. He would have been very proud of you.”

Julian’s throat tightened.

Her eyes wandered over the faded patches on the quilt. “He was a smart man, too, and very level-headed. Not a starry-eyed fanatic like some.”

Did she mean Saul? He would have to move carefully into the conversation he planned to have with her.

Nana kissed the photo. Her hand trembled as she set it down in its usual place on the nightstand.

"Let me make you something to eat, Nana."

She looked startled. "Did I miss our lunch? Is your friend here?"

"No," he said. He wasn't going to get into how Annette had lied to him. "She's not coming."

He persuaded her to get up and wash her face while he went into the kitchen and heated up a bowl of tomato soup for her. She joined him a few minutes later. She had combed her hair, put on a pair of earrings with a cluster of sparkly stones and changed into a pink sweater with a red apple applique. He remembered the sweater from when he was in high school, but back then it had fit her. Now it hung on her frail frame, making the apple look like it was wilting.

"Soup's ready," he said, adjusting a pillow behind her back as she sat down.

He brought the bowl to the table and took a seat across from her.

She took a small taste of soup. "This is wonderful, Julian. Thank you."

They sat in silence surrounded by the low-tech past—the Philco refrigerator with its rounded edges and giant handle, a green and white O'Keefe and Merritt gas stove, even the original double-basin cast-iron sink with a checkered green skirt to hide its legs. Julian remembered sneaking off behind the curtain, under the sink, trying to block out the arguments between his mother and grandmother. His mother crying. *You never even hugged me. Not once.*

Hadn't he said something just like that to Essie the other day?

There'd been a palpable distance between Nana and his mother, and that same lack of affection had been passed down to ruin the relationship between Essie and him. But why hadn't Nana hugged her daughter?

He eased into the subject. "I went to see Rhonda this morning."

She sipped the soup from her spoon. "You and your sister should spend more time together."

"She gave me something. I'll be right back." He got the thick folder from the foyer and set it down on the kitchen table.

Nana started. "What are you doing with that?"

"Rhonda told me you gave it to her years ago. She said you were afraid you'd burn it if you kept it. Why is that, Nana?"

She pushed her soup bowl out of the way. "Please, let me see them."

He slid them toward her. She went through the sketches quickly, stopping to look at a Buck Rogers drawing, then continuing until she reached the one of her mother.

"Mama," she said softly, her eyes watering. She looked up at Julian. "This is the only picture of her, except for the one on her headstone."

"Why did you give these to Rhonda? What made you say you were going to burn them?"

"I wasn't thinking clearly. Rhonda had found the sketches when she and your mother were visiting. Your mother became very angry when she saw them."

"Why?"

She shrugged.

"Did they remind her of the painting you'd hidden from her when she was a girl?"

"Who knows," she said. "We started arguing. I told Rhonda to take the folder away. I don't know what I was thinking. I suppose I'd hoped if I didn't have anything of Saul's here, your mother wouldn't find a reason to argue."

"Why were you so determined to keep Saul's artwork from her?"

She shook her head fiercely, like a child not willing to give up a favorite toy.

"This all happened years ago, Nana. Why is my mother still angry with you?"

"It's nothing. It's all in her head."

He was frustrated. "What's in her head?"

She ran a trembling finger over the image of her mother, not quite touching it. "I had forgotten this was in with the other drawings. I never would have given this to Rhonda if I had remembered."

His grandmother wasn't going to tell him. At least, not yet. And he knew that trying to pressure her would only cause her to shut down.

He took in a deep breath, and looked more closely at the picture of his great-grandmother. "There's a lot of heart in this sketch."

"Saul loved our mother very much. We both did." Her voice quivered. "She died when Saul was seventeen. He took it hard. Wouldn't get out of bed for a month."

"That must have been difficult for you, too."

"Yes." She reached across the table for her soup and moved the spoon back and forth without eating it. "Finally, Saul snapped out of it and threw himself back into his studies. He graduated from Brooklyn College when he was eighteen and went on to Princeton. He completed his PhD in physics when he was twenty-one."

Julian quickly did the math. "1943. The U.S. was involved in World War II then." He knew enough history to see where this was heading. Many scientists, particularly those in physics, had been scooped up by the government to work on the Manhattan Project. "Jesus," he said. "Was Saul sent to Los Alamos?"

She put her hand over the red apple on her chest. "It doesn't matter anymore. He's gone. Why do you want to dig up the past?"

"So he was at Los Alamos, wasn't he?"

"He was young and naïve, still a boy really," she said. "The government promised him things they knew mattered to him. Working with the brightest minds in the world. Getting involved with science at a level that was beyond his dreams."

"My god, Nana. Did he work on the atomic bomb?"

"They brainwashed him," she said. "They told him he would be serving his country. Helping humanity by ending the war."

Goddamn. His great-uncle Saul had been involved with the development of the atomic bomb. Was that what the hostility between his mother and Nana had been about?

The image of the painting in his mother's living room came to him. A spreading stain of red. Not a geyser, as Julian always thought, but more like a giant mushroom. His uncle had painted a red mushroom cloud surrounded by radioactive objects. These weren't reminders of Buck Rogers, but of Saul's own horrible experiences.

"It took him a while to understand what he was creating." Nana put her spoon down, splattering red soup on the tabletop. "But what could he do? If he objected to his assignment, he would have been seen as a traitor to his country."

"So he helped develop the atomic bomb," he said. "And died with a guilty conscience."

She stared at the red splatters of tomato soup.

"But first he made a painting of his guilt and gave it to my mother."

CHAPTER 29

Mariasha jerked her head up too quickly, causing a painful crick in her neck. "You know nothing of guilt."

"Then tell me what happened, Nana. Why did Saul make that painting?"

She had already told her grandson too much, but a memory was pushing to get out and she couldn't seem to hold it back.

"Saul was a good man," she said. "But being good can't always protect you from evil."

December 1944

Mari was surprised by the knock on the door. Had Aaron forgotten his key? She checked the time. Not quite five. Her husband had a late class tonight and wasn't due home until after six.

"Who is it?" she called through the door.

"Your favorite *trombenik*," the voice said.

"My god. Saulie? What are you doing here?"

"Would you mind letting me in?"

She unlocked and opened the door, delighted to see her brother for the first time in months, since he'd left for some secret job in the middle of nowhere that he wasn't allowed to talk about.

"Look at you." He gave her a hug. "A regular *balabusta*. But I was expecting to see you with a big belly."

Mari felt her face grow warm, but her brother meant well. He had no idea he'd hit a sensitive spot.

She smiled brightly so he wouldn't notice. "Well you finally look like a grown-up man."

"I think the moustache helps," he said, smoothing out the thin line of golden red hair above his lip.

She stood back and took him in. Still delicately built with his mop of curls, but there were a few lines on his forehead and by his eyes that hadn't been there when she'd waited with him to catch the train for Albuquerque six months before.

"So I'm starving to death and I smell something good," he said.

"I made brisket."

"You must have been expecting me."

"It's Aaron's favorite."

"And mine, too, at the moment."

She served him a platter of brisket with cooked carrots and potatoes and a healthy dollop of horseradish on the side. He ate as though he hadn't eaten in months, although she'd been mailing him packages with salami and cheese each week. Finally, he pushed back the kitchen chair and patted his belly. "That was delicious, Mari. Just like Mama's."

Mari felt a bittersweet tinge. She and Saul had come a long way from the ragamuffins who played on the tenement stoop. If only Mama were here to see them.

She poured him a cup of hot tea with honey and set out a platter of mandel bread. "So what's it like for you in the middle of nowhere?" she asked.

"Not too bad." He dipped a slice of the hard pastry into his tea just like he did when he was a child. "You know, it sure isn't run much like a secret military installation. Sometimes I feel like I'm at a movie set for the Keystone Cops."

"What do you mean?"

"No one follows the rules. We sneak in and out of the facility without the guards noticing. Secret documents are lying all over the place for anyone to see. And you've got people wearing red badges wandering into areas that are supposedly for white badges only."

"Red badges? White badges?"

"Red is for people with intermediate clearance. Blue is for the laborers who have lowest access. White is for the scientists like me."

Mari had concluded from not-very-subtle remarks in her brother's letters that Los Alamos was engaged in building some incredibly powerful weapon that would end the war. Though occasionally, Saul would write jokingly that they were 'developing windshield wipers for submarines.'

"Aren't they worried about someone leaking information?" she asked.

Saul stuffed half the mandel bread into his mouth. "Everyone who works there had to get clearance," he said as he chewed. "So I guess they figure the information is safe, at least amongst the guys who work there." He reached for another cookie. "But I don't exactly agree with all the secretiveness."

"What do you mean?"

"We're doing important, ground-breaking research. Our findings should be made available to all our allies in the scientific community, not kept hidden away. It isn't right."

"You mean the Soviets."

"Well, of course. The ally that everyone treats like an unwanted stepchild."

"The Soviets have been unpredictable," Mari said. "They only begged to join the Allies when Germany turned on them."

"And can you blame them for being leery of us? The U.S. hasn't exactly been a fan of the communists, even when Papa was alive. Our government has always been terrified that the Reds are going to upset our nice cushy capitalistic society."

"So your point isn't about sharing scientific advances, but rather giving the communists a leg up."

"We're all on the same side now, Mari. If we work together instead of mistrusting each other, we're more likely to end the war sooner."

"Who have you been talking to?"

He broke a fresh slice of mandel bread in two and picked out a nut. "I just hate this damn war and the number of people who are dying. Anything we can do to accelerate its end is a good thing."

"I suppose I can agree with that."

He rolled the nut between his thumb and forefinger. "I saw one of your old friends, by the way."

"One of my friends? Who?"

"Flossie. She's staying in Albuquerque to be near her boyfriend Joey. You remember Joey? He was at the first Popular Front meeting I ever went to."

She remembered. The good-looking fellow Flossie had attached herself to. So he and Flossie were still together, though never married. She felt sad that she and her friend had lost touch all these years.

"Is Joey at Los Alamos with you?" she asked.

"No. He's taking the cure. TB."

Mari knew that people suffering from tuberculosis frequently went to sanitariums in New Mexico because the climate was supposedly good for them.

How selfless of Flossie to devote herself to him.

"Flossie had some people over for dinner a couple of weeks ago and invited her cousin Bertie. Bertie's at the installation with me, but he's only a machinist with intermediate clearance."

"I remember him, too," she said. Bertie had been another of Yitzy's friends, though she decided against bringing up Yitzy's name. Saul had been very angry when Yitzy left for California after their mother died. Never forgave Yitzy for not saying goodbye to him. "Bertie also went to City College," she said. "A heavyset fellow."

"You're being polite," Saul said. "More like a tub. Anyway, I had the weekend free so Bertie invited me to hitch a ride with him to see Flossie and Joey. We had a swell evening. It was like a home-coming. Even that fellow who was the speaker at the Popular Front meeting was there. Anton Dubrovski. Would you believe it, he remembered me."

Mari recalled the night at the meeting. How interested Dubrovski had been in Saul's accomplishments and background in physics and engineering. Had Dubrovski kept an eye on her brother all these years? Having a Party sympathizer of Saul's caliber on the inside of Los Alamos would have been very useful to the communists. Maybe this was why Saul was showing so much enthusiasm for sharing scientific secrets with the Soviets.

"I'm not surprised he remembered you," she said.

"I wasn't either," her brother said. "But I was surprised that he remembered you."

"Dubrovski remembered you?" a voice asked.

Not Saul's voice. Saul was dead. It took Mariasha a moment to clear her head and return to the present.

"You told me Dubrovski had been watching you at the Popular Front meeting years ago," her grandson said.

"That's right." There was a dull ache in her shoulder. She massaged it.

"Why?" Julian asked.

She considered how best to answer this. "I was very attractive as a young woman. I didn't recognize it at the time. I always thought of myself as too skinny and plain, but when I look at photos or remember back, I can understand why men often stared at me."

"So what happened between Saul and Dubrovski?" Julian asked. "Saul was obviously sympathetic to the communist cause. Did Dubrovski recruit him to be a spy?"

Julian was pressing her for the truth, but she could never reveal everything to him. "Dubrovski tried to recruit him," she said finally.

"And?"

"Saul told me about Dubrovski's proposition. Part of him wanted to do it, but Saul also understood the risk he'd be taking. I told him idealism was overrated. He needed to consider the evil forces he was up against. I didn't trust the Soviets."

Her grandson had leaned forward waiting for an answer to his question. "So did he?" Julian asked again. "Did Saul spy for the communists?"

Mariasha moistened her lips with her tongue and forced the words out. "No. He did not."

CHAPTER 30

Arnie Weissman's theories spun through Annette's head as she stepped out of his apartment building into the frosty, late-afternoon air. A government conspiracy? Bill had also suggested as much, but that would be almost impossible for her to prove. The best way to publicly vindicate her grandfather was to identify the true spy. But how could she find the traitor who had evaded identification for over sixty years? Most everyone associated with the trial was dead. And Mariasha Lowe, who may or may not have been close enough to the family to know the truth, was no longer an option.

The smell of roasted chestnuts drifted toward her from a stand at the entrance to Central Park and a couple of joggers ran past into the park.

Bill might be able to help. She pulled out her cell phone.

"Well if it isn't Annie-get-your-gun," he said, sounding unusually exuberant. "I haven't heard from you since Sunday night. How's the romance with the grandson coming along?"

"It isn't."

"Gee, that's too bad."

"Do you have time to get together for a little bit?"

"I'm picking Billy up at six and bringing him back here for a special dinner. Come on by if you don't mind watching me cook."

She told him that was fine, and then took the uptown train to his apartment near Columbia University.

Since his separation from his wife six months before, Bill had been renting a studio on the sixth floor of an old building near Riverside Park. It had an elevator, but Annette couldn't remember a time when there wasn't an 'Out-of-Order' sign covering the control panel. She huffed up the stairs and found the door to Bill's apartment slightly ajar. Bill had a bad habit of leaving his door unlocked. She knocked and walked in. "I'm here."

The large room smelled like fresh baked bread, apples and cinnamon.

She hung up her ski jacket by the door and bent down to stroke Woodward, Bill's gray tabby named for the Watergate investigative journalist. Then, the cat slinked off to its bed on the windowsill, near the ancient radiator.

The apartment faced Riverside Park and the Hudson River, but a rusty fire escape and soot on the windows obscured most of the view. Inside, Bill kept everything clean and orderly, despite multiple coats of peeling paint on the walls and over-shellacked wood floors. A beige futon sat on a shaggy area rug in the center of the room, and a double bed with a black iron headboard and a small Parson's desk were pushed against the far wall. The low room divider was filled with books, and several stacks of books cluttered the coffee table and desk.

Bill was in the kitchen alcove wearing a red and white striped apron, a huge bandage on his right pinkie.

"What happened to you?" she asked.

"Clumsy," he said. "I got carried away peeling apples and sliced off a piece of my finger."

"*Quelle horreur*!"

"It's fine," he said. "I ran over to the ER and they stitched me up. Gave me oxycodone if the pain gets too bad, but so far Tylenol is keeping the edge off."

"You're awfully cheerful under the circumstances."

"It feels great to cook for a change. I'm making Billy's favorites. My famous meatloaf and gravy with garlic mashed potatoes. And I'm baking an artisan boule and Dutch apple pie."

"Lucky boy."

"No. Happy daddy. I'm really excited. Kylie's letting him spend the night."

"I wish you wouldn't act like she's doing you a favor. He's your son, too."

"I hear ya, but now's not a good time to make waves. I'm sure Kylie will come around if I cooperate with her."

"I hope so." She sat down at the small oak breakfast table next to the fireplace that probably hadn't worked in fifty years. Above the fireplace was the framed Pulitzer certificate Bill had been awarded when he was a young reporter with the *Washington Post*. William Turner, it said. He had been runner-up in the 'feature writing' category, a tremendous accomplishment. Had that bothered him, never again achieving such heights in his career?

Bill was shaping the meatloaf in a casserole dish, holding his bandaged finger up and away from the chopped meat.

"Do you want help with that?"

"I'm good. Thanks." He ripped off a piece of aluminum foil, covered the dish and put it in the oven. "So what's going on with the grandson?" he asked, his back toward her.

A bottle of Tylenol was beside a sealed bag from the pharmacy on the breakfast table. "Nothing," she said.

Bill turned to her, his brow furrowed. There was a light dusting of flour on his tortoise-framed glasses. "And his grandmother? Did you at least have a successful meeting with her last Sunday?"

"She's a lovely woman, but I think there are better ways for me to get at the truth about Isaac Goldstein. That's why I wanted to talk to you."

“Whatever I can do to help.” He put a bowl full of cooked potatoes on the counter and began to mash them with determination.

“This afternoon I went to talk to the son of the attorney who defended my grandfather.”

He stopped and held the potato masher up out of the bowl. “That’s an interesting development.”

“It is. His name’s Arnie Weissman.” She ran her fingernail against a crack in the wood. “He gave me a little more insight into the type of person my grandfather was. Charming. Charismatic.”

“I hear a ‘but.’”

“I’ve been so focused on proving his innocence that I hadn’t accepted that even if he hadn’t passed atomic-bomb secrets to the Russians, he was still a communist and possibly a spy.

Bill went back to mashing the potatoes. “You know better than to think of people in terms of black and white.”

“I just need to adjust my expectations,” she said. “But something bothers me. The government was convinced Isaac knew the identity of the true spy. They believed by threatening him with execution, they could get him to reveal that person.”

“But he didn’t,” Bill said. “Do you think it’s because he was the traitor?”

“No. I’m sure he wasn’t, especially after talking to Weissman. But how can I figure out who the true traitor was?”

“Do you believe your grandfather knew?”

“And give up his life to protect this person?” She shook her head. “I just can’t imagine him doing that, knowing how his execution would destroy his family.”

“Maybe he wanted to die.”

She looked over at Bill. His head was bent over the mixing bowl so she couldn’t read his face. “That’s an odd thing to say.”

He kept mashing.

"If he wanted to die, that would suggest he was guilt-ridden," she said.

"Maybe he was. But guilty about what?"

Woodward hopped down from the windowsill and came over to watch Bill mash the potatoes.

"I'm just saying as a journalist you should look at this from every angle." Bill came around the counter with a spoonful of potatoes. "Have a taste."

She licked the spoon. "Good."

The cat jumped up on the counter, sniffed the empty spoon, then slinked over to the bowl.

"There now," Bill said. "Woodward still has his investigative instincts."

"Right." She laughed. "I guess I'll just have to keep sniffing around some more."

CHAPTER 31

It was in a part of Queens that Julian had never been to before. The streetlights came on as he hurried past a check-cashing store, a grocery, beauty shop, Chinese restaurant, and the shell of a graffitied building, whose interior was littered with loose bricks, weeds, and garbage partially covered by dirty snow. He checked the address she'd given him over the phone, then looked across the street and saw a block-letter sign above a brightly painted storefront, 'Sandman Pediatric Care Center.'

What the heck? His mother operated a free clinic? Julian knew nothing about this.

He crossed to the clinic, taken aback by the beauty of the windows, covered with paintings of families and children in a primitive, urban-art style. Probably done by some local artist. Julian followed the colors inside, where the walls continued the family motif, and the room was filled with a dozen or so adults and children sitting on red, yellow and green plastic chairs. At first glance, it seemed like an experimental primary school, but quickly Julian heard the sounds of suffering beneath the smooth beat of Beyoncé. Children crying, soft moans, gentle hushing.

He went to the check-in window. To his surprise, there was a framed photo of his father on the wall. His father was laughing, looking much like Julian liked to remember him. Beneath the picture was a plaque. *In Memory of Tom Sandman.*

So the clinic was named for his dad, not his mother. How come she'd never told Julian about any of this?

"Can I help you?"

He turned to the slim black woman behind the window. She had a full head of beaded braids. "I'm here to see Dr. Sandman," he said. "She's expecting me."

She looked confused for a moment. "Oh. Doctor Essie. You must be her son." She smiled. "Come on back."

He went through the door, noticing a long hallway with several closed doors, each with a colorful number.

"She's in Room Three," the woman said. "We're happy for the help."

I'm not here to help, he was about to say, but she'd turned away to speak to a new patient.

He knocked first, then opened the door to an oversized examination room. A toddler sat on the exam table, held by her mother, as Essie stitched the child's brow. Sitting on the floor were two other young children, crying softly. Then Julian noticed the blood-soaked bandages.

"What happened?" he asked.

"Car accident." His mother wore a pink lab coat that said 'Dr. Essie' on the pocket. "LaTanya and Tanice need stitches. I'm handling Ajay and Mom."

"I'm on it," Julian said, washing and disinfecting his hands in the sink.

"Doctor Bruce called in sick. A bad time for him to get the flu. I only have one other doctor working tonight."

"Shouldn't they have gone to the ER?" he asked.

The children's mother widened her eyes and shook her head in a near panic.

Essie gave Julian a quick, stern look. "These are my patients, practically family," she said, patting the mother's arm. "They know I'll never turn them away."

Practically family. He felt a twinge of envy. Her patients were more her family than he'd ever been.

"I understand," he said, crouching down to examine LaTanya and Tanice. He hadn't practiced medicine in several years, but his ER training came back to him quickly. LaTanya's cuts were more serious and he carefully lifted her up to the examining table.

Out of the corner of his eye, he watched his mother. He'd known she was a dedicated physician, but he had only been aware of her pediatric-oncology practice, not this free-clinic project. Her manner was gentle and reassuring.

As he cleaned LaTanya's wounds and told her to be brave, he remembered his own pain as a child.

A few days before Julian turned five, his father had taken him and Rhonda to see the July Fourth fireworks. Julian couldn't recall his mother being there. She'd probably been working at the hospital that day. The black evening had started out frightening. Loud sudden blasts, terrifying whistling sounds. But quickly, Julian became transfixed by the light show in the sky, thinking that God was making the startling colors and lights. He wandered a short distance away, where a group of older boys were swinging sparkling sticks back and forth like wands, making their own magic. One of them threw a firecracker into the air. It exploded with an eruption of bright light and the boys laughed. Julian smiled and stepped closer. He watched the boy throw a second firecracker. Julian froze. It was coming at him. The firecracker exploded, hitting Julian in the chest with an excruciating burst of pain.

He didn't remember going to the hospital to be treated for second-degree burns on his arms. And until just now, he hadn't remembered his father washing him in the shower to remove the dead skin. The agony as his father ran lukewarm water over his arms and cleaned the burned area. His own screams echoed in his head. Tears ran down his father's cheeks. *I'm so sorry. I'm so sorry I wasn't there to protect you.*

But where had his mother been when Julian wanted her to protect and comfort him?

He finished stitching up LaTanya and lowered her to the floor. "You're very brave," he said. "Now how about you, Tanice? Are you as brave as your sister?"

He carefully picked up the little girl, who was as light as a goose, even though she was probably three or four years old.

This wasn't what he'd planned to be doing when he had left his grandmother's apartment earlier. Nana's revelations about Saul had raised fresh questions, which he believed only his mother could answer. But with a waiting room full of people who needed immediate care, his own priorities had changed. These people needed attention. Saul would have to wait.

After a couple of hours of treating young patients with high fever, diarrhea, and ear infections, the waiting room was finally clear. His mother invited him back to her small office—more of a large closet with a metal desk and a guest chair squished in. Essie took a couple of containers of orange juice from a small refrigerator, handed one to Julian and stuck a straw in the other. "Do you want to eat?" she asked. "I can have Chloe order you something."

"I'm good, thanks." He drank down the juice, surprised by how good it tasted. In fact, the satisfaction he felt was something he hadn't experienced in a very long time.

Essie handed him another container. "Thanks for helping out. It isn't usually so hectic."

"I didn't realize you ran a clinic, too."

She shrugged. "I started it a few years ago. It's staffed by volunteer physicians and physician assistants during the week and I generally just work on weekends." The straw made a sucking sound as she finished her juice. "Anyway, you didn't come out here to practice medicine. What's up?"

He leaned against the hard chair. "Nana's been filling me in on Saul. I had no idea he'd been involved with the Manhattan Project."

Essie pushed a strand of hair out of her eye and behind her ear, but continued looking down at her desk blotter. It was covered with scribbled words and numbers.

"She told me the communists tried to recruit him," Julian said, "but he refused to help them."

She met his eye. "Is that what she told you?"

"Yes. Do you know something different?"

"If that's what my mother told you, it must be true," she said. "So what do you want from me?"

"The painting he made in our living room. It depicts his guilt over helping to create the atomic bomb, doesn't it?"

"That's as good an explanation as any."

"But it wasn't like Saul had a choice. He was recruited to work on the bomb. He did what he was told. Why would Nana hide the picture? It's as though she was ashamed of him, and yet she speaks of him with great love."

"Why are you asking me? She's the one who has the answers."

"I can tell she's holding back. That she doesn't want to tell me what really happened."

"Then why do you assume I know anything?"

"Because you and she have been at odds about something my entire life. I think it has something to do with Saul. But whatever it is has affected how you raised me."

She glanced at the scribbles on the blotter. Behind her, shelves were neatly stacked with medical supplies. "You're letting your imagination get away from you, Julian. You have a tendency to do that."

"This isn't about me."

"Really? You just said it was."

"Why do you hate her, Essie?"

His mother rubbed her temples. "Why does she hate me?" she said in a small voice.

The phone buzzed. Essie answered it. "Thanks, Chloe. I'll be right there." She stood up. "More patients, but one of my physician assistant volunteers just arrived, so I won't need you." She slipped past him and opened the door. "Thanks again for your help."

"She's ninety-five," he said. "She won't be around forever."

He heard her footsteps down the hallway, then a door closed.

Damn it. What the hell would it take to get his grandmother and mother to finally tell him the truth?

CHAPTER 32

Annette left Bill's apartment and headed over to Columbia's Butler Library, where she still had stack privileges.

First, she went through the catalog to see if any source documents relating to Isaac Goldstein were housed here. She found all of the books she'd already identified, but in addition, she discovered that a trial attorney named Louis Spiezer, who had written a famous analysis of the Goldstein trial called *Implosion*, had left seventeen boxes of documents to the library. The ones relating to Goldstein were in Box 20, shelved in the Rare Books collection, but required two days' advance notice to retrieve the box.

She went up to Rare Books and Manuscripts on the 6th Floor and was delighted to find that the librarian on duty was a friend of hers. She and Lopez had been in one of Bill's journalism classes together and Annette had given him her notes a few times, so he owed her. Lopez told her he'd get the box while she waited. An hour later, Annette was seated at a table with a carton filled with Spiezer's yellowed notes, newspaper clippings and correspondence. She had read snippets of Spiezer's *Implosion* and found it slanted in favor of the prosecution. Still, she was hoping there might be letters or memos suggesting the identity of the real spy in Spiezer's research. It was not uncommon for researchers to ignore or honestly overlook hints that didn't support their theses.

After hours of poring over papers, she found no fresh insights. At around ten thirty, Lopez came to tell her he needed to close up for the night. She thanked him and left, tired and discouraged.

She wasn't ready to go home. It would be too quiet and that would give her time to think about Julian. Instead, she headed toward the Black Sheep. It felt like the temperature had dropped to below zero. She walked carefully, avoiding patches of ice, the frozen air stabbing her lungs with every breath.

She pushed open the door to the Black Sheep. Only a handful of people were at the bar and most of the booths were empty. She sat down on a barstool. The manager, a middle-aged guy named Doug with a shaved head and a body fine-tuned by Crossfit workouts, was working the front alone. "Everyone call in sick tonight?" she asked.

Doug laughed. "Yeah. My two bartenders claim to have the flu, but I think they just didn't feel like going out in this cold. What can I get you?"

"A glass of cabernet and a vegan burger."

"Want any tofu or bean sprouts on it?"

"Nope. I'll take it straight."

He put the order in with the kitchen and poured her wine. "You look a little strung out tonight."

"Just tired."

"I thought maybe you've been with Bill."

She took a sip of wine. "Bill? Why do you say that?"

Doug wiped up the counter with a white cloth. "Well, he was pretty messed up himself when he came by earlier."

"Tonight?"

"Yeah. He came in around seven looking like he was going to mow down the place."

She sat up straighter. "Are you sure? Bill was making dinner for his son. Billy was spending the night."

"Maybe that's what was supposed to happen, but he told me when he went to pick up his kid, his ex-wife's apartment had been completely cleared out. No furniture. No clothes. No kid."

"But she can't do that. That's kidnapping."

"Whatever," Doug said. "Bill sure gave me an earful about it. He said she left a note. Called him a terrible influence and said she would make sure he'd never see his son again."

"Oh no. He didn't have a drink, did he?"

"Seriously? This is a bar."

"But Bill has a problem."

"I told him to go easy, but sometimes people just need to let loose."

"He's an alcoholic. He can't handle it."

Doug held up his hands. "Hey, I'm sorry, but it's not my job to babysit everyone who comes in here wanting a drink."

"When did he leave?"

"A little before you came in."

"Was he going home? Did he say anything when he left?"

"He wasn't making a lot of sense," Doug said. "It sounded like 'guilt' and 'absolution.' And then he said, 'Maybe the poor bastard just wanted to die.'"

The breath snagged in her chest. *Oh god, Bill. Please don't do anything stupid.*

She slid off the barstool and ran out of the Black Sheep.

Ran down the frozen streets, slipping and scraping her hands on the rough sidewalk.

She picked herself up and ran.

Ran so fast she could barely fill her lungs with the frozen air.

Ran into Bill's apartment building and up the five flights of stairs.

Gasping when she reached the top, she heard a loud meow. Woodward outside the apartment.

Please be all right, Bill.

The door was unlocked. She pushed it open and was hit by the smell of burnt meat.

For an instant, she was disoriented by the ransacked apartment. Chairs, tables, and the room divider thrown over. Books everywhere. Broken dishes. The walls splattered with potatoes and apples. A torn striped apron. Bill's tortoise-framed glasses on the floor.

"Bill," she shouted, stepping over the cracked framed Pulitzer certificate.

Then she saw him lying on the other side of the futon, mouth open, eyes glazed. An empty prescription bottle was on the shag rug.

"Oh, Bill. What have you done?"

She punched 911 on her phone and touched his neck. There was the lightest pulse. He was breathing.

"Please state your emergency," said the voice on the phone.

"Drug overdose. He's still alive. Just barely." Annette gave the address. "Sixth floor. The elevator's broken. Hurry. Please hurry."

"Keep him on his side with his legs bent at right angles. If he stops breathing, administer CPR. Do you know how to do that?"

"Yes."

"Good. Keep him warm and make sure he keeps breathing."

"Keep breathing," Annette repeated.

She rolled him on his side and covered him with a blanket. Then she sat down with his head in her lap and watched him breathe. So slowly. So shallow, like he wanted to give up.

"Keep breathing, Bill. Keep breathing."

Tears rolled down her cheeks, splattering as they hit his short, graying afro.

She stroked his cheek. "Don't die. Please don't die."

The tears came faster, the pressure inside her unbearable. She cried, harder than she'd ever cried in her life. Cried for her dear friend. Cried for her mother. Her grandmother. For Isaac Goldstein. She cried for herself. For loneliness and sadness and guilt.

She sat on the floor, surrounded by chaos and the smell of burnt meat, her dear friend's head on her lap, and sobbed her heart out.

Because the world made no sense.

And she didn't know what else to do.

CHAPTER 33

Annette sat in the ER waiting area, while somewhere deep in the bowels of the hospital doctors pumped Bill's stomach and tried to save his life.

Maybe he wanted to die, Bill had said earlier tonight. She'd thought he was talking about Isaac Goldstein. She hadn't considered Bill might have been thinking of himself. And she should have, but she'd been too preoccupied with her own problems to pay attention. Now, because of her, her dear friend might die.

The waiting area resembled a refugee camp with all the people stretched out on chairs or on the floor. Students from Columbia. Men, women, children from the surrounding neighborhoods—Morningside Park, Harlem. The huddled masses. A TV suspended from the ceiling showed the news, the sound barely audible over the coughing, crying, and moaning.

Annette had never felt more alone in her life.

Across from her, a pale woman clung to her sick child. Annette stared at her cell phone and thought about calling her mother. But that would only leave Mama worried and agitated.

Her finger hovered over Julian's name, even though she willed it not to. He had called her a liar. He had lied to her. He had a girlfriend. It was a mistake to call him.

Her finger didn't listen. It touched his name.

She almost hit 'end' when a sleepy voice said, "Annette?"

"I'm sorry. I shouldn't have called."

"What's wrong?" His voice became alert. "Are you all right?"

"My friend. He tried to kill himself."

"Is he going to be okay?"

"I don't know."

"Where are you? Is anyone with you?"

"I'm alone. At St. Luke's by Columbia. He took pills and he'd been drinking. I don't know if I got to him in time."

"Stay there," Julian said. "I'll grab a cab. There won't be much traffic."

"I shouldn't have called."

"I'm glad you did. Just hold on. I'll be there soon."

She ended the call. A feeling of tentative calm spread over her and she clung to it like a life raft. Julian was coming. She wasn't alone.

He came through the ER doors less than thirty minutes later, a wool hat pulled low over his ears, and searched the crowd until he spotted her.

"Hey," he said, slouching down in front of her since there was nowhere to sit. "Any word?"

She shook her head.

"I'll check. What's his name?"

"Bill. Wait, no. He's registered as William Turner."

Julian went up to the admitting desk. She watched as he talked to a woman standing behind the check-in person.

Julian's cheeks were shadowed. He probably hadn't shaved since she'd seen him yesterday afternoon. With his pale skin and bloodshot eyes, he looked a lot like the first time she'd met him. When was that? Saturday? Only three days ago? It felt like she'd known him forever.

She wondered what he'd said to the redhead when he rushed out of his apartment to be here.

She shouldn't have called him. She had no business interfering with his relationship with that girl, whatever it was.

He was coming toward her, his face in a grimace.

Oh god. Bill's dead.

Julian must have read the expression on her face. "He's alive," he said quickly. "They pumped his stomach, but he may be unconscious for a day or two. Hard to say at this stage whether there will be any long-term effects. The nurse said to go home. There's nothing to do for now. They won't let you in to see him. Family only. Does he have any?"

"Just his almost ex-wife who disappeared with their son."

"Is that what set him off?"

She nodded. "I should have seen it coming. He was too happy. I should have known he'd crash."

"We can't predict what other people will do. We're not that wise."

"I suppose." She took in a deep breath. "But I'm glad you're here. I didn't know who else to call."

"You live nearby?"

"A few blocks."

"I'll walk you home."

She knew she should tell him 'no' and that she was fine. He had a girlfriend. He had lied to her. They had lied to each other.

"Thank you," she said. "I'd like that."

It was incredibly cold outside. She pulled up her hood and shoved her hands into her pockets, but it hardly helped. The icy air numbed her face, and the aestheticized sensation seemed to spread through her veins. And then, she felt his arm around her, his body sheltering her from the wind, and she could feel her nerve endings thaw.

She told him about Bill as they walked huddled together. How fragile he was, and his guilt about being gay. Bill would have seen Kylie's actions as having been his fault.

"He probably believed he deserves to lose Billy," she said.

"But he's done nothing wrong."

"In his mind, he has."

She led Julian up the stoop to her brownstone, then into her apartment.

He crisscrossed his arms and thumped his chest and shoulders. "Damn, it's cold."

"I can make *chocolat chaud*," she said.

"Hot chocolate. That sounds good in any language." He kept his hat and jacket on and sat on a kitchen stool while she heated milk in a saucepan.

She'd give him a cup of cocoa, thank him for coming, and then say goodbye. It was clear that was what he had planned, as well.

"I want to explain," he said. "About Sephora."

She added the bittersweet chocolate she'd bought the last time she was in Paris, and stirred, watching the melting dark brown swirl through the hot milk. Just like when Grandma Betty used to make it for her.

"She isn't my girlfriend," he said. "I'd already broken up with her."

Annette poured a little brown sugar into the boiling mixture.

"I didn't lie to you about that."

She bit her lip. "But I lied to you."

"Not exactly." He took off his wool hat and turned it around in his hands. "I thought about what you said. You had a legitimate reason for using a cover story. You didn't know anything would develop between us."

She glanced over at him. So something had developed between them? It wasn't all in her head?

"I probably would have done the same thing in your situation," he said. "The problem is, once you start lying, it's pretty tough to go back and undo things."

She poured the cocoa into two mugs and put them on the counter. Was he saying it was too late for them?

"Thank you." He unzipped his jacket, then held the mug with both hands. He looked like he was debating with himself.

"What is it?" she asked.

"I like you." He put his hand over hers. It was warm from the mug. "A lot."

She wanted to tell him that she liked him, too, but the words got stuck. She shouldn't be thinking about such things while her friend lay close to death in the hospital.

He took his hand off hers and tapped his fingertips against the countertop. "I think we need to finish that conversation we started."

"Conversation?" She was confused.

"About your grandfather."

"Are you sure?"

"I think it's what you want to talk about," he said. "Or at least what you need to talk about."

She sipped the cocoa. It went down warm and sweet. She would have to trust Julian or there could never be a future for them.

"Why do you believe he knew my grandmother?" he asked.

"They were together in old photos."

"Seriously?"

"I'll show you." She went and got the album from the trunk, put it on the counter, and sat down on the stool next to his.

He turned the pages slowly. "Good-looking guy. He looks nothing like the Isaac Goldstein I learned about in school."

"I know," she said.

He paused at the photo of the Lowes and Goldsteins at the Laurels Hotel in December 1943. "My god. These are my grandparents. Nana has a honeymoon photo that was taken around the same time." He turned to the next page and studied the photo of the two couples in dress clothes at the Starlight Roof restaurant. "They look like good friends."

"It seemed that way to me. That's why I wanted to talk to your grandmother."

He continued going through the photo album, stopping at the last page. The two little blonde girls holding hands in front of a brick apartment building.

"That's my mother." His voice was filled with amazement. "Essie Lowe." He scowled. "Is Sally your mother?"

"Yes."

He rubbed his head. "So your mother and my mother were friends as children."

"That's right," she said. Now what? Would he understand why she had to speak to his grandmother?

He turned back to the photo of his grandparents and hers at the restaurant and studied it. "What are you hoping to find out about your grandfather from Nana?"

"I think Isaac Goldstein was a scapegoat," she said. "Maybe he was a communist or even some kind of low-level spy, but I don't believe he gave significant atomic-bomb secrets to the Russians."

"Is that what the spy book you had with you the other day said?"

"Yes. And my research supports that theory."

"But it's still a theory. No proof."

"That's right." She took another sip of cocoa. "I was hoping your grandmother could tell me something. Maybe she knew one of the others in the spy ring and why they testified against my grandfather. Florence Heller or Albert Shevsky or Joseph Bartow. Remember, she told us how she went to an anti-war rally at City College. Shevsky and Bartow went to school there."

"You're ignoring the elephant in the room," he said.

She felt herself flush. There were several elephants she was ignoring, and the biggest one was sitting so close to her that their elbows were touching. "What do you mean?"

"Nana's practically come out and admitted she was a communist. Do you think she was involved in the spy ring?"

"I don't think so," she said. "Many people were communist-leaning at that time. That didn't make them spies. And her name hasn't come up in anything I read." She hesitated.

"What?" he asked.

"Please don't be angry, but I did wonder about your grandfather."

"You think he may have been a spy?"

"As an economics professor at NYU, Aaron Lowe was very much in the heart of things. And he published a few articles on how central planning would work in the United States."

"How do you know that?"

"I *am* a journalist. I didn't lie about that."

He gestured for her to continue.

"And when I think about your grandparents and mine in those photos, isn't the likely explanation that Aaron and Isaac were the friends?"

"Communists and friends. I guess that nails it then. They must have been in the same spy ring."

"Please, Julian, don't get upset. That's not what I'm saying. I don't know anyone's true connection. All I know is that these four people had been friends. At least three of them had communist leanings. Your grandmother is the only one alive for me to talk to. I just want to find out the whole story."

He gripped the mug of cocoa.

"Someone was passing atomic-bomb secrets to the Russians and I don't believe it was my grandfather," she said.

"And you think my Nana knows?"

"*Je ne sais pas*, Julian." She got up from the stool and went to sit on the sofa. Her back hurt. Her head hurt. Her heart hurt.

Julian followed her and sat down near her, not quite touching.

"Here's the thing," she said. "I'm pretty sure my grandfather's innocent, but unless I can prove someone else was the traitor, I won't be able to clear his name. And I need to do this for my mother and for my grandmother's memory."

"And for you."

"Yes." She leaned back against the cushion and closed her eyes. "And for me."

She felt a warm breath near her face, then the press of soft lips against hers. She kissed back, melting like chocolate in simmering milk.

His arms tightened around her, holding her so tight that she could feel the tension and fear of the last few hours dissolve. She dug her hands under his jacket, touching his hard muscles, feeling the heat come off him in waves.

Abruptly, he pulled away.

She opened her eyes.

He was breathing hard, a sheen on his face. "I'd better go."

No, her mind shouted. *Ne vont pas*.

"This isn't the right time," he said. "We're both overtired. You're worried about your friend. There are things we need to work out first. Let's not complicate the situation."

He snapped up his jacket and pulled on his hat. "I'll call you later, okay?"

So close to safety, and suddenly it had been jerked away. But he was probably right. Now wasn't the right time.

He placed his hand against her heart, pressing so tightly she could feel his pulse pounding along with hers. Then he kissed her gently and left the apartment.

She couldn't believe she'd let him go.

CHAPTER 34

Annette had slept poorly, checking her text messages throughout the early morning. The last one pinged at a little after five. *Got home ok. Let me know about Bill.* Then a minute later. *Miss you already*. Nothing after, but Julian was very likely still asleep.

She finished her second cup of coffee and rinsed out the cup, putting it in the dish drainer beside the mug Julian had used for hot chocolate. She ran her finger over the rim where his mouth had been. Perhaps their closeness a few hours before had been an illusion and what she'd taken for attraction was just his way of comforting her.

But enough jumping to conclusions. She wasn't thinking clearly, with images of Bill's unconscious body mingling with the memory of Julian's soft lips pressed against hers. The awful and the sweet. She hoped that wasn't a foreshadowing of her future with Julian, but right now, she had other things to deal with.

She phoned the hospital to see if there was a change in Bill's condition. There wasn't. Then, she headed over to Bill's apartment to straighten up. One of Bill's neighbors had taken Woodward in and promised to keep the cat until Bill returned.

Annette righted the furniture, cleaned off the splattered potatoes and apples from the walls, picked up broken dishes, and arranged his books on the bookshelves, telling herself that Bill would be home soon. It took her a couple of hours to get things almost back to normal. She left his apartment with his eyeglasses in her satchel, and carrying his broken framed Pulitzer certificate, which she planned to have reframed.

Once back in her own apartment, she called the hospital. A familiar voice answered and Annette said, "I'm calling for an update on William Turner."

"No change from the last time we spoke." Then a sigh into the phone. "Look, I understand you're concerned. Why don't you leave me your name and number? I promise I'll call you if there's any change in Mr. Turner's condition."

Annette left her information, frustrated. *Mr. Turner's condition.* Anger began boiling up inside her. How could Bill have taken such a drastic step? Couldn't he have at least called her to talk it through? If she hadn't gone to the Black Sheep last night, she wouldn't have learned about Bill's meltdown and he very likely would be dead.

"*Stupide,*" she muttered under her breath. A stupid, unnecessary tragedy. All because Bill's wife was a cruel, heartless woman.

Cruel, heartless.

Cousin Linda had used those words the other day. Even your grandmother finally admitted that he was a cruel, heartless man.

When would Grandma Betty have said that? The two sisters had communicated mostly by mail, but Betty hadn't written anything about Isaac being cruel or heartless in any of the letters Annette had seen. So why would Linda have said that Betty had made such a comment? Unless Linda had read it in a letter she hadn't given Annette.

She thought back to walking past her great-aunt Irene's room the day Jen had dropped the bomb about Isaac Goldstein. Irene had been sitting on her bed, surrounded by a pile of letters, Prettybird on a perch behind her.

She tried to picture the details in her mind's eye. Irene in a pink quilted robe, a piece of white paper in her trembling hands. White envelopes strewn over the green floral bedspread. Squat ones with hand-written addresses, that had made Annette conclude, even at that moment, that the letters had been personal.

Prettybird squawking, 'Mail's here. Mail's here,' in Irene's voice.

Had Irene been eagerly waiting for her sister's letters all those years before?

Annette sat up straight. White letters in white envelopes. Not blue like the airmailed letters from France that Linda had given her. The letters Grandma Betty would have sent her sister before Isaac Goldstein was executed.

So where were those letters now and, if Linda knew, why had she kept them from her?

Annette arrived at the Dobbs Ferry train station at 11:02. She hurried off the platform with the handful of other passengers, relieved to see a taxi waiting. She gave the driver Linda's address, sat back in the seat and played with a tear in the upholstery. She hadn't called ahead, not wanting to give Linda an opportunity to come up with more excuses or worse, hide the letters.

She had the driver let her out a few houses down from Linda's, then briskly walked up the winding street. The snow had been shoveled on either side of the path that led to their brick house, and a layer of ice had formed over it. Kenny's old red Corvair was parked in the driveway. No sign of Linda's yellow Volkswagen.

Was Linda not home? Annette quickly changed her strategy as she rang the doorbell. She could hear Prettybird calling, "Mail's here."

Kenny opened the door, a screwdriver in his hand. Linda's husband was a tall, lanky man with flyaway gray hair, thick glasses, and stains on his orange T-shirt and blue jeans.

"Annette. Come on in. Linda's not back from grocery shopping yet. " He looked beyond her, into the street. "How'd you get here?"

"A friend dropped me off," she lied. She was getting pretty good at lying. "I figured I'd stop in and say hi."

"Great. Well, Linda should be back soon." He rubbed his face, transferring grease from his fingers to his cheek. "I'm just fixing a leak under the sink, if you want to watch."

"Actually," she said. "Linda found a few letters for me. I think they're in Irene's old room."

"Oh good." He seemed relieved that he didn't have to entertain her.

"How's the Corvair running?"

He gave her a big smile. "Great. You'd never know she's almost fifty years old. Want to take her for a spin?"

"Thanks. Maybe next time. I'd better go get those letters." She headed up the stairs, before Kenny reconsidered letting her loose in the house.

Her heart pounded as she stepped into the room Irene had lived in when she could no longer stay by herself in her big house in Boston. The room looked smaller than Annette remembered it and smelled stale, but the same floral bedspread covered the bed. The bureau, dresser and nightstands were a dark, dull wood and looked very old, as though they may have been Irene's original bedroom set.

On top of the bureau were several black-and-white photos in antique frames. A wedding picture of Irene and her husband, Irene holding a tiny baby in a blanket—probably Linda—and a photo of a young woman and a teenage girl standing behind an old woman who was seated at a table. Betty and Irene and their mother. The two sisters, in flapper dresses and headbands, had their arms around each other's shoulders. On the table were three sets of brass candleholders, all identical, just like the ones Annette had taken from Grandma Betty's apartment. And the embroidered tablecloth looked like the one Betty had stowed away.

The apparent closeness of the two sisters in the photo made her even more certain that Irene had been Betty's confidante. But where would Betty's letters be?

She opened the sliding closet door. Irene's pink quilted robe was hanging with blouses and dresses. Several pairs of flats and sneakers filled a shoe rack. Irene had been dead for two years, but it didn't look like Linda had changed a thing. The letters were very likely still in this room.

She looked up at the top shelf of the closet. Too high for an old woman. Irene would have kept the letters where she could get to them easily.

A clanking noise from below startled her. Kenny working on the kitchen sink. How much time did she have before Linda returned?

She went to the bureau and opened each drawer. A sweet-sour smell drifted toward her as she rooted beneath underwear, scarves, folded blouses and sweaters, looking for a stash of envelopes. Nothing. She started on the drawers of the mirrored dresser. The top drawer was filled with costume jewelry, old watches, hairpins, combs. The next drawer was harder to open. She gave it a tug. Envelopes! Stacks of them. Bank statements. Insurance letters. Long, commercial envelopes. Nothing personal. She closed the drawer. Checked the next one, then the bottom drawer.

Something hard clattered downstairs. "Shit," Kenny cried out.

She went to the doorway and called down. "You okay?"

"Yeah, yeah." His voice was muffled. "Damn wrench slipped."

She returned to her search. Where do you keep the things that are most personal to you? Her eyes lighted on the bedside table. Of course.

She opened the nightstand drawer, and there they were—a stack of white envelopes and loose letters. Written in Grandma Betty's hand!

She felt a moment's elation, followed by fury. How dare Linda lie to her and claim she didn't have these? But she wasn't going to wait around and ask her. She shoved the letters into her satchel and ran down the stairs, eager to get out of the house before Linda returned and tried to intercept her.

As she got to the foyer, Prettybird called out, "Mail's here."

The door opened. Linda came in, pulling off her orange mittens. "Oh my goodness. Annette." She smiled, then frowned. "Had you told me you were coming? Was I supposed to meet you at the station?"

Annette shook her head. "It was a spur-of-the-moment visit."

"Oh good. Terrific," Linda said. "I'll make coffee." She hung up her coat in the closet, then started toward the kitchen.

"I came here to pick up my grandmother's letters."

Linda stopped and faced her. "I gave them to you the other day."

"Not those letters. The ones my grandmother wrote while my grandfather was in prison."

Linda tugged on a strand of long curly hair.

"I found them in your mother's nightstand."

The muscles in Linda's face tightened. "How dare you go through my mother's things?"

"How dare you lie to me?"

Linda sagged against the wall. She rubbed her cheek. "He was a terrible man. Why do you want to prove to the world that he was a hero?"

"Not a hero. Just not a monster."

"But he was a monster. How can you do this to your grandmother's memory? After all she went through, it's shameful for you to make it seem like he wasn't at fault. He was."

"It's my business, not yours. These were my grandparents. You had no right to keep these letters from me."

"Take them, then. Read them. Learn the truth about who your grandfather really was." Linda straightened up, then went to the front door and held it open. "I was only trying to protect you. I thought you and your mother and grandmother had already suffered enough."

Annette stepped outside. She turned to tell Linda that her mother couldn't stop suffering until Isaac's name was cleared, but Linda had already closed the door with a hard slam.

CHAPTER 35

The phone rang in the bedroom while Mariasha was in the kitchen putting peanut butter on slices of apple. Probably a telemarketer selling life insurance. No one else ever called. Except for Julian.

The phone rang again. She went as quickly as she could to answer it, cursing herself for not putting an extension phone in the kitchen like her grandson had suggested repeatedly. The shrill bringing sound was like an ambulance. “I’m coming,” she called. "I’m coming.”

She was breathing hard when she picked up the phone on the nightstand. “Hello?”

“It’s me,” said the soft voice Mariasha hadn’t heard in far too long.

She sat down on the bed, her insides contracting as though from a labor pain. “Hello, Essie.”

“I was just calling to see how you are.” The voice was shy, hesitant.

Mariasha wanted to jump through the phone and hold her daughter in her arms, but too much time had passed for displays of affection. Instead, she said, “I’m still alive.”

“Yes,” Essie said, after a moment. “I can see that.” Her voice had turned icy.

Mariasha looked at the pillows piled high on the bed. Remembered how Essie used to climb under the quilt between her and Aaron when she was a tyke. How sweet her cold little toes felt.

“Julian’s been to see me,” Essie said.

"He told me." *Tell her you love her*, a voice whispered in Mariasha's head. Aaron's voice. But the words were frozen inside her.

"Why do you hate me?" her daughter asked. "Would you please tell me that?"

I don't hate you. I love you.

"Julian asked me why I never try talking to you," Essie said. "Well, I tried."

She could hear the click as her daughter hung up the phone.

"I don't hate you, my darling girl," she said to the hard piece of plastic in her hand. "It's me I hate."

December 1944

If it hadn't been wartime, they probably would never have gotten a table at the Starlight Roof on a Saturday night. If it hadn't been their one-year anniversaries, they would never have splurged. And if Yitzy hadn't insisted they go and Aaron been such a good sport, they would more likely have dined at a coffee shop in Times Square.

But Aaron had warmed to the idea. "We only have our first anniversary once, darling," he'd said to Mari.

And so, here they were, in this elegant art deco room, seated some distance from the Big Band orchestra. But even hidden from the main crowd in a dim corner, Mari was uneasy in the blue silk dress and rhinestone earrings Aaron had bought her for the occasion. She was a Brooklyn girl who grew up in a tenement. She had no business acting hoity-toity at the Waldorf Astoria. But the others at the small table didn't seem to share her discomfort. Yitzy had ordered a bottle of champagne and the four of them, not accustomed to drinking, were growing more and more tipsy as the meal progressed through their Waldorf salads and beef Wellington. The waiter set the apple strudel that Yitzy had ordered on the table, but Mari didn't think she could eat another bite.

Betty gazed longingly at the couples swirling across the dance floor. She looked pretty tonight, her hair in an upsweep, a velvet choker with a white orchid around her neck.

"My dear wife wants to dance," Yitzy said, "and I'm of absolutely no use." He patted his bad leg.

"Oh, I'm perfectly happy watching," Betty said.

"No you aren't. Sometimes I catch you dancing around the apartment with a broomstick."

Betty giggled. "He's making that up."

"Aaron," Yitzy said. "Would you do me the very great honor of escorting my wife around the dance floor?"

Aaron's eyes met Mari's and they exchanged a split-second non-verbal message that a year of knowing each other's moods and minds had perfected.

Aaron stood and held out his hand for Betty. "The honor would be mine."

Betty glanced at Mari. "You don't mind?"

"Not at all. Enjoy yourselves."

Mari watched her husband lead Yitzy's wife to the dance floor. Most of the men were in their dress military uniforms or tuxedoes, but Aaron looked just as handsome in his dark suit. Throughout the night, Mari had noticed how even the waiters seemed to look through Aaron but smile at Yitzy with his medals gleaming in the glow of the chandeliers. It made Mari sad for Aaron. She knew her husband was as big a hero as they came.

The band was playing 'Moonlight Serenade' and Aaron gracefully waltzed Betty around the floor.

"I've been meaning to thank you for taking Betty under your wing," Yitzy said. "You've been a good friend to her."

Mari started at his voice, his breath so close to her ear. The four of them had become regular companions, going out together almost every Saturday night, but she and Yitzy were rarely alone. She could feel the heat coming off him, smell his scent. She shifted away from his nearness. "It's no chore. She's been a good friend to me."

"You seem preoccupied tonight."

Yitzy could always read her, often better than Aaron did.

"Tell me," he said.

"Saul was home last week."

He nodded. Yitzy knew Saul was at Los Alamos and probably understood better than Mari about the project Saul was involved with.

"He told me he'd been approached by a communist handler to gather information for them."

"And you're worried he'll do it?"

"He promised me he won't," she said. "But Saul's always been a bit of a fanatic when it comes to the Party. You know that."

He smiled, as though to acknowledge his own commitment to communism.

"I'm afraid the temptation for him to help them will be too great."

"And what concerns you, Mariasha? That your brother will be putting himself in danger, or that you don't want him supporting the communist principles you no longer believe in?"

It took her a moment to answer as the beautiful strains of the 'Moonlight Serenade' floated around her. "Both," she said. "Maybe communism works in theory, but it isn't the solution to society's problems.

The communist leaders have their own agenda—power and control. Equality for all and social justice are just the maxims they use to get the masses to buy in to their program."

"And you think that's any different from democracy?" Yitzy said with a half smile.

"Maybe not. I suppose every political system is ultimately corrupted by the powerful minority that controls it."

"You sound bitter," he said. "But then, that's the curse of your name."

"I'm not bitter. I'm worried that these superpowers fighting for their own brand of politics will destroy mankind."

"So if not political systems, what do you now believe in, Mariasha?" Yitzy sliced off a piece of strudel with his fork, taking her back almost ten years to the coffee shop where they had eaten apple pie after the anti-war rally.

"Peace," she said. "And I'm pretty sure that's what you believe in, too."

"Sometimes I think you hold me in higher esteem than I deserve."

"I'm not mistaken about you."

He brushed her denial away with his hand. "But you may find this enlightening. It seems the Party is out in full force."

"What do you mean?"

"I bumped into your friend Flossie on my way home from work a couple of days ago. Of course, thinking about it now, I'm sure she planned it. She was all rouged up and smelling like honeysuckle."

Mari leaned back in her chair. "I thought Flossie was in Albuquerque."

"She was, but she came back to New York to take care of a few things. She begged me to have a cup of coffee with her to catch up for old time's sake."

The band had switched to a fast number, 'Chattanooga Choo Choo' and Aaron was spinning Betty between the other couples around the crowded dance floor.

"She mentioned you," Yitzy said.

"Me?"

"She seemed surprised we're friends." He took another bite. "We didn't talk for too long about the past. She was clearly on a mission. She told me her cousin Bertie was thinking of helping out Anton Dubrovski. "

"Dubrovski? He's the one who approached Saul."

"Well this Manhattan Project is a big deal and the communists are pursuing every avenue to get as much information as they can. Flossie said they need someone to help them out at this end. Ideally someone without obvious connections to Los Alamos. She asked me."

Mari's heart slammed against her chest. "What did you tell her?"

"Absolutely not. I'm not going to be a spy against my own country." His shoulders edged back as though conscious of their responsibility to the uniform.

"So I was right about you."

"Perhaps." He smiled. "Flossie wasn't very happy about my position. Or maybe she wasn't happy that I didn't succumb to her feminine charms. I think I bruised her ego, because she said, 'I'm sure you'd do it if Mari asked you.'"

She felt her cheeks grow warm.

"Then she stormed out of the coffee shop."

"She always liked you," Mari said.

"And she was always jealous of you."

Mari watched the couples spinning out on the floor. Betty laughing. A flush in her cheeks. "I hadn't realized it at the time, but that's probably why our friendship ended."

"Flossie was right, you know," Yitzy said.

She turned back to him.

He was holding a piece of apple on the tip of his extended fork. "I would do anything for you."

CHAPTER 36

The sky was covered with dark clouds and there was a biting chill in the air, as Annette hurried toward the Dobbs Ferry station. She kept her hood up and hands buried in the pockets of her ski jacket. She wasn't surprised that neither Linda nor Kenny came after her to give her a lift. After today, her relationship with Linda was probably over. Which was fine by her. She didn't need more lies and deception in her life.

When she reached the outskirts of downtown Dobbs Ferry, she stepped into a coffee shop. It was an old-fashioned place with a counter for ordering, a black-and-white checkered floor, and painted chair railings along the walls. For an instant she was reminded of Yonah Shimmel's Knishery, sitting across from Julian, both of them still mysterious strangers. She checked her phone, but he hadn't called or texted. Nothing from the hospital, either.

She ordered a coffee, then sat down at a table in the back to read the letters. A few were in envelopes, most weren't. She skimmed them. Although the loose letters weren't dated, they appeared to be in date order based on the mixed-in postmarked envelopes. She decided to read them as they were arranged to get context.

A few of the early letters from before 1949 were long, filled with mundane details about meals that Betty had prepared using the cookbook Irene had given her. Betty had written about how much Isaac enjoyed her cooking. How baby Sally was doing. Teething, walking. Details of a contented life.

And then, in an envelope postmarked August 13, 1950, Annette found this.

Oh my dear sister,

How much I need you right now. As I told you on the phone, Isaac was arrested three days ago. He had assured me that it was a mistake and he would be released as soon as they realized it. But as each day passes, the news reports say otherwise. They say Isaac is a spy. How can that be? My Isaac?

Betty

The next letter was in an envelope, postmarked September 12, 1950, one month after the arrest.

Dear Renie:

I cannot express in words how grateful I am to you for coming to New York and staying with me these last few days. I don't know how I would have managed without you. I'm doing a bit better. At least I'm able to get out of bed and take Sally to school, though this morning she clung to me and screamed not to leave her. My heart breaks over what this is doing to my little girl. The children are cruel to her, which doesn't surprise me considering the looks I'm getting from their mothers.

She stopped reading. A young woman with a stroller had come into the coffee shop and taken a seat at the table next to hers. The woman gave her a little smile, then broke off pieces of a muffin, which she fed to the toddler in the stroller. Annette returned to the letter.

Our lawyer, David Weissman, is encouraging. He says that he spoke to the prosecutors and if Isaac gives them the names of the people who got him in this mess, they'll release him. Everyone seems to know that Isaac isn't capable of doing what they're accusing him of.

Your loving sister,

Betty

She absorbed this. Early on, it appeared that the prosecutors were looking for bigger fish than Isaac Goldstein. So what happened? Had the government given up on finding the real spy? Had they built a case against Isaac Goldstein because he was the best option they had? From what Arnie Weissman had said, the government was determined to make someone an example.

She read another short, undated letter.

Dearest Renie:

Thank you, dear sister, for your offer for me and Sally to come stay with you in Boston. I appreciate it more than you can imagine, but I can't possibly leave Isaac. Although he's quiet and distracted when I see him, I think he treasures my weekly visits to the detention center. At least, I tell myself he does. I wish he would speak to me. The trial is scheduled for March 13, two months from now. That will make seven months that Isaac will have been apart from me. I know once the trial is over, everyone will see that he isn't guilty and he'll come home to me.

Betty

Poor Grandma Betty. Annette could hardly imagine what she must have been going through.

Dear Renie:

I want to scream. Doesn't he understand what he's doing to me and Sally? How can he maintain this silence? Why won't he come forward and tell the FBI what they want to know? There's talk that they will be asking for the death penalty at his trial. Our lawyer says that's just a scare tactic, but it's certainly working on me!

Today, I met him as usual in the visitor room, but it was as though seeing a stranger. He has lost so much weight, that there's very little left of the man I loved and married. I begged him, "Isaac, can't you give them a name? Please tell them what they want." He looked at me and began to cry. "I'm sorry, Betty. I can't."

God help me, but I'm starting to believe he could be the monster they say he is in the news. Why else wouldn't he speak out to save himself unless he was guilty?

Your poor Betty

Annette took a deep breath. So even Grandma Betty had believed he was the traitor. And yet, from the next letter, she wasn't willing to give up on him.

Dear Renie:

I appreciate your concern, but I can't divorce Isaac. I just can't. It would make him look all the more guilty in the public's eye if I were to desert him. The trial is depleting all of our energy. Sally is still having nightmares. She wakes up in the middle of the night screaming. She's sleeping in my bed now, but I'm not sure it helps.

Betty

The next letter's envelope was postmarked April 5, 1951, one day after he had been convicted.

My dear sister:

I want to stay in my bed and sleep until I no longer wake up. I barely have energy to write. Sally lies here beside me, sucking her thumb like an infant, although she's six years old.

My husband is a convicted spy, sentenced to the electric chair. I say these words over and over, hoping the repetition will numb the pain. It isn't working.

Betty

"Are you all right?" The woman with the stroller stood beside Annette's table.

Annette touched her wet cheek and looked down at the water spots on the letter. She forced a smile for the concerned woman. "Yes, thank you."

The woman glanced at the letters, nodded, then pushed the stroller out of the coffee shop.

She wiped her cheeks and blew her nose in a paper napkin. She went through the rest of the letters. Irene had apparently stayed with Betty in New York for a while after the conviction. Then Isaac's lawyer filed a number of appeals over the next two years.

Mr. Weissman assures me that the conviction will be overturned in our next appeal.

But Betty's optimism was quashed as each appeal failed. Her last hope hinged on presidential clemency, but the pardon from Eisenhower never came.

And then Annette came to an envelope postmarked June 11, 1953, the day before the execution. There was no letter inside, but the last loose undated letter must have belonged in it. It was scrawled in a shaky handwriting, like the writing on the envelope.

Dear Renie:

Did you know that the FBI has a phone line at the prison that goes directly to J. Edgar Hoover? Mr. Weissman told me that the FBI expects Isaac to name the real spy rather than die in the electric chair. I told this to Isaac today, expecting him to say what he's said for the past two years. Instead, he looked up at me and said, "This is a sacrifice I must make"

Annette sucked in her breath. What? He knew? She continued reading.

I was stunned. "You know who the spy is?" He nodded, unable to look me in the eye. "You've rotted away in prison these two years" I said. "You've left me and Sally to be treated worse than lepers, and all this time, you knew? He kept his head down, and I screamed at him. "Tell them. Tell them now. I can't live like this another minute."

He brought his eyes up to mine. "I can't," he said. "I won't."

And then he called for a guard to take him back to his cell and left me in my rage.

I will tell you something, my dear sister. I have mourned for this man for almost three years, believing that he was as trapped in this nightmare as I. Now I learn that all this time, he had the ability to set himself, me, and Sally free. All this time, he had at his fingertips the means of avoiding public disgrace and the electric chair, yet he's chosen to protect someone else. Not me, not his daughter, but a traitor to our country.

Annette felt numb. He had known all along, but chose to die. Chose to let his wife and daughter live in shame when he could have freed them.

Why would he have done that? And whom was he protecting?

CHAPTER 37

It took Annette a moment to realize she'd received a text. She checked her phone, relieved to see a message from Julian.

Just woke up. How r u? Any news on Bill? Want to meet at ER park ?

ER Park? Emergency room parking lot? Her heart bounced. Why would Julian want to meet there? Then she reprocessed it. East River Park.

She wrote back. *No news on Bill. I can be at the park by 2.*

Julian replied. *See u then. I'll bring lunch.*

She took the train back to Grand Central, then transferred to the subway to get down to the East River Park. It gave her plenty of time to reread Grandma Betty's letters and consider her grandfather's actions. Although she didn't agree with what Linda had done, she could certainly understand her cousin wanting to keep these letters from her. With each rereading, she felt a spike of pain for Grandma Betty. She wanted to believe her grandfather had an admirable reason for destroying his family, but she couldn't imagine what, or how she would ever learn what it was.

As she put the letters away, it occurred to her that she hadn't come across the phrase 'cruel, heartless man,' though the sentiment was clear enough in the letters. Linda must have paraphrased Grandma Betty's words.

She got out at Delancey Street at a few minutes after two. Dark clouds hung low in the sky, looking like they'd burst open at any moment. She was breathless when she got to the park. It was practically deserted except for some kids playing football in a slushy field. On the bench beside the old oak tree, she could see the back of a man in a black wool hat and green army jacket.

Julian turned, as though sensing her presence, and waved her over.

She sat down beside him, awkward for the moment. Were they on the brink of a relationship, or were they supposed to keep a distance?

He seemed to hesitate, then he reached over and gave her a hug. "How are you doing?" he asked when he released her.

"Still no news on Bill. I feel like I'm in limbo."

"I understand. Here's lunch. Maybe that will help."

He gave her something wrapped in foil. She opened it. A hotdog covered with sauerkraut and mustard. She took a bite, the combination of flavors waking up her senses.

"It's what my dad and I always ate when we came here. Hotdogs, Cracker Jacks and orange soda." He handed her a bottle of Fanta. "Unfortunately, the vendor didn't have Cracker Jacks."

She finished the hotdog while Julian ate his. "I didn't realize how hungry I was," she said.

"Lack of sleep will do that." He reached over and rubbed something off the corner of her mouth. She started at his touch. He held up his finger and showed her the mustard, then he licked it off.

She turned away, chagrined by what she was feeling when she should have been thinking about Bill and dealing with her grandfather's treachery. The football kids were cheering someone's touchdown. She looked out over the river at Brooklyn's low skyline. Many of those buildings and smokestacks had been here when her grandparents lived on the Lower East Side. Had they ever come to the park? Had Isaac loved Betty? She'd cooked his favorite meals for him. They'd had a child together.

But her grandfather had chosen to protect someone and die a traitor despite all they may have shared.

Julian gathered up their trash, threw it away, then sat back down. "It's kind of strange," he said. "Being here reminds me of my father, but it also makes me think about my mother. At least her absence."

"Are you angry with her?"

"No, not today. I'm starting to realize that her life has always been much larger than just being a mom."

"Something happened?"

"I went to see her yesterday at her clinic."

"*Her* clinic?"

"She runs a free clinic."

"I thought she was a pediatric oncologist."

"That, too."

"Wow."

"Yeah. You know, I spent so many years resenting her that I never really thought about how much she gives to others."

Annette nodded. "What happened at the clinic?"

"There was a rush of patients. One of her doctors hadn't come in, so I helped out."

"I forget you're an MD. How did it feel getting back into it?"

"Good." He ran his tongue over his lips. The same lips that had kissed her a few hours before. "Real good."

"You've never felt that before?"

"No. Isn't that crazy? But when I went for my MD, I had this negative attitude that I was doing it for my mother. I hadn't realized how much it meant to me to actually heal people."

She studied the reflection of low-hanging clouds in the river. "I'm mixed up, too," she said. "I don't know what I really want out of life, yet here I am trying to understand all these people in my family. My grandparents, my mother, even my cousin Linda."

He shifted closer to her on the bench until their shoulders touched. "Talk to me."

She let her weight slump against him, letting him share her burden. "Linda was holding back letters my grandmother had sent her sister while Isaac was in prison. I found them at Linda's house this morning." She patted her satchel. "Of course, now that I have them, I've uncovered a whole other level of my grandfather's deception."

"What do you mean?"

"Isaac Goldstein was a traitor to his family."

"Not to his country?"

She shook her head. A dirty candy wrapper blew past in the wind. "Apparently he knew who the real traitor was, but chose not to give him up."

"He went to the electric chair for someone else?"

"That's right."

The football game was breaking up. The mud-covered kids were leaving in groups of two and three, crossing in front of them on the riverfront path.

"You're not alone anymore," he said. "I know you wish you'd grown up in a nice, normal family, but family can be just someone who understands you."

She looked into his eyes, darkened by the overcast sky. "You're not alone either."

He reached for her hand. A large, cold raindrop splattered against her cheek.

Julian brought her fingers to his lips and kissed them, just as the sky opened up, pelting them with rain.

CHAPTER 38

Julian grabbed Annette's hand and they ran for cover under a tarp at the pedestrian entrance to the Williamsburg Bridge. They were both drenched when they reached it. Rain drummed against the tarp. A train screamed by, causing the russet metal beams to shake.

He held her close, chilled by the rain and freezing air. Annette was hurting, but he might be able to help her. He wanted to help her.

"Do you still want to find out who the real spy was?" he asked.

She pulled back from his chest and looked up at him. The hood of her red ski jacket covered her head, but tendrils of hair clung to her wet cheeks and forehead. "I honestly don't know anymore. The deeper I dig, the more I think my mother and grandmother were right to run away from the past."

"So you're good with leaving things where they are? With never finding out whom he was protecting?"

"Good with it? No, I'm not good with it. I'm angrier than ever that my grandfather hurt my family so much." She frowned. "Why? Do you know something?"

"I'm not sure. Nana told me some things that might make more sense to you than to me."

"About Isaac Goldstein?"

He shook his head. "No. She hasn't mentioned him, but she's told me about her brother Saul. He was a physicist involved with the Manhattan Project."

He felt her tense. "Working on the atomic bomb?" she asked.

"Apparently." He took in a deep breath. "And he was approached to spy for the Soviets."

"*Mince alors*! Did he do it?"

"Nana said he didn't."

"But how would she have known? Maybe her brother decided to spy and didn't tell her the truth."

He stared at the graffiti-covered girders. "It's possible."

"Then Saul may have been the spy Isaac Goldstein was protecting."

Cars splashed by as they drove over the bridge.

Julian shook his head. "I think you're reaching. We don't know if Saul agreed to spy. Or if he did, if he provided the Soviets with any important information. Also, we don't know if Isaac Goldstein even knew my great-uncle, so why the heck would he protect him?"

"But I'm sure this is an important connection." Her lips were trembling. Excitement or the cold? "Saul worked on the atomic bomb. Isaac was good friends with Mariasha and Aaron Lowe. Saul was Mariasha's brother."

A train roared by overhead, shaking the bridge.

She was right. The connection was definitely there.

"Slugger," Annette said. "Oh my god. I think I figured it out. Saul had wanted to play ball for the Yankees. The Louisville Slugger was a popular bat. It makes sense that Slugger would have been the code name he chose."

"No," Julian said, a bit too emphatically before he caught himself. Saul could very well have been an atomic-bomb spy. Maybe that was why he had died of guilt.

The thrumming of rain against the tarp subsided. A frozen mist floated in the air.

"I'm sorry," Annette said. "I'm jumping to conclusions."

He took her cold hands between his, rubbing them to make her warm. To make himself warm. "No, *I'm* sorry.

You and I need to work together on this. We're after the same thing—the truth about what happened in our families' pasts. I need to know what my great-uncle did, and you're trying to understand your grandfather. I think my grandmother has answers for both of us."

Tiny beads of moisture had gathered on her lashes, surrounding her intense blue eyes. "You realize that one of us may be badly hurt by what she tells us," she said.

"Yes." He tightened his arms around her. "But whatever it turns out to be, we'll still have each other."

CHAPTER 39

Annette sat at Mariasha's kitchen table across from Julian, chilled by her rain-drenched hair despite the wool blanket over her shoulders. Mariasha hobbled around the small old-fashioned kitchen, ignoring an open jar of peanut butter and a plate of brown slices of apple—perhaps her uneaten lunch.

The old woman arranged chocolate-covered marshmallow cookies from a red cookie jar shaped like an apple, then set the platter down on the table. She had insisted that she didn't want or need any help. Shakily, she carried two mugs of tea to the table, then finally sat down on a kitchen chair with a pillow behind her back. The fisherman's knit sweater she wore was much too big for her and she had rolled up the sleeves two or three turns.

Julian held his mug of tea in both hands without drinking. "I know a lot of what you've been telling me is personal, Nana, but I really want Annette to hear about this."

Mariasha's eyes flitted toward her, then returned to Julian.

"I told Annette that Saul worked at Los Alamos," he said.

"That's going pretty far afield from my sculptures."

"Well, she's also interested in what was going on with the communist movement at that time," he said before Annette could respond herself.

His grandmother frowned.

"I told her Saul had been approached to pass information on to the Soviets but he didn't do it."

Mariasha fingered one of her large gold button earrings. "That's not exactly accurate."

"What do you mean?" He looked as surprised as Annette felt. "You said he didn't spy for them."

"The situation wasn't so cut and dried."

"Sure it is," he said. "He either provided the Soviets with what he knew about the bomb, or he didn't."

"Saul agreed to pass information to the Soviets."

Annette let a tiny gasp escape. She covered her mouth with her hand.

Mariasha turned to her. "You think that made him a traitor?"

"I know that another man was executed in the electric chair for doing less." Annette avoided Julian's look of warning. On the way over, they'd agreed not to mention that Isaac Goldstein was her grandfather. But Mariasha had just admitted her brother had spied for the Soviets.

Mariasha took a cookie and picked off the chocolate shell. "You're speaking about Isaac Goldstein."

"That's right." The wool blanket was making her too warm. Annette shrugged it off her shoulders. "Did you know him?"

Mariasha looked up hard.

Annette's heart was pounding. She didn't want to reveal who she was, but she needed to learn the truth. "Goldstein lived in this neighborhood. You've said your family was sympathetic to the communist cause. I assume you may have met."

Mariasha picked apart the cookie, separating the marshmallow from the vanilla wafer. She seemed to be deciding how to answer. "Yes," she said finally. "I knew Isaac and his wife Betty. Their daughter Sally was friends with my daughter Essie." She glanced at her grandson. "Julian's mother."

Julian's face was tight. He simply nodded. He'd seen the photo of the two little girls in Grandma Betty's album, but hearing his grandmother acknowledge this must have really brought the facts home. His grandmother had known the Goldsteins. Had known them well.

"Was Isaac Goldstein acquainted with Saul?" Annette asked, when what was really on her mind was, *Did Isaac Goldstein die for your brother, the real traitor*?

There was no sound in the kitchen except for a slow drip from the sink faucet.

"My brother was a hero," Mariasha said, her voice so unexpectedly loud that it startled Annette.

Julian put his hand on his grandmother's arm. "A hero because Saul believed he was doing the right thing to fight the Nazis?"

"Certainly not." She looked down at her fingers. They were smeared with dark chocolate. "Saul gave the Soviets bad information."

Ca alors! Annette thought. Bad information?

"What are you talking about?" Julian asked.

"Saul altered the diagrams and formulas. The Soviets couldn't have built a working bomb from what he gave them."

"My god," Julian said. "So he was a hero."

Annette processed this. Saul had sabotaged the Soviets by deliberately giving them faulty data? It didn't add up. "Then why didn't Saul go to the government when Isaac Goldstein was on trial and admit what he had done? They would have honored him and set Goldstein free."

Mariasha tilted her head, as though trying to see Annette from a different perspective. "Are you so naïve as to believe that's what would have happened?"

Her comment ruffled Annette. "I suppose I am."

Mariasha sighed. "You're not unlike most people. Unfortunately those with special interests don't care about doing the right thing." She rerolled the cuff of her sweater, smearing it with chocolate. "In the early fifties, the government was on a rampage to execute an atomic-bomb spy. You see, the Russians had detonated their own bomb in 1949 and that was terrifying to Americans. Our government wanted to show we were a force to be reckoned with. If Saul had told them he'd undermined the Soviets, do you think it would have been advantageous to the U.S. to believe him?" She made a spitting sound. "They would have arrested him along with Isaac and murdered them both. They were on a witch hunt for traitors, not heroes."

Annette opened her mouth to object, but wasn't that what Arnie Weissman had also said? It had served the government's purpose to unite Americans against a common threat, in this case, the Red Scare.

"I don't know, Nana. I think I agree with Annette," Julian said. "If Saul was heroic enough to risk his life passing bad information to the communists, then he would have spoken out to save Isaac Goldstein's life, even if there was a chance he'd be vilified, as well."

Mariasha studied him, something hard and unreadable on her face.

She wasn't telling the whole truth, Annette was certain of that.

"Why didn't he speak out, Nana? You've been telling me how smart and idealistic Saul was. Was that true, or was he really a coward?"

"Saul a coward?" she said softly. "No my darling Julian. I was the coward."

CHAPTER 40

Mariasha stared at the brown slices of apple on the kitchen counter, uncertain how much time had passed since Julian and the girl had left. A column of tiny ants marched from the edge of the sink to the apple slices. She crushed them with a sponge, watching several black dots wiggle and scatter.

One more time, she recalled the tight expression on her grandson's face as he asked her questions she refused to answer: Why had she called herself a coward? Why hadn't Saul spoken out? Why had he died consumed by guilt?

She had sat there mute, devastated by the realization that her words had been leading directly to an inescapable abyss, until at last Julian pushed out his chair and led Annette from the apartment.

She never should have told Julian about Saul. But once she'd begun, the memories and the words kept flowing and she was almost powerless to stop them. Why? So she could finally be free and die without the burden she'd carried inside for most of her life? But what about Julian, and Rhonda, and Essie? Was it fair to lay her burden on them?

The black column of ants was reforming, moving once again toward the brown apples. She picked up a slice. Brown and shriveled.

Guilt could do that to a person's soul.

January 1945

Mari sat on a bench beside a leafless oak tree and looked out over the snow-covered path that ran along the East River. The low Brooklyn skyline of her childhood was forlorn against the gray sky, and a stale fishy smell blew in off the river. She shivered despite the plaid blanket she'd wrapped around herself. She was cold, yes, but she was also filled with second thoughts about her plan. I promised Mama and Papa, she repeated like a mantra. I promised them. But was it right to put Yitzy at risk?

She heard him approaching. One firm step cracking through twigs and ice, followed by the swishing sound his bad leg made as he dragged it through the snow.

"Is this seat taken?" Yitzy asked, touching a spot on the bench beside her, his voice far too cheerful for the occasion. Of course, he didn't yet know the reason for the rendezvous. Last Saturday night when they were leaving the movie theater with their spouses, she had found a moment to whisper to him. "Meet me at the East River Park next Friday at four?" She knew he got out of work early on Fridays for the Sabbath. Yitzy had simply nodded.

Now here he was, bundled in his overcoat, a tweed cap on his head, the tips of his ears and nose red from the cold, grinning like the time he'd first sat down at her table at Camp Kindervelt. He'd given her a bite of his apple. Now she was going to give him a taste of hers.

"I need to ask you for a favor," she said.

CHAPTER 41

Julian pushed into the subway car after Annette just as the doors closed behind them. They were packed in against dozens of other rain-drenched commuters. He leaned against the door for balance, his arms around her. Holding onto her tight, because he had lost his grip on Nana.

What the hell was his grandmother hiding, and why? Had she been uncomfortable opening up in front of Annette? But then why hadn't Nana simply said she didn't want to discuss family business instead of completely shutting down the way she had?

There was something she didn't want them to know that would explain why Saul, after heroically tricking the Soviets, had chosen not to come forward to clear Isaac Goldstein. But Julian was pretty sure where he could get answers.

"Where are we going?" Annette asked over the screeching train noises. She'd pulled her hood down. Her hair had dried in golden ridges.

"Forest Hills."

"Where you grew up?"

"That's right. There's something at my mother's house I want to see again."

"That might explain Saul's actions?"

"I'm hoping."

The train went through a tunnel. The lights went out, then came back on.

"Something occurred to me about Saul," Annette said. "Maybe he didn't come forward to clear Isaac because he was afraid the communists would zap him for double-crossing them."

"That's a good possibility," he said. "And it would also explain Saul's guilt and why he may have viewed himself as a coward."

"But what about Isaac?" she said. "Why wouldn't he have given Saul's name to the government if he knew Saul had acted in the best interest of the U.S.?"

"Maybe he felt like Nana did. That the government wouldn't believe him and they'd both end up dead."

Annette held onto his arm for support as the train sped to the next station. "But my grandfather wasn't just sacrificing himself by keeping silent. There was his wife and daughter. Did Saul have some kind of hold over him that would have kept my grandfather from turning him in?"

"Maybe Isaac didn't know Saul was the spy." The train lurched and Annette fell against him. He held her tighter. "Did your grandmother's letter mention Saul?"

"No. My grandfather was cryptic. He'd said to Betty, '*This is a sacrifice I must make*.' But why? For whom?"

"There are a lot of unanswered questions. For you and for me."

The train took them into Queens, finally stopping at 71st Street in Forest Hills. They exited the station, preparing themselves for the onslaught of cold, stinging sleet, but a soft snowfall was coming down from the black sky, the flakes brightened by streetlights.

He led them away from the wide, heavily trafficked Queens Boulevard, past low-rise apartment buildings, then through the neighborhood of sprawling Tudors. The streets were covered with a rug of snow, which muffled the noises of traffic and their own footfalls.

He stopped on the corner and looked down the street at the house where he'd grown up. A couple of downstairs lights were on, but no smoke was coming out of the chimney. Why had he hoped there'd be a fire going in the fireplace? His mother probably wasn't home, and even if she was, it was foolish of him to believe he'd gotten through to her the other day. His mother would never change. Her resentment toward Nana ran too deep, like the submerged portion of an iceberg.

"That's where my mother lives. The white Colonial."

"Different from the others," she said. "I like it."

"I doubt anyone's home. My mother works late and it's only a little after five."

"She leaves lights on?"

"Maybe she doesn't like coming home to a dark house."

They walked up the snow-covered walkway. He was surprised to see footprints leading to the side entrance. He unlocked the front door and they stepped inside, stomping the snow from their feet. Voices were coming from the living room, but stopped abruptly.

"Essie?" he called. "I'm here with a friend."

"You call her 'Essie'?" Annette asked quietly.

"Yeah." He took their jackets and hung them on a couple of low pegs. It was notably chilly in the house.

"Third time in one week. This must be a record." His mother stood in the living room doorway, a glass of red wine in her hand. He was again surprised to find her drinking. She wore a black wool dress and black stockings. No shoes. Her cool blue eyes assessed Annette.

"Nice to see you, too," Julian said.

His mother took a step forward and extended her hand to Annette. "I'm Essie Sandman."

"Annette Revoir." She shook Essie's hand. "Good to meet you, Dr. Sandman."

His mother was quite a bit taller than Annette, even in her stocking feet. "Rhonda's here, by the way," she said to Julian.

"Wonderful. Now I'm sorry I didn't drag Nana along. We could have had a family reunion."

His mother gave him a stern look, clearly not appreciating his sarcasm.

He guided Annette into the living room. Rhonda was sprawled out on the sofa, holding a glass of wine. Her wiry graying hair jutted out in all directions and she wore an unraveling rust-colored sweater over another sweater, over a wool jumper, and god knew how many other layers.

He noticed Annette surveying the room, taking in the corner game table, the bookshelves, the fireplace.

"This is my sister Rhonda. She's a law professor, so she thinks she knows everything. Rhonda, my friend Annette."

"Nice to meet you," Annette said.

"You, too." Rhonda made no move to get up. An open bottle of wine sat on the coffee table next to her. "And I don't think I know everything," she said, her laconic voice conveying boredom. "But I certainly try my best to learn all the facts before reaching a conclusion."

"Would you like some wine?" Essie asked, maybe to break up the sibling raillery.

"We'd love some, thanks." He went to the painting over the mantel. "Saul made this," he said to Annette.

She stepped closer, and studied the intense watercolor behind the non-reflective glass.

Essie handed a glass of wine to Annette, another to Julian. "Why don't you give it a rest, Julian?"

"I wish I could, but it won't seem to let go of me." He took a sip of wine. "Nana's been telling us some interesting things about Saul."

"Both of you?" His mother sounded surprised.

"Annette's a journalist. She's very interested in the atomic-bomb spy rings in the early fifties."

His mother stood straighter. "What does that have to do with Saul?"

"According to Nana, Saul spied for the Soviets during the war, passing them information about the bomb."

Rhonda and his mother exchanged a look. He couldn't tell if this was something they both knew, but they didn't seem surprised.

Essie perched on the arm of one of the chairs and picked up her glass. "Yesterday you told me your grandmother said Saul refused to help the communists."

"Right, but she hadn't told me the whole truth and you knew it, didn't you? You knew he'd been a serious atomic spy."

She looked down at her glass.

"Did you also know that Saul doctored up the information he passed on to the Soviets, making it effectively useless?"

"Holy crap." Rhonda lifted her feet off the sofa and set them on the floor. "He sabotaged what he gave the Soviets? Is that true, Mom?"

Essie continued staring at her glass.

"Saul may have been a spy, but he was also effectively a hero," Julian said. "So why didn't he come forward to clear Isaac Goldstein instead of letting him die in the electric chair?"

"My mother's lying," Essie said.

"No she isn't," he said. "She has no reason to lie."

"How can you be so sure?" his mother said. "You think she's a kindly old woman, but she's the devil."

His anger flared up. He felt Annette's hand on his shoulder. He took a deep breath. Getting sucked into a fight with his mother wasn't the best way to learn what he'd come here for.

"Let's back up a second." Rhonda plucked on her wiry curls. "Mom, is it possible Saul sabotaged the bomb information he passed on to the Soviets?"

Essie shook her head.

"Don't reject it out of hand," Rhonda said. "Saul spied for the Soviets in 1945."

So Rhonda knew this, too.

"The Russians didn't produce a working bomb until 1949," Rhonda continued. "If what he gave them had been correct, it wouldn't have taken four years."

"He didn't sabotage the Russians," Essie said. "I don't know why your grandmother made up that story, but Saul was a traitor during the war."

Nana's words came back to him. *Saul was a hero.* Julian glanced over at Annette. She seemed to be struggling to hold back her emotions. What was the truth?

He looked again at the painting, at the red mushroom cloud, the rotting black oval shapes, the neon green dots that seemed to glow like ghostly fireflies. "I think I understand," he said. "Even if Saul had misled the Soviets, he also helped build the atomic bomb." He turned back to his mother. "That's why Saul felt guilty, wasn't it? Because he was a traitor to himself."

Essie drained the rest of her wine, then ran her finger around the rim of the glass. It made an eerie high-pitched noise.

"Why did he give you the painting?" he asked. "And why did Nana hide it?"

Essie reached for the wine bottle and refilled her glass. Her eyes met Annette's. "Do you come from a close family?" she asked.

Annette tensed. "Not as close as I'd like."

"That's too bad. My mother and I have never been close." Essie took a sip of wine. "I suppose that's why I adored my Uncle Saul so much. He was my mother's brother, but he was her antithesis. Warm, friendly, funny. A little man with curly red hair. He reminded me of a leprechaun and I always looked forward to his visits when I was a child."

Interesting that Essie's description of Saul matched Nana's.

"I hardly recognized him when he showed up on my thirteenth birthday. He'd become as skinny as a starvation victim. His hair had fallen out and there was an awful sore on his lower lip."

"He died shortly after," Julian said.

"That's right." Essie looked him directly in the eye. "Radiation sickness."

"Really?" Annette said. "From exposure at Los Alamos?"

Essie shook her head. "No, after that. He stayed with the Manhattan Project after the war when it became the Armed Forces Special Weapons Project, and they moved to the Sandia Base in Albuquerque."

"Whoa," Julian said. "Saul kept making bombs after the war? That makes no sense."

Rhonda and his mother exchanged another look.

"Did Nana know he had continued making bombs? Was that why she was angry with him and hid the painting?"

Essie stared at her glass of wine. "Not exactly."

"Then what the heck was going on? Why would Saul keep making bombs and put himself at risk of developing radiation sickness?"

His mother rubbed her leg. There was a run in her black stocking.

"Tell me, Essie."

His mother wet her lips with her tongue. "Because it was the best way he could accomplish what he needed to do, and he was willing to accept the consequences."

"Needed to do? What did he believe he needed to do?"

"Save the world," Rhonda said. "Make it a safer place."

He shook his head in disbelief. "By building bombs?"

"There's no point in keeping this a secret, Mom," Rhonda said. "I'm going to show them. It's time."

"You're right," Essie said softly. "It's time."

A chill ran through him. A secret. This couldn't be good.

Rhonda got up from the sofa and shuffled over to the fireplace. She stared up at Saul's painting for a moment, then turned back to Julian and Annette. "What do you see in this painting?"

They stepped closer. "I assume the spreading red is an atomic mushroom cloud," Julian said. "The neon green probably symbolizes radioactivity."

"And these?" Rhonda pointed at the black oval shapes piled up on the bottom of the canvas.

"They look like bombs," Annette said. "Spent bombs?"

"Not spent. Duds."

"Dud bombs?" Julian said.

Rhonda nodded. "From 1945 through 1958, Saul systematically sabotaged the United States stockpile of bombs by modifying their sensors so their nuclear cores wouldn't go critical and produce fission."

"You mean so they'd fail during detonation?" Julian said.

"That's right."

"Jesus! Saul sabotaged American bombs?" The idea blew Julian away. His great-uncle had undermined the United States government. "How could he do such a thing?"

"You have to understand the context," Essie said from her chair. "Saul was traumatized by Hiroshima and Nagasaki. He'd never imagined the magnitude of the atomic bomb when he helped build it. Then when the bombs were dropped, he became deeply distressed. He felt personally responsible for the more than two hundred thousand people who died from the explosions and from burns and radiation sickness. Years later, the effects of radiation were still visible in the survivors who developed leukemia and other cancers, in stillborn babies and in children born with birth defects." Essie shook her head. "Such horrors." She softened her voice. "Grotesque deformities. Babies with extra body parts, missing parts, distended brains. Saul had seen the photos."

No one spoke. A dog barked outside, a car swished by in the wet snow. Had this been why his mother had gone into pediatric oncology and opened the clinic?

"There were other scientists who felt the same as Saul," Rhonda said. "Deceived by the government. Tricked into creating something they'd believed would only be used in the defense of America. Not as an aggressive weapon."

"But the U.S. government claimed that by dropping those bombs, it ended the war more quickly and saved many more lives," Julian said.

"Saul didn't buy that," Rhonda said. "He felt betrayed, and he was determined to do whatever he could to keep mass destruction from happening again."

"Ironic, isn't it?" his mother said. "In trying to prevent more radiation poisoning, Saul knowingly exposed himself to radiation and it killed him."

Annette was twisting a strand of hair around her finger as she stared at the cold hearth. "So he effectively committed suicide to do what he believed was right."

"Yes," his mother said.

Julian walked back and forth in front of the fireplace, deeply disturbed by these new revelations. Could his great-uncle's actions somehow be interpreted as heroic? "Wait." He stopped pacing. "How could you possibly know all this about Saul?"

"Because he chronicled it." Rhonda lifted the painting from the wall, grasping it with both arms extended, then set it on the rug glass-side down. Carefully, she removed the backing. It was obvious she'd done this before.

The inside of the large rectangular insert was completely covered with tiny writing in black ink.

Julian crouched and examined it. He could make out dates and other numbers. Hundreds of entries. Probably the serial numbers of the bombs Saul had sabotaged. *Jesus*, he said under his breath. He looked up at his mother. "Did Nana know about this?"

"Most likely," his mother said.

"Why wouldn't she have destroyed it?" he asked. "It documented that her brother was a traitor."

Annette had gotten on her knees to study the canvas. "That depends on your perspective," she said. "Was the government justified in developing and stockpiling thousands of bombs with such terrible potential?" She sat back on her heels and twisted a strand of blonde hair around her finger. "If yes, then the person who intervened to keep the bombs from working could be considered a traitor to his country."

She paused. "But others might regard him as a hero to the world."

CHAPTER 42

Her cell phone buzzed, pulling Annette out of her absorption in the implications of Saul's final message. She recognized the number of St. Luke's Hospital. She answered, her heart pounding. As she listened to the nurse's update on Bill, Annette felt an enormous weight lift. "*Dieu merci*!" Annette said.

"Is Bill okay?" Julian asked when she got off the call.

"He's awake and out of danger. He wants to see me."

Essie and Rhonda looked at her with curiosity.

"My friend had a serious accident," she said, choosing not to share that Bill had attempted suicide. "He has no family. I'm sorry, but I must leave to see him now."

"Of course," Essie said. "Anything I can do?"

She was touched by the concern in her face. So there was a caring person behind the façade. "That's very kind of you, but he seems to be getting good care."

"Don't hesitate to call me if you think I can help."

"Thank you. And thank you for sharing your family's secrets with me. I won't abuse what you've told me."

"Saul's long gone. It won't matter to him." Essie turned to Julian. "But I suppose it's good you know the whole story." She patted her throat, in that instant reminding Annette of her own mother.

This hard, unhappy woman, with her core of kindness, had been her mother's childhood friend. It occurred to her how similar Sally Goldstein Revoir and Essie Lowe Sandman were, even though they'd been separated by over sixty years and almost four thousand miles. But Annette understood why her mother was so injured. What had caused Julian's mother to develop her shell?

"Thank you both." Julian kissed his mother and sister on their cheeks, which seemed to surprise them.

"The answers are never simple," Essie said.

"No, they aren't," he said.

That was an understatement, Annette thought. The more she learned, the further she seemed to be from understanding the truth about her grandfather.

The taxi that Julian had called for arrived a few minutes later. It smelled like gasoline and vanilla air freshener and made Annette sick to her stomach. Snow had turned to sleet, which hit the windshield hard. Julian put his arm around her as the taxi bounced over a pothole. "Bill will be fine."

She snuggled against him in the backseat, taking in his scent and blocking out the unwelcome smells and sensations from the rest of the world. "Bill doesn't have much of a support structure."

"He has you."

"I once thought so, but it's weighing on me that he didn't call me when he was falling apart."

"He probably didn't want to be talked out of what he'd decided to do."

The windshield wipers squeaked as they pushed the icy rain back and forth.

"I don't understand being so depressed or guilty that suicide seems like the best option," she said.

"Because you're not built that way," he said. "You're a fighter. Even when you're knocked down, you don't stay down." She could feel his chest expand and contract beneath her shoulder as he took a deep breath. "Apparently Saul wasn't a fighter."

"I think he was," she said. "Even though he felt guilty about developing the bomb, after the war he tried to keep America from committing even more acts of destruction."

"Fighters don't kill themselves."

"Saul didn't kill himself—he died fighting," she said.

The taxi sped along the Grand Central Parkway, splashing through puddles. Muted lights from the traffic leaving Manhattan inched toward them from the opposite direction like a Chinese-lantern parade.

"Do you think Saul sabotaged the information he gave to the Soviets during the war?" she asked. "Your mother was adamant that he hadn't."

"But why would Nana say that he gave the Soviets bad info if he didn't?"

"*Je ne sais pas.* Maybe she was trying to protect Saul's reputation." The driver hit the brakes, pitching her forward, but Julian held her tight. She settled back against him. "I wonder if we've been thinking about this the wrong way," she said. "Could the real issue be what Saul did after the war? Perhaps Isaac didn't turn Saul in because he didn't want to expose what he was doing to the post-war bombs."

"Are you saying your grandfather supported Saul sabotaging those bombs?"

She thought about her grandfather's words to Grandma Betty. *This is a sacrifice I must make.*

"If he knew about it, yes. I see that as a possibility. As a final act of bravery."

"Whoa." Julian let go of her. "You think it was a noble act for Isaac Goldstein to hide the possibility that hundreds, maybe even thousands, of U.S. bombs wouldn't work?"

She turned to face him. "I'm just saying my grandfather may have viewed it as heroic and tried to keep this secret. Especially if he shared Saul's opinion that detonating those bombs would be more destructive to the world than the U.S. not having them as weapons."

"Then he was playing God," Julian said. "They both were—Saul and Isaac."

"You sound like you don't agree with what they did."

"Saul's actions potentially put the United States in a terrible position with respect to our national defense."

"But what about as an aggressor?" she said, feeling a surge of anger. "Do you really believe the U.S. needed to bomb Japan to end the war promptly? I've read that Japan tried to surrender before the bombing. Dropping the atomic bombs was more an act of the U.S. flexing its muscles than one of defense."

"That's not what the history books say."

"Whose history books? The ones you read in the United States? Did it ever occur to you that not everyone in the world sees America as the center of the universe?"

"Spoken like a French patriot."

"I'm also American, Julian. That's not what I'm talking about. I just happen to believe in looking at all sides and perspectives, not wearing blinders."

"So I'm wearing blinders?"

The taxi hit another pothole and jolted her. She was breathing hard, but she wasn't finished. She was angry at this country, which played by its own rulebook, and had executed her grandfather because it needed a scapegoat. "I'm just saying, what if the U.S. government took it upon itself to bomb countries they considered threats, killing and poisoning another few hundred thousand people?" She looked Julian in the eye "You don't like the idea of Isaac and Saul playing God, but isn't that exactly what the government did?"

His eyes widened. The lights from oncoming traffic made patterns on his face, creating a kaleidoscope of emotion.

"Someone has to play God." She leaned back against the seat. "I guess the question is who should be making those decisions?"

"Maybe God should," he said softly.

She stared forward, through the slush-splattered windshield, at the approaching Manhattan skyline, trying to picture where the World Trade Center had once been. "If there is a God," she said. "Let's just pray that he really has humanity's interest at heart."

CHAPTER 43

Annette jumped out of the taxi in front of the hospital, her hood shielding her from the deluge, until she reached the main entranceway.

Julian followed close behind. "You go on up," he said. "I'll wait down here."

She hesitated. They hadn't spoken for the remainder of the drive into Manhattan. She couldn't tell if he was angry with her or trying to make sense of her rant about playing God. She touched his arm. His unshaven face was wet with icy rain. "I didn't mean to come across like I was attacking you. I—"

"Go." His voice was gentle. "Go to Bill. I'll be waiting right here for you."

Bill had been moved out of acute care to a regular wing. Annette found his room at the end of an antiseptic-smelling corridor. He was propped up against the elevated bed, his face ashen. She was taken aback. Her once larger-than-life professor looked small and wasted.

"Wow." She tried to sound upbeat. "I didn't think I'd ever call you pale."

He forced a smile. Tubes and wires connected him to various machines. One behind him beeped every few seconds. "It's good to see you, Annie," he said in a raspy voice.

She sat on the edge of the bed, rather than on the ugly orange chair. There was a moveable tray with a water pitcher and a plastic glass with a straw. No flowers anywhere. She should have brought him flowers. No one else would.

"Do you want your water?" she asked.

"Wouldn't mind."

She handed him the glass and he sipped through the straw. He still had a bandage on his pinkie where he'd cut himself the day before. It seemed so long ago. If only she had picked up on the signs.

He met her eye. His eyes looked naked.

She reached into her satchel and pulled out his tortoise-framed glasses. "Thought you might like these."

"Wonderful." He adjusted them on his nose. "Much better. Where did you find them?"

"On the floor of your apartment. With your smashed dishes and overturned furniture. I stopped by earlier to straighten up. And by the way, Woodward's staying with one of your neighbors."

"Thank you," he said softly.

"You're welcome."

He stared at the bandage on his finger. "You're angry with me."

"I'm angrier with myself. I should have known something could go wrong last night. That Kylie would pull something."

"So now you're clairvoyant, my Annie?" He gave her a weak smile. "You can blame me."

"Oh don't worry. I'm furious with you, too. How would you feel if I hadn't called you when I had a problem and then overdosed on pills and alcohol?"

"I'd give you an F."

"Glad you find it funny."

"I'm sorry." He closed his eyes. "It just hurt so bad. What she'd done. I couldn't bear it. Losing Billy."

"But you haven't lost him. It's a temporary setback. You'll track them down, take her to court."

"Stop." He held up his hand. One of the machines made a beep of protest.

"Okay." She softened her voice. "We shouldn't talk about this now."

"I know you want to fix things," he said. "You can't help yourself. That's why you're my Annie-get-your-gun." Another smile, this one stronger.

Her eyes watered. "Damn you, Bill." She leaned over to hug him. "You're my best friend. You know how much I love you."

"I do."

"Promise me," she said, her voice too choked to continue.

"I promise," he said. "I'll call you if I ever feel low."

She nodded and wiped her cheek. "And I promise I'll try to be a better friend."

"You're a great friend, Annie. Most of the time." He winked. "But it took you long enough to get here. Where the hell have you been?"

She was relieved that he was able to joke. "Are you up to talking about my stuff?"

"I sure as shit don't want to think about my situation. Please, tell me what's been going on."

"Julian and I went to see Mariasha Lowe this afternoon."

"Julian? Yesterday you said that was over."

At least Bill's mind was crystal clear. "Over and back on," she said.

"I hope my situation had something to do with that happy resolution."

"It did. But please don't feel obligated to attempt suicide every time I have relationship issues."

He let out a full-bodied laugh.

Tres bon. He's back to himself.

"And did Mariasha shed any new light on Isaac Goldstein?"

"Quite a bit, though I don't think she realized it."

"She still doesn't know your relation to Isaac Goldstein?"

"No," Annette said. "But I told Julian everything."

"Did you now?" He pursed his lips and gave a quick nod, reminding her of when she'd give an answer in class that he approved of.

"Anyway," she said. "Mariasha had a brother named Saul who was a physicist working on the bomb at Los Alamos."

"My, my."

"Saul was recruited by the Soviets to pass technical information on to them."

"And?"

"Apparently he did."

"There's a promising development. Saul may have been the spy the government was looking for."

"I think he was, but it gets better. Mariasha claims that Saul deceived the Soviets. He modified the formulas he gave them, so any bombs they built wouldn't work."

"Ballsy," Bill said.

"If, in fact, he was the saboteur. There's some question about that. I'm wondering if Mariasha made that part up because she wanted to believe her brother was actually a hero."

"Hmm." Bill rubbed his chin, causing the machine to give beep of protest. "Do you think Isaac knew Saul? They may have met through Mariasha."

"Yes. And I'm pretty sure my grandfather knew Saul was spying."

"Interesting," he said. "But if Isaac knew about Saul's involvement, either he would have been Saul's handler or someone else in the spy ring was. How is it possible Saul's name never came up? Was there any mention of him in anything you read?"

"Just the Slugger reference," she said. "And I'm sure Saul was Slugger."

"So why do you think Isaac didn't give Saul up to the government to save himself?"

"It gets complicated," she said. "Apparently, Saul was so mortified about the devastation caused by the bombs dropped on Hiroshima and Nagasaki that he continued working for the government after the Manhattan Project was disbanded. But this time, Saul sabotaged the American bombs. He modified the sensors so the bombs wouldn't detonate."

"Whoa," Bill said. "That's huge. So America had a stockpile of dud bombs?"

"That's right. I believe that's the reason my grandfather didn't turn Saul in. He must have agreed with Saul's scheme. It was the sacrifice Isaac made to keep the world safe."

"Sacrifice?" Bill sucked on the straw, draining the rest of the water. He handed her the empty glass. "Maybe I'm a little slow tonight, but either you're leaving something out, or you're jumping to conclusions."

"Sorry. I left something out." She reached into her satchel for the pile of her grandmother's letters, found the last one Betty had written, and handed it to Bill. "It was written on June 11, 1953."

"The day before the execution." Bill squinted at the letter, and read aloud. "*This is a sacrifice I must make*."

"Where did you get these letters?"

"I found them at Linda's house. She'd lied about having them."

"Why would she have done that?"

"She said she wanted to protect me from learning how terrible my grandfather really was. But now that I know why he made the sacrifice, I realize he had an impossible choice. His family or saving humanity."

He rubbed his chin. “This letter isn’t dated. How do you know it’s from June 11?”

“The postmark on the envelope.” She handed him the empty envelope at the back of the pile of letters.

He studied it, then put the envelope down on the bed. “Why are you so certain Isaac knew what Saul was doing and that he agreed with him?”

“Because it all fits.”

“Really? Just like that?” He frowned. “Think of Nassim Taleb’s Black Swan theory, Annette. We talked about this in class. For every event or set of circumstances, there are an infinite number of explanations for how it happened, all of them fitting the known data. Are you sure you’re not making the pieces fit because you want to believe this? Because it makes your grandfather into a hero?”

Wasn’t that what she had just accused Mariasha of doing with her brother?

“I’m not making up the stuff about Saul. It comes from Mariasha and a painting Saul made that documents what he was doing.”

Bill scratched his arm where an intravenous tube was held in place by tape. “I’m not saying Saul didn’t do those things. I just don’t see the connection to the letter.”

“My grandfather admitted his guilt to Grandma Betty the day before he was executed, so it’s effectively a confession.”

“*This is a sacrifice I must make,*” Bill read, again, then handed her back the letter. “That’s too general to be a confession.”

It was a bit general, but everything fit so nicely. And yes, she couldn’t deny she wanted to believe the scenario she’d painted of her grandfather’s *beau geste.*

She looked at the letter her Grandma Betty had written the day before her husband was executed. She studied the shaky blue penmanship. A letter, understandably written in fury. She wished she could tell her grandmother that Isaac Goldstein's death hadn't been in vain. Maybe Grandma Betty would have even agreed with his sacrifice.

She picked up the envelope lying on the bed. June 11, 1953 postmark. The same shaky handwriting.

In black ink.

Not blue.

Her heart hiccupped. This wasn't necessarily the letter that had been mailed in this envelope. She had made the wrong assumption.

Again.

CHAPTER 44

She left Bill with a hug and a promise to visit the next day with the books he asked her to bring. Her brain was churning. How could she have been so rash, jumping to conclusions about the date of that letter? And she had also conveniently explained away Linda's reference to Isaac being "a cruel, heartless man" rather than searching for the letter where Linda had very likely read the remark. Now, Annette realized, it must be in the missing letter.

She wandered down the hallway, relieved to find an empty waiting room. She turned the volume on the TV to mute and called Linda, wondering if her second cousin would talk to her after their ugly confrontation that morning.

The phone rang four times before Linda answered. "What is it, Annette?" Her voice was chilly and flat.

"I know there's another letter. My grandmother sent it the day before Isaac was executed. I have the envelope." She could make out droning voices in the background, perhaps the news. "Do you have the letter?"

"What if I told you I destroyed it?" Linda said.

"I don't think you did."

Linda didn't say anything. In the background, the newscaster's voice sounded harsh and robotic. Finally, Linda gave a little cough. "My mother always told me what a monster he was and how deeply he hurt her sister, but I never understood to what extent. When I found the letters after you asked me to look for them, I read them for the first time. I wanted to destroy all of them, but I couldn't. Aunt Betty had written them and I knew I'd be destroying a part of her, as well. But I kept out that last letter, planning to burn it."

"But you didn't."

"No. I didn't."

"Please, Linda. I need to read it."

"Can't you leave it alone?"

"I wish I could."

There was a female newscaster speaking now on Linda's end, all chipper, probably giving the weather report.

"Please, Linda. Let me come by tonight and pick it up."

She seemed to be thinking. Finally, she said, "I'm going into the city in a few minutes to pick up Kenny. I'll drop off the letter then, but I don't want to see you right now."

"Thank you," Annette said. "Thank you so much."

"I don't think you'll be thanking me after you've read it."

The rain had slowed to a drizzle and turned into a frosty mist blurring the cars and buildings as she and Julian walked home from the hospital. They went down slushy streets and she filled him in on her discovery about the letter her grandmother had written just before her grandfather's execution.

"Linda told me she'll bring me the letter tonight."

"And then what? The letters you already have are pretty harsh. Your grandfather chose to die a traitor and basically ruined your mother's and grandmother's lives. But Linda has a letter that could be even more damning. Are you sure you want to read that?"

Gray steam rose from the manholes in front of Annette's brownstone. Her apartment was dark, as she'd left it. She looked up at Julian. His black wool cap was dotted with ice crystals. "I have to," she said. "Because as awful as it may turn out to be, I need to know the truth."

They went inside the building. She could smell a chicken roasting. Her mother made roast chicken for special occasions. Maybe it had been a dish Mama remembered from her childhood. Friday night dinners from 'before,' when she'd lived with both her parents on the Lower East Side. When her life had been simple, secure, and happy.

She hung up their jackets and went into the kitchen alcove to open a bottle of wine. She filled two glasses then brought them to the sofa and sat down beside Julian. They drank without talking. She leaned back against the sofa cushions and closed her eyes. The wine made her woozy, the strain of the day and lack of sleep finally hitting her.

Julian's arm slipped around her shoulders. His breath warmed her ear and sent shivers down her back. "You know, Annette. You already have your truth. You have a plausible explanation for your grandfather's actions. He was a flawed and complex man who grievously hurt your grandmother and mother by choosing to follow his convictions."

"If that's all there is."

"Do you think it's possible to know the complete truth about anything?"

"Probably not." She opened her eyes and took another sip of wine. The edges in the room were blurring. The bookshelves, bricked-up fireplace, soft blue sofa, the old trunk. On it was the photo album, open to her grandparents' wedding picture.

"Then if Linda brings the letter, tear it up, burn it," he said. "Let it go."

His face was close to hers. His blue eyes closing in. *Let it go.*

He was right. She had her truth about her grandfather. A flawed and complex man. Not a monster. She'd let it go.

Her lips touched his.

And a sound, gentle as a flapping bird wing came from the front door.

She turned toward it. On the floor, partially stuck beneath the door, was a manila envelope. The letter she no longer wanted to see.

"I don't want to read it," she said.

"Then don't."

She struggled with herself. Rip it up. Burn it.

"But I have to." She put her empty wine glass down on the trunk and went to pick up the manila envelope. She felt a loosening in her gut as she took out the letter in her grandmother's handwriting, written in same shade of blue ink as on the envelope postmarked June 11, 1953.

She sat on the sofa and read her grandmother's words, as Julian looked over her shoulder.

Dear Irene:

My husband is a cruel, heartless man.

There, finally—Betty's remark, just as Linda had said.

Isaac will be executed tomorrow and to Hell with him. I pray that no legal tactics or further stays of execution will intervene. I wish him gone from my life forever.

As I was arriving at the prison today, I saw a woman dressed completely in black leaving. She was stooped over and a veil shaded her eyes. There was something familiar about her, but I couldn't place her, and the handkerchief she held prevented me from seeing her face. I think she had seen me and knew who I was because she left in a hurry. Somehow I knew she had just been to see Isaac. That she had come to say goodbye.

When I saw Isaac shortly after, I was left with no doubt. His eyes were red and he was unable to look at me. And then, without warning, he dropped to his knees and grabbed hold of my ankles. "Forgive me," he said. "You don't deserve any of this."

My heart felt like it had been ripped from my chest as I listened to my husband of almost ten years tell me he loved another.

Annette gasped. He loved another? Her grandfather had loved someone other than Grandma Betty? She glanced at the photo album on the trunk, open to the wedding photo of Betty and Isaac.

And then, as though loving another woman wasn't enough to destroy what little of me is left, he told me that he loved her so much he was willing to make this sacrifice. He was going to die for her.

"*Ce que l'enfer?*" Annette said, stunned. There had been no grand gesture in her grandfather's death. He hadn't died for his principles, but for this mystery woman.

She met Julian's eyes. "He was no hero." She spit out the words. "Isaac Goldstein went to the electric chair because he was in love with someone else."

CHAPTER 45

Her apartment felt too small, too close, no air to breathe.

The old photo album sat on the trunk, filled with pages of false dreams. It was too difficult to look at her grandmother's young happy face, knowing the pain that was in store for her.

"Let's get out of here," Julian said.

She was only vaguely aware of a hustle out of her brownstone into the street. A taxi ride huddled against Julian, then into the lobby, up in the elevator, and into his overheated apartment.

She sat on the black leather sofa now, a glass of something stronger than wine in her hands. She took another sip, felt the burn. Cognac. But it couldn't burn out the anger she felt toward her grandfather.

Julian was beside her, his arm draped over the back of the sofa, the fingers of one hand tapping against the leather, a glass in his other hand.

At least it was over. Her search for the truth was over.

"I turned the heat down," Julian said. "It's been on since last night."

She processed that. Last night was when Bill had almost killed himself and she had called Julian to help her. She'd hardly slept since.

She stared out the window. Distant, blurred lights from lower Manhattan broke through the darkness of the night. "I guess I got what I was looking for," she said. "Now I know the truth about Isaac Goldstein. Not a traitor to his country, but he sure hung my mother and grandmother out to dry."

"It seems that way."

"I'm sorry I ever got involved."

"Are you?" Julian brought his arm around her, tightened it. "But then we never would have met."

She rested her head in the crook of his neck and closed her eyes. Inhaled his smell, sweat and something like the licorice candy she loved as a child.

He took the cognac glass out of her hand. She heard the clink of glass against glass as he set it on the coffee table. Then his soft fingertips touched her face. Gently massaged her temple, her cheeks. Deeper.

Her breath quickened. No, she wasn't sorry.

She leaned toward him, her mouth open. His sweet breath mixed with hers. Then his lips pressed against her lips. His tongue against her tongue. His chest against her chest. The ugliness of the last few days faded. Bill's near death. Isaac Goldstein's deception. Only one face remained.

Julian.

She dug her fingers into his back. Felt his kisses up and down her neck, behind her ear. His hands in her hair, squeezing her shoulders, running down her spine. Digging deeper, deeper. Kneading out her childhood loneliness and shame. Expelling the knots in her life as she flinched beneath his strong fingers.

Hot. It was too hot. Her sweater came off. His shirt. Her pants, then his.

Their naked bodies burned up against each other's. Burned up the hate, the bitterness, the lies, the deception.

She cried out. A moment later, she felt him shudder, then lie still. She buried her face in his chest and drifted off to sleep, dreaming of licorice.

The sound of clicking fingernails awakened her. Against the windows, icy snowflakes, or perhaps hail.

A dull light filled the room. For a moment, she stayed perfectly still. Her head rested in a nest of soft hair and hard muscles. Julian was breathing deeply, his breastbone expanding and contracting. Gently, she pushed herself up and watched him sleep. His face was relaxed. The tension gone. Thick black eyelashes. Pale veins on his eyelids. Full lips. Tiny cleft in his chin. High forehead in a perfectly shaped head. She'd never seen him like this before. Hadn't realized how beautiful he was.

She could make out the time on the microwave. 10:03. Had they only been asleep an hour? She blinked again. It was morning. And everything had changed.

Julian shifted beneath her. Opened his eyes. Blue and clear. He smiled. "Hello."

"Good morning."

He stretched. "Is it morning?"

"It is. We've been asleep for twelve hours."

He pressed his hand against her heart. She could feel his pulse pounding along with hers. Then he kissed her. And the heat began again.

At some point, they realized neither one of them was going anywhere. They didn't need to squeeze a lifetime into an hour. They showered. He made coffee. She poured juice and popped four frozen waffles into the toaster.

Julian, in gym shorts and a T-shirt, came up behind her and put his arms around her waist. "I like your shirt." She was wearing one of his old jerseys, sleeves rolled. "But I'd like it better off."

"First, we eat," she said.

"Tough task-master."

They carried the juice, coffee, and plates of waffles over to the glass coffee table and sat on the sofa.

Julian brought his last forkful of waffle dripping with syrup into his mouth. "Man. I was actually starving." He leaned back against the cushions and gazed out toward the window. The snowflakes had formed a frozen shield making it impossible to see out.

"So cold out there," she said. "I don't want to leave our cocoon."

He brought her close to him. "Then let's not."

She picked up her mug of coffee. The cognac glasses from last night were still on the coffee table. They reminded her that their cocoon wasn't impenetrable.

"You okay?" he asked.

"I was just remembering my grandmother's letter. I wish I could forget all about Isaac Goldstein."

"Like your grandmother and mother did?" Julian said. "They tried to erase him from their lives and it didn't work out very well for them."

The room felt chilly. The magic gone. "What are you suggesting? That I invest more of myself in this bastard who brought nothing but pain to his family?"

"A few hours ago you labeled him a hero because he didn't give Saul away."

"A few hours ago, I didn't know he'd sacrificed my grandmother and mother for another woman."

"It's got to make you wonder though, doesn't it?" he asked, rubbing his thighs. His arms and legs were muscled like a runner's.

"What?"

"How strong his love for the woman in black must have been."

"Don't romanticize it, Julian."

"Can't help it. I'm in that kind of mood." He pushed her hair away from her neck and kissed her ear.

She wiggled away from him. "I understand about being in love, but he had responsibilities. A wife. A daughter."

"He still may have been covering for Saul," Julian said. "That would make him somewhat heroic."

"*Bien*. Let's leave it at that."

"But something doesn't make sense to me. How come no one seems to know of Saul's career as a spy?"

"The Soviets knew," she said. "Saul was Slugger."

"Maybe. We've been assuming Isaac was protecting him, but in your grandmother's letter, Isaac said he was dying for the woman in black."

She folded her bare legs under her on the sofa and took another sip of coffee. As much as she wanted to move on from Isaac Goldstein, the analytical journalist side of her brain protested. Grandma Betty's letter didn't support their theory that Isaac Goldstein had been protecting Saul. "You're right," she said. "We need to figure out who the woman in black was."

"And what she did that Isaac was willing to take the fall for." Julian frowned. "You realize the significance of this. The woman in black was very likely the traitor."

A crackling noise came from the window, as though the expanding ice was about to break up.

"Maybe," she said. "But it's also possible that Isaac was so guilty about loving her that he chose the electric chair as a form of suicide."

"Suicide out of guilt?"

"Why not?" she said. "Saul effectively committed suicide through radiation poisoning. Bill tried to kill himself with pills. Both of them felt tremendous guilt."

Julian shook his head. "Your grandmother's letter said Isaac was making a sacrifice for the woman in black. That doesn't sound like guilt."

"True." She thought about Betty's letter. "The word sacrifice sounds more like he was covering for her."

"I'm sure we can figure this out," Julian said. "Nana's told me stories relating to Saul and you've read about the communist movement and the players in the thirties and forties. Let's pool what we know."

The fear of discovering something else that would hurt her held her back, but the need to see this through won out. "Okay." She put her coffee mug down on the table. "Let's start with the known players in the spy ring. There was Florence Heller, who gave the most damaging testimony against Isaac."

"Do you think she may have been the woman in black?"

Annette worked the possibility through. "Why would he be willing to make a sacrifice for Heller if she was pointing the finger at him?"

"Love can make a person do strange things."

"True. But Arnie Weissman believes Heller was protecting Joseph Bartow."

"Maybe there was a love triangle and Heller chose Bartow over Isaac. That may have been the reason he was willing to go to the electric chair."

"There are other pieces that don't fit," she said. "Supposedly Albert Shevsky, who was working at Los Alamos, was the point person leaking the information, but he only had intermediate clearance, so it was highly unlikely that he would have had access to the atomic-bomb technology."

Julian scowled.

"What?"

"I'm just remembering something Nana told me." He rubbed his forehead. "She told me about a dinner Saul went to when he was at Los Alamos where he met the Soviet agent Dubrovski."

"The one who was at the Popular Front meeting?"

"That's right," he said. "I'd assumed that was when Dubrovski recruited Saul, but now I'm wondering about the other people who were at that dinner."

"Who?"

"Nana's friend Flossie had organized it. She was in Albuquerque to take care of her boyfriend Joey, who was at a tuberculosis sanitarium. And Flossie's cousin Bertie was working over at Los Alamos as a machinist with intermediate clearance."

"Intermediate clearance," she repeated. "Like Albert Shevsky."

Flossie. Joey. Bertie. The names hung in the air as the ice on the window snapped. And then everything snapped into focus for Annette.

"*Mon dieu.* They're nicknames. Flossie, Joey and Bertie are nicknames for Florence, Joseph, and Albert. It couldn't be a coincidence. Florence Heller, Joseph Bartow and Albert Shevsky were part of the spy ring that Isaac was accused of masterminding."

Julian rubbed his unshaven cheek. He looked disturbed about something. "Flossie, Joey and Bertie also all knew Nana's friend Yitzy."

Annette felt a spasm of nausea as a troubling idea came to her.

"What's wrong?" he asked. "You just got very pale."

She picked up the mug of coffee and took a sip. It was icy cold. "I'm not sure I want to go there, but do you think Isaac was Yitzy?"

"That occurred to me, too, but let's not jump to conclusions until we talk it through."

She nodded, though she was terrified of where this was heading.

"Okay," he said. "We know from Nana's stories that Yitzy was her age, so he would have been born around 1918. He was an outspoken communist who attended City College in the late thirties and majored in engineering."

Just like Isaac Goldstein, Annette thought.

Julian's forehead was in a scowl, as though he was working through a math or logic problem. "Isaac, call him 'A', was friends with Florence, Joseph and Albert, call them 'B'," Julian continued. "And Yitzy, call him 'C', was friends with Flossie, Joey and Bertie, call them 'D'. We're hypothesizing that B equals D. So logically, if A is to B, as C is to D, and B equals D, then it follows that A equals C."

Isaac equals Yitzy. Julian hadn't needed to say it aloud. It was plain enough to her.

"It's still just a theory," he said. "There are probably lots of other ways all these pieces could make sense."

She watched sections of ice slide down the windows, creating crevices of visibility. She didn't want to look at it, but she couldn't help herself. If Isaac had been Yitzy, there were implications to consider. Mariasha had been in love with Yitzy. But that had been a youthful infatuation. It wouldn't have continued once they were married, or could it have?

"Let's think about this hypothetically," Julian said. "If Isaac was Yitzy, then everyone in the spy ring was connected, possibly as early as 1935." Julian ran his hand over his cheek. "That's when Nana and Flossie went to the anti-war demonstration at City College. Then later they all met Bertie and Joey and Dubrovski at the Popular Front meeting."

Annette was only half listening. She remembered something in Grandma Betty's letter. Betty had seen a woman at the prison who seemed familiar, but Betty couldn't place her. A disturbing possibility was forming in her head. She needed to stop Julian, but he was too wound up, his grandmother's stories suddenly coming together for him.

"But it goes back even earlier," Julian said. "Nana became friends with Yitzy at summer camp. She was supposed to meet Yitzy at Yankee stadium by the baseball-bat smokestack, but Saul got sick and she never went." Julian chewed on his lower lip. "My dad took me there when I was a kid. He told me the smokestack was patterned after Babe Ruth's bat. The Slugger."

No, Julian. Don't go there.

"I wonder if the Slugger code name wasn't a reference to the bat, but to the smokestack where Yitzy and my grandmother were supposed to meet." He took in an abrupt breath as though startled by something. "Damn," he said. "Yitzy may have been Slugger."

"I don't think so." She didn't want to say the words. Saying things aloud could make them true and the repercussions of this truth would be devastating. But she knew it was only a matter of time before Julian arrived at the possibility himself. "If my grandfather was Yitzy," she said. "Then your grandmother was Slugger."

"Nana?" he said, shaking his head. "Slugger?"

Annette felt the sting of her words just before they dropped from her mouth like hailstones. "Yes, Julian. And she was also very likely the mystery woman in black."

CHAPTER 46

Slugger. The mystery woman in black. That person couldn't be Nana, Julian thought. And Yitzy couldn't have been Isaac Goldstein.

They had to be mistaken. Because if they were right, that would mean Isaac Goldstein had been in love with Nana and had sacrificed himself for her. And it also meant his grandmother had been the traitor.

"It's impossible." His voice sounded too loud in his own ears. "There has to be another explanation."

Annette looked at him with sad-urchin eyes. "Like what?"

"I don't know," he said, standing up to get dressed. "But I have a feeling my grandmother does."

Julian could tell that Nana was perplexed when they arrived at her apartment. She smiled at him uncertainly. His gaze brushed over the crimson sofa, the turquoise chairs, the sculptures in front of the windows. It was all familiar, yet everything seemed slightly off, as though he was viewing it through a hangover.

Annette squeezed his hand. *Whatever the truth turns out to be, we're in this together,* she had said as they walked over from his apartment. It was almost exactly what he'd said to her yesterday when she was confronting her grandfather's demons. And now, they certainly would be in this together if their theories turned out to be correct. The truth hinged on whether Nana's old flame, Yitzy, was in fact Isaac Goldstein.

A record was playing on the old Victrola. Over the scratches, a young man's voice sang, sweet and trembling.

Believe me, deceive me
Darling, just don't leave me.

Nana reached up and touched Julian's face. "What's wrong?"

"Let's sit down, Nana."

She gave a little nod, then wobbled to her favorite chair, so shaky it seemed she would topple over. She hoisted herself into it. Her black sweater and black stretch pants hung on her tiny frame.

The woman in black? Impossible. Nana would explain everything.

You are the apple of my soul
If you love me, don't let me go.

He and Annette sat close together on the sofa, their hands intertwined. He thought he could smell their lovemaking from a few hours before. Could Nana have had a love affair with Annette's grandfather? Impossible.

"Nana." His voice came out rough. He cleared his throat. "Nana, who was Yitzy?"

She started, like a bird hearing a loud noise. "Yitzy. I told you. He was the boy I met at camp. Then we met again in college."

"What was his real name?"

She looked from Julian to Annette, then back to Julian. "He was a young man from my past. That's all."

"Did you stay in touch with him after college?"

Nana rubbed the arthritic bump on her pointer finger. "What difference does it make?"

"I don't know," he said. "If it doesn't make a difference, why won't you tell us?"

One promise I will make to you
Wherever I am, whatever you choose.

"That's Yitzy." She gestured with her chin toward the Victrola.

The voice on the record. The boy from summer camp, and then from college. Why was she still playing his record? Unless she was the woman in black.

He could hear Annette's strained breathing next to him. He didn't dare meet her eye.

"What was Yitzy's real name?" he asked his grandmother again.

"Certain things are better left unsaid."

"Like what you didn't tell me about Saul?"

His grandmother flinched, then turned to stare at the sculpture of *Boy Playing Stickball*. The boy seemed forlorn in the dull light coming from the window.

"I went to my mother's house last night," he said, his voice gentler. Attacking Nana wasn't the best way to approach this. He was sure she'd have a logical explanation for all the half-truths she had told him. "We talked about the painting, Nana. The writing on the back. We also talked about the fact that Saul was sabotaging U.S. bombs after the war."

His grandmother closed her eyes and became utterly still.

"Nana?"

She slowly opened her eyes.

"Did you know Saul was modifying the sensors of American bombs so they'd fail during detonation?" he asked. "That he'd incapacitated hundreds, maybe even thousands, of them?"

"Yes." The word came out as a whisper.

"Whose idea was that?"

She didn't answer. The radiator clanked off. "It was Saul's," she said. "I had no idea what he was doing until he told me shortly before he died. He also told me he deliberately exposed himself to radiation."

"It wasn't exactly deliberate," Julian said. "The radiation was a consequence of modifying the bombs."

"But he knew he was exposing himself," Nana said. "Saul knew it would kill him. He did it anyway, even after all I'd sacrificed for him."

After all Nana had sacrificed? What had she sacrificed for Saul? And then an unsettling possibility came to him. "What about during the war?" he asked. "Had it been Saul's idea to alter the formulas in the documents he passed on to the Soviets?"

The record ended, the needle scratching around and around in the run-out groove.

"That was my idea," Nana said finally.

Annette let go of his hand. He could feel her tense up beside him. "Your idea?" she asked.

"Yes," Nana said. "I didn't want the Soviets to have such a powerful weapon. I hated what the communists had become. I didn't trust them. I persuaded Saul to modify the documents in a way that would make it impossible for the Soviets to build a working bomb from them."

"But how do you know Saul did this?" she asked. "He could have lied to you about what he was passing on to them."

Nana narrowed her eyes at Annette. "I'm telling you the formulas and data were wrong."

"Did you see the documents Saul gave the Soviets, Nana?"

She rubbed her pointer finger. "Yes."

He tried to keep his voice matter of fact, though his heart was pounding. "Were you working with the communists?" He waited a beat. "Were you Slugger?"

The needle scratched around and around the run-out groove.

"Yes. I was Slugger."

Even though he'd been expecting her answer, he felt a jolt. It was one thing to speculate about it, another to hear it confirmed. His grandmother had been a communist spy, the go-between running atomic-bomb secrets from Los Alamos to the Soviets. Maybe her intention had been to protect the U.S. by passing the Soviets bad info, but the magnitude of her revelation was overwhelming. And a bigger issue was gnawing at him. Did this mean his grandmother had been the woman in black? Impossible.

Annette leaned forward on the sofa. "Even if you'd seen the documents, you couldn't have known Saul had modified the information. How can you be so certain?"

"I told you the formulas and data were wrong," Nana said. "The Soviet bombs wouldn't have worked."

Why was his grandmother being so defensive? And then it hit him. "Saul wasn't the one who altered the documents, was he?"

The phonograph needle went around and around.

Nana stared at her swollen fingers. It took her a long time before she answered. "No, it wasn't Saul. I lied about that."

He felt Annette squirm beside him. Essie had been right. Nana was a liar.

His grandmother met his eye. There was desperation in hers, as though she was begging him to believe her. "Saul insisted that I pass the original documents he'd stolen to the Soviets," she said. "He believed science should have no barriers and all our allies should share scientific information." She shook her head. "But I couldn't let that happen. I knew this bomb of ours was a terrible, terrible weapon. I couldn't let the Soviets build one, too. I was afraid we would all destroy each other."

Interrogating his grandmother like this, causing her so much obvious pain was as difficult for him as it had been to let his father wash off the burned skin caused by the firecracker explosion when he'd been a little boy, but just as then, Julian had to do this.

"So if Saul wasn't willing to change the formulas, who was?" he asked. "You didn't have the expertise."

"But Isaac Goldstein did," Annette said. "He was an engineer with a strong physics background. He could have altered the formulas and measurements credibly. Were you and Isaac Goldstein working together?"

His grandmother didn't move. She stared at the three sculptures.

"Nana, did you take the documents Saul stole from Los Alamos to Isaac Goldstein, ask him to make the data unusable, and then pass them on to the Soviets?"

His grandmother took in a deep breath. "Yes."

Heroic, he tried to tell himself. Nana and Isaac Goldstein had been heroes.

"*Mon dieu.* You could have saved Isaac," Annette said. "You knew he wasn't a traitor."

"Perhaps I could have saved him, but if I had, my own brother would have been sent to the electric chair. It was an impossible choice." She shuddered. "Impossible."

"So you chose to let Isaac Goldstein die?" Annette asked.

Julian reached for her hand. "Isaac could have saved himself, Annette." He turned to his grandmother. "Why didn't he, Nana? Why did he keep your secret?"

Nana eased herself out of her chair and went to the phonograph. She lifted the tone arm and picked up the old record. Her hands trembled as she held it. The gesture reminded Julian of the moment before the boy had thrown the firecracker at him.

"Who was Yitzy, Nana?" he asked. "Was he Isaac Goldstein?"

Nana looked at him with such tenderness that Julian wasn't prepared when she answered. "Yes. Yitzy was Isaac."

Annette's fingernails dug into his palm.

Yitzy was Isaac, which meant his grandmother had once been in love with Isaac Goldstein. But that didn't mean their love had continued after they were both married to others.

Nana pressed the record against her chest. "I went to see him in prison the day before he was executed."

Oh god, he thought. *No please. Don't be the woman in black.*

"He told me he was sick over what the publicity and upcoming execution were doing to his wife and daughter," she said. "My heart went out to Betty and Sally. I knew how much they were suffering. Betty was especially tormented about how this was affecting her little girl."

He could feel Annette cringe beside him.

"But then, Yitzy told me that he'd decided to report my brother to the FBI."

Annette let out a tiny gasp, but Nana didn't seem to hear it.

"I begged him not to turn Saul in. 'Tell them I'm the spy,' I said. But Yitzy refused. He didn't trust the government. He was certain they would make me the scapegoat regardless of the truth." She wet her lips. "What could I do? I had to take care of my brother. I had promised my parents." Her cheeks drooped like a melted mask. "So I told Yitzy that if he exposed Saul, I would turn myself in."

Julian dared not look at Annette. Her grandfather had died and gone down in history as a traitor because of his grandmother. It was no longer possible to deny it. Nana was the woman in black.

"So you saved yourself and your brother." Annette's quavering voice was monotone, but Julian could hear the undercurrent of rage. "I get that. What I don't get is why my grandfather was willing to sacrifice himself and destroy his family."

Nana put the record down on the credenza and teetered back to her chair. Was she buying time, trying to make up a fresh lie to tell them?

She settled herself in the chair and gazed at the photo of Julian, Rhonda and their parents on the coffee table. "Yitzy wasn't sacrificing his entire family," Nana said, staring at the photo. "Maybe I did the wrong thing, but I was determined to protect her at all costs. And so was Yitzy."

"Protect her?" he asked, bewildered. "Protect who?"

Tears ran down Nana's wrinkled cheeks. "Our daughter. Mine and Yitzy's." She looked directly into Julian's eyes. "Your mother."

"My mother?"

He felt Annette's hand pull away. A chill invaded the room.

"What are you saying, Nana? That Isaac Goldstein is *my* grandfather? But that's impossible. Isaac Goldstein is *Annette's* grandfather."

CHAPTER 47

Julian was Isaac Goldstein's grandson.

The man she had just fallen in love with, had just made love to, was her half-cousin. How could she have not seen it? This beautiful man, with whom she'd felt a connection deeper than anything she'd ever experienced before, shared her blood.

Annette could hardly breathe. She was frozen. Unable to speak, or scream or even move.

Julian drew her close, his heart pounding. And although she could feel her own heart respond, her mind couldn't. It was frozen.

"It's okay," he whispered.

It isn't okay. It can never be okay.

She pulled away. She hated her grandfather, who had not only had an affair with Julian's grandmother, but had had a child with her. Hated him because he'd chosen to protect his mistress and their child rather than his own wife and legitimate daughter. Hated him because she loved his grandson.

Across from her, Mariasha sat in the huge turquoise chair, looking tiny and dark like a trapped animal. Annette hated her, too, for causing so much pain to her grandmother, her mother, herself, and now Julian.

She heard her own voice, small, sharp and unfamiliar. "Do you realize what you did?"

Mariasha slowly raised her head and met her eye. "Of course," she said softly. "I let him die."

This woman deserved to suffer as Annette's family had. As she and Julian now were.

"Not Isaac Goldstein," Annette said. "My grandmother and mother. Do you understand what you did to them?"

Mariasha tilted her head. She looked confused.

Annette forced the words from her icy throat. "My grandmother was Betty Goldstein. My mother is Sally Goldstein."

She watched Mariasha's face blanch.

The freeze broke and her voice came out loud and clear. "I am Isaac Goldstein's grandchild. Just like Julian."

CHAPTER 48

Isaac Goldstein's grandchild.

Mariasha pressed her hand against her pounding heart as she looked across at the two young people, agony twisting their beautiful faces.

She wished she'd died an hour ago listening to Yitzy's sweet voice on the old scratchy record. Wished she'd died before her grandson had come here. Before she had told him the truth.

And the girl.

She should have recognized the clear blue eyes the first time she'd met Annette. Yitzy's eyes. Like the cat's-eye marble she'd had as a child. But Mariasha had been distracted by Julian's attraction to this warm, lovely girl. So happy he'd finally met someone he deserved.

A moan escaped her lips. Hadn't she destroyed enough? Yitzy. Saul. And now Julian and even this unsuspecting girl.

With each destruction, she had felt her own death. And yet, God had kept her alive to suffer with her pain and guilt. *Dear God. Why didn't you take me an hour ago?*

She tried to get up from her chair to comfort these poor children, but she had no strength. All she could do was watch them sitting a few inches apart, no longer able to comfort each other.

Her grandson stood up first, his face ghostlike. He gently pulled Annette up from the sofa by her arm, then he took a step toward Mariasha. "We're leaving," he said, his voice raw. "I don't know what to say to you."

Mariasha ran her tongue over her lips and nodded.

Julian leaned toward her. Hesitated. Then he swooped over and grabbed her head in both his hands. She could feel the pressure of his palms against her ears, for a moment sealing her inside a snow globe. Then he pressed his lips hard against her forehead.

He pulled away abruptly and started toward the door. "Let's go, Annette."

He wasn't a traitor, she tried to call after them, but no words came out. *Yitzy was a kind, generous man, who had been caught in the web of my love. Who was unable to protect his family. All of you.*

The door slammed after them.

"Don't hate him," she whispered. "Hate me. I am the traitor."

January 1945

Snowflakes came down hard around them, coating the park bench, settling in his cap and on his eyelashes. He reached beneath the plaid blanket for her hands. Their eyes met. The world seemed to freeze. And for a moment, Mari felt as though they were sealed inside a snow globe. Safe, untouchable.

"Anything," Yitzy said. "You know I'll do anything you ask."

"My brother is about to make a terrible mistake. I need your help."

A foghorn sounded off the river, penetrating the stillness and shattering her illusion of safety.

He dropped her hands and looked out toward the thick snow falling over the river. His features had gone from boyish happiness to a cold hardness. She didn't understand the change that had come over him, but she continued.

"Saul has agreed to steal secrets for the Soviets, even though I begged him not to. He believes scientific knowledge belongs to everyone."

"You and I have taught him well," Yitzy said.

"Saul's being naïve," she said. "Like you and I talked about the other night, what my father believed, what you and I once believed, doesn't work. Social democracy is a myth."

"That's right," Yitzy said. "You told me you're no longer a good communist."

"And I don't believe you are either, despite the act you put on. I think you're someone, like me, who believes in peace, not the violent destruction of the world so that a particular political agenda can prevail."

He turned to her and rapidly blinked the snow off his eyelashes. "But you're also thinking about your brother, aren't you? What could happen to him if he's caught."

Mari looked away. There were small black holes in the blanket of snow that covered the ground. Weeds that had pushed their way through. She had promised Mama and Papa to always watch over Saul.

"What is it you want me to do?" Yitzy said.

She took a deep, cold breath that stung her lungs. "If I give you the documents that Saul steals from Los Alamos, would you be able to modify them in such a way that the weapons won't work if the Soviets build them?"

The world around them was silent, all sound muted by the snowfall.

"Do you realize what you're asking?"

"Yes."

Yitzy stood up from the bench and shrugged the snow off his lap and shoulders. "Bring me whatever you need me to change." He started to walk away, dragging his bad leg through the thick snow.

Mari felt miserable. She believed she was doing the right thing, and not just to protect Saul. If this terrible weapon got into the wrong hands, the potential was devastating. But she was putting Yitzy at grave risk.

"Yitzy," she called, as she ran after him.

He stopped and turned. There was something like hope in his face.

"I'm sorry." She held the wool blanket over her head as the snow cascaded around her. "I had no right to ask you to do this."

"I told you, Mariasha. I would do anything for you."

"I know, and that's what isn't fair. Forget what I asked you to do. I don't blame you for being angry with me."

He drew his head back. "You think that's why I'm upset?"

"Isn't it?"

"Oh, Mariasha." His voice broke. "You can't imagine how I felt when you asked me to meet you. It was all I could think about all week. I was hardly able to eat or sleep."

Mari let out a little gasp. Yitzy had misinterpreted the reason for their rendezvous today.

"I'd hoped you and I..." He looked at her with a terrifying intensity, his blue eyes just like the cat's-eye marble she'd had as a child.

Her heart thumped hard inside her chest. Had she been hoping for that, too? Had that been the real reason she'd asked him to meet her today?

"I love you," he said. "I've loved you since the first moment I saw you."

Stop, she tried to say. You have a wife who adores you. I adore my Aaron. But images of the handsome boy who had sung so sweetly at Camp Kindervelt, the passionate college student who had held her at Coney Island, the young man who had once been her life, blocked her words.

"Say you haven't stopped loving me." Yitzy grabbed her hands. "Say it."

The smell of damp wool was suffocating. "Oh, Yitzy. This is wrong." She tried to pull her hands out of his, but he held fast.

"I can't help myself," he said. "Believe me, I've tried, but you're the one I think about when I'm falling asleep, when I wake up in the morning. Please, Mariasha. Tell me you feel the same."

"You left me," she whispered. "When Mama died and Saul was sick. You left me when I needed you most."

"Oh my darling, I was a stupid fool. I've regretted that more than anything I've ever done. You are the love of my life."

She willed her heart to stop pounding, her breathing to slow down, but her body wouldn't listen. Reason had left her. Nothing seemed to matter as much as Yitzy. The feelings from all those years of yearning for him rose up. And when he leaned forward to kiss her, she couldn't pull away. She felt his warm lips against hers, gentle at first. And then he pushed against her with ferocity and crushed her against him.

"Mariasha," he whispered. "You are my life."

She was dazed and breathless as Yitzy led her from the park in the deepening snow. They walked north, farther and farther away from the familiar tenements and shops, away from thoughts of Aaron, to a place where everything was shrouded in white, as though reality had been erased. And although she told herself to stop, to turn back, her legs and heart propelled her forward.

Yitzy unlocked the door to a store and bundled her inside. Around her pipes and copper spheres, the smell of oil. Yitzy mumbled something about an army buddy, store closed early for the Sabbath, as he led her to the back room.

Then, as though there were no other possible choice, they fell into each other's arms.

And after they made love, Mari lay on the narrow daybed in Yitzy's arms and listened to the beating of his heart. Snow completely covered the small window, shutting out the world. Safe and untouchable.

Yitzy began to sing softly.

One promise I will make to you
Wherever I am, whatever you choose.
I will love you till my last breath's drawn
I will love you long after my time is gone.

All around the dim room were pipes and rods and copper spheres shaped like heads. Faces. Watching her.

She sat up abruptly.

"What's wrong?" Yitzy asked. "What is it?"

Mari pressed her hand over her pounding heart. She felt sick inside, knowing that as much as they loved each other, they had just done something unforgivable.

She promised herself it would never happen again.

And that no matter what, no one would ever learn of what she and Yitzy had done.

CHAPTER 49

Annette had been unable to look at Julian, nor speak to him in the elevator ride down from Mariasha's apartment. They stepped outside into the courtyard and their eyes finally met.

Please don't say you'll call me, she thought. *Don't demean what we had.*

He reached out to touch her cheek, then drew back his hand. He spun around and headed down the street toward Brooklyn or somewhere far away.

She walked in the opposite direction, increasing the distance between them with each step, not knowing where she was going, but only that she needed to get away from this place.

Her quest for the truth about her grandfather was over. She now knew exactly who Isaac Goldstein had been and what he had done, but there was no satisfaction in her discovery, only more pain.

She kept walking and walking until the sound of children's laughter broke through her anguish. She was at the entrance to a small playground. Mounds of cleared snow were piled up against the fence. She sat on a bench and watched children in colorful snowsuits climb the jungle gym, hang from swings, run shrieking down the snow-cleared paths. It reminded her of the playground near where she grew up in Paris. Her mother used to take her there when she was little.

Mama. What would the truth about Isaac Goldstein mean to her?

He hadn't been the traitor the world believed, that Mama had believed. Yes, he had been a communist spy, but he had sabotaged the information that was passed on to the Soviets. So, in one sense, he had acted valiantly. But what he'd done to his family—could that ever be excused or forgiven?

That was not for her to decide.

She took out her phone, oddly relieved as she pressed the speed-dial number and listened to it ring on the other end.

The familiar voice answered, tinged with the usual worry. "Annette? Is everything all right?"

She looked up at the sky. Blue. No clouds. The air was warmed by the sun.

"Mama," she said. "It's time for you to come home."

CHAPTER 50

His feet were moving, taking him farther and farther away from Annette. It wasn't until Julian had crossed the Williamsburg Bridge that he realized he was in Brooklyn.

Brooklyn. Where Nana had been born. Where she'd watched her brother play stickball and mended his overalls. Where her stories of the past had their beginning.

But there would be no more of Nana's stories for him. No more stories, and no more gentle counsel. One of the worst parts of his grandmother's deception was that she could never again be a trusted haven for him. He had no one safe to turn to. Even Annette was gone.

He was startled by the sound of a boat horn. His wandering had taken him to the edge of the East River. Across the rippling blue-black water was Manhattan. The park where he and Annette had sat appeared very different from this perspective. Rolling mounds of white. Broad, leafless trees. Skyscrapers, not low-rise buildings, against a blue sky.

The sky was just as clear as the first time he'd gone to the park with Annette last Sunday, when they'd hardly known each other. They had talked about their childhoods and how their mothers had been unable to show them love.

A small boat sped along in the river, passing a slow-moving cargo ship.

Would knowing the truth help his mother heal from her own wounds? All he knew for certain was he was tired of lies and deception. His grandmother had pre-empted fate by deciding who should live and die. He would not make that choice. He would tell his mother what he had just learned and let her handle it her own way.

He took out his cell phone and touched the speed-dial number.

His mother answered, her voice concerned. "Julian?"

"Mom," he said. "We need to talk about Nana. I'm coming home."

It was only after he disconnected from the call that he realized this was the first time he'd called her 'Mom' in almost twenty years.

CHAPTER 51

Mariasha shivered. Why was it so cold in the room? She got up carefully from her chair and went over to the radiator. There was no heat coming out of it. She banged it, hurting her hand. She brought her fingers to her lips. Cold. No heat coming from her body.

Over. Everything was nearly over.

She found a sheet of paper and a pen in one of the credenza drawers, then put Yitzy's record on before she returned to her chair.

His beautiful voice rang out.

Embrace me, disgrace me
Just don't erase me.
You are the apple of my soul
If you love me, don't let me go.

The music transported her back to that Friday afternoon when she and Yitzy had made love in the back room of his friend's store. They had both agreed. They would remain friends because the idea of never seeing each other again was unbearable to both of them, but they would never again come together as lovers. And then they swore that they would never speak to each other or anyone else about this one lapse. This one blissful and unpardonable afternoon of ecstasy.

And perhaps she would have been able to keep their secret, but destiny wasn't finished with her games. A few weeks later, when Mariasha realized she was pregnant, she knew she had no choice but to tell Aaron. She was prepared for him to throw her and Yitzy's baby out of his life. But Aaron was too kind a man for such things. He accepted her promise that she would never again cheat on him and took the birth of their daughter to be a blessing.

For almost five years, only Mariasha and Aaron knew the truth about Essie's real father. But that changed one beautiful summer's day.

August 1950

Mari recognized Yitzy, even from behind. He was sitting on their bench beneath the lush oak tree. There was something about the upward slope of his shoulders and the way he held his head. Proud and confident, just like the fourteen-year-old boy who had once stood in front of a room of campers to sing the *Internationale.* Yitzy was wearing a straw hat and throwing breadcrumbs at the sparrows that pecked in the grass around his feet.

He turned when she was still a few feet away and stood up, favoring his good leg. His smile lit up his face. "I thought that was you sneaking up behind me."

They gave each other a hug, as had been their practice the past few years when they would get together with their families. But this time, it seemed Yitzy held her a moment longer than usual. Her heart skipped. Maybe she shouldn't have come. Even after all this time she wasn't sure she could trust herself alone with him.

"Glad you could make it," he said.

The Saturday before, when they'd been out to the movies with Betty and Aaron, he'd slipped her a note asking to meet.

"Is everything all right?" she asked.

She followed his gaze to the wide avenue behind them where a black car slowed, then sped up until it was out of sight.

"Let's sit down," he said. "We may not have much time, so I'll get right to the point."

His tone alarmed her.

"That car was probably the FBI. They've been keeping a close watch on me."

"On you?"

"I'm sure you read in the papers that they arrested Bertie Shevsky and Joey Bartow."

"I have." In the last few months, people with communist leanings had been picked up and questioned. And since the Soviets had detonated a test atomic bomb recently, there had been a number of investigations into the leaking of secrets from Los Alamos. "But you had nothing to do with Bertie or Joey," she said. "Why would the FBI be watching you?"

"Apparently they brought in Flossie Heller for questioning. She told them I was part of Bertie's and Joey's spy ring. In fact, she said I was the one calling the shots."

"But that's a lie."

"Of course it's a lie." He threw another handful of crumbs at the birds. "But it's a good way for Flossie to get Bertie and Joey lighter sentences and keep herself out of prison. Right now, the FBI's game is to bring in people they think have information about atomic spy rings and give them 'get-out-of-jail-free' cards if they provide the name of someone higher up in the system."

"Have they questioned you yet?"

"They did indeed. Right after Flossie pointed her finger at me."

Mari took a deep breath to settle her panic. If they had questioned Yitzy, then Saul might be next. And for Saul there was no get-out-of-jail-free card.

"What did you tell them?" she asked.

"The truth. That I had nothing to do with any of Flossie's crowd during the war."

"But they're still watching you. Do you think they know about Saul?"

He shook his head. "It doesn't seem that way to me. In fact, these guys are pretty clueless. I think they're under some pressure from the politicians to come up with a scapegoat to persuade everyone the Soviets stole the bomb from the U.S."

She was quiet. There were people picnicking on blankets in the grass. Couples walking hand in hand along the path beside the river. Across the water, she could see the low, familiar Brooklyn skyline. It was a beautiful summer day, but her stomach was in knots. "Do you think you're in any danger?"

"Nah," he said. "They'll never be able to prove a connection between me and Bertie or Joey."

"But there's a connection to Saul."

"No one's looking for Saul," he said. "Stop worrying about him.

"But what if they pressure you to give them a name?"

He jerked his head back and studied her from beneath the brim of his straw hat. His right eyelid drooped like a falling curtain. "You think I'd ever give your brother away, Mariasha?"

"No. I'm sorry. I shouldn't have said that." She took off her white gloves, looked at the gold wedding band Aaron had given her. She was worried, but what could she say? She had to trust him.

Yitzy rested his hand over hers. "It's going to be all right."

She let out a shaky breath.

"I know you and I promised each other we would never talk about that afternoon," he said, "but I'm going to break that promise."

"Let's not, Yitzy. Please."

He held up his hand. "I told you then how much I love you, Mariasha. That hasn't changed. It will never change."

She couldn't meet his eye. Her mind didn't want to go there, but her heart was making its own choices. It ached inside her.

"I think about that afternoon every single day," Yitzy said.

"Me, too," she said softly.

"You do?" His voice lifted. Just like it did in the song he'd recorded for her.

"Not that way," she said quickly, then felt her cheeks grow warm.

He frowned. "What way then?"

"Nothing. I didn't mean anything."

"Yes, you did." He looked across the river at the tugboats pushing larger ships. "Essie's birthday is in October."

Mari felt an awful weight pressing against her.

"I always wondered." He threw a few crumbs at the birds. They attacked them. "Her blue eyes. Her blonde curls. But Aaron's such a loving father that I stopped hoping."

"You hoped?" she said, stunned.

"Of course I hoped. Do you think anything could give me greater joy than for us to have made a beautiful child like Essie?"

"I promised Aaron I would never tell you she's yours."

"Essie's my daughter," he whispered. His eyes watered. He rubbed them with the back of his hands.

She had never guessed her secret would affect him so deeply.

"And you're saying that Aaron knows the truth?"

She nodded.

"Aaron's a great man."

"Yes," she said. "He is."

"I want you to know something, Mariasha." He lifted her chin with his finger. "Even if Essie never learns that I'm her real father, I love her as much as I love her mother, and I promise you that I will do whatever's in my power to keep her safe."

The record was over. The needle made an ugly sound as it went around and around in the run-out groove, but Mariasha didn't have the strength to get up and set it back on the record.

She shivered. It was so cold that she could hardly hold the pen in her hand, but she had to write this letter. She needed to tell Essie what she had never had the guts to tell her before.

She began to write.

Precious Daughter of my Heart:

My Essie. You were named for my mother, Esther, the strongest woman I've ever known. If only I could have been more like her...

CHAPTER 52

Essie heard the door close as her son left the house after telling her of her mother's treachery. It was ironic that despite the awfulness of the situation, Julian was more her son than he'd been since his father died. 'Mom,' he called her for the first time in twenty years.

So perhaps she should be grateful to her mother for this. But how could she be grateful to Mariasha Lowe for anything after all the years of pain? Now this fresh insult. Would it ever end with this hateful woman? But one thing Essie realized was if she didn't confront her mother now, she would never be free of her.

A taxi dropped her off in front of her mother's building. Essie's childhood home, where she'd played hopscotch on the sidewalk, thrown a pink rubber ball against the courtyard wall. She used to play with Sally Goldstein. They'd been best friends until Sally and her mother moved away. Essie had only vaguely understood there was shame in the Goldstein family. She knew it the last couple of times the two girls had played together, Sally unable to laugh or meet Essie's eye.

I could have been that little girl.

She used the key she still kept on her key ring to get into the building, then took the elevator up to the fourth floor. The elevator seemed smaller than she remembered it, as it often did when she returned.

When was the last time she'd been here? Two years ago? Three? Longer, since she'd seen her mother? Essie called her mother from time to time, but always felt even more discouraged after each brief conversation. She tried to persuade herself that Mariasha didn't matter to her, but that didn't work. Essie had been drinking more and more in the last few years, trying to numb an ache that wouldn't go away. An ache she'd inadvertently passed on to her son.

Sure, she could blame Julian for pulling away from her, but he had been a child. She was his mother. She should have tried harder, but she didn't. She receded into an ice chest, just as her mother had done with her.

At the front door, she hesitated. She could turn around and leave things alone. Live with her anger, just as she always had.

No. No more avoidance. She was finally going to have it out with her mother.

She knocked, her heart beating wildly.

No answer.

Perhaps she was napping or showering. Essie used her key and stepped into the foyer.

Memories flooded her. Her mother calling. *Leave your shoes in the foyer, sweetheart.*

Her father hugging her. *How's my Esseleh? Did you have a good day at school?*

There was a scratching sound coming from the living room. She listened. The needle from the old phonograph at the end of a record. She remembered the sound from her childhood.

She peered into the living room. It was exactly the same as when she was growing up. The bulbous art deco sofa and chairs. Coffee table shaped like a boomerang. TV cabinet with the old black-and-white television that hadn't worked in thirty years.

Her mother was asleep on the turquoise chair. It had always been her favorite place to sit. It faced the picture windows and three sculptures. *Woman Wearing New Hat, Man Reading, Boy Playing Stickball.* Her mother's parents and brother. Still Essie's family, even though she now, apparently, had a different father.

She took a step closer to her mother. She didn't want to wake her, not just yet. Didn't want to end these few minutes of memories with an ugly confrontation.

Her mother's head was against the arm of the chair, eyes closed, mouth open. Essie's heart jumped. How tiny she looked in her black sweater and pants against the large chair. She had seemed like such an enormous presence when Essie was a girl. A beautiful, famous sculptress with a larger than life personality. She was beautiful still, even with her wrinkles and sunken cheeks.

There was something on her lap. A book. On top of it a paper. A letter she was writing? A pen had fallen to the floor.

The phonograph needle went around and around.

She took another step, finally admitting to herself what she had known the moment she'd entered the room and seen her mother absolutely still. No movement in her chest. No fluttering in her eyelids.

Mariasha Lowe was dead.

"My mother is dead," Essie said to the room. She waited for the stab of pain that had hit her when she learned of her father's death, and then again when her husband died. But she felt nothing.

"Good," she said. "I'm glad you're dead."

Nothing. No pain. No joy. Just the sound of scratching as the phonograph needle went around and around.

She moistened her lips and approached her mother's body.

There would be no confrontation now. No resolution. Her mother was dead.

She reached for the letter in her lap. The handwriting was barely legible, but as soon as she'd read the first couple of lines, she knew things weren't completely finished with Mariasha Lowe.

Precious Daughter of my Heart:

My Essie. You were named for my mother, Esther, the strongest woman I've ever known. If only I could have been more like her.

Esseleh, your father called you. Oh, he loved you more than life itself, even though he knew he hadn't made you. He forgave me for that. No, more than forgave. He thanked me for giving him a daughter, because he'd been unable to have children of his own. And you lit up his life, as you did mine.

I wish I had told you how much I love you, but my world was forever darkened the moment Yitzy Goldstein was executed. Every time I looked at you, I remembered that I was responsible for your father's death. Guilt kept me from hugging you, kissing you, telling you how much I love you.

Oh my darling girl, how can I ever make up to you the pain I've caused you?

I can only tell you that Yitzy Goldstein, the father who made you, was a good man. A kind and generous man. And you were the product of the purest, the most beautiful love. I only wish ...

The letter ended there, the 'h' in 'wish' running off the page.

Essie stood without moving, as the phonograph needle scratched around and around, making a shrill noise like the scream that was forming in her head.

"Liar," she said. "You're such a liar."

She went to the old Victrola and lifted the tone arm.

The record was ancient, with a hand-written label.

For Mariasha, it said. *From Yitzy.*

A heavy pressure pushed against her chest. She cranked up the phonograph and cued the tone arm.

A wistful voice sang a cappella. Soft and distant, like it was coming to her from another world. But the words were clear and strong.

Believe me, deceive me
Darling, just don't leave me
You are the apple of my soul
If you love me, don't let me go.

Her real father.

She thought about her mother's letter. *You were the product of the purest, the most beautiful love.* Was that part true?

Essie sank down beside her mother on the chair and held her small, stiff body. Hugged her tight. She smelled the citrusy fragrance that had always been her mother's and a memory came to her.

Her mother combing her hair when she was very little. *You have your father's golden curls.* Then a kiss. *I love you, Essie. More than you'll ever know.*

The pain started deep, deep inside, taking her breath away, as her father continued to sing.

One promise I will make to you
Wherever I am, whatever you choose.
I will love you till my last breath's drawn
I will love you long after my time is gone.

Tears ran down Essie's cheeks as the pain erupted.

"I love you, too, Mommy. More than you'll ever know."

CHAPTER 53

The cemetery reminded Julian of a park. Low rolling hills, paths, benches, lots of thick-trunked trees that had probably been here for a hundred years. If not for the rows and rows of headstones, this could have been Central Park.

He had never been to a cemetery, at least not one where people he knew were buried. When his father died, there had been a service at a funeral home, but no burial. A few months afterward, his mother and sister had taken his father's ashes to be scattered in the bay, but Julian had refused to go with them. He hadn't wanted yet another reminder that his father was gone.

With Nana, though, it was different. Rather than upheaval, he had a sense of quiet, as though something significant had come to an end. Then why couldn't he feel anything?

He stood arm-in-arm with his mother at Nana's grave as they listened to the rabbi speak and recite prayers in Hebrew. Rhonda was on Julian's other side, next to her husband.

Only a handful of other people had come. A couple of Mariasha's neighbors. A man who introduced himself as a collector of her sculptures. Someone from a museum. Most everyone from Nana's past was dead.

Julian hadn't cried when his mother had called him with the news on Thursday evening. He hadn't cried in the two-and-a-half days since he learned of her death. Would he ever mourn her? Ever forgive her?

A grave had been dug beside Aaron Lowe's. Half the headstone read '*Aaron Lowe 1910-1984. Loving husband, father, and grandfather.*' The blank side was for Mariasha, as per her instructions.

Nana had chosen to be buried beside her husband. Out of duty? Devotion? Love? Julian wondered where Isaac Goldstein was buried.

The weather had been unseasonably warm over the last couple of days, confusing a few of the trees where Julian noticed tiny green buds.

The rabbi finished his eulogy. Julian was surprised when his mother dropped his arm and turned toward the mourners.

"My mother was a complex woman, who had been faced with an impossible choice in her life," she said.

Impossible choice. Nana's words, too.

"But she was human, which meant she made mistakes. But whatever she may have done wrong, I know in her heart, she loved her family. All of us."

The rabbi picked up the shovel, scooped up dirt, then flung it into the grave, over the coffin. His mother did the same. Then Rhonda. Julian shook his head when the rabbi handed him the shovel. Maybe his mother and sister were able to move on, but Julian wasn't quite there.

The rabbi led the group in the Mourner's Kaddish, the traditional prayer for the dead. Julian remembered his mother reciting it when his father died.

The ceremony was over. The neighbors and the others came over to the family and expressed their condolences, then left.

Julian stared down into the open pit at the casket that held Nana's physical remains.

"How are you doing, Jules?" Rhonda asked.

"Still numb."

"Are you able to forgive her?"

"Are you?"

"It's different for me," his sister said. "I'd written her off years ago, but I know how much you loved her."

"I haven't cried," he said.

Rhonda touched his shoulder.

Their mother was beckoning them. She was a short distance away with the rabbi, her hand on top of a dark gray headstone, which looked much older than the ones near Nana's gravesite.

"I don't think anyone's visited these graves in many years," she said, as Julian and Rhonda approached.

He read the headstone his mother's hand rested on. Below several Hebrew letters, it said, '*Beloved Mother, Esther Hirsch. Died March 15, 1936, Age 42 Years.*' There was a well-preserved photo in the upper right-hand corner of a young woman, hair piled on her head, a determined expression on her face. Very different from the sad, broken woman in the sketch Saul had made of her.

"Esther Hirsch was my grandmother. Your great-grandmother." His mother's voice caught. "I was named for her."

That's what Nana had written in her final letter.

"And this." His mother touched the headstone beside it. "This was my grandfather."

'*My Beloved Husband and Our Dear Father Abraham Hirsch. Died June 8, 1925. Age 34.*' There was a place for a picture, but it must have fallen out some time ago.

"They were both so young," Rhonda said.

Woman Wearing New Hat, Man Reading, Julian thought. Nana had kept them in her life right until the end. She had made them a promise to always watch over Saul.

"And here's my uncle's grave," his mother said.

'*Saul Hirsch. My Brother. Died October 23, 1958. Age 36.*' And beneath his name, an epitaph, very likely written by Nana. *'If only his dream to play baseball had come true.'*

Boy Playing Stickball.

If only. Would Isaac Goldstein have been executed? Probably not. Without Saul at Los Alamos, it was unlikely Isaac would have been involved with the information passed on to the Soviets. Would Isaac have had an affair with Mariasha? That was something he could never know. But one thing he did know was that if Isaac and Mariasha hadn't consummated their love, Julian wouldn't now exist.

The rabbi was reciting the Mourner's Kaddish.

Yit-gadal v'yit-kadash sh'mei raba

Julian didn't know what the Hebrew words meant, but he found the cadence of the prayer comforting.

He thought about Nana losing both her parents when she was young. Only seven when her father had died. Then her mother. And all she had was her kid brother.

Impossible choice.

He was only just beginning to understand the complexity of what Nana had been faced with. Saul wasn't simply her brother, he had been her responsibility. And so, she protected him up to the end, but in doing so she sacrificed the man she loved.

Oseh shalom bim'romav hu ya'aseh shalom

Aleinu v'al kol Yis'ra'eil v'im'ru

The rabbi met his eye. "Now say '*Amen*'."

Julian's mother and sister said, '*Amen,*' but he said nothing.

"*Amen,*" said a shaky unfamiliar female voice behind them.

He turned to the woman, tall like his mother, who stood beside a tree. She wore a camelhair coat that hung loosely on her narrow frame, and had thin white hair and blue eyes. A petite woman in a long black coat came from behind the tree and slipped her arm through the woman's.

It took a pulse beat for him to process her without the red ski jacket, then his heart lurched. Annette!

The two women approached. "I hope you don't mind our being here," Annette said to Julian's mother. "I read that the funeral was today."

"You're very welcome here." His mother stared at the tall woman. "Sally?"

"Essie," she replied, in a small childlike voice.

The two women studied each other, perhaps trying to find something in each other's faces of the children they'd been so many years before.

Julian felt something in the pit of his stomach he couldn't identify. They were daughters of the same father. Two women whose lives might have been reversed had Nana chosen differently.

"I'm very sorry about your grandmother." Annette was only inches from him. Agonizingly close. "Whatever she did doesn't change that she loved you very much."

He couldn't bear to look at her or smell her now-familiar scent. "Thank you," he said, focusing instead on their mothers.

The two women had taken each other's hands. For an instant, he was reminded of the two little girls in the photo. Then Sally kissed Essie on both cheeks, and walked quickly away.

He felt the gentlest pressure on his chest. Annette's hand. He wanted to clamp it against his heart with all his might, but he knew she would pull away.

Her eyes were shiny, brimming with sadness, maybe even regret. "*Au revoir,* Julian."

"*Au revoir*," he whispered.

"Remember," she said. "Revoir means to see again, not goodbye." Then she turned and hurried after her mother.

He remembered. Their first conversation about her name. Annette Revoir. She had said *revoir* meant to see again, not goodbye.

Would he ever see her again?

The blue sky, rolling hills, thick old trees, and rows and rows of headstones pressed in around him. It was quiet, as though something significant had happened and the world would never again be the same.

He sank to his knees by his grandmother's grave, overwhelmed by a pain so crushing it took his breath away.

Nana was gone. Nana, who had watched over him when he felt he had no one else, who had always loved him unconditionally.

Gone.

He inhaled sharply, the smell of sweet, rich earth and budding trees filling his lungs. Then he threw a handful of dirt into her grave, and at last felt her release.

"*Au revoir*, Nana."

CHAPTER 54

Au revoir, Julian.

Annette and her mother hurried from Mariasha's gravesite. No backward glances. Would she ever see him again or did *au revoir* really mean goodbye?

"Thank you for making me go to see Essie," her mother said, as they stepped outside the cemetery gates. "*J'avais peur.*"

"I know you were afraid."

"She's my half-sister," Mama said, more to herself than to Annette. "I thought it would be strange to see her, but it wasn't. I think I always felt a special bond with her."

"I'm glad."

The heels of their shoes tapped against the sidewalk as cars sped by on the wide boulevard.

"I like her son," Mama said.

Annette didn't answer, afraid her voice might break.

When they got home from the cemetery, Mama sat on the sofa while Annette went to the kitchen alcove to make them *chocolat chaud*. She brought the milk in the saucepan to a slow boil, whisked in finely chopped bittersweet chocolate, then added a little brown sugar, just like Grandma Betty used to make it. Just as she'd herself done a few days before for Julian. The memory hurt, but she tried to ignore the pain. She and Julian had shared many beautiful things. Even if they never saw each other again, she wasn't going to block out her sweet memories the way her mother had done of her own past.

She brought the two mugs of cocoa to the sofa, where Mama was thumbing through Grandma Betty's photo album.

Her mother took a sip. "This tastes just like your grandmother's."

Annette nodded, and sat beside her, close enough to see the photos. The first time she'd shown Mama the album, just after Grandma Betty had died, her mother had been reluctant to look at the old photos. Now, she lingered on each one.

Mama turned slowly past her parents' wedding photos, past the pictures of the Goldsteins with the Lowes, past pictures of family and friends long dead. Something slipped out from behind one of the pasted-in photos. It had apparently been stuck there all these years. Mama picked up the faded black-and-white snapshot, and Annette studied it over her shoulder. Her mother as a young child with her parents.

The three of them were sitting on an Adirondack chair, Grandma Betty on one of Isaac's knees, Mama, her hair in two thick braids, on the other. Grandma Betty wore a halter and shorts and Isaac was in a striped T-shirt. They were all laughing.

Mama turned the photo over, read it, then handed it to Annette.

With the two loves of my life in the Catskill Mountains, July 1950.

The penmanship was stronger and less fussy than Grandma Betty's, and Annette realized it was her grandfather's handwriting. He'd probably put the photo into the album, perhaps intending to paste it in some day. She wondered if Grandma Betty had ever seen it or had known it was there.

The photo had been taken a couple of months before Isaac was arrested—so Mama was only five—and it was very likely the last one of her mother and grandparents together.

"I remember this day," Mama said. "I remember being happy."

With the two loves of my life, Isaac had written.

Annette took a sip of cocoa, tasting the bittersweet chocolate.

Whatever Mariasha had meant to him, her grandfather had loved his wife and daughter, too. Annette believed that. And as much as he'd hurt Mama, and Grandma Betty, and even herself, she understood the impossible choice he'd been forced to make, and it saddened her that he'd been put through that.

Mama slipped the snapshot in her pocket, then closed the album and hugged it against her chest, as she stared across the room at the bricked-in fireplace.

That's what Mama had always been, Annette realized. A bricked-in hearth without enough oxygen for fire to burn in it. Unable to love or be loved. But now, perhaps, that was changing.

For both of them.

Annette put her mug on the trunk and scooted closer to her mother. She slipped her arm around her mother's shoulders. Her mother winced at the touch, then relaxed.

"You know I love you very much, Mama."

Her mother looked at her, narrowing her eyes as though she was troubled. Then she reached out and touched Annette's hair. "Would you like me to braid your hair like Grandma Betty used to do?"

Forever hugs.

"*Oui,* Mama. I would like that very much."

CHAPTER 55

The morning after Nana's funeral, Julian awoke to warmth. Without Sephora there to prop open the balcony door, his apartment was no longer cold. But it wasn't enough to make him want to stay. He got out of bed and wandered around the sterile rooms for the last time. It had never felt like home and never would.

He called the landlord and agreed to forfeit his security deposit to get out of his lease. Then he sent Sephora a text message that she was welcome to all the furniture. He glanced at her headshot on his phone, but felt nothing except relief that she was gone from his life. He deleted her from his contacts.

His clothes all fit in a large suitcase, and his chess set in his backpack. He carried his art portfolio separately, and stepped outside his apartment. He stared at his reflection in the black lacquered door for the last time. Still blurry.

Goodbye, whoever you are, he thought. *I hope you find your real self soon.*

His mother had sounded pleased when he called to ask if he could stay in his old room for a few days until he found a new apartment. He got to Forest Hills in the afternoon, while his mom was still at the clinic, brought his suitcase and backpack upstairs, and put his portfolio on his childhood desk. He hadn't been up here in years. His old microscope, protected by a vinyl cover, was still there, along with the four boxes of slides he'd once examined with fascination. No dust anywhere. Had his mom kept the room clean all this time?

The bedroom was mostly unchanged from before he'd left for college when he was sixteen. Blues and grays and a large window that overlooked the backyard where he and his dad would occasionally toss a ball around. The smell was even the same. Like unwashed gym socks. It made him feel as though he'd never left.

He plopped down on the too-soft mattress on his bed and put his arms behind his head like he always did as a kid. On the wall to his left were several pen-and-ink superhero drawings he'd made as a kid. Funny—he'd thought he had thrown these away. Now, he remembered how he'd carefully framed each one, then hung each drawing so he could see it from his bed. Why had he forgotten that?

He took in his collection of anatomical posters on the opposite wall—the skeletal, muscular, vascular, and nervous systems. He used to stare at them in the semi-darkness before he fell asleep and recite the specific details he'd memorized, but couldn't see.

He turned to the left, then back to the right. Art and medicine. There hadn't been any conflict between them. They'd always been two halves of the same whole.

That's when the truth hit him. He had always wanted to become a physician. No one had stopped him from following his dreams. No one, except himself.

The revelation was thrilling, and he wanted to tell Annette. He reached for his phone and scrolled to her contact info. There was her headshot. She was smiling at him, and his heart contracted in a spasm of pain. Annette was no longer in his life. He could delete her from his contacts, but he knew he never would. He clicked off his phone and closed his eyes.

He awoke with a start, smelling smoke. Where was he? Then he remembered. His childhood bedroom. His mother had probably gotten home while he had dozed off and made a fire in the fireplace.

He went downstairs. With the fire going, the living room was warm and homey, like it had been when Dad was alive. Saul's painting was gone from above the fireplace mantel. In its place was an enlarged framed family photo taken on Julian's sixth birthday, right here in this living room. Rhonda was sixteen, her curly black hair in ripples on her shoulders like a gypsy's. Dad was grinning, his arm around Rhonda. Julian, wearing Ninja Turtle pajamas, was on his mother's lap, cuddled against her. Both of them were smiling, as though this was the most natural thing in the world.

"I hope I didn't disturb you," his mother said from the entrance to the room. "I saw you were napping."

"I guess I was more tired than I realized."

"It's been a strain," she said. "I've got dinner going, but it'll be awhile. Are you interested in a game of chess?"

"Sure," he said, relieved to have something to occupy his thoughts other than Annette, though surprised his mother had suggested a game she rarely played.

He brought his wooden chess pieces down from his room, then arranged them on the game table. He and his mother sat down to play. The strategies came back to him quickly, even though it had been years since he'd played. He was surprised by how challenging an opponent his mother was, matching his moves with her own. The game was almost at a stalemate. Then his mother moved her queen, blocking most escape routes for his king. It was clear to him that it was only a matter of a few moves before he would lose.

He gently tipped over his king. "I resign," he said, following the chess etiquette instilled in him as a child. He reached over the table to shake her hand. It was soft and warm, her grip strong. Something familiar about it. "Good game," he said.

"I had a lot of practice," she said.

"You did? When?"

"When you were young, you and I played most nights and weekends."

"We did?" He was perplexed. "I only remember playing with Dad."

But now, it was coming back to him. Feeling upset with himself for losing a game. His mother on the other side of the chess table. How he'd reach across to shake her hand. Soft and warm, her grip strong.

"What else do you remember about your father?" she asked.

"He took me to ball games. We'd shoot hoops." He thought for a moment. "And I remember after I got hit by the firecracker when I was a kid how he took me into the shower to wash off the dead skin on my arms. I think he cried harder than I did."

"That was me," she said quietly.

"You?"

"I was the one who went into the shower with you. Your father was too squeamish, and I'm the doctor, after all."

How could he have been so mistaken? Then the real memory started to take hold. His arms began to tingle with remembered pain. The spray of water in his eyes. The agony growing. *Stop! Please stop.* His mother in a blue one-piece bathing suit. Water running through her hair and down her face. Tears glistening in her eyes. *I'm sorry. I'm so sorry I wasn't there to protect you.*

His mother had said those words, not his father. She had always loved him, even though Julian had denied it.

A piece of wood crackled in the fireplace. Julian turned. His eyes were drawn to the photo of his family above the mantel.

Had he been misleading himself about other things because it was easier than accepting the truth?

"You know, Mom," he said. "I spent most of my life convincing myself that my unhappiness was your fault. That everything I did was to please you. I gave up painting for you, went to medical school for you, got a PhD for you. I created a barrier between us, and reinvented a past that had you playing the villain."

She looked away. "But I was the villain. After your father died, I should have reached out to you."

"Maybe, but even if you had, I probably would have pushed you away." He leaned toward her. "I've been my own worst enemy, haven't I?"

"It seems to run in our family." Her eyes looked pained. "I did the same thing with my mother."

"Maybe it's time to stop blaming ourselves and each other," he said. "Maybe it's time for us to move forward."

"I'd like that."

He reached across the chessboard and took his mother's hand. Soft and warm, her grip strong. Just as it had always been for him.

CHAPTER 56

Three months later

The East River Park was filled with people, some on blankets in the grass, others jogging along the waterfront path. The park was completely transformed from three months before, the last time Annette had been here with Julian. The trees were no longer barren, and the patches of dirty snow and mud were gone from the fields. Instead, oaks, elms, and maples gushed pale green leaves, and a thick rug of grass covered the grounds.

Annette hugged the thick bundle of papers against her chest, as she crossed the wide field where kids had been playing football that last time. In front of her, the Williamsburg Bridge stretched across the blue-gray river, the low silhouette of Brooklyn backlit by the morning sun.

She sat on their bench, shaded by the enormous oak, and left the heavy Sunday newspaper unopened on her lap. She could smell the still-fresh newsprint and shuddered.

Had she made a mistake?

But everyone had been behind her to do it. Bill especially. He'd said that not only was it important for her as a journalist, but she needed to write the article so she could finally emerge from the shadow of her grandfather's false legacy. She'd been hesitant, worried about reopening old wounds and hurting fresh victims. But much to her surprise, both Essie and Rhonda had wanted her to write it. All of it, they'd insisted—including their Uncle Saul's controversial role. It was important to them that the world learned to what lengths some people would go to safeguard peace. They didn't care that they might be tarnished by their previously unknown relationship to Isaac Goldstein.

What amazed her more, though, was how supportive her mother had been, despite having already suffered from enough public exposure to last a lifetime. But this time was different, Mama had said. This time, it was the complete story. This time, it was Annette's story.

But it was also Julian's. And although he'd responded to her email about writing the article with a terse, "OK with me," he probably hadn't considered all the implications. Of course, at the time she'd conceived the article, she hadn't either. She had sent it to a minor editor she knew at the *New York Times*, expecting a rejection, or at best, a shortened, watered-down version of her submission that would be buried somewhere in the middle of a weekday edition. So when she'd received the call from a senior editor, she had been elated. Then shock and dread set in. How would Julian cope with this very public exposé of his family? Had Annette inadvertently relegated him to a life of shame and shadows, like she had known as the granddaughter of the treacherous Isaac Goldstein, or would Julian see beyond that?

A flock of small brown sparrows settled on the grass near her.

When she'd emailed Julian about meeting this morning, her thoughts had been muddled, her emotions still raw and exposed. Aside from that brief email exchange about her writing the article, they hadn't communicated or seen each other since Mariasha's funeral. But that didn't mean she'd stopped thinking about him. The truth was—she couldn't stop thinking of him.

A shuffling sound startled her.

She turned, and there he was.

Her heart crashed against her lungs, taking her breath away.

A smile lit up Julian's face. His black hair was longish and his face clean-shaven, making the dimple in his chin more pronounced. He wore light blue scrubs, covered with what looked like scribbles. He looked…happy.

Was she about to take that away from him?

He slid next to her on the bench. He hesitated for barely an instant, then his arms tightened around her. She fit against his breastbone, beneath his chin, just like she remembered, and it felt so right. She filled her lungs with his rich licorice scent, not wanting to let go—ever.

The weight of the newspaper on her lap pressed against her. She pulled away.

"Thanks so much for coming," she said, hearing the strain in her voice.

He glanced at the newspaper, then ran his hand through his hair. "I'm glad you emailed me," he said. "It's really good to see you."

She draped her arms over the paper, not yet ready to end this. There was so much they needed to say to each other before the article took their words away.

"You look well," she said. "You look…you look like I always imagined you were supposed to look. Like you."

"That's because I am me." He smiled again. "I'm living in Brooklyn, like we'd talked about. And I'm working with my mom at her clinic. It's what I always wanted, even though I'd refused to accept that."

"And your art work?"

He ran his hand over his scrubs, and she realized the scribbles were beautifully executed ink-drawings of superheroes. "I make these to entertain and distract the sick kids," he said. "That's satisfying enough for me. That, and helping to get them well."

"So you're happy," she said.

"Almost." His intense blue eyes held hers. She looked away. "What about you?" he asked softly.

Almost.

The sparrows pecked at the grass by their feet.

"I miss you, Annette."

*I miss **you**.*

He rested his hand on her shoulder. "Show me the article," he said.

Not yet. She wasn't ready. She wanted to hold onto these few moments with him for as long as she could.

"It's okay," he said softly.

She took a settling breath, then opened the newspaper and thumbed through the different sections until she found the magazine. She pulled it out.

The cover story, as the editor had told her.

***Traitors or Heroes**? By Annette Revoir*

She couldn't bring herself to look at Julian, anxious about what he was thinking and feeling to see his grandmother and real grandfather revealed like this. Instead, she stared at the prints of the two black-and-white photos she'd submitted along with the article, the newsprint around their faces slightly smudged.

Mariasha was dazzling in her rhinestone earrings. Her dark eyes wide and intense. So young. So beautiful. So different from the old woman whose revelations had torn Annette's heart.

Isaac seemed to be gazing longingly at Mariasha, and she, at him. He was wearing his U.S. Army uniform, medals and ribbons clearly displayed. So handsome. So charismatic. Not the monster in the photo that had been on the 'Death to Goldstein' posters.

Her grandfather.

But they were both Julian's grandparents. He gently took the magazine from her and turned the pages as he skimmed the article. He already knew what it said. He'd heard most of the story himself.

He closed the magazine, a thoughtful expression on his face, not the hurt she'd feared.

A boat horn sounded—melancholy and far-away.

"Do you suppose they ever came here?" he asked, his voice wistful. "Maybe even sat on this bench, beneath this oak tree, and looked out at the river?"

"I believe they did."

"They really loved each other," he said.

Was he only speaking of Mariasha and Isaac?

"Thank you," he said. "Thank you for setting them free. For setting all of us free."

Free? She was relieved by his words, but she didn't feel free.

"It took a lot of courage for you to write this."

"Not courage," she said. "It was something I had to do. I only hope you won't regret it."

"Regret the truth?" He shook his head. "This is my past. It's who I am. Who *we* are." He picked up the newspaper from her lap and set it down on the other side of the bench.

He was right. It was *their* past. And at last, she no longer felt its crushing weight.

"I won't deny the past," he said. "And I won't deny how I feel about you." His eyes seemed to penetrate her. "I love you, Annette."

A shift in the wind unsettled the sparrows. They rose up, up, up. Above the park, over the river, toward the infinite blue sky, until they became tiny specks.

Free. They were all free now.

She placed Julian's hand over her heart, pressing so tightly that she could feel his pulse pounding along with hers.

And then she kissed him.

ACKNOWLEDGEMENTS

When I was a child, my mother mesmerized me with her stories about growing up in Brooklyn during the Great Depression. How her father died when she was seven, and how her mother, penniless and illiterate, went to extraordinary measures to survive with three small children (my mom was the oldest!) Despite the adversity in her life, my mother went on to graduate from college and lived a happy and rewarding life, but her memories of being a 'red-diaper baby', influenced by socialism and later communism, often seemed to take her to another place. The mention of Julius and Ethel Rosenberg, who had been executed as atomic-bomb spies in 1953 would bring tears to her eyes. The Rosenbergs were a young married couple with two small children. They had lived in the same Lower East Side neighborhood as my family and my oldest brother had gone to elementary school with one of their sons. Had they deserved to die? It was a question that haunted me.

The idea to merge my mother's early years with the story of the execution of an atomic-bomb spy seemed inevitable. Of course, the result—this book—is very much a work of fiction. My mother didn't have a secret life like Mariasha did. She and my father were perhaps the most loving, devoted couple I've ever known. But I believe both my mom and dad would have been pleased with this story of Mariasha, Isaac, and their offspring, and of their desire to do the right thing.

While my mother's stories were the basis for many of the flashbacks and memories in *The Other Traitor*, I worked hard at getting the details and atmosphere right. The Internet provided me with some wonderful source material, including Brooklyn College's *Spotlight* magazine. But above all, Sam Roberts's brilliant biography, *The Brother—The Untold Story of the Rosenberg Case,* enabled me to enrich my fictitious world.

There are many others to whom I'm grateful for helping make this book a reality. My early readers and support system—Delia Foley, Maureen O'Connor, Jack Turken, Arnold Weiss, and Neil Nyren, who gave me encouragement and focused me on my theme of the past haunting the present. My wonderful critique partners—Christine Jackson, Kristy Montee, Miriam Auerbach, Christine Kling, and Neil Plakcy, who once again played muse for me. Kelly Nichols, who designed the amazing cover. The photo, by the way, is one of my favorites of my children's *other* grandparents—Susie and Frazier Potts.

As always, my remarkable husband Joe, the force behind Churlish Press, made sure I got the details right—the little ones like commas and spelling, the big historical ones, and everything in between. It's convenient to be married to a genius, but even better to be married to one as supportive and encouraging as mine!

ABOUT THE AUTHOR

Sharon Potts is the award-winning, critically acclaimed author of five psychological thrillers, including *In Their Blood*—winner of the Benjamin Franklin Award and recipient of a starred review in *Publishers Weekly*. A former CPA, corporate executive, and entrepreneur, Sharon has served as treasurer of the national board of Mystery Writers of America, as well as president of that organization's Florida chapter. She has also co-chaired SleuthFest, a national writers' conference. Sharon lives in Miami Beach with her husband and a spirited Australian shepherd named Gidget.

56074458R00208

Made in the USA
Charleston, SC
14 May 2016